# MASTER ARCANIST

## FRITH CHRONICLES, BOOK VI.V OF VII

### SHAMI STOVALL

# Contents

Published by
**CS BOOKS, LLC**

This is a work of fiction. Names, characters, places, and incidents either are the product of author imagination or are used fictitiously, and any resemblance to actual persons, living or dead, business establishments, events, or locales, is entirely fictional.

Master Arcanist
Copyright © 2022 Capital Station Books
All rights reserved.
https://sastovallauthor.com/

Cover Design: Darko Paganus

Editors: Amy McNulty, Nia Quinn, Justin Barnett

**IF YOU WANT TO BE NOTIFIED WHEN SHAMI STOVALL'S NEXT BOOK RELEASES, PLEASE VISIT HER WEBSITE OR CONTACT HER DIRECTLY AT**

s.adelle.s@gmail.com

ISBN: *978-1-7347587-2-6*

*To John, my soulmate.*
*To Justin Barnett, who has helped me in so many ways.*
*To Beka, forever.*
*To Gail and Big John, my surrogate parents.*
*To Henry Copeland, for the beautiful leather map and book covers.*
*To Brian Wiggins, for giving a voice to the characters.*
*To Mary, Emily, James & Dana, for all the jokes and input.*
*To my patrons over on Patreon, for all the support.*
*To my Facebook group, for all the memes.*
*And finally, to everyone unnamed, thank you for everything.*

# CHAPTER 1

## PRIORITIES

The last twenty-four hours had been rough.

I stood outside the shattered walls of Thronehold, the capital of the Argo Empire. The cries of the injured and mourning rose with the smoke into the air. The armies—soldiers and arcanists familiar with war—celebrated their victory and the rightful queen's restoration, despite the surrounding rubble and bodies. I wanted to rest, to spend time with Evianna and the others, but I didn't have that luxury.

I was the World Serpent Arcanist, the Warlord.

Too many problems needed my attention.

Last night, I had killed Theasin, but the Second Ascension had stolen away with his soul forge. From what I knew, the god-creatures couldn't survive without their arcanists. The soul forge was surely dead, but now its corpse was in the hands of the enemy. The Second Ascension had used the skeleton of the apoch dragon to make fearsome weapons, and I had no doubt they'd use the soul forge for the same villainy.

That was a serious threat, but without knowing where the corpse had been taken, there little I could do about it right now.

To make matters worse, several of my friends and family had been infected with the arcane plague during our battles. I had thought the plague was no longer a threat. I had helped a friend, Vethica, bond with a khepera, a creature with the power to revert the corrosive damage caused by corrupted magic. Then I had allowed that information to be spread widely—I wanted everyone to be cured.

But now Vethica was gone. She had vanished during the battle, and I had every reason to think the Second Ascension had taken her.

Now I had to find a way to help those infected, as well as locate Vethica.

The mounting pressure to find the Second Ascension's lair weighed on me. How would we find it? As well as the other god-creature I suspected had already bonded. Was that god-arcanist a member of the Second Ascension? So many problems...

Another complication—the fenris wolf, a god-creature of extraordinary ability—was nearby, here in the Argo Empire, somewhere close to Thronehold. Someone had to bond with it, but Queen Ladislava had declared all god-creatures in her realm belonged to her. Would she see reason and allow us to send someone into the lair of the wolf?

The final problem was a personal one.

During the fight for Thronehold, the soul forge had used its heinous abilities to steal life from people, and then given it to the corpses of mystical creatures. Those corpses... They had risen from the dead.

Even Luthair.

A white hart stood next to me, stomping his golden hooves and shaking his head. "Where am I? Why am I here?" When he turned to face me, his white fur shone in the bright afternoon light. "I don't understand."

Arthur, the white hart, was the eldrin of an assassin who had tried to kill me—Adelgis's sister, Venae. His golden antlers had been sliced from his head during our fight, but they had grown back during his resurrection, large and pointed, just as glorious as before.

I had almost forgotten about him. My thoughts were on so many other things.

Thankfully, Evianna was with me as well. She waited by my side, a look of determination etched onto her face. Her white hair, pulled back in a tight ponytail, fluttered in the wind. Loose strands glittered with a metallic edge, beautiful and mystical, in a way no one else was.

Her bluish-purple eyes...

Evianna stared at me without saying anything, but I knew she was waiting.

I had to decide what to do.

Which problem had the highest priority? Rescuing Vethica? Finding someone to bond with the fenris wolf? Stopping the Second Ascension from using the body of the soul forge?

Saving Luthair?

Thinking of Luthair caused a twinge of pain to lance through my chest. I turned to the white hart. He had been brought back to life—perhaps he would have answers for me.

"Are you still bonded with Venae?" I asked.

The mighty beast twitched his ears. "I don't know who you speak of."

"You don't... recognize Venae's name?"

Arthur shook his head. "My Trial of Worth has been completed. I can... sense it. But I have no arcanist. I need to find her. We need to bond."

"You know your arcanist is a woman?" I asked.

The white hart didn't answer for a long moment, perplexed.

But it was all I needed to hear. Arthur couldn't remember his old arcanist, but he sought to bond with her regardless. Was that what Luthair had felt when he awoke? Had he felt an urge to find me and bond with me? Or was it just because Venae remained unbonded?

Again, my chest hurt. I hated... the thought of him searching endlessly for me. I hated the thought I wasn't there for him.

"Volke?" Evianna asked. She placed a hand on my shoulder and stepped close to me. "Are you okay?"

"I will be," I managed to say.

"We still have Venae in custody."

"I... I know."

I didn't care whether she bonded with her white hart again. I just *didn't*. Someone else could handle that. Right now, I needed to focus on the big issues.

Out of all the problems, which could I handle the fastest? Obviously, the fenris wolf was nearby. I could speak with Guildmaster Eventide, and we could escort someone into the lair of the beast. We had the wolf's runestone. Everything was ready —we could have another god-arcanist on our side before nightfall, assuming we all didn't die from the perils of the lair.

And then we'd stand a better chance against our enemies.

Those who were infected with the arcane plague... Their eldrin had a few days, maximum, before becoming twisted monsters. The arcanists had longer, since they weren't completely magical, but it wouldn't matter if their eldrin fell first.

It would probably take weeks or months for the Second Ascension to use the soul forge to create powerful artifacts. Especially now that Theasin wasn't there to help them.

Heading to the fenris wolf's lair was the best choice.

At least, I hoped it was.

"Evianna," I said.

She tensed and then held herself a little straighter. "Yes? What is it?" Before I could answer, she hastily added, "Do you need something? What can I do to help?"

"Can you gather the other master arcanists of the Frith

Guild?" I shook my head. "Or anyone else on our side? I need to speak with them."

The white hart snorted. "What of me? You said you knew my arcanist. I want to meet her!"

I waved my hand at the creature. "Evianna, can you... take care of him as well?"

The shadows around Evianna's feet flickered and fluttered, like bats trapped in the darkness. She replied with a single nod, and then her knightmare, Layshl, stepped out of the inky void.

Layshl's leathery scaled armor, black as midnight, didn't take to the sunlight well. Her empty cowl and dragon-wing cape seemed thinner than usual. Knightmares didn't care for the light. They became weaker when it was bright. An unfortunate downside.

With careful and silent movements, Layshl stood next to the white hart. Her gloved hand—disembodied, as though worn by an invisible person—stroked the brilliant white fur of the creature. Arthur calmed and allowed the knightmare to stroke his shoulders.

"Layshl and I will handle this," Evianna said. "You should rest a bit."

She pointed to the encampment just outside of Thronehold. The many tents had once been for Queen Ladislava's soldiers, but now that she had the city, they were empty. Eventually, the whole lot of tents would be torn down and packed away. The commander's tent—larger and positioned near the center of the encampment—was a quiet location, sitting in the middle of the tent graveyard.

"You've been through a lot," Evianna said, the concern in her voice genuine. When she touched my shoulder again, it was gentle. "I promise I won't take long. I just... I worry about you. Everything you've been through. It's so much."

"I'll handle it," I said, more confidence in my voice than I felt in my heart.

She smiled up at me. "I know. But I want you to be okay at the end of everything, too." Then Evianna threw her arms around me in a tight embrace. "No more near-deaths. No more close calls. Do you understand?"

The more she squeezed, the more I could feel her concern. I returned the hug, thankful she wasn't too angry with my recklessness. "Sorry for worrying you."

Evianna broke away from me and placed her hands on her hips. Her clothing—a high-quality button-up shirt and riding trousers that fit her perfectly—had been dirtied during the fighting, but still retained their elegant qualities.

"No more apologizing," Evianna stated. "We can't have excuses. You rest, I'll handle the white hart, as well as gathering everyone for a discussion. Everything will be taken care of. You have my word."

Although the smoke from destroyed smokestacks in the city stung my nose, I managed a smile. Evianna was dependable. I could relax for just a moment in the command tent while I thought of a plan.

---

I slept for a short while.

The dreams I had were fleeting. I relived my bonding with Terrakona. The inside of the massive tree—Terrakona's lair—had been a gauntlet of obstacles. The insides had consumed the others, and then we had faced Evianna's brother in a dark confrontation.

Luthair...

He had killed the grim reaper to save me.

That was when I first met the hatchling world serpent. The massive beast had bonded with me. My arcanist mark—a twelve-pointed star over the heart of my chest—marked me as one of the strongest arcanists in the world.

As a world serpent arcanist, I could move the earth, control the water, summon fire and plants, and reshape terrain. A warlord on the battlefield that was how the last world serpent arcanist had become a legend.

But I still thought about Luthair. I couldn't abandon him.

I owed him my life. More than once over.

The sound of air popping jerked me awake. I stood from my chair, half-groggy and confused by my surroundings. The table in the center of the command tent was massive—it was made from solid wood and had to weigh more than two horses. A *Tactician's Charm* was rolled out on top of the table—a magical trinket map that detailed the surrounding area, including the weather.

The tent walls were held up with shelves, and half a dozen chairs were positioned around the table. In the midafternoon sun, the tent was warm. It didn't help wake me.

When I glanced around, I noticed my sister, and I immediately tensed.

She stood at the opposite end of the table, quiet and careful, as always. Her eldrin—the adorable white rizzel, Nicholin—sat on her shoulder like an extra-long ferret. His silver stripes shimmered in the lantern-light as Illia walked around to greet me.

Although we weren't related by blood, we were siblings. I knew her emotions long before she said a word. The eyepatch over her face, stitched with the image of a rizzel, couldn't obfuscate her dread. Her one eye remained locked on me until we were mere inches apart.

I was taller than her, but even when afraid, she had an innate confidence that practically added a few inches to her stature.

"Volke," she said, her voice unusually soft.

"What's wrong?" I asked.

The fear in her voice, coupled with my own frayed nerves, caused me to jump to the worst-case scenario—the Second

Ascension had returned for Thronehold. I stepped around Illia and headed for the flap of the tent. "Let's go. If there are more members of the Second Ascension around, I'll—"

Illia grabbed my elbow and yanked me back. I turned around to face her, my brow furrowed.

"Illia?" I asked.

She shook her head. "It's not the Second Ascension."

"Then what is it?"

In that moment, she hesitated. It wasn't like her. Nicholin said nothing—which *really* wasn't like him. The little ferret creature didn't look me in the eyes. His paws gripped Illia's coat, and his white tail wrapped around her neck.

Their silence gave me chills.

"We won't find Vethica in time," Illia whispered. "And the other khepera arcanists who are part of the Frith Guild are barely trained in their magic. Even if we somehow made it back to Fortuna—where they are—it wouldn't be fast enough."

"For Zaxis, you mean?" I asked.

Illia tightened her hands into fists. "Yes. For Zaxis." She glared up at me with her one eye. Her shoulder-length hair, wavy all the way from the roots to the tips, had been beaten down by rain, mud, and sweat. When she went to run a hand through it, her fingers got caught in tangles. Illia ripped her hand through, her frustration apparent in the simple act.

"Guildmaster Eventide separated him from the others," Nicholin muttered, his gaze on the floor. "And he hasn't complained, but... He's really worried."

"I'll help him," I said. "I promise."

"How?" Illia demanded.

"I... I'll think of something."

Only creatures and people with magic could become twisted by the arcane plague. If worse came to worse, we could kill Zaxis's eldrin—his phoenix, Forsythe—in order to save his mind from falling to madness. That wasn't the *ideal* route, but it was something.

But I knew I couldn't default like that.

I grabbed at my arm and idly rubbed the spot on my shoulder where a plague-ridden creature had once bitten and infected me. What could I do?

I had cured myself of the plague when Luthair achieved his true form. I couldn't force Zaxis to do the same with Forsythe, but another thought crossed my mind. Terrakona had said that a mystical creature achieving its true form was the same as touching the *purest magic*—and the purest magic couldn't be corrupted by the plague.

Terrakona had also said that his lair—his birthplace—had been steeped in the purest magic.

We were too far away from Terrakona's lair, but the fenris wolf...

It was nearby.

"Listen," I said, placing a hand on Illia's shoulder. "I have an idea. I don't know if it'll work, but I'd rather try it than never know."

## Chapter 2

# Lair Of The Fenris Wolf

Terrakona wrapped his gigantic serpentine body around me. I climbed up the side of his body and took a seat on his scaled back.

He was too large to fit into Thronehold without destroying something. He was at least a few hundred feet in length, his body thick with snake-like muscle, and his head was wide, like a python's. The crest of crystals around his head flared out, similar to a mane or the hood of a viper.

The crystals sparkled with a black inner beauty. For some reason, they reminded me of knightmare magic.

**"Warlord,"** Terrakona telepathically said, his voice deep and regal—but youthful and hopeful. I appreciated that about him. **"The arcanists of the Frith Guild are gathering inside the city. It would be best to join them."**

"I will in a moment," I said, as I stared out at the destruction around the shattered walls of Thronehold. The wind carried debris and ash over the cracked roads. The sight fueled my determination.

I wouldn't let the Second Ascension do this again.

**"Why hesitate?"**

"I'm waiting for Adelgis."

We needed Adelgis more than ever. He was the only one who could detect the location of the god-creatures. And... I needed to thank him for that. At first, Adelgis hadn't been able to use his ethereal whelk magic on god-creatures—he couldn't even hear my thoughts. But Adelgis was more talented than people gave him credit for.

Adelgis had spent all his free time mastering his manipulation—his ability to alter dreams—to find the dreams of the god-creatures. Ever since then, his magic had been able to affect god-creatures and their arcanists. He could hear my thoughts—and he could sense the dreams of the fenris wolf.

"Volke?"

Adelgis's quiet voice drew me out of my thoughts. I turned and spotted him on the ruined road outside of Thronehold. He walked over to Terrakona and I, his eldrin floating through the air by his side.

His ethereal whelk—a shimmering sea snail the size of a human head—had once been a bizarre sight to me. Now, I enjoyed her presence. Felicity was one of the few mystical creatures who maintained a tranquil demeanor at all times. Plus, she reminded me of the ocean. Her spiral shell, iridescent in color, like oil on the surface of water, looked like the shells I would find on the beach of Ruma.

Felicity had tentacles that hung from her sea slug-body, though. That was odd.

"Good afternoon, Volke," Felicity said as they approached.

Her voice was as light as the breeze.

I leaned forward and rested my elbows on my knees. "How are you two doing?" I asked.

Adelgis smiled up at me. It was forced. I could tell in an instant.

He was tall and slender, but right now he stood with drooped shoulders and his robes sloppily tied. That wasn't like

Adelgis. Even his long black hair, which he usually spent some time maintaining, had been tied back in a knot. A few strands were loose and fluttered in the wind.

"Volke, allow me to apologize," Adelgis said, not even bothering to answer my question. "I know I already did through telepathy, but I owe you the respect of saying it in person."

"Don't worry about it."

"No. Please, listen." Adelgis walked to the side of Terrakona and placed his hand on my eldrin's emerald scales. Terrakona didn't move away or otherwise react. Then Adelgis pressed his forehead into Terrakona's side, hiding his face from me. "All of this is my fault."

"What're you talking about?" I asked.

After a long exhale, Adelgis replied, "I was so concerned about stopping my father, that I failed to think of all the many things the enemy was capable of." He kept his forehead on Terrakona, staring down at the ground. "The plague, *their* enemy agents, *their abilities*. I... I should've devised a better strategy. I should've coordinated more. I should've—"

"We have other arcanists with us," I said, cutting him off. "You don't need to put this all on yourself. Even Guildmaster Eventide and Master Zelfree were caught off guard by the enemy."

"You don't understand. They don't know my father like I do."

"It's okay," I said with a dark chuckle. "He's dead now. That much we accomplished. He won't hurt anybody anymore."

Adelgis shook his head. "Don't you understand? My father never did anything halfway. Look what happened to Thronehold. He used his god-arcanist powers to resurrect the fallen mystical creatures here. He used them to create an army for the Second Ascension."

"We'll find them," I said with a shrug. "We have ways. Like the Occult Compass."

Adelgis didn't respond.

Wasn't this part of being a leader? Helping others when they felt low? Even though I felt like I had just fought through a hurricane, I had to maintain my confidence and extend Adelgis a helping hand.

"I can hear you," Adelgis muttered into Terrakona's side.

I rubbed my face. "Right. Sorry. I'm just... Trying to think of something to help." Even though I knew he could read thoughts, I just always forgot.

"I'm afraid that I'll overlook something my father left behind," Adelgis muttered.

"Look, he was a talented man, but you don't need to be afraid of him anymore."

"I barely ever saw him... But he still terrified and inspired me. Even now... I'm worried."

For a long moment, I mulled over the comment. Adelgis was right. We had chased the shadow of Theasin Venrover across ocean and land. He had always been ahead of us—plotting and planning—but did we really need to fear his schemes when he wasn't around to execute them? Who was more competent than Theasin?

"The Autarch," Adelgis murmured in response to my inner monologue.

I didn't know much about the Autarch. All I knew was he led the Second Ascension, and that he was bonded to a rare gold kirin. From what we had gathered, the Autarch's plan was to bond with multiple god-creatures and then rule as the sole sovereign over all nations.

If he had gotten the world serpent, the Autarch would've won already, but he hadn't.

"We'll be fine," I said as I slid off Terrakona and landed on the road next to Adelgis. "Don't worry about it."

Adelgis finally removed his forehead from my eldrin and turned to face me. The black bags under his eyes didn't reassure me. "My father set up an arranged marriage for me when I was five," he said. "A whole *decade* before I was a man, my father had already planned my wedding. Trust me. My father left instructions for the Autarch—for my siblings—and for the Second Ascension. I just... I just need to think of what they would be." Adelgis rubbed at his chin. "What would've been my father's next move?"

His ethereal whelk floated in the air around his head. Her tentacles grabbed his long hair and gently tugged. "Listen to Volke. Everything will be fine."

I placed my hand on Adelgis's boney shoulder. He snapped his gaze to mine.

"Forget about your father for a moment," I said, my tone serious and my words exact. "I need you to locate the fenris wolf. All right?"

Adelgis nodded once. "You needn't worry. I felt the dreams of the wolf before we arrived in Thronehold. And now that the fighting has ended, the wolf dreams again." He turned on his heel and pointed to the south, beyond the fields, and straight into a forest. "He's there. In his lair."

**"I can sense him as well,"** Terrakona said, his eyes narrowing into harsh slits. **"The fenris wolf slumbers."**

"Do you think you can lead us straight to the door of the lair?" I asked. When we had discovered Terrakona's lair, it had been locked. Only the world serpent runestone had allowed us to open it.

Adelgis faced me with a half-smile. "I failed you before, but I won't fail you on this."

"You've never failed me," I said, curt. "Don't even think that way."

"Even if you forgive me for not outsmarting my father, you must admit that... That it's my fault Luthair might be in the hands of the enemy. I should've... I should've thought about—"

"*Don't talk about Luthair,*" I snapped. Then I forced myself to breathe—to enjoy the crisp midafternoon air—and allow my rage to subside. "Everything will be okay. We just have to focus on one problem at a time."

Adelgis didn't respond. Part of me knew he would still blame himself, but I didn't know how to convince him otherwise. He had complete control over people's dreams, but this wasn't a dream. He couldn't control *everything*.

It was in *all* our hands to set things right.

"I'm going to speak with the master arcanists about our plans," I said to him. "All I want from you is to make sure we have a path straight to the wolf."

Adelgis nodded, and his whelk spun around like a wagon wheel.

"Thank you," I said, clasping his shoulder. "Trust me—without you, I'd be lost. Stop blaming yourself. You're one of my closest friends and allies."

I didn't know why, but Adelgis stood a little straighter. "R-Right. Well, I'll try not to disappoint you."

"You have until sundown to locate the entrance." Then I turned on my heel. "That's when I'll return with the others."

---

There were only twelve god-creatures in total. From what I knew, they spawned one at a time, all across the world. The world serpent was first. The soul forge had been second. The fenris wolf was third.

It was all I could think about as I paced the study room in the Thronehold library. The toppled bookshelves and cracked windows made the library feel like a refugee camp. The lanterns hanging on the wall were new, though. Scribes had been busy cleaning everything, but Guildmaster Eventide had asked them to leave.

Now it was just me, Eventide, and the Ace of Cutlasses in

the large stone room. The books at our feet were battered, but not destroyed, and I took a moment to kneel and examine everything.

Guildmaster Eventide stood near one of the bookshelves, her eyes on the tomes.

The Ace of Cutlasses—Yesna, the siren arcanist—stared at the large window with a frown. She wore a simple tunic and trousers, which was different from her typical swashbuckling gear. Her two blades were secured to her thick leather belt, and I wondered why she didn't like to wear armor.

Then again, Thronehold was safe. In theory. Perhaps she didn't think armor was necessary.

Her black hair had been braided, similar to Eventide's, but the tie didn't look like it would hold. Her hair was thick and puffed and looked like a powder keg ready to explode from all restraints.

Despite all that, Yesna was beautiful—athletic and confident, and her eyes bright with adventure. She reminded me of old tales, like the stories of Gregory Ruma.

"We don't have much time," Yesna said. She kept her gaze on something beyond the window. "Queen Ladislava said she would be preparing some of her knights to escort us into the fenris wolf's lair."

"We don't need an escort," I said.

Guildmaster Eventide picked up a ruined book. She dusted the cover and then walked over to the nearby desk. "She's not sending them to protect us. She's sending them because she's hoping one will be accepted by the fenris wolf to bond."

Ah. Right. Ladislava wanted someone from the Argo Empire to be the next god-arcanist.

I sighed. Why was everyone so much trouble?

Then again, I still didn't know who I would recommend to bond with the beast. What if one of the knights was a suitable match? Then we wouldn't run the risk of someone from the Second Ascension bonding to a god-creature.

I gritted my teeth, my mind going to dark places.

What if there was a traitor among the knights? What if they bonded, and then betrayed us?

Guildmaster Eventide placed her hand on the desk, her gaze drilling a hole into the book. She seemed... older. Worse than before. Her hair had always been gray, but now it seemed frayed. She had once moved with such energy and gusto—now her movements seemed stiff and forced.

Eventide touched the edge of her tricorn cap and pulled it down a bit, hiding her face in shadow, preventing anyone from seeing the dark marks under her eyes.

"We should send only a handful of people into the fenris wolf's lair," she said.

"Why is that?" Yesna snapped back. "Let's just send in the whole damn guild and see who can bond with it."

Eventide held up a finger, but her gaze never left the book. "When Volke traveled through the world serpent's lair, it was filled with traps."

"They weren't deadly." Yesna shrugged. "Everett said he got caught, but he didn't die."

"Only because Volke bonded with the world serpent." When Eventide glanced up, her eyes were narrowed in a glare. "If Volke *hadn't* bonded, everyone caught in the traps would've stayed there. And died."

The statement sent a shiver down my spine. Illia had been one of the few unfortunate people to get caught. I could still recall her being swallowed by the floor. The sight haunted my thoughts.

"We should send in only a few people—those who can help get others through the lair, and those who we think can bond."

"Also, Zaxis and Odion," I said. "They're both infected with the arcane plague, but I have an idea." I walked over to the desk and stood next to Eventide. "Please. I'll go. I'll watch them."

Guildmaster Eventide offered me a weak smile. "You needn't ask my permission on this. If you think it's wise to take them—for whatever reason—do so."

I held my breath and tapped the tips of my finger on the desk. For years, I had considered Eventide my *guildmaster*. She had been the one in charge. But that had changed when I had become a god-arcanist.

Before I could say anything else, Eventide asked, "Who do you think would make a suitable god-arcanist?"

I had been thinking about that for days, yet nothing ever came to me. I blamed the fatigue. The answer had to be obvious.

"Have you ever considered your adopted father?" she asked. "William Savan was a naval officer back in his heyday."

The suggestion struck me like a punch in the chest. My throat tightened, and I dwelled on the thought for a full minute. Why hadn't I thought of that before?

Guilt twisted in me, but I slowly realized why. Gravekeeper William had once told me that he had tried to bond to a creature, but he had failed the Trial of Worth. In my mind, I never pictured him as an arcanist, even in these dire situations. He was just... my father. The one who had raised me. The kind man who had taught me my love of books—and of honor.

Could he be a god-arcanist?

Even now, the thought seemed crazy to me.

But plausible.

"He's back in Fortuna," I whispered. "We'd never be able to get him here in time."

"In time for what?" Yesna barked from her position near the window. "And speak up! There's nothin' about this that needs hushed voices."

Eventide waved away the comment. Her hand was wan and

shaky, though. I stared at it a bit longer, even after she put it back down at her side.

"Then perhaps we should consider him when it comes time to find the other god-creatures," Eventide stated. "There are many others. We should think of who we want to go through their Trials of Worth."

How many other creatures were there? "I know we have more than half the runestones," I muttered. "Which ones do we have?"

"The jade runestone, for the world serpent. The shale runestone, for the fenris wolf. The red jasper runestone, for the typhon beast. The lapis lazuli runestone, for the scylla waters. The opal runestone, for the tempest coatl. The sandstone runestone, for the progenitor behemoth. And finally... we have the bauxite runestone, for the corona phoenix."

Which meant the Second Ascension had the runestones for the sky titan, garuda bird, the abyssal kraken, and the endless undead...

And *one* of those creatures had bonded. Since the Second Ascension had the runestone, I could only conclude that they had another god-arcanist in their midst.

It would be helpful if we had more information on these creatures. Who would make good partners for the god-creatures? Some of them sounded fearsome. Others...

"*Volke*," Adelgis said to me telepathically.

I tensed, my whole body prepared for a fight. "Adelgis?"

Yesna and Eventide both turned to face me. They, too, looked like they were ready for anything.

"*I've found the door to the lair. It isn't far from Thronehold. Please bring the shale runestone so we can enter.*"

# CHAPTER 3

# A TEAM OF SIX

Guildmaster Eventide walked with me to the broken walls of Thronehold.

Although most of the trek was in silence, whenever I glanced over, she offered me a confident smile. Her long coat was made of patchwork materials. Leather from various mythical creatures, including a minotaur, was sewn together with thick thread. I had never examined the thread before. It appeared to be the golden mane of a unicorn.

"Did you imbue that coat yourself?" I asked once we reached the foot of the wall.

Eventide shook her head. "A friend of mine did. It was a gift." She grabbed the edge of the coat and lifted it so that I could see the hem at the bottom. Patches of void-black fur were used in the construction, giving the coat a frayed appearance. "These are from a rare black sphinx."

While I wanted to ask a hundred questions—about Eventide's friends, and her adventures across the world—I knew I didn't have much time. I turned my attention to the wall. "I'm ready for the fenris wolf. I won't come back until the way is secured, and we find someone to bond."

"Afterward, we should head back to Fortuna and regroup," Eventide said. She released her coat and then reached into a pocket and withdrew the shale runestone. It was no larger than her hand, with arcane runes on one side, a picture of a fearsome wolf on the other. "Who all are you taking?"

"Odion and Zaxis." I held my breath, trying to think of others in the nearby area. "Illia and Master Zelfree."

"Everett won't be joining you."

I met her gaze with a lifted eyebrow. "Why not?"

"He's insisted on watching the prisoners. The Second Ascension members who were caught during the attack on Thronehold."

Eventide said the statement as though it meant nothing, but I saw through her words. Master Zelfree was staying behind to watch Calisto. That madman had almost died in the final battle, but Illia had captured him instead. *Someone* had to watch the dread pirate, even if his manticore was dead.

He wasn't an arcanist anymore—the moment someone's mystical creature died, their connection to magic faded—but that didn't mean his black heart would change. Calisto was a cutthroat, and if we allowed him to escape, I had no doubt that he would find a new creature to bond with, and then terrorize the seas all over again.

"Okay," I muttered. "I'll take Illia, Evianna, and Captain Devlin."

Illia had her rizzel magic. Teleportation and the ability to manipulate gravity were impressive.

The world serpent's lair had been pitch dark. Evianna's knightmare augmentation would allow us to see in the dark.

Devlin was a master arcanist, capable of using all his magical abilities, almost with ease. He was one of the few arcanists I knew who could even produce his aura without difficulties. Although I didn't know the man well, Devlin had proven himself to be dependable time and time again.

Guildmaster Eventide smiled. "Excellent. Then you should hurry." She glanced up and stared at the orange-tinted sky. "You should return before dawn. And remember your guild pendant."

I touched the guild pendant hanging around my neck. Unlike most guild pendants—which were made from copper, bronze, or silver—mine had been crafted from the bone of an atlas turtle. On one side it read: Volke Savan the World Serpent God-Arcanist. On the other side was the Frith Guild symbol, an ornate sword and shield with a star of magic between the two.

It could protect me from attacks.

Ever since Eventide had given it to me, I hadn't taken it off.

"Thank you, Guildmaster Eventide," I said. "I won't let you down."

She sighed. "How many times do I have to tell you? Call me Liet."

"Well... It just feels unnatural." With a nervous laugh, I added, "But I'll try."

"I'd go with you, if I could." Eventide exhaled, this time with obvious fatigue. "But Gentel is so far from me... And after that battle, it feels as though my soul has been ripped and frayed."

"I understand."

Eventide—no, Liet—placed a hand on my shoulder. "When we return to Fortuna, we'll have a chance to recover. Until then, don't let your guard down. If any members of the Second Ascension escaped us, they might be nearby, just waiting for an opportunity to strike."

She always had insight and advice that I hadn't considered.

The fourth step of the Pillar. *Preparation. Without it, we leave our fate to chance.*

"I won't let you down," I said.

Terrakona rushed across the fields of the Argo Empire. He was massive, and his concertina movements allowed him to move with surprising speed. Sometimes I forgot he was the world serpent—I feared he would destroy the landscape, and leave the Argo Empire a smoking wreck—but then I glanced behind us, and saw that the ground moved to accommodate Terrakona's movements.

Whenever he moved, the very land would part to create a smooth path. The trees, the rocks, and even the water would be peeled away, like the skin on a banana, and then the earth would stitch itself back together once Terrakona had passed.

There were some minor hiccups—sometimes the ground didn't lineup quite right—but it was basically the same as before. No harm to the wilderness. No damage to the farms or crops.

Evianna and Illia held on to Terrakona's emerald scales, clinging to his back as we traveled. Evianna's knightmare remained hidden in her shadow, and Illia's rizzel clung to her shoulder. Every once in a while, Nicholin would poke his head up through her wavy hair and allow the wind to play with his soft, white ears.

High above us, on a white two-headed dragon, was Odion, the King of Javin.

His eldrin was a juvenile twilight dragon. They were fearsome beasts who changed colors depending on the time of day. While the sun was up, they were a bright white. Once the moon dominated the sky, twilight dragons were a bluish-black. Currently, Odion's twilight dragon, Hasdrubal, was a brilliant white. Once dusk hit, he would shift to a grayish color, and then finally to his raven-black form.

Zaxis rode on the dragon alongside Odion. The two of them were infected with the arcane plague, and while *I* was immune, Illia and Evianna weren't.

Zaxis's phoenix, Forsythe, glided through the sky, his scarlet wings out wide. Soot and embers trailed off of him as his inner fiery body pulsed with life.

And while we all stayed together, Devlin had shot out ahead. His massive roc, Mesos, could be seen from a mile away, so I didn't fear losing him, but I wished he would've stayed close.

Since rocs were man-eaters, they were immune to blood diseases. Devlin was the only other one in our group immune to the terrible effects of the arcane plague.

While I dwelled on everyone's capabilities—trying to think of strategies long before we reached the lair of the fenris wolf—Terrakona brought us to the forest. The trees parted as we went deeper into the woods, and before I had any real time to formulate a plan, Terrakona came to a stop.

I grabbed the crystals of his mane to keep my balance.

**"Adelgis is nearby, Warlord,"** Terrakona telepathically said.

"Thank you."

I slid off his head, down his back, and then off the side of his gargantuan body. I hit the ground hard, to the point it hurt my knees, but I quickly brushed off the sensation. As a god-arcanist, my ability to heal was superior to most.

Illia disappeared with a pop and glitter. Then she appeared by my side. She touched her eyepatch and offered me a smirk.

As though not to be outdone, Evianna dramatically leapt off Terrakona and then dove into the darkness like it was a pool of ink. She emerged on the other side of me, walking out of the shadows with all the confidence of an assassin.

Evianna fluffed her white hair. "I'm ready for this challenge. I'll make it to the end of the lair this time."

"You need to be on your toes at all times," Illia said. "The lair of the world serpent was no joke."

"Who said I was joking?" Evianna placed a hand on the hilt of her short sword. "When I say *I'm ready*, I mean, *I'm ready*."

Nicholin once again poked his head out of Illia's hair. "Okay, children. Everyone put their smiles on because I am *not* getting eaten by a tree this time." He squeaked and ruffled his white fur. "This lair will be different. We won't be messing up."

"You don't need to worry—I'm here," I said, more confident than I felt.

For whatever reason, it seemed to calm the others. Both Illia and Evianna acknowledged my statement with nods, and I wondered if the lair would even allow me in. From what I could remember, Terrakona's lair had practically been a living thing. The massive tree had attacked us.

Would the fenris wolf tolerate my presence?

Captain Devlin—who had flown so far ahead of us—had to angle his roc back around. He circled once and then leapt off his bird-like eldrin a good fifty feet from the ground. Right as he was about to hit the ground, he evoked wind to buffer his fall. With a *whoosh* of dirt, leaves, and icy wind, he landed among us, his tricorn cap still snugly secured to his head.

The man stroked his thin chinstrap beard and looked us over.

"Eh," Devlin said with a grunt. "I keep forgettin' how young you all are." He sighed and rolled his shoulders. "I suppose it's up to me to carry the team."

Evianna placed her hands on her hips. "I'll have you know that I'm quite accomplished."

"*For your age,*" Devlin quipped. "But you're no master arcanist, trust me." He pointed his thumb at his chest. "I'll be the one dealin' with the traps." Then he lifted his cap a bit to show off the arcanist mark on his forehead.

His was a seven-pointed star with a giant bird woven around the points. The image was clean and clear—the darker the lines, the longer the arcanist had been bonded. His mark didn't glow, though, which meant his eldrin wasn't true form.

Evianna's mark—a seven-pointed star with a cape and a

sword—wasn't nearly as prominent. She had only been bonded for a year.

"I can still carry my own weight, thank you very much," Evianna stated.

"Uh-huh. Sure." Devlin waved away the comment. "I'm gonna tell you the same thing I tell my cabin girl, Biyu. Just stay behind me when it comes to a fight. I'll handle the rest."

I had never seen Evianna press her lips so tightly together. With her cheeks red, she turned away from Devlin and stomped off toward the shadows of the forest. Illia said nothing and followed her, unconcerned with Devlin's bluster.

Illia had never really listened when told to stand back and do nothing. Why would now be any different?

A rush of wind caught my attention. The twilight dragon descended into the forest, his feathered wings a beautiful sight to behold. Unfortunately, the trees were too close together, and Hasdrubal had difficulty landing. Eventually, the massive dragon manipulated the shadows to form blades of hardened darkness. Then the dragon cut at the branches until he could land.

Both heads of the twilight dragon chomped at the branches and leaves, his anger on full display.

From what I could remember, there weren't many trees in Javin. The tiny island nation was more well-known for its brutal lifestyle.

Odion leapt off the back of his dragon. His armor—gleaming full plate that was the color of snow—glittered whenever he walked into pillars of light streaming through the forest canopy. His white hair was similar to Evianna's, but cut short and kept neat.

When he turned his blue eyes to me, I was reminded of his intensity. The man always gave me an odd feeling.

"We're close?" he asked.

I replied with a curt nod. Then I pointed in the direction

Evianna had headed. "Adelgis is that way. He's waiting at the entrance."

Captain Devlin gave the king the once over. "Curse the storm-ridden tides. You're young, too, aren't ya?"

Although he was young in terms of arcanists, Odion was at least seven years older than me, likely twenty-five. Still younger than Devlin, though.

King Odion didn't dignify the question with a reply. Instead, he offered me a formal bow. "I'll see you at the entrance then, my liege."

I really disliked it whenever people said that, but now wasn't the time to complain. Odion straightened himself and headed toward our destination. When he passed Devlin, he shot the man a glower.

Devlin replied by straightening the crotch of his pants.

I suspected this would be an interesting adventure.

Zaxis dismounted from the twilight dragon at the same time his phoenix flew through the forest canopy and landed at my feet. With sluggish steps, Zaxis walked over to me, his gaze on the dirt the entire time.

His red scale armor didn't glitter like Odion's, but it did seem to have an inner fire that was hard to describe. It had been crafted from the hide of a salamander—a creature of pure flame—and it was immune to all forms of heat.

Forsythe walked alongside his arcanist, his heron-like head craned upward to stare at his arcanist.

Once Zaxis reached me, he hardened himself and straightened his posture. His red hair looked messy and limp, like he hadn't done anything with it in a long while. His green eyes were clear, but his brow remained furrowed, like he couldn't dispel the last of his anxiety.

"You're not dead yet, son," Captain Devlin said.

When Zaxis met my gaze, I froze.

He seemed so serious.

"Do you remember Gregory Ruma's wife?" he asked me.

I swear my heart froze for a moment. How could I *forget* Ruma's wife, Acantha? She had been nothing more than a shambling zombie. Ruma had kissed her on the forehead and whispered sweet nothings to her, despite the fact she was just a corpse.

Zaxis exhaled. "Her phoenix was plague-ridden, right?"

I nodded once, already knowing where this was going.

"Somehow the corrupted magic of the phoenix kept Ruma's wife alive far longer than was natural." Zaxis gritted his teeth and stared at his boots. "I just... keep thinking about that."

Once mystical creatures were infected with the arcane plague, they became twisted monsters. But if they consumed enough magic, they achieved their *dread form*, the exact opposite of a creature's true form. It was the hideous pinnacle of corruption.

A true form phoenix could resurrect the dead, in theory.

A dread form phoenix could... keep a body moving. Even if it was infested with maggots.

I placed a hand on Zaxis's shoulder. "Don't worry. You were infected before, remember? We cured you. We can do it again."

"Forsythe wasn't infected then."

I couldn't deny that.

"Stop worrying about it." I withdrew the shale runestone from my pocket. "We have a plan. Find a source of pure magic in the fenris wolf's lair. Maybe that can cure you."

"*Maybe*," Zaxis repeated the word with venom.

I almost punched the man. That would've gotten through to him.

But I didn't have the anger necessary to jolt him out of his depression. I felt his fear. I, more than anyone else, understood. I remembered the terror I had felt after being infected—I remembered running from the Frith Guild because I hadn't wanted to accidentally infect anyone else.

So all I could do was offer confidence.

"The previous god-creatures single-handedly stopped the Blight of the Sky," I said. "If they can do that, I'm sure they can cure a single person of the plague. We just have to find this one."

Captain Devlin grunted in agreement.

Zaxis listened in silence, then closed his green eyes and took a deep breath. Opening them again, he turned his gaze to the woods. "Fine. Let's do this. Let's make it through this damn wolf's lair and go home."

# CHAPTER 4

## THE LAIR OF THE FENRIS WOLF

Adelgis waited for us in the forest, his eldrin floating around his head, orbiting him in a slow rotation. The old oak trees created thick shadows throughout the area. Adelgis stood by a mound of dirt and rock, one large enough that it could've been a house, or a small cave. On the side of the hill was a circular door made of stone, nearly fifteen feet in height.

I recognized this door. This was the same as the door to the world serpent's lair.

Well, not entirely.

The world serpent's door had been carved with a stunning image of Terrakona. *This* door was marked with a wolf—the same one on the shale runestone. The wolf image was carved intricately and deeply, with such detail that I could see the mighty fangs and claws. Frost covered the edges of the door, and for a brief moment, I was reminded of Fain's wendigo.

I wished Fain had come with us, but Liet was right about keeping the numbers low. The lairs of the god-creatures were dangerous.

Since this was made of stone and earth, I briefly wondered if my god-arcanist powers would work. I could control the terrain, after all. In small amounts, at least. I waved my hand and attempted to open the hill—or perhaps make a new hole, so we didn't have to open the door.

The dirt around my feet shifted, and the trees nearby shook hard enough that acorns fell to the ground by the dozens.

But the hill never budged. It was as if the hill wasn't made of earth—but something else disguised as earth. Perhaps magic itself. That was what I hoped, anyway. Perhaps the inside of the lair *would* have the magic necessary to cure Zaxis and Odion.

"I'll keep the Frith Guild informed of your activities," Adelgis said matter-of-factly as I walked up to him.

I checked my equipment. I had my sword, Retribution. I had my shield, Forfend. I had my guild pendant. I had the runestone.

"You won't be coming in with us?" I asked. "You can evoke light, can't you?"

Adelgis replied with a slow nod. "I'll do whatever you think is best, but I'd rather act as a coordinator. Ever since... the abyssal leech left my body... I can't function like I used to. It's better if I specialize. That way I can be useful—and not a liability."

I really didn't like it when Adelgis spoke of himself as a burden. Unfortunately, I didn't have the time to change his mind. I patted his arm and offered him a smile. He probably knew everything I was thinking anyway, so best to just go along with it.

Illia, Evianna, and Zaxis stood near the stone door, their eldrin around them. The phoenix, knightmare, and rizzel were all small creatures, even when they were adults.

Odion and Devlin, however...

Hasdrubal was a juvenile twilight dragon, but he was still massive, and had two heads. Mesos was a fully grown roc. Her gigantic wings—while beautiful and golden—would never fit through.

And then there was Terrakona.

I glanced over my shoulder. His head stuck out above the forest's canopy, his black crystal mane sparkling in the fading midafternoon light. He stared down at me, the pupils of his eyes wider than normal.

**"Warlord?"** he asked with a hint of curiosity.

"Protect Mesos and Hasdrubal," I said, gesturing to the two. "I'll be right back."

Terrakona stuck out his snake-like tongue. **"Were you aware that snakes eat birds and other lizards?"**

I held my breath, my chest tight. What *did* Terrakona eat? I hadn't thought about it before, and now it frightened me. He was the largest creature I had ever seen in my life. Would he have to hunt creatures like fully grown rocs in order to survive?

"Should I be feeding you?" I asked.

Terrakona lowered his head through the branches of the oak trees. Leaves fell around me like rain. I didn't move away as Terrakona's python nose poked me gently in the side of the head. He was so massive, I stumbled back a step.

For some reason, it made me smile.

**"A creature my size is sustained through pure magic,"** he telepathically said. **"I consume magic with every breath—stealing it from the world to maintain my life."**

I placed a hand on the scales of his snout. With a chuckle, I said, "When you say it like that, you sound evil."

**"There is a reason the apoch dragon comes for the god-creatures, Warlord."**

I really didn't want to think about the apoch dragon. Not at a time like this. In order to keep my mood high, I simply smiled and said, "So you *won't* eat Mesos and Hasdrubal, right? I don't have to worry about that?"

Terrakona's tongue flicked from his mouth. He almost

toppled me over, but I managed to recover. **"I suppose I will not eat them."**

"Make sure nothing happens to them. They shouldn't be injured."

**"By your command, Warlord."**

I stepped away from my eldrin and headed for the stone door. Everyone else waited with bated breath—especially Illia and Evianna. They had been inside the world serpent's lair with me before. They knew this would be a gauntlet of trials.

"Are we ready?" I asked.

Devlin and Odion both replied with quick and curt nods.

"A warrior is always ready," Odion stated.

He played with a bracelet on his wrist, one with multi-colored silk threads. His colors were black, blue, green, white, and red, and each represented someone's death. Black for the enemy. Red for brothers-in-arms.

Green for loved ones.

Odion had given me a similar bracelet for my birthday celebration. He called it a *warrior's mark*. I glanced at my own—there were just two colors, green and black. Black for the several enemies I had killed in the past, and the green... for Luthair.

Should I even have it? Now that Luthair had cheated death and likely been taken by the enemy?

Odion must've seen me staring, because he withdrew a thread from a pouch secured to his belt. It was small—thin and delicate—but also beautiful.

It was a gold thread.

"For slaying a god-arcanist in battle," Odion said. "I feel you should have it before we proceed."

"Why is that?" I asked as I took the thread and wrapped it into my bracelet. It was easy to secure into place, but it also felt sturdy.

"We don't know what we'll find in the lair of the fenris wolf."

Captain Devlin scoffed. "Listen to you. We'll be fine."

"These lairs are a Trial of Worth in and of themselves."

"Do you even know what you have to do to impress a roc?" Devlin scoffed again, this time louder and more indignant. "I've seen the worst of things, kid. Trust me. With this group, we'll all make it to the end."

He had enough confidence for the rest of us. Which was good, because Zaxis looked like he had all the conviction of a sandwich. He just glowered at the ground, never even acknowledging the conversation.

I withdrew the shale runestone from my pocket and held it close. "Are we ready?"

The others replied with murmured affirmatives.

With steady steps, I walked over to the stone door and placed the runestone flat against it. The grayish-black of the shale glittered, and the door reacted in kind. The outline of the wolf glowed, and the fangs pulsed with power.

Then it became so bright I had to close my eyes.

Shining and wondrous, the door opened inward. Once it stopped, and I could open my eyes again, I glanced inside. The door had opened to reveal a downward tunnel, like a slide into the pit of the earth. The pitch black didn't frighten me, but the foul odor of blood and death did.

"You needn't fret," Evianna declared as she walked around the group. She touched everyone on the shoulder, pausing for a brief moment to allow her knightmare magic to work. "I'll augment you all so that you can see in the dark."

"Useful," Devlin muttered.

Zaxis murmured his thanks.

When Evianna reached me, she smiled. I returned it, and then leaned down to kiss her. When our lips touched, the tingle of her magic infected me, and I shuddered. Her face grew hot and red, but I knew she preferred to pass her augmentation to me in this way.

I preferred it too, though I hadn't admitted that to anyone.

Except now Adelgis, who watched us with a blank stare.

"Thank you, Evianna," I whispered as I touched her white hair.

"Of course." She turned on her heel and then motioned to her shadow. "Layshl and I will do whatever it takes to help." The darkness around her feet flowed up her legs like ink defying gravity. Layshl coalesced on Evianna's body, pieces of scale-leather armor forming from shadow to encase her.

Layshl was still a young knightmare. She was a cape, a cowl, two boots, a chest piece, and a single glove of armor—not yet a complete set. Once Layshl was mature, she'd be an entire suit of armor, much like Luthair had been.

Now that Evianna was merged with her knightmare, they would live and die as a single individual. I remembered the cold power that went along with wearing a knightmare. But I couldn't dwell. I rubbed at my arms and stepped forward, glancing down at the slide into the dark.

"I'll go first," I said as I stepped onto the steep incline.

No one protested.

I slid down into the ground, keeping my balance as I went. The incline of the slide was enough that I quickly gained speed. I held my breath and touched the curved wall. The whole tunnel was a circle, perfectly cut. My fingers dug into the dirt, and I slowed myself a bit as I went deeper and deeper.

Evianna's magic allowed me to see in the dark. The dirt of the walls gradually became stone, and I cut my fingertips on something jagged as I went.

When I reached the bottom of the slide, I stumbled forward, but kept myself upright. Once again, I tried to use my magic on the dirt and rocks around us. My manipulation did nothing. I couldn't alter it or bend it to my will.

So I held out my hand and stared at the creases in my palms.

Magma slowly oozed from the creases of my skin as I used my evocation.

Steam wafted from the blazing-hot magma. I glanced around, and quickly discovered why.

The cavern around me was covered in thin amounts of ice. Again, I was reminded of Fain and his wendigo. Fain could evoke ice. And the nearby rime seemed similar. The chill of the cavern dug deep into my thoughts as I turned my attention to the opposite side of the "room."

There was another tunnel—not a slide, but a corridor. Icy winds rushed out of it, creating a haunting howl that echoed up to the tall cavern ceilings.

Illia, Evianna, and Zaxis slid in. They all kept their footing and glanced around.

"Ice?" Zaxis growled. "Of course."

He evoked fire in his hand and waved it around, creating a bit of heat for the rest of us.

Odion and Forsythe slid in next. Forsythe flapped his wings and embers went flying, also adding to the heat. Odion, on the other hand, shivered and placed a hand on the hilt of his blade. He didn't seem content with our situation.

"The Kingdom of Javin never gets this chilly," he said, glaring at our surroundings.

Devlin slid in last, but his wind allowed him to control his descent. He landed with a flourish, his arms up, like we'd cheer. No one said anything, and he fidgeted with his cap.

"Well?" he barked. "Let's get this over with."

I went ahead, molten rock held tightly in my hand. Obsidian formed near my knuckles and elbow, an odd side-effect of my evocation. I didn't mind it, though. The longer I evoked magma, the more rock-like I became. Even my bones became basalt, hardening enough that I could withstand blows from swords.

It was an interesting defensive measure.

I entered the icy tunnel. It stretched on for a long while, and the foul odor I had detected before slowly became a wet-dog scent. Bones littered the ground, but not human skeletons—they were the gnawed remains of animals. Deer. Boar. Rats. Fang-marks lined everything, like they had been chewed for hours.

Everyone followed closely behind, their steps tense and cautious.

Forsythe stepped on a shard of bone, and it snapped. The tiny noise caused everyone to jump, including Devlin.

"S-Sorry," Forsythe muttered as he ducked his head down to his body.

Nicholin poked his head up through Illia's hair. "Okay, everyone listen up. The walls are going to eat us. Be prepared for that!"

Illia placed a hand on his face. "That was in the world serpent's lair. This is different."

He squirmed out of her grip. "No, it's not! We have to be ready! I'm telling you—this place is going to eat us!"

The floor beneath me shuddered. I held my breath, my senses heightened. I felt the tremors of things moving. Multiple things. Multiple four-legged creatures. They were heading our way... But inside the wall?

I glanced to either side of us, confused by the stone. I felt the creatures on the other side. They were heading our way. A dozen of them.

"Something is coming," I whispered as I pulled out Retribution.

It had gotten so cold that my breath came out as a fine mist.

"Coming from where?" Odion asked.

I shook my head. "The... walls."

Howls, barks, and panting flooded the chilly corridor. A song of wolves. They were nearby—so many of them. Did the fenris wolf have a pack? Or was he a creature like the Mother of Shapeshifters, where he could be multiple creatures at once?

Evianna pulled her short sword, Illia readied a dagger, and Zaxis held up white-hot metal knuckles. We had been in dozens of fights together. I knew they could handle themselves.

And then the wolves grew closer, their growls and cries growing so loud they almost hurt my ears.

# CHAPTER 5

## DIRE WOLVES

"Enough of this," Devlin growled.

He thrust his hands out, and the wind obeyed his call. A blast of hurricane weather exploded from his palms, screaming as it shattered ice and smashed against the walls of the cavern with enough force to crack stone. The room shook from Devlin's attack until he finally allowed his evocation to wane.

The wolves quieted themselves, and I no longer felt their footfalls. I shivered at the chill winds, wondering if the cold came from the fenris wolf's lair, or from Devlin himself.

Devlin stopped evoking his storm winds and took a deep breath. When he glanced around, he did so with squinted eyes. "I'm seein' nothin'."

"It's a narrow corridor," Zaxis quipped. "Of course you're *seein' nothin'*, old man."

"*Old man?*" Devlin ripped off his cap and gritted his teeth. "You listen to me—roc arcanists have superb eyesight. Better than anything you have, that's for sure."

"Congratulations. You don't need spectacles. You can console yourself with that fact when you get wooden teeth."

I turned on my heel and shot them both glares. "Enough."

Everyone came to a halt in the middle of the stone corridor. The conversations stopped, and everyone tensed, as though this would turn into a fight. That wasn't what I wanted, though. We just needed to stay focused. Sarcastic comments and bickering weren't helpful.

"We need to—"

Then the floor rumbled. I caught my breath, my thoughts halted. The tremors beneath my feet told me that the floor was rearranging itself. A pit was being created underneath the floor. Blades made of ice filled the bottom of the pit, creating a trap that would impale anyone who fell into it—or give them frostbite, even if they lived after the fall.

"The floor is about to open up!" I shouted, my voice echoing.

I went to jump into the shadows by instinct, but I cursed myself when I stepped hard onto the shadows, and nothing happened. Instead, Evianna grabbed me and took me with her into the darkness. The cold protection of the void helped ease my anxiety. When we emerged, we were twenty feet down the hall.

Devlin jumped with his wind, avoiding the pit by practically flying. Illia grabbed Zaxis and teleported to safety. The only person who didn't get out of the way in time was Odion. He seemed caught off guard, and he tried to leap away, but it wasn't enough. The ground opened, and he tumbled downward toward the ice blades—they were basically spikes, ready to skewer the king.

He hit two, but his armor protected his torso. His armor didn't fully encase his leg, though. An icy blade cut into the back of his leg as he fell, breaking skin and causing him to bleed. Normally, the small amount of blood wouldn't bother me, but Illia and Evianna could still be infected with the arcane plague.

I couldn't allow that to happen.

The rumbling stopped, leaving the corridor split in half. Illia, Evianna, Zaxis, Devlin, and I stood on one side, and Odion was down below us, at least fifteen feet at the bottom of the pit.

"Are you okay?" I asked.

Illia stepped forward to teleport down, but I held her back. When she glanced at me with her one eye, I shook my head.

"I'm fine," Odion said. He shoved himself away from the ice skewer and stood between two of them. "That was my fault. I was distracted."

"You can step into the shadows like a knightmare arcanist," I said. I remembered when he did it against me. "Why didn't you?"

Odion glanced up, his brow furrowed. "I told you, my liege. I was distracted." He offered me a forced smile. "I've never been touched by corrupted magic before. It weighs heavily on my mind."

Before I could reply, Odion slipped into the darkness like he had stepped into a bottomless puddle. When he rose out of the shadows, he was on the ledge next to Captain Devlin, his white armor marred on his left leg with a small trickle of tainted blood.

"I'll heal him," Forsythe said, his phoenix-voice beautiful and comforting in our dark atmosphere.

He hopped forward, a soot trail left in his tracks. The fire of his inner body lit up our cave like surroundings. When he got near Odion, he poked his beak closer to Odion's injury. Typically, phoenix healing didn't have a visual component. Phoenixes, and their arcanists, could touch someone, and then augment the individual to stitch together their flesh.

Instead of that, Forsythe's body glowed a gentle gold, and a sparkling yellow flame wafted off his body. It was small, but it was something. The heat helped warm the whole corridor.

The golden flames washed over Odion, healing his leg, but charring the clothing underneath his armor. He leapt back and patted his trousers. "What is this?" he barked.

Zaxis leapt forward, his eyes wide. "Forsythe! Is that... your healing and your fire mixed together? L-Like Atty?"

His phoenix eldrin turned to him, his golden eyes the same shade as the healing fire. "Yes, my arcanist. I've been practicing with Titania. I thought... I thought you'd be impressed, and that it might be useful."

"Healing *fire*?" Odion asked as he examined his injured leg. "I've never heard of that before."

No one had until recently—mixing evocation and augmentation was unheard of. Atty Trixibelle had managed to develop it, though. She was clearly talented with her magic, but it had cost her. She hadn't been involved in *anything* else since she started down the path to achieving true form with her phoenix eldrin.

Atty studied her magic, focused her mind, and did nothing else.

Now her eldrin had taught Forsythe the secret to her development.

Perhaps I would have to speak to her at some point as well. I hadn't yet developed my augmentation, and I worried about it.

Zaxis knelt down and petted his phoenix. "I'm really impressed, Forsythe. Truly."

With his head held high, Forsythe fluffed his scarlet feathers. "Thank you. I'm trying to be more like you, my arcanist. I'm going to be *surprising*."

Although I wanted them to celebrate their magic and accomplishments, we didn't have time for this. I held Retribution tight in my grip, and then used it to point down the corridor. "We need to press forward. If we see anything harmful, we should eliminate it. No one hesitate."

We had to clear a path, just in case we had to bring other people through the lair to bond with the wolf.

As a group of six arcanists, we continued forward.

When we reached the next cavern-like room, I caught my breath.

It was...

A forest.

An underground forest. Complete with pine trees, snow, icicles, and a winding path. My mouth dropped open when I stepped into the "cavern" and noticed that the roof wasn't a cave. It was a *sky*. Stars twinkled overhead, glittering with a brilliant intensity. I knew it wasn't night, though. It had been the afternoon when we had entered.

"What is this?" Illia asked as her boots crunched the fresh snow.

Nicholin poked his nose out of her hair. "Rizzels aren't fond of the snow, I'll have you know." He sniffed deep. "And be careful! The trees are going to consume us."

"Everything will be okay," Evianna said in her double-voice, rolling her eyes.

"It won't. I'm telling you! We'll be eaten for sure!"

No one said anything to Nicholin. He remained in Illia's hair, shifty-eyed as we continued into the mysterious forest. Odion and Devlin regarded the area with disgust, but Zaxis seemed delighted. He summoned fire and threw it across the forest, melting the snow.

"Why is there a sky?" he asked.

I shrugged. "I'm not sure. It's not *actually* the sky, though."

With my tremor sense, I could tell we were still underground. The sky was fake. I felt the roof. I felt the stone. The sky was probably an illusion. And once I had that thought, I turned my attention to the trees. I couldn't feel them either.

More illusions?

The cold felt real, though. My breath came out as an icy mist.

Then the howling and the grunting returned. Wolves were nearby. Everyone stopped and glanced around, their attention on the cluster of pine trees. It was Devlin who spotted something first. He homed in on far off movement.

"There they are," he muttered as he pointed to the distance. "At least six of them."

"Twelve," I corrected. They couldn't hide their numbers from me. "They're circling around us. Six are somewhere over there." I pointed in the opposite direction. "They're trying to trick us."

"What are they?" Odion asked.

"Based on their size... I'd say they're dire wolves."

"The island of Javin isn't familiar with wolves."

Dire wolves were powerful creatures. They were immune to any sort of ice or cold, and they were large—the size of a horse. When they bit someone, their powerful jaws could shatter bone, and their howls could cause hallucinations. Most were considered aggressive, and they typically only bonded to individuals who were cutthroat and forceful.

What were dire wolves doing in the lair of the fenris wolf?

Then again, there had been creatures in the world serpent's lair... But they hadn't been actual creatures. They were constructs created either by the world serpent, or the lair itself, I was never fully certain.

The wolves were likely a test. A part of the Trial of Worth. We probably had to deal with them.

Devlin whistled and then motioned to everyone. "Okay, kids. Gather up here. We need to stick close. Dire wolves attack the weakest first. Or the person most separate from the group. We gotta outthink them, you understand?"

"I could teleport around and confuse them," Illia said, the cold breeze sending a flurry of snowflakes around us. "Or maybe even pick off a few of them before they strike."

Everyone turned to me. I thought over the options for a moment, then nodded to Illia. "Okay. Go ahead. Confuse the wolves. The rest of us will stay together as a group."

Illia touched her eyepatch and then replied with a nod. She disappeared in a puff of glitter, leaving the rest of us in the snowy forest. I glanced upward, my eyes on the stars. I evoked some molten rock as I thought about Luthair's cape.

I didn't want to disappoint him. I had to solve this and find him.

Evianna manipulated the shadows and created pools of writhing darkness. At first, I wasn't sure what she was doing, but then I realized they were traps. She positioned them between the trees, and near the edge of the pathway.

Odion and Devlin went back-to-back. Devlin was the only one who wasn't shivering, and I suspected it was because of his roc magic. Rocs were often in cold weather, and they soared at the highest heights.

Zaxis approached me. His metal knuckles were white-hot, and he held them up, ready to fight. Forsythe stayed on the ground near his arcanist. We made a small team of three, and Evianna, with her knightmare, stayed by my side.

I closed my eyes and felt the tremors of the wolves. My heart beat faster and faster each time I felt Illia appear. She caught the attention of the wolves, and they angled for her. Then one wolf disappeared from my "sight." Where had it gone? Had she teleported it? She hadn't killed it. I would've felt it hit the ground...

But then the other eleven wolves charged at us.

"They're coming," I called out.

I held up my black sword, and so did Odion. His white blade was a harsh contrast to mine, but it matched the white of the snow.

The dire wolves wove through the trees. Their feet crunched the snow, and their heavy breathing sounded like husky growls. I spotted them in the darkness of the false forest, rushing toward us in groups of two. Everyone tensed when I lifted a hand.

The first wolf that charged hit one of Evianna's traps. The

shadows sprang to life and stabbed at the wolf as it ran over the pool of darkness. The beast was *huge*, though. Much larger than a standard horse—it was a draft horse in size, thick with muscle. The dire wolf had a mouth of fangs, and its eyes were oddly unfocused.

It seemed crazed.

But I had seen worse. I had fought hundreds of plague creatures at this point. A rabid dire wolf didn't frighten me.

The second dire wolf leapt over Evianna's trap and went for the group. Zaxis and Forsythe were ready. After a deep inhale, Forsythe breathed a torrent of flames. The fire burned the underside of the wolf and it yipped. Zaxis leapt forward and punched the creature in the neck, his knuckles hot enough to melt off the creature's fur.

It smelled of cooked meat and burnt hair.

Evianna controlled her shadows to crush the dire wolf in the trap. The darkness rose up as tendrils and wrapped around the creature. Like a snake, the shadows tightened and crushed down on the wolf. With each exhale, the creature became more constricted.

A third wolf dashed out of the snowy pine trees.

I was ready.

It leapt at me with its mouth open, its fangs slick with saliva. I swung my blade at its head and sliced it clean in half. I didn't even feel the impact. My blade cut through magical flesh without any resistance, even through bone.

The dire wolf died instantly, but it still crashed into me due to its momentum. I grunted and stumbled backward, but I kept my footing. The beast's blood smeared across my clothing and the front of my shield.

When a fourth dire wolf came for me, I stepped up onto the warm corpse of the first wolf and leapt at the enemy. I slashed with my sword, cutting deep into the beast's chest and killing the second one as just quickly as the first.

My sword was made from the bones of the apoch dragon, and it was a magic destroyer.

Odion's sword, the White Curse, didn't slice through the wolves as quickly, but his weapon was heavy, and it cleaved through flesh just fine. Devlin evoked winds and knocked the wolves into more of Evianna's traps. The tendrils grabbed them and kept them in place.

But then one of the wolves howled. The sound rang in my ears. Instead of falling victim to their hallucinations, I clamped my hands over my ears. Molten rock fell onto my shoulder, and I shook off the hot sensation. Heat didn't hurt me, but it did damage my clothing.

I glanced around.

Curse the abyssal hells.

I hadn't told the others about the hallucinations, and I cursed under my breath for not telling them what I knew. The only other person who had covered their ears was Devlin.

The others swung at the air, flailing about as though they were fighting wolves—but they weren't. It was just them and the wind.

Then I noticed four black wolves in the trees. They were watching the fight with intelligent eyes, like they were evaluating us all.

I readied Retribution and Forfend.

# CHAPTER 6

## DETERMINATION

The four wolves lunged from the forest, all in different directions, surrounding us like only a pack could. One of the wolves leapt over Evianna's shadowy trap and went straight for her throat. Like any good knightmare arcanist, she stepped backward and fell into the darkness, easily dodging the jaws of the massive dire wolf.

When she emerged from the shadows, a second wolf went for her in an obviously coordinated attack.

I turned to help her, but the other two wolves came for me, like they were expecting my actions. One came at me from the front, and the other behind. I slashed and then whirled on my heel, trying to keep both at bay. They lunged, snapped their jaws, and then darted back, their hot saliva splattered across my shield.

It happened a second time—one at my front, the other behind—and when I swung this time, it wasn't with as much power as before. The wolves darted away just the same, and then I realized...

The wolves were just distracting me.

The other two wolves focused their aggression on Evianna. They weren't playing games. They were snapping at her body, making plays for her legs, and circling with a fierce intensity. Evianna dodged through the darkness, but she wasn't fast enough for two giant wolves.

One wolf caught her arm and she shouted.

"Evianna!"

I evoked magma and threw it around me. The molten rock hit the ground and heat wafted around the cavern, raising the temperature. The wolves leapt away, their hackles raised. I ran to Evianna, but the wolf on her arm pulled her toward the tree illusions. Its fangs pierced deep into her flesh, and her concentration broke.

Evianna shouted again, and her shadow-puddle traps disappeared. The darkness returned to its normal state.

"Leave her alone!"

I threw Retribution in an act of desperation, fearing that if I lost sight of Evianna, she'd disappear forever. My blade slashed the wolf's shoulder, effortlessly removing a chunk of its flesh and fur. The beast howled and scrambled away, its intelligent eyes on me.

These lair beasts seemed... different. The beasts in the lair of the world serpent weren't nearly as coordinated or tactical. They had attacked and then vanished. No strategy. No games. It was like the wolves *wanted* to separate us.

Now free, Evianna shadow-stepped away from the monster wolf and appeared at my side. She took a deep breath, her arm ragged.

"Volke," Evianna muttered, her voice mixed with Layshl's. "I'm sorry. I'll be more careful."

She manipulated the shadows to grab the hilt of Retribution. With a quick tug, she yanked my blade over to my feet. I knelt and scooped up my weapon.

The ground beneath our feet shook. Evianna grabbed me— as if to steady me—and while I was rocking back on my heels, one of the wolves lunged. I slashed the wolf's face, right over an eye. The canine yipped and then stumbled to the side, its paws touching my magma, which burned its pads.

While the wolf was unsteady, Zaxis leapt over with a punch and struck the beast in its snout. His knuckles shattered bone and caused the wolf to hit the stone floor. When the beast was down, Zaxis punched it again, and again, and again, pummeling the head until it couldn't move.

With a deep breath, he straightened. "What's going to—"

But then the rumbling intensified. Evianna used her shadows to keep me and Zaxis on our feet, but everyone else wasn't so lucky. A crack formed in the stone, opening wide like a chasm. It reminded me of the world serpent's lair... when it opened and swallowed Illia whole.

"Illia!" I shouted, desperate to find her. "Illia, where are you!"

I ripped myself free of Evianna's shadows and ran for the forest illusion. Evianna and Zaxis both held out hands, trying to stop me, but I ran out of their grasp. I didn't want to wait. I jumped over my magma and continued into the shadows of the trees. Zaxis and Evianna followed me. The footfalls of their running echoed behind me as I went.

"Devlin!"

Was that Odion? I ignored him. I kept going, the ground shaking but my feet were steady. My world serpent magic couldn't seem to manipulate the ground of another god-creature's lair, but it seemed to help me remain upright.

I heard a pop of air, and my heart jumped. I turned in that direction, and found a glittering mist of silver. "Illia!" Thankfully, she wasn't far away.

Illia stood next to one of the trees, trying to keep her balance by holding onto it. Unfortunately, it was an illusion, and couldn't support her weight. The ground opened, and Illia was about to fall, but I rushed over and grabbed her arm.

She teleported the both of us in the matter of an instant.

Her magic yanked me through space, twisting my insides. When we appeared in a different area of the forest, my head spun.

Then the rumbling stopped.

No more earthquake.

"Volke?" Illia asked. She touched my shoulder, her one eye narrowed in concern.

Nicholin stared at me from her shoulder. "I told you. The lair tried to eat us! *No one listened to me.*" His fur stood on end. "I'm always right!"

I took Illia by the elbow and steered her back toward Evianna and Zaxis, both of which were searching through the fake trees in order to find us. Once we reunited, we hurried through the undergrowth and headed for the main road. As we ran, the trees, starry sky, and vegetation all shimmered and slowly faded away.

We reached the "road" right as everything disappeared.

Only Odion was waiting for us.

He stared at the ground, his shoulders tense and his brow furrowed. His sword—normally held with two hands—was held limply in one. Odion took in deep breaths, sweat dappling his skin.

I rushed over. "Where's Devlin?"

Without the trees, I could see the entire cavern. No one was here. Not even the wolves. When I tried to sense our surroundings with my abilities, I couldn't detect anything. We were alone.

"Devlin was swallowed by the ground," Odion muttered. Then he turned his attention to me. "He saved me from that terrible fate."

I waited with my breath held, uncertain of what to say.

But Zaxis didn't hesitate. "That sounds like Devlin." He rubbed at his heated metal knuckles. "Let's keep going. The faster we find the fenris wolf, the faster we save him."

The others didn't protest. Illia, Evianna, Zaxis, and Odion

stuck close, their attention on our surroundings, each vigilant. Forsythe flew in and landed next to us, his feathers ruffled. He hopped alongside his arcanist, his head up and his beak pointed toward the rock ceiling.

We walked across the empty cavern, and I wondered if the ground had opened up because we had failed at some level. If we had defeated the wolves faster, would we have avoided that punishment?

"Listen," I said, my gaze on the ground as I spoke. "I've spoken to the first world serpent arcanist before."

The only one surprised was Odion. He seemed curious and confused, but he didn't say anything.

"The first world serpent arcanist—his name was Luvi—told me about the first fenris wolf arcanist. He said the man who bonded with the wolf was clever. He was a strategist, but he was also a man who was relentless and determined."

"What was his name?" Odion asked.

"Balastar."

"Why bring this up?" Illia whispered. Her eldrin regarded me with a questioning tilt of his head.

I glanced back at the empty cavern. "The illusions... The wolves... I think whatever challenge is ahead, we need to keep what I just said in mind. We need to think like strategists."

Evianna, Zaxis, and Illia nodded along with my words.

"That was the *first* fenris wolf arcanist," Odion stated. "I don't think we need to match him perfectly."

"Just keep it in mind."

We entered another stone corridor in silence. Forsythe's blazing body provided light, but Evianna went around and touched us all, renewing her augmentation on us so we could see in the thickest of darkness.

A few hundred feet into the corridor, I heard a howling of interesting intensity. It didn't sound like an animal—it was the type of howl only the wind could produce. We quickened our steps until I finally saw what was making the noise.

A snowstorm.

The room ahead of us—it was a blizzard trapped underground. Snow, hail, and sleet swirled through the air at ferocious speeds. To my surprise, the blizzard never entered the corridor. It stayed in the cavern. Not even a single snowflake exited the storm and entered our space.

I walked up to the invisible barrier that kept the weather at bay and I examined our obstacle. It was too difficult to see through the snow. The white-on-white might as well have been a blanket over my eyes.

"What're we supposed to do?" Evianna asked, her eyebrows knitted. "Do you want me to drag you all through the shadows?"

The storm battered the ground. It made it impossible for me to sense anyone's steps or tremors. What if the last of the wolves were waiting in the storm? I couldn't tell.

Odion shook his head. "Perhaps we should have our phoenix arcanist clear us a path."

"Step aside," Zaxis said. He walked over to the edge of the snowstorm and held up a hand. "I'll handle this."

Flames erupted from his palm, pouring out into the harsh winter. His fire melted some of the snow, and defeated the hail and sleet... But it didn't kill the storm. The hurricane raged on regardless.

"I don't think that's going to work," I muttered.

With a stroke of my chin, I tried to think about this strategically. What sort of *tactics* could we use to solve this dilemma?

"What're we waiting for?" Zaxis asked.

"We don't know how much storm is in this cavern." I pointed to the violent winds. "And if this *isn't* an illusion, the snowstorm could really harm us."

"I thought you said we needed to be determined? And

relentless." Zaxis rotated his shoulders. "This is a Trial of Worth, isn't it? We shouldn't sit around dwelling. We should show the wolf what we're made of."

While I applauded Zaxis's cavalier attitude, I couldn't match his enthusiasm. We were supposed to be looking for raw magic. Just rushing forward seemed like a foolish idea. On the other hand, I *had* mentioned Balastar's determination. Perhaps Zaxis was right.

Without warning, Zaxis stepped around me.

"W-Wait," Forsythe squawked.

Before I could stop him, Zaxis stepped into the storm. I tried to hold out my hand, but he just kept going—straight into the cold.

"*Zaxis*," I shouted.

His phoenix hurried after him, running into the freezing winds.

It was like they were disappearing into a curtain of ice. One second, they were in the warm corridor, and the next they were gone. Swallowed whole by the sheer amount of snow in the air.

Illia didn't wait for me to say anything. She, too, rushed into the winter cold, chasing after Zaxis and his eldrin. Evianna and Odion didn't budge, though. They both watched me, waiting for a command or a plan of action.

"We should stick together," I said as I motioned to the storm. "Let's go."

Unlike with the forest illusion, where I couldn't sense the trees with my tremors, I *could* sense the snow. Which meant—at some level—it was real.

And it felt real the moment I stepped into the next cavern. The howling winds assaulted me from all sides, slamming me with hail. Evianna tried to manipulate the shadows to shield herself, but it wasn't enough. Odion attempted to cover his face, but his armor wasn't suited to defending against weather.

When I held up Forfend, the shield pulsed with an inner

magic. Normally, Forfend could reflect magical attacks—it had never reflected ambient weather, though. Then again, the storm was clearly magical in nature. Was Forfend storing up the power of the blizzard? I kept that in mind as I held my shield close.

My teeth chattered ceaselessly. I couldn't stop. And the snow was so high, it came up to my waist. I had to follow in Zaxis's trail just to avoid trudging through the worst of the ice.

The winds became so bad, I had to close my eyes. Odion and Evianna followed suit. Evianna eventually hugged my arm, keeping herself a tiny bit warmer with my heat and allowing me to lead the way. Although I couldn't "see" much with my tremor sense in a storm, I could sense enough to stay within Zaxis's pre-made furrow.

Hail and sleet got into my ears, and the cold became so great, it felt like I was on fire. It was an odd sensation—even taking in a breath hurt. Especially my nose. It seemed like the cold was tearing me apart from the inside.

I took a deep breath.

What would Terrakona say?

He would tell me that rocks wouldn't freeze.

When I exhaled, steam rushed out with my breath. I was warm. The heat of my molten rock kept me warm. Obsidian sprouted from my elbows and shoulders, disturbing my clothing —some so sharp, they jutted out.

Evianna had to watch her grip.

The cold was no longer a problem. At least, not for me.

Once I was warm, and steam wafted off my body at a rapid rate, Odion moved closer, like approaching a small campfire. He kept his shaky hands near my body.

The howling of the wind prevented us from saying anything, but it wasn't long until the winds lessened, and the storm eventually waned. When I managed to open my eyes, I was shocked to find we were in another cavern identical to the last. Well, except for the huge piles of snow.

Now that the storm had cleared, I easily spotted Zaxis, Forsythe, Illia, and Nicholin, all at the far end of the cavern. They stood next to a circular door, their eyes on the giant carving of the fenris wolf.

With as much energy as I could muster, I pushed through the snow. My warm body melted anything I touched, leaving a stream of icy water in my wake. Evianna grabbed me and then dropped into the shadows. I went with her, traveling in the darkness until we both emerged near Illia.

Odion had done the same, though he still shivered and rubbed at his arms.

"You have the shale runestone, right?" Zaxis asked, holding out his hand.

I nodded once. I dug the runestone out of my pocket and handed it over.

Zaxis held the palm-sized rock close and then touched it to the giant stone door. Just like at the entrance, the door split in half and then opened, this time the wall rumbling.

It reminded me of my meeting with Terrakona.

Beyond the door, far from the snow of the underground blizzard, was a garden of marble, bone, fur, and ice. And while it looked cold, it was far from chilly. The inner sanctum had the heat of a well-kept home, and the moment we all stepped inside, I breathed easier.

It really was a garden of wonder. Blue flowers. White furs. Bones of animals who looked to have died peacefully in their sleep. Carvings of battles and dogs were on every surface. This appeared to be a place for tranquility and reflection. It surprised me. I had expected something violent and blood soaked, but a part of me wondered if the smells near the entrance had also been an illusion.

Had the fenris wolf been attempting to scare us away?

"This is it," I muttered.

"What?" Zaxis asked.

"This is the heart of the lair."

Illia spun around, her one eye searching. "But... where is the wolf?"

The garden was small enough that I could see the back wall. I remembered meeting Terrakona... He had been hiding in the pool of water. Was the fenris wolf around here as well?

"Listen," I whispered. "The wolf is here, even if you can't see him right now." I held up a hand. "But don't worry about that just yet. Everyone should split up and search. When I met Terrakona, his lair had star shards and raw magic. This place should have them as well."

"You want us to loot the god-creature's lair before he's even bonded?" Zaxis asked, deadpan and sardonic.

I shot him a glower. "Yeah? Is there a problem with that?"

"No. I just wanted to hear you say it."

I ran a hand down my face. "Look. I just want to make sure you and—"

Zaxis placed a heavy hand on my shoulder, cutting me off. "No, I get it." Then he met my gaze. "I appreciate you doing this for us."

His phoenix hopped around his feet. "Hm. I agree with my arcanist."

"Then you should get searching," I whispered. "The wolf is nearby. I can feel it."

# CHAPTER 7

## THE HUNTER

The icy garden of the fenris wolf was soaked in magic. I felt it with every step. And while snow and rime covered every surface, I wasn't chilled. The temperature remained at a pleasant level, even though my breath came out as a glittery fog.

I searched through the blue blossoms of the crystal flowers, and then around the decorative boulders placed along the edges of the regal garden. A pathway made of pebbles had been laid out in a figure eight, looping throughout the massive cavern but ultimately leading nowhere.

Everything seemed tranquil and inviting, like a regal oil painting of a fantastical snowy landscape.

While I searched through the leaves of blue ferns, Illia and Nicholin approached.

Her face...

Her nose was a bright red, and the tip had ice. Even her ears looked frosted, but she didn't shiver or indicate she was cold. Was it just a cosmetic effect of the cavern? Everything looked cold, even if it wasn't?

"Volke?" she asked.

I stared at her eyepatch. It looked... frozen. "Are you okay?" I asked.

"I think so." Illia glanced at her body. "Does something look wrong?"

"You look cold."

"I feel fine." She put down her arms and then lowered her voice. "I'm actually a little worried. The lair of the world serpent seemed... More dangerous than this lair." She brushed back her hair with pale-white fingers. "Maybe it's because I was swallowed by the tree last time, but this place doesn't seem too dangerous."

"An indoor blizzard and a pack of wolves *isn't too dangerous* for you?" I half-laughed. "In theory, someone without an eldrin is supposed to complete this Trial of Worth."

Nicholin twitched his ferret-tail from side to side. "We had a world serpent arcanist with us, and we *still* lost someone." He squinted at the sapphire flowers. "And I don't like this place. Something is wrong."

Although his fur was coated with ice, and the fingers of his paws were stiff, Nicholin didn't shiver or chatter his teeth. Both he and Illia were the picture of *hypothermia*, but that didn't change their behaviors.

I closed my coat a little tighter, anxious.

We still hadn't found the fenris wolf. And while there was obviously magic here, it wasn't like with Terrakona. I hadn't found a single star shard. *Not one.* There had to be some sort of mistake.

"I think we're fine," I said with a shrug. "We just need to search harder, okay? Odion and Zaxis are relying on us."

Illia glared at me with her one eye. "You don't think I know that? I want to save Zaxis more than anybody."

"S-Sorry. I didn't mean to imply otherwise."

She softened immediately afterward. With a curt nod, she said, "I'm sorry. Let's just focus." Illia patted Nicholin's head. Even her hand was stiff. "We'll find something."

When we parted ways, I returned my attention to the "vegetation." Sure, there were flowers, ferns, and vines, but they weren't any real plants I had ever seen in my life. Few flowers grew in the frosty north—I knew of the *summer snowflake*—it was a golden flower with six distinct petals. The summer snowflake could grow anywhere, and when someone touched the plant, it was warm to the touch.

On rare occasions, a seven-petal summer snowflake could be found. The seeds were spicy, or so I had heard, and the old tales said that if you ate them, you'd have a year of good fortune.

I had never seen a seven-petal summer snowflake—I had never seen the flower, period—but I loved reading about the unusual and magical flora of far-off places.

Once I reached the beginning of the figure-eight loop, I sighed.

Curse the abyssal hells. I hadn't found *anything*. The feeling of magic persisted, but that wasn't helping. Where *hadn't* I searched? The fenris wolf wasn't even appearing. Had we done something wrong? Had the wolf left?

No. We had used the runestone on both doors. It had to be here.

Zaxis and Forsythe wandered down the trail. Unlike Illia and her eldrin, Zaxis wasn't frosted at all. As a matter of fact, steam wafted off his body at a steady rate. Same with Forsythe. Their ability to heat themselves kept the frost from claiming their flesh.

I glanced down at my fingers. They seemed devoid of blood circulation. I tried to curl my fingers, but it was difficult—they were frozen. I brought them to my mouth and blew hot air on them, but I felt nothing. No heat. No cold.

That was odd.

"Are you sure this is the heart of the fenris wolf's lair?" Zaxis asked as he drew close. "Nothing is like I imagined it."

Forsythe nodded once. "It smells like dog in here. But I don't see it."

I blew more hot air onto my hands. Still, I felt nothing.

With a sigh, I replied, "Have you found any raw magic? I think that's more important."

"Are you okay?" Zaxis asked as he crossed his arms. He gave me the once-over. "You look like you're about to collapse."

"I do?"

"You're an ice block. By the abyssal hells, button up your coat or something. You want frostbite?"

I pulled my coat on even tighter, but nothing seemed to happen. I couldn't feel anything.

And then it struck me.

Maybe... this *wasn't* the end of the Trial of Worth. Maybe this was one final test. The forest with the wolves had been an illusion. The flowers and ferns here all felt real, but what if the *temperature* was an illusion? What if I wasn't feeling cold because something was tricking me into feeling okay?

I tried to voice my concerns, but it was already too late. My lungs hurt. I tried to take in a deep breath, but I couldn't. I stepped backward, my nose stuffed up, and my breath shallow.

Zaxis furrowed his brow. "What's wrong?"

I hit the ground on one knee, closed my eyes. With effortless concentration, I evoked my magma. The heat of my magic flooded my being. It dispelled the frost and rime in a heartbeat, freeing me from the oppressive clutches of the ice. I gasped down air, my body warmed by the magma that coursed through my limbs.

I hadn't thought to keep myself warm because I wasn't feeling cold.

I stood straight and clenched my fist. Obsidian jutted from my skin, like rock claws. "This room is freezing."

Zaxis sarcastically widened his eyes. "Is *that* what all this frost is?"

"No. You don't understand." I glanced around, worried about the others. "It never felt cold. I guess you're always warm... but no one else is."

"What're you saying? They're in trouble?"

"We need to find them. Right now."

Without waiting for a reply, I took off down the stone path. I had *just* seen Illia. Where was she? The room was large, there were plenty of plants and boulders, and I couldn't see anyone else—not Odion, Illia, or Evianna.

With frantic movements, I pushed the ferns aside, then the flowers. I even tried to manipulate the terrain again, but it wouldn't work. Something about the god-creatures' lairs made it difficult to alter.

Damn.

But then I found something—a hand on the ground, poking out from another cluster of blue ferns. I dashed over and ripped the plants aside, only to find Illia. She and Nicholin both had heavy layers of ice over their bodies. They must've collapsed.

I knelt down and evoked some of my magma. I couldn't touch them with it, but I kept the superheated rock close enough to melt most of the frost. Then I gently shook Illia's shoulder, hoping to wake her with enough heat.

"C'mon," I said. "Get up."

After a few minutes exposed to my heat, the ice had left her body. Then sweat dappled her skin, and her eye fluttered open. "What's... going on?"

"Are you okay?" I shook the magma from my palms—it burned into the ground—and then I helped Illia to her feet. "What do you remember last?"

"I remember... feeling tired." She rubbed at her head. "Nicholin?"

He was at her feet, curled into a little ball. I evoked more magma and brought it closer to his ferret body. He was much larger than I remembered. He was the size of a fisher—nearly eight pounds.

When Nicholin stirred, he immediately hissed and arched his back. "How *dare* you," he said through his grogginess. "I will *not* be eaten again!"

I picked him up—he was too disoriented to see straight—and then placed him on Illia's shoulder. Now that they were safe, I ran down the path again, frantic to find Evianna.

This room *had* been a trap, and I had almost fallen for it.

When I reached the starting point of the path, Zaxis, Forsythe, and Odion were waiting.

But no Evianna.

"Where is she?" I demanded. "Where is Evianna?"

Zaxis shook his head. "I don't know." He opened his mouth, like he was about to ask for Illia, but she came stumbling down the path on her own. "Oh, thank the good stars." He rushed over and hugged her, his smile larger than I had seen it in days.

Illia hugged him back. And then Nicholin got in on the embrace, rubbing his little weasel-like face into Zaxis's red hair.

"I missed your warmth," Nicholin muttered.

I wanted to search the whole cavern over again for Evianna, but I knew the truth of the matter. She was gone. The lair had swallowed her because she had failed the test, just like Devlin had. It was the world serpent's lair all over again.

Without warning, a terrible chill filled the room.

The ferns wilted. The flowers died. The boulders were coated in a layer of thick ice.

A rumbling echoed between the cavernous walls, followed by a deep and guttural growl. It sounded louder and larger than almost anything I had encountered before. Not larger than Terrakona—or the leviathan, Decimus, or the king basilisk, Nyre—but still large enough to send a shiver down my spine.

**"What have we here?"** a foreboding voice asked, its tone

masculine, yet playful. **"Three Children of Balastar, and one Child of Astros. An unlikely fellowship."**

I glanced around, trying to find the source of the voice. It had to be the god-creature. I'd recognize that forceful and mystical tone anywhere.

"Oh, great and powerful fenris wolf," I said. "Please, forgive us. We came to search the heart of your lair."

**"What's that, small one? You lie. You came here to kill me."**

"W-What?" I asked, taken aback by the question. "Of course not. Why would you think that?"

**"Why else would a god-arcanist come into my lair? You've come to hunt me—but I am no one's prey. I am the greatest hunter of all time."**

"That's not true," Zaxis yelled, anger raw in his voice. "We didn't come here for that!" He also glanced around, looking for the wolf. But it was nowhere to be seen. "Show yourself! If you're such a *mighty hunter*, you shouldn't be afraid! We've come to speak with you—and maybe find a cure for a magical corruption."

Forsythe fluffed his feathers. "That's right, great wolf hunter. We mean you no harm."

Everyone else remained quiet, myself included.

A prolonged second stretched between us.

Then the fenris wolf appeared, as though he had dropped his invisibility.

I hadn't even sensed him. Perhaps he had appeared out of thin air?

My breath caught in my chest even as frost crawled up my clothing. The wolf was massive. He could play with a horse the same way a cat played with a mouse. But it was the beast's majesty that rendered me silent.

The wolf's fur reminded me of Luthair—metallic darkness streaked with frost. His eyes glowed with the light of a full moon on a winter night. Chains wrapped around his neck and down his torso, each link branded with runes in a language I did not know, but somehow understood it promised power.

His teeth and claws gleamed as if forged from winter silver. Every slight movement of the beast caused its corded muscle to ripple beneath his fur. His ears stood erect, twitching in the direction of new sounds, including when Nicholin uttered a quiet, "*Goodness.*"

This wolf was the incarnation of winter's fury—a death that approached almost gently, then struck without mercy.

The beast opened his mouth, his insides were an icy blue, and his tongue pure black. With each exhale, the gigantic fenris wolf washed us all in snow.

**"I am the embodiment of winter—and winter is the greatest killer of life. My name is Vjorn the Second Fenris Wolf, and I will crush the skulls of any who think they can slay me in my own lair."**

"We didn't come to slay you," Illia said, one hand up.

"Can't you hear our thoughts?" I asked, stepping forward. "Terrakona could hear the thoughts of everyone who entered his lair. Can't you tell we're telling the truth?"

**"I can hear you,"** Vjorn said with a growl. **"That's why I know you've come to kill me. One of you thinks my blood could cure the arcane plague."**

I didn't even need to ask. With a slow turn, I faced Odion.

The man slicked back his white hair, a neutral expression on his face, though a twitch of his eyebrow told the truth.

"I didn't come here planning to kill it," King Odion said. "I only thought... that if all else failed... the world serpent arcanist could likely cut the beast down."

The fenris wolf wasn't as large as Terrakona, but I wasn't confident in my ability to kill him in his own lair. The world serpent was the incarnation of dominion, the soul forge was the manifestation of primal life. The fenris wolf was the epitome of what it meant to be a killer. Vjorn's magic was perfect for single combat.

I shook my head, dispelling the thoughts. Then I returned my attention to Vjorn. "Please, listen to me. We came here for two reasons."

**"Fool,"** the god-creature barked, his voice so loud, I had to cover my ears. When it echoed throughout the room, I thought I would go deaf. **"Have you forgotten that I can hear your thoughts? I know why you've come. To steal the raw magic of my lair and feed it to your companions—and to clear a path for some other person to bond with me."**

"That's right," I said in a sheepish voice. "I'm sorry, Mighty Vjorn, but there weren't many options for us."

The gigantic wolf relaxed a bit, his frosty fur resting back against his muscular body. He looked younger—almost puppyish—and I remembered that he hadn't been alive long.

**"Fret not,"** the fenris wolf said. **"I can sense the turning of an age. It is time for me to usher humanity in the right direction. I will bond with a mighty warrior, and they will become the Hunter. Together, we shall purge the world of weakness and impurity."**

I took a deep breath and then said, "Can we please have access to the raw magic of your lair?"

**"It won't cure the corruption in their veins,"** Vjorn stated. **"The Child of Balastar, and the Child of Astros, will soon succumb."**

Zaxis and Odion exchanged glances, both of them pale.

"There has to be some way," I said as I stepped closer to the beast. His icy breath caused goosebumps to appear across my skin.

**"Perhaps there is,"** Vjorn said. **"But first—one of you must bond with me."**

# CHAPTER 8

## A GOD'S MAGI CROSS

There were only four of us here.

Illia, Zaxis, Odion, and myself.

"We know other people who can bond with you," I said. "People worthy of becoming god-arcanists. I can go get them."

**"We needn't look any further,"** the fenris wolf said. **"There are three people here worthy of my magic. I can feel it in their veins, with every beat of their heart. The Child of Astros is bathed in blood, and the Children of Balastar both harbor desires for strength."**

Nicholin shivered. With his ears back against his skull, he whispered, "Well, I'm plenty strong."

The frozen lair reminded me of the stories I had heard of the first fenris wolf and his arcanist. They had been a team who had hunted down other god-arcanists and their creatures. Not just *any* god-creatures, but the ones who had created *armageddon auras*. According to the first world serpent arcanist, the fenris wolf duo had had a habit of acting on their own, with reckless abandonment of their own safety.

Illia often did things on her own. She had gone after the Dread Pirate Calisto when she had barely been an apprentice arcanist. She wanted power to right the wrongs of pirates—to erase them from the oceans and seas.

Zaxis was as reckless and impulsive as they came. He often threw punches first and asked questions later. If he were any more overzealous, he'd be dead. He wanted power. Not because he *needed* power, but because he hated being weak. Like me, he wanted to defend others, not passively watch as evil affected the world.

And Odion... I had known Odion for only a few short months. He was the king of a nation, but he was also young and audacious. We'd had a duel to the death the first day we had met. Who did that? And I knew he valued power over all else. I sometimes wondered if he had sworn his loyalty to me only to learn enough so he could become a god-arcanist himself, somehow.

I understood why Vjorn thought they were arcanists worthy of his illusions and ice.

"Mighty Vjorn, I don't want to bond with you," Illia stated. She placed a hand on top of Nicholin's head and backed away. "The day I met my eldrin in the Endless Mire is the day I finally felt in control of my destiny."

"Yeah," Nicholin said, his ears shooting straight back up and his tail wagging. "I'm a master of fate!"

Illia closed her one eye and smiled. "And to be frank... Master Zelfree has helped me understand that sometimes physical strength is not the only way to handle my problems." She offered Vjorn a slight bow of her head. "I'm honored you consider me worthy, but—"

"I'm *more* worthy," Nicholin interjected.

"—I have to decline," Illia said with a slight smile.

A tightness settled in my chest. I had felt this way once before, but I was struggling to remember why.

"I'm sorry, Mighty Vjorn," Zaxis said as he stepped closer to his phoenix. "I already have an eldrin."

Forsythe quietly chirped—a sound both sad and hopeful. "My arcanist... I'm tainted."

"I don't care." Zaxis knelt and then wrapped his muscular arms around his delicate phoenix. "I'm not going to desert you. We'll do this together, just like we've done everything else."

The phoenix wrapped his scarlet wings around his arcanist, his heron-like head nestled on Zaxis's shoulder. For a long moment, no one said anything. The tightening in my chest didn't relent. Anxiousness consumed my thoughts. What were we going to do?

"I have an idea," I said, my voice an icy echo in the cavern. "What if... we found a relickeeper arcanist? They have an ability to freeze people and things in a sort of stasis. Maybe then we can halt the progress of the corruption and find Vethica to cure you and—"

"We don't have enough time for that," Odion stated, no emotion in his words. "Once a mystical creature is infected, there's not much time. Less than two days. It'd take longer than that for us to get to someone."

Technically, I knew the location of a relickeeper—he was studying the Crystal Lake—but Odion was right. We'd never get there in time. Even if we had left yesterday. He was too far away.

"I have no qualms with reality," King Odion said as he turned to the wolf. "I'm ready. If you need, I'll summon Hasdrubal to my side and free myself from the bond with my own hands."

Vjorn turned his canine head, his fangs visible.

"No!" Forsythe cried. He leapt away from Zaxis, his wings spread, the fire of his body burning brightly. "My arcanist deserves the very best." With a few powerful flaps, Forsythe took flight. He swirled around, blazing and bright, his soot sprinkling down. Then he landed next to the wolf's paw. "I implore you.

Bond with Zaxis. I won't be the reason he stumbles at the door of greatness."

"*Forsythe*," Zaxis growled. He pointed to his feet. "Come back here. Right now."

The phoenix turned his head away—defiant and confident. "Never."

In that moment, I could see Zaxis's personality clear as day in his eldrin. So stubborn. So assured he was right. The old legends said an eldrin became like their arcanist because they grew by feeding on the arcanist's soul. I agreed. It eventually happened.

The fenris wolf chuckled, his breath as wintry as the end of the year. **"Indeed, you are both worthy, but I only wish to bond with someone sure of their path—and ready for the strain of leading the world."**

"I'm ready," Odion said.

"Zaxis is ready," Forsythe stated, no hesitation.

"Don't do this." Zaxis stomped forward, his shoulders tense. "We're leaving, you understand, Forsythe? I don't want this."

His phoenix flew away before Zaxis could reach him.

**"If you are truly ready, there should be a way to pick amongst you. The best of the best."**

"Zaxis doesn't want to," I said.

Odion nodded. "I agree. I'm the best by default. There's no competition."

"No!" Forsythe swooped back down and landed next to Odion, his feathers fluffed. "*I'll* be your competition. I want Zaxis to become a god-arcanist. It's his destiny."

Zaxis turned on his heel and faced Illia. "Teleport and catch him! I don't want to lose Forsythe."

A brief moment of still silence filled the lair. The wolf watched with keen eyes. When he opened his mouth, his black tongue shimmered with saliva. **"Enough. To settle this, we will have a duel."**

"I agree," Odion immediately said. "A magi cross." He pointed at Zaxis. "You and I will fight this out."

Zaxis said nothing.

"If my arcanist refuses, I'll fight in his place," Forsythe proudly stated.

**"So be it,"** Vjorn said. **"The arcanist—or mystical creature—who survives the fight shall have the right to decide who bonds with me."**

Odion nodded once.

"But—" Zaxis caught his breath, his hands balled into tight fists. "I don't want this."

Forsythe's body brightened again with a flare of inner fire. "You're only as good as the things that stop you, and you're much better than this arcane plague. I don't want to be the reason you falter on your path to greatness."

"You're the only reason I'm on this path to begin with." Zaxis stepped closer, slower and more confident. "Please don't make me do this. I don't want to say goodbye."

His phoenix's inner fire waned a bit, a little colder and dimmer than before. But then he held his head a little higher, his golden eyes twinkling. "We're a team, aren't we?" His voice slightly cracked as he said, "And teammates don't hold other teammates back."

**"I care not who fights in the duel, so long as they understand the terms,"** Vjorn said. He stomped a paw, and the cavern iced over again—a drastic change happened all at once. The plants disappeared, the walls became smooth, and the path disappeared. Only the boulders remained.

The icy cavern had become smooth and wide open, like an arena for battle. Odion clearly knew what it was for, and took his position on one side. When Forsythe went to take his position on the other, Zaxis stepped in front of him.

Instead of having another argument or hashing out what had already been said, they just stared at each other, having a silent conversation all their own. Finally—reluctantly—Zaxis headed for the opposite side of the arena. His eldrin hopped to the side, to a position from which to better watch the battle, and I suddenly remembered where I'd felt this odd twist in my chest before.

Evianna's sister had died during a fight to the death.

I had been forced to watch from the sidelines as Lyvia had fought her brother, Rishan. The moment she had died had scarred my soul. To this day, I sometimes had dreams where I swooped in to save her.

Would I be forced to watch the same thing happen to Zaxis?

Before that could happen, I took a hesitant step toward him.

"Don't," Zaxis growled, like he could hear all my inner turmoil. "I've made up my mind."

"But—"

"I'm not going to change my mind. Don't watch if you can't handle it."

Illia glared at him, her lips tight. "You better not lose," she whispered, though it was much too quiet for Zaxis to hear. "If you do, I'll never forgive you." Nicholin nodded along with her words, his nose twitching, his blue eyes watery.

He never turned to face her, and I wondered if it was because he was afraid to.

Odion stood in his white plate armor, and Zaxis in his red scale armor. They weren't properly matched. Twilight dragons were creatures of light and dark, and phoenixes were beings of healing and flame. If I had to guess, Odion had the advantage.

Technically, they both wore rings I had crafted for them. They were *knight trinkets*—symbols of their loyalty to me—and they had been crafted to give people enhanced regeneration abilities. I wanted to protect those I cared about, which was why I had handed them out.

The rings had a twelve-pointed star, a cape, and a sword

etched into the side. They were small, and shimmered with an iridescent color, like oil on the surface of water.

Both Odion and Zaxis removed the rings. In a magi cross, you were only allowed magical items you had created yourself.

Vjorn moved to the edge of the arena, his frosted black fur standing on end. Licking his lips, he said, **"The last one standing is the winner. Child of Balastar, Child of Astros, are you ready?"**

Both Odion and Zaxis nodded.

**"Then you may begin."**

In similarly brutal opening moves, Zaxis lifted his hand, and so did Odion. Without much need to aim, Zaxis unleashed a torrent of fire across the room, melting more of the ice and creating a wave of steam that filled the area. Heat and pressure mixed in equal parts, and for a moment, it was difficult to breathe.

Odion didn't evoke anything nearly as destructive. He flashed a light so brilliant and blinding, anyone staring in his direction would be affected for at least a couple of minutes. Even Vjorn turned away, his eyes squinted.

I held up a hand, one eye burned by the light, and the other eye shielded just in time. With half my sight blurry from light, I watched as Zaxis stopped his evocation and rushed forward. He practically ran through his own flame to throw a superheated punch, his metal knuckles glowing hot.

The flames and light cleared just in time for me to see Zaxis strike Odion across the face. I thought the fight would be over in that one blow—the knuckles took a chunk of burnt flesh, maiming Odion's face.

Forsythe's feathers fluffed, his eyes going wide. Illia and Nicholin smiled, both practically on their tiptoes.

But I had fought Odion—I should've known he wouldn't go down so easily. He stumbled back, and then grabbed for his two-handed blade. In a fluid motion, in which he regained his stance and slashed at the same time, Odion twisted around and cut with his blade.

Zaxis jumped back. When he went to lunge forward, Odion was ready. With expert skill, Odion slashed Zaxis along the arm, cutting part of Zaxis's armguards in the process. Plague-ridden blood splashed across the half-melted ice.

The sword was a longer-range weapon. It gave Odion reach. Zaxis's punches hurt, but they were limited by Zaxis's arm length.

Zaxis's arm healed in mere seconds—it was the phoenix's ability he had the best grasp on. But he must've known he was at a disadvantage, because he held up his hand a second time and evoked more heat. Then there was more steam. More melted ice. It was difficult to see.

This time, Zaxis didn't even bother approaching. He backed away, evoking more and more fire. He created a river of flames that coursed through half the cavern.

But I knew it wouldn't last. Odion had the ability to shadow-step. He could dive into the darkness and move away, just like how knightmare arcanists could. I held my breath, waiting to see where Odion would appear.

"The tension is killing me," Nicholin said, his voice quiet and strained.

The entire time, all I could think of was Lyvia. In her fight, I had thought she would win, only to slowly watch her lose right at the end. Would that happen here?

That was when Odion stepped out of the darkness. He rose from the shadows, his sword in both hands. He appeared behind Zaxis—a classic maneuver, something even the wolves in the forest illusion had tried against us.

Thankfully, Zaxis was ready for it. He spun around and evoked fire from his other hand as well, creating a small tornado of flame that startled Odion. The two separated, and Zaxis tried to hit him with even more fire. Unfortunately, Odion evoked another flash of light, his twilight dragon magic so strong, it burned my eyes.

I couldn't see.

# CHAPTER 9

## THE FENRIS WOLF ARCANIST

I just heard the fighting as Zaxis and King Odion continued their magi cross.

There wasn't the clang of metal swords, or the bashing of shields—it was just the whoosh of hot fire, the hiss of burning steam, and shouts of pain and frustration as both fighters persisted. I rubbed my eyes, desperate to see the details, but also fearful of what I might find.

"You've got this, Zaxis!" Illia shouted from my side, her voice strained, but loud. "You can do it! I know you can!"

Even Nicholin added to the cheers. "I take back everything negative I ever said about you! If you win, I won't pester you anymore, I promise!" He squeaked out a sad noise. "Please don't die!"

Could they see? I didn't know.

Finally, bits of my vision returned. At first, it was shapes, and then vibrant colors. When my sight fully returned, Zaxis was bleeding from both his arms, and Odion was mostly unscathed. Whenever Zaxis took in a breath, his whole body shuddered. He kept his mouth partially open, gulping down air whenever he could.

I stepped forward, tense. Although I didn't want to play favorites, I couldn't help myself. I had known Zaxis all my life. He had been with me on the Isle of Ruma, on Calisto's pirate ship—even fought with me during the Sovereign Dragon Tournament.

"Zaxis, you never give up!" I shouted. "Don't start now!"

He straightened his posture and brought his metal knuckles up.

Odion lunged forward, his two-handed sword held high. Nicholin squeaked and covered his eyes with his tiny paws.

Although he was clearly exhausted, Zaxis expertly side-stepped out of Odion's swing. The white blade nearly caught his shoulder, but he managed to flow with more fluidity than I had ever seen from him before.

As Odion stumbled forward, Zaxis unleashed another torrent of fire, this time striking Odion on the back.

Odion's armor managed to take the brunt of the attack, but to my surprise, Zaxis lifted his other hand and evoked *more* fire —just not at Odion. He washed the ground in a torrent of red flames. At first, I didn't understand why he would do such a thing, but then I realized.

The fire was dispelling the shadows.

Odion couldn't step into the darkness if there was no darkness.

Unable to quickly escape, Odion shouted in agony. The phoenix fire engulfed him in heat, burning most of his silvery hair and charring his smooth skin. In a display of sheer willpower, Odion managed to concentrate long enough to evoke a third flash of light.

This time, I shielded my gaze before I was blinded again.

Zaxis wasn't as lucky, however. He gritted his teeth, growled some sort of curse, and then flailed his hands around, throwing wave after wave of flame around their mini arena.

The fenris wolf stood and paced, his giant tail swishing,

kicking up winter winds with each movement. His eyes never blinked as he observed the battle, as though he couldn't risk missing the smallest detail. I didn't know what he was looking for, but I hoped it wasn't for an excuse to deny either of them.

Forsythe took off from the floor, flapping his scarlet wings with enough force to circle over the battle arena. His gold eyes glinted as he watched—it seemed like he wasn't blinking, either.

The tornado of fire didn't stop Odion.

He gripped his blade, waited until there was a slight opening in Zaxis's flailing pattern, and then rushed forward.

I gritted my teeth, my heart slamming against my ribs.

Still blind, Zaxis didn't get out of the way in time. Odion slashed down with his sword, cutting through a portion of Zaxis's salamander armor and then straight across his chest, a vertical slice splashing blood across the charred floor.

Zaxis shouted as he stumbled back, unable to evoke his fire since losing focus.

Odion hefted his weapon, smoke lifting off his weakened body.

I didn't know what to do. I watched, unable to breathe.

To my surprise, Illia placed her hand on my shoulder, her fingers digging into my flesh. I felt her anxiety and dread as she tightened her grip, her attention squarely focused on the magi cross.

Without Zaxis's fire to hinder him, Odion dove into the darkness, shifted across the floor, and then stepped out of the shadows a few feet behind Zaxis. He lifted his sword—obviously struggling to do so—and then went for the final strike.

This was it.

The fight was over.

I almost did something. Almost used my magic. *Almost stopped the fight.*

Odion stepped quickly, with power behind his overhead swing. He brought it down, and even though Zaxis's back was to him, Zaxis lunged to the side, dodging the blow. He tumbled, still weeping blood at a hideous rate, but leapt back to his feet. While Odion was still gathering his strength to lift his blade again, Zaxis stepped in for a punch.

He struck with his knuckles, punching Odion hard across the jaw. Then he threw another punch. And another. Using both hands to pummel the twilight dragon arcanist.

Forsythe screeched in triumph as Odion hit the ground, his face raw, bloodied, and misshapen.

Zaxis jumped on top of the man, his fist poised to strike again, but...

Nothing happened.

Odion was on the ground, his nose so broken, he couldn't breathe through it. He took in wet gulps of air, practically cooked from the levels of flame that Zaxis had created.

Now the fight was over. All that was left was for Zaxis to finish the deed.

But still, nothing happened.

Zaxis stared down at the broken Odion, his fist still held high. His knuckles—red hot—burned away all blood and skin. When he couldn't bring himself to kill a defenseless man, Zaxis stumbled off of him and then crumpled to the floor, his own injuries too much.

They were both dying.

Illia let go of my shoulder and ran forward. Vjorn stepped in her path, preventing her from interfering. His cold winter fur, and intense eyes, were enough to give a combat veteran nightmares.

"The fight is over!" Illia shouted, her arm held out.

**"They both still live."**

"Zaxis won't kill Odion." But Illia didn't have the patience to explain why she knew. Instead, she disappeared in a puff of silvery glitter, and then popped into existence next to Zaxis, completely ignoring the fenris wolf's wishes.

Illia knelt next to Zaxis and gently touched the side of his face. Then she touched the slash wound on his chest. Zaxis flinched slightly, shuddering from the obvious pain. Odion's sword, The White Curse, was an artifact of considerable power. It made healing difficult... Zaxis had a harder time recovering.

It didn't look like many of his injuries had healed at all.

"Everything will be okay," Illia whispered.

Zaxis ran a shaky hand through her hair, but didn't reply.

**"Leave him be, Child of Balastar,"** the wolf commanded, his voice a cold chill all its own. **"Let them finish what they started. Or else I'll have to end this myself."**

I motioned to Illia to return to my side. She clenched her jaw, clearly upset, but when she was given no other options, she teleported away from Zaxis, and reappeared next to me, her silvery glitter puffing into existence with each quick teleport.

Then Zaxis stood—like Illia's mere presence had somehow given him the strength to keep going. He pushed his way to his feet, and then stumbled over to Odion. With a sigh, he turned to face Vjorn.

"I've won," Zaxis said, his voice raspy. "The fight is over."

**"The Child of Astros still lives."**

"I don't care. He's... He's..." Zaxis placed a hand on his face. He rubbed his eyes, and then his nose. "Master Zelfree said I needed to learn to rely on others more... To not think I had to do everything myself. King Odion helped us in the fight against the Second Ascension. I relied on him... And he never let me down. I can't kill him now. Not when he can't even fight back."

**"He will die on his own. No help is required."**

Zaxis struggled to stand. With a haggard breath, he turned to Odion. I knew what he was thinking. He wanted to heal the man. But he didn't have the energy, or the concentration to pull it off.

"I don't want to win," Zaxis said, weak and his volume fading. "I didn't want this."

Forsythe circled down. With a few gentle flaps of his wings, spreading soot across the blackened floor, he landed next to his arcanist. "You won. I knew you would, my arcanist."

Zaxis dropped to one knee and hugged Forsythe tightly. His phoenix draped his wings around his shoulders, returning the embrace with loving heat.

They remained still for a long moment. I wanted to walk out and speak to him—to tell him there weren't many other options —but Forsythe knew. Zaxis's eldrin had forced him into this, knowing their time was limited.

"It's t-time," Forsythe said, his voice catching with emotion. He broke away from Zaxis's grasp and then took to the air. "I wanted more time—maybe to become gigantic, or true form, like Luthair—to finish the adventure."

His body blazed with an inner fire, intensifying brighter and brighter.

"But I'm not afraid. I learned from you, my arcanist. You push forward... No matter the fear, no matter the challenge, no matter the consequence... I'm so glad I learned from the best."

His body pulsed with fire, becoming a brilliant gold, growing to the size of a pyre.

Then the flames exploded outward, a burst so glorious and brilliant, I couldn't look away. The gold flames washed over everyone. Me. Illia. Nicholin. Odion. Zaxis. Even the fenris wolf, who didn't flinch or look away, his cold gaze locked on to the phoenix throughout the entire explosion.

I thought the flames would hurt, or at the very least, burn my eyes.

But they didn't.

They felt warm. And comforting. And like... they were filled with an unstoppable energy that needed to fuel us all.

Once the flames died away, leaving the room aglow with magic I had rarely felt, I had to wipe tears from my eyes. Forsythe had been as bright as a star. And he had proved that, without a doubt.

When I finally turned my attention to Zaxis, I nearly caught my breath.

He was healed. Completely. Forsythe's healing flames had cured him of all injuries. And it was the same with Odion. The King of Javin pushed himself to his feet, his face no longer pummeled, his body now whole.

Despite being healthy and unharmed, Zaxis fell back to his knees, the arcanist mark on his forehead fading into a dull scar—a slight indent in his skin.

"Forsythe..."

King Odion took a deep breath, and then exhaled. He didn't look at me, nor did he turn to Zaxis. He just stiffened his shoulders, and then headed for the tunnel out. He walked with weak steps.

"Wait," I called out. "Odion! There might be other ways to—"

But he didn't stop or even turn to me. He continued outward, his white armor blackened from the intense fire. And although he had been healed, it hadn't restored his hair. He reminded me of a corpse I had once helped Gravekeeper William bury, but the thought didn't stick with me long.

Vjorn bounded out into the arena as golden embers rained down around us, like fireflies falling to the earth. Bathed in glorious healing magic, Vjorn stood directly in front of Zaxis.

**"Zaxis Ren,"** the fenris wolf said. **"Your eldrin's thoughts, as he immolated himself to save you, would've been enough to convince the apoch dragon to bond with you."**

"I don't want it," Zaxis whispered, his gaze on the ground.

**"There are people in this world who brought a deadly plague to you and others. They infected your blood, and**

your eldrin, and now you wish to waste your eldrin's gift by giving up?"

Zaxis snapped his gaze up, heat in his movements, even as he got to his feet.

"A hunter's job is to make sure those same people are brought to the ultimate justice. The world serpent needs conviction, but we need to make sure this crime never happens again."

Zaxis couldn't speak. He stood with confidence, his shoulders squared and stiff.

"I'm so glad I'm here for this," Nicholin whispered. "Forsythe is in my memory forever, as golden flames."

Zaxis held out his hand.

"We will be the winter hunters, bringers of justice." The fenris wolf exhaled hard, rushing his frost breath over the room, covering everything in thin rime. "The time is nigh. Bond with me, Vjorn the Second Fenris Wolf, and become an unparalleled hunter of corrupted magic."

# Chapter 10

## Two Pillars Of Light

Vjorn touched his large snout to Zaxis's hand. At first, I thought they would bond, but when nothing happened, I remembered what Terrakona had told me. He had wanted to bond outside, where the light could see us.

Sure enough, Vjorn took his nose away and then snorted. **"Come. The oldest source of light must be a witness to our bonding."** With swift and powerful movements, Vjorn turned and bounded away.

Left alone with Illia, Nicholin, and Zaxis, I held my breath and waited. No one said anything for a short moment. Then Illia teleported to Zaxis's side, her glittery reappearance smoother and more ethereal than normal.

Illia slowly wrapped her arms around Zaxis. He was stiff, and it wasn't until Nicholin wrapped his paws around his neck that he shifted and returned their embrace. I wanted to go over and join them—to say something profound or comforting—but I couldn't think of anything.

I waited on the sidelines, remembering how Luthair's death had shaken me.

What could I say to ease Zaxis's loss?

Nothing. There had been no words for me—just as there were no words for Zaxis.

But knowing that I'd had the Frith Guild had helped me through the moment. And I was, perhaps, the only person who could truly understand Zaxis's situation. I had to be there for him. Because whenever push had come to shove, Zaxis had always been there for me.

I walked across the charred stone of the fenris wolf's lair until I reached everyone else. Zaxis and Illia ended their embrace, and Zaxis turned to me, his eyes sunken and his breathing shallow. He seemed tired, or perhaps mentally exhausted.

"Where do you think Odion went?" Zaxis asked, much to my surprise.

I shook my head. "I don't know. Probably not far."

"What about Devlin? And Evianna? Are they coming back?"

Nicholin's fur stood on end. "I told you! *The lair ate them*. That's what happened to Illia and me back at the world serpent's tree. And then, after Volke bonded, we were released!"

"Will that happen?" Zaxis asked me. "You're sure?"

I nodded once. "I hope so." If I had lost Evianna, I didn't know what I was going to do with myself.

Illia placed a gentle hand on Zaxis's shoulder. "We should go."

Together, we walked out of the lair, our footfalls echoing in the dark and icy rooms. The illusions were gone—the forests vanished—and the wolves who had hounded us were no longer in the caves. I couldn't feel their tremors, and I wondered if the fenris wolf had taken them with him.

The walk was quiet, but Illia held Zaxis's hand the entire trek, occasionally giving him a concerned sidelong glance.

When we reached the exit, I eagerly headed for the late afternoon light. The warmth of the outside was what I craved.

The lairs of the god-creatures were basically gauntlets of trials and tribulations, and I was happy to put this one behind us.

Terrakona, Adelgis, Mesos, and Vjorn waited for us outside.

No Odion, or his eldrin, the massive twilight dragon.

I headed straight for my giant serpent. His scales shimmered in the bright light.

"What happened to King Odion?" I asked.

**"He left, Warlord."**

"Do you know where?"

The gargantuan serpent shook his head once. Then he leaned down and poked me with his snout. His cold scales were a mild comfort. I hugged him and patted his nose. When Terrakona's black tongue forked out, it tickled my side.

Odion... I wished I had said something more to him. Perhaps he was back with the other members of the Frith Guild? He couldn't have gone far...

Zaxis went straight for the giant wolf. Illia hung back, along with her eldrin.

Mesos, the massive roc, turned her eagle-like head toward the entrance of the lair. Then she glanced at me, her golden feathers ruffled.

"He'll return," I said. "Your arcanist is safe."

Her piercing gaze went to the lair's entrance. I wondered how long she would wait there for Devlin. A day? A month? A full year? How long had they been bonded? Devlin seemed older than most arcanists I knew. Perhaps they had been together for centuries.

I didn't think he would ever give her up.

Zaxis held up my hand. "I'm ready to bond." With icy confidence in his voice, he said, "Let's do this. Let's hunt down all magical corruption and put an end to once and for all."

Vjorn huffed and replied with a canine smile. Then he lowered his head, the chains on his body clinking as the tip of his nose touched Zaxis's palm.

**"With the oldest source of light as our witness, I
intend to intertwine our destinies."**

A wave of magic washed over the area, disturbing the canopy
of leaves over the forest, and washing dirt up into the air. I
shielded my eyes, but Terrakona quickly wrapped a part of his
body around Illia and me, protecting us from the sheer power
that rolled off of the fenris wolf.

Then the sun disappeared.

I had seen this thrice before. Once when I had bonded to
Terrakona, once when Theasin had bonded to the soul forge,
and once over the ocean after the war. The sun melted into the
sky, as if it had never existed, and everything was thrown into
utter darkness.

A silvery light rose up from the fenris wolf and shot into the
sky, creating a pillar so brilliant and majestic, it stole my breath.
And as I stared, I was reminded of something...

The Pillar on the Isle of Ruma, the one with the steps that
circled around... This pillar of light seemed so similar. It made
me wonder, had the structure on my home island been made to
look like this? Was it a reference to the bonding of the first god-
arcanists?

I wished I knew someone I could ask.

Then the pillar of silvery light disappeared. The sun
returned to its position in the sky, blanketing the world in warm,
forgiving light. For half a second, the glow of the sun reminded
me of Forsythe.

Terrakona removed his serpentine body. Illia and I walked
over to Zaxis. He tugged at his salamander armor. Some of it had
been cut by Odion's blade—enough that he was able to yank it
down to expose his chest.

A god-arcanist mark had appeared. Just like mine, the
twelve-pointed star was over his heart. The mark spiraled
outward, forming a wolf and chains over his shoulder, down his
arm, and across his ribs. The wolf had its fangs exposed and its

claws extended, and the fragmentation of snowflakes coursed the edge of his marking.

Zaxis touched the chains on his shoulder, and then ran a hand over the faded etching on his forehead. He didn't say anything, but I could feel the weight of his loss.

**"Brother,"** Vjorn said as he turned his canine head to face Terrakona. **"We have never met, but the bonds of time have brought us together. It must be fate."**

Terrakona didn't reply. He stayed close to me, his irises thin lines that watched all of the wolf's movements.

Adelgis cleared his throat, reminding me of his presence. I turned around, and he strode forward. He had a regal sophistication about him—he didn't seem bothered by the turn of events, or even surprised by who had come out and who hadn't.

"You needn't worry," Adelgis said as he placed a hand on my shoulder. "Devlin and Evianna are heading out now."

I forced myself to smile. "Thank you."

"I already told the Frith Guild of the outcome. Guildmaster Eventide is happy Zaxis won the magi cross."

"You could see that?" I asked.

He shook his head. "It's all Zaxis has been thinking about since he arrived... And the fenris wolf doesn't like that I can hear his thoughts. He thinks it's a mistake—and I'm violating his sovereign authority."

"Okay..." I rubbed at the back of my neck. "What do you want me to do about that?"

"Well, I think he might try to attack me," Adelgis said with a nervous laugh. He moved a bit closer to my side. "Would you mind telling him that my ability to read his thoughts stems from my mastery of ethereal whelk magic and abyssal leech tampering? He'll probably listen to you."

Sure enough, when I glanced over at the massive wolf, he was glaring at Adelgis, his fangs visible.

"I'll talk to him," I muttered.

"Thank you, Volke."

Before I could wander over and explain everything, the sky went black *again*.

Everyone gasped, and Adelgis even grabbed hold of my arm.

**"Another one,"** Terrakona said to me, his telepathy filled with disbelief.

Another pillar of light filled the sky. This one wasn't silvery, but white. It had a glorious glow that drew everyone's attention. I could see it through the opening in the forest canopy as easily as I could see the sun or moon hanging in a clear sky.

The light was emanating from somewhere distant, but I couldn't estimate the exact location. I wasn't familiar with the Argo Empire, nor was I certain which direction I was facing. I had gotten so turned around while in the fenris wolf lair, that I barely remembered where we were.

**"The sky titan,"** Vjorn growled.

Someone in the Second Ascension had become a god-arcanist as well.

"What is a *sky titan*?" Illia asked, her one eye glued to the shining light.

**"A gigantic bird with no form,"** Terrakona replied. **"It is a creature of pure air, unable to be touched—not even by light."**

"It's invisible," Adelgis murmured.

The pillar of light vanished. Then the sun returned, and everything was as it should have been. The late afternoon glow brought the forest to life a second time.

That was when Adelgis released me. He offered a nervous chuckle as his only explanation.

"Invisible?" I asked. "And unable to be touched?"

"Incorporeal." Adelgis brushed his long, black hair over his shoulder. "That means nothing solid can touch it. Much like the wind, it's both there, and not really there. A creature of powerful magics."

Vjorn lowered his head and growled. **"It is one of the mightiest god-creatures. How can you kill the wind? There is no way."**

"It *can* be killed," Zaxis said, his voice rusty. He glanced up, no mirth or joking in his hard-set expression. "Because its *arcanist* isn't incorporeal."

That was much darker than I had expected from Zaxis. If we killed the god-arcanist, their eldrin would die. Very few people knew that—only god-arcanists and anyone they had told.

I understood Zaxis's sentiment. Whoever was working with the Second Ascension was likely someone like Theasin. A foul fiend we needed to do away with in order to protect the peace and order of the world.

Before we could discuss anything else on the matter, both Devlin and Evianna emerged from the depths of the fenris wolf's lair. They panted and smiled as they reached the light.

"Volke," Evianna said as she rushed to my side. Then she threw her arms around me. "I'm so sorry. I never meant to fail like that."

"It's okay," I said as I hugged her back. "Everything is fine, now."

Devlin went to his roc, and his bird cooed a happy welcome. She leaned her beak down, and Devlin scratched around the sides of it. His clothes were shredded, and he no longer had his tricorn cap—but somehow his thin beard was still in order. That was a mystery I would never solve.

"Did you miss me?" Devlin asked as he held his eldrin close. "I'm sorry, girl. I got careless."

Evianna released me and then placed her fists on her hips. "Who bonded with—" She caught her breath when she glanced over at Zaxis. For a prolonged moment, she said nothing. Then she murmured, "But Forsythe..."

I shook my head, hoping she wouldn't say anything too loud. Right now wasn't the time.

"Guildmaster Eventide wants us to return," Adelgis suddenly said, breaking me away from my thoughts. He turned in the direction of Thronehold. "Queen Ladislava wants to know what's happening. And Master Zelfree says he wants Illia's assistance with questioning the Dread Pirate Calisto."

Illia's one eye went wide. A second later, she reined in her shock and controlled her face to hide away any emotions. "All right. We should return."

While speaking with the dread pirate would surely be terrible, I was already hating the thought of speaking with the queen. She had wanted someone from the Argo Empire to bond with the fenris wolf...

But we couldn't undo that now.

## CHAPTER 11

---

## THE FALLEN PIRATE

Terrakona lowered his head, and I took hold of his crystal mane and lifted myself up. Evianna joined me, and I offered her a smile as she positioned herself by my side. Captain Devlin went for his roc, Mesos, but this time, we didn't have Odion or his majestic twilight dragon...

They were gone. And even when I glanced around, searching the forest as far as my gaze allowed, I saw nothing.

"Devlin," I called out. "Do you see Odion? Or his eldrin?"

The captain glanced around, his sight enhanced by roc magic. It was a passive ability—an eagle-like sight. The longer he searched, the more I feared we may never see Odion or his dragon again.

"I think he's traveling in the darkness," Devlin finally stated. "The birds of the forest keep taking flight, but I'm not seeing anything. When he surfaces from the shadows, I think he's startling them."

"Do you know which direction he's heading?"

"I'd say north. But I might be wrong."

My chest tightened. I gave thought to chasing him, but I

knew he'd try to evade me. Perhaps someone he couldn't avoid would be able to talk some sense into him.

Which was why I turned my gaze to Adelgis.

He stared up at me, his eyebrow raised. "I doubt I can convince him to return."

"Please try, Adelgis," I said. "His dragon doesn't have much longer before it's corrupted by the arcane plague. It'll become dread form, and then..."

I didn't finish the sentence. Adelgis didn't need me to. He simply replied with a single slow nod, his expression pensive. A part of me blamed myself for the outcome. As a god-arcanist, it was my duty to usher humanity into a new age free of this magical corruption.

And while we had accomplished something great today, I needed to return to Thronehold to deal with the Second Ascension, even if it was just to draw up battle plans. I would never be able to eradicate the plague with them constantly hounding me.

Zaxis must've seen something in my expression and felt the same. He jogged over to his wolf, Vjorn, and then grabbed the chains like a rope and hoisted himself onto the wolf's back. The mighty creature shook his head and allowed Zaxis to get comfortable.

"C'mon," Zaxis said, his teeth gritted. "The Second Ascension won't escape us now that we're both god-arcanists. I mastered fire and healing. I can master ice and death. *We're going to bring the entire Second Ascension to its knees.*"

I had never heard him quite so angry before. He wasn't even yelling—his dark tone conveyed everything.

Illia teleported onto the back of the wolf. It was a large beast, capable of holding two people, but I wondered if it bothered the god-creature to be used as a horse.

Hopefully not, since I had been riding around on Terrakona for quite some time now.

I patted his serpentine head.

**"Warlord?"** he asked me through telepathy.

"Take us to Thronehold," I said. "If you don't mind."

"I'll stay here for a bit," Adelgis said to me.

"That's fine."

My eldrin turned and headed for the capital of the Argo Empire. As he moved through the forest, and then through the fields that surrounded the city, the very terrain moved to accommodate him. The ground cracked, the trees parted, and then everything stitched itself back together afterward.

I watched the ground with mild fascination the entire trek, trying desperately not to dwell on Odion and the sickness running through his veins.

---

Thronehold pulsed with life and reconstruction.

The war that had been fought here was still apparent in the scars of the city, but the citizens were quick to pivot. Wood and stone were being brought in by the cartload, and arcanists were using their magics to help with the repairs. Gargoyle arcanists were manipulating stone to fix the walls, and sylph arcanists controlled the winds to allow for easier work.

Before we entered the city, however, I tapped Terrakona on the head and pointed to the ground. My eldrin let me off just near the western gates of the city. Evianna dove into the shadows and emerged near my side, her knightmare magic making me smile.

The fenris wolf arrived shortly afterward, a cold mist surrounding his very presence. Illia teleported off, a puff of silver popping into existence both when she disappeared and when she reappeared on my other side.

Zaxis leaned and stared down at me from the back of his black wolf.

"I'm going to find Guildmaster Eventide and then speak with the queen," he said, no emotion in his voice.

Vjorn's ears twitched, but the god-creature offered no comment.

"Stay with Eventide," I said. "Once she's been informed of everything that's happened, perhaps we can speak to the queen together."

Zaxis half-shrugged. "It has to be dealt with."

"You should recover before speaking to anyone of importance. You look terrible." I motioned to his half-shredded armor and slumped shoulders. "Trust me. Just give yourself time. The queen can wait. Even if she's angry, there's little we can do about the bonding now. Vjorn won't bond with anyone else—we'll just have to make sure she knows that."

Zaxis could probably handle speaking to the queen, but I still wanted to make sure he was okay. Eventide would know what to do, especially when it came to Zaxis's health. Well, *Liet* would know what to do. She had asked me to start calling her by her first name, but I just couldn't bring myself to think that way for very long. I had always known her as my guildmaster.

Zaxis pointed to the city, and his wolf walked to the gates. The soldiers, and the will-o-wisp arcanists, stood aside, their gasps and mutterings so audible, I heard them from fifty feet away.

After a long sigh, Illia turned to me. "Why aren't you going with him?"

"I could ask you the same question," I said.

"I need to speak with Master Zelfree about Calisto."

I nodded once. "That's why I wanted to be with you. Just in case you needed me."

Illia stared at me for a long moment, her one eye searching my gaze. She obviously didn't *need* me to stay with her. She had fought Calisto not too long ago, during the fight just outside of Thronehold. Calisto had only lived because she hadn't dealt the final blow—she had killed his crewmate, and helped Zelfree kill Calisto's eldrin... But something about Calisto's tired and defeated response had stayed her hand.

Illia fidgeted with her fingers as her gaze drifted to the dirt.

Nicholin shifted around on her shoulder, poking his head through her wavy hair and then wrinkling his nose. "We don't have to do this," he said. "Zelfree said he would handle everything, if you wanted."

I almost laughed.

Zelfree hadn't been able to bring himself to kill Calisto, either. At least with him, I knew why. They had been longtime friends before Calisto had earned himself the title of Dread Pirate. In Zelfree's mind, Calisto was still *Lynus*, a boy who had grown up with him—a man Zelfree had once referred to as something more than a friend.

The winds around Thronehold remained still due to magic. I wished I had something to think about other than the situation.

Evianna placed a hand on my shoulder, offering quiet reassurance. She brushed back her white hair and then smiled up at me. I couldn't help but return the gesture.

"Volke," Illia muttered. "Apparently, Calisto knows a lot about the Second Ascension."

"I know."

"Even without Adelgis, he gave up all his secrets when questioned. He's refusing to eat or drink anything, and according to Master Zelfree, he barely sleeps. He just sits in his cell in the Iron Dungeon and does nothing."

I crossed my arms and nodded along with her words. "Okay."

"Do you think we should just let him rot away underground?" She finally managed to bring her gaze to me. "Or..."

"We should execute him." I had said the words as a gut

reaction to the question, but I probably responded too quickly. I took a moment to mull it over. "His crimes are vast, and I don't trust him. But... I did promise Zelfree we wouldn't."

Although, I knew Zelfree wanted to speak with Illia on the matter. If they both decided, it would happen. I wished they would, but I wouldn't stop them from finding their own solution.

Illia stared at Nicholin, and then stroked his white and silver fur. "I had dreamt of this moment for a long time," she whispered. "But... nothing is as I imagined it."

Nicholin puffed up his fur. "I imagined we'd be fighting him on the edge of a cliff, and then we'd just be so much better and more skilled and more powerful, that we'd push him to the edge and then knock him off and then throw a boulder on him." He took a breath, and his fur went down. "But then I remembered Hellion flew, so that fantasy didn't work very long."

"I had just imagined him fighting until the very end," Illia said, her voice so quiet, I almost didn't hear it. "So... I asked Adelgis to show me some of his memories..."

What a terrible idea.

I had no idea what kind of memories the Dread Pirate Calisto would have, but none of them could be pleasant.

"I want to speak with him," Illia finally said. "I don't think I'll be happy until..."

I waited for the end of that sentence, but it never came. Perhaps she wanted some sort of resolution that could only come through truly understanding the man—I didn't know. But whatever her reason, I still wanted to be with her.

"I'll go with you," I said.

Illia half-smiled. "Okay." Then she held out her hand. "I'd like that, Volke. I think you and Gravekeeper William are the only ones I really want to have with me for this."

"*Hey*," Nicholin barked.

"Sorry. You know I always want you around."

He swished his tail. "That's good. Because you're not getting rid of me. I'm here for the long haul."

I placed my hand on Illia's. Then I gave Evianna a glance over my shoulder. She motioned for me to go, and I figured she would go find the rest of the Frith Guild, but I didn't ask. When I turned to Terrakona, he tilted his massive head.

**"I will be here,"** he telepathically said. **"You needn't worry about me."**

Luthair would sometimes say that, and now look at what had happened.

But I didn't say that part aloud. Instead, I allowed Illia to teleport us both away from the walls of Thronehold. Her magic carried me along—it was an odd sensation. When I had stepped through the darkness, I had been in control, but with Illia, it was like I was being dragged behind a boat.

We appeared somewhere in the city, and I caught my breath, silver glitter in my eyes. Then we teleported again. And again. The changing sights and new surroundings left me disoriented. First, we were in an alleyway. Then we appeared on a rooftop. Then near a bakery.

When we arrived at the Justice District, it took me a long moment to recognize our surroundings. The courtyards, shrubs, and fountains were all decimated. The fighting had been so intense, not even the decorations had been left unscathed.

Nicholin rubbed at his face. "There's still time to turn back, you know."

"I'm not the kind of person who backs down from a challenge." Illia petted her eldrin. "Let's go."

We turned and headed for the courthouse and dungeon. I had never been to the Iron Dungeon, but I knew it was a location meant for mortals—non-arcanists. Unlike the other dungeons that were built with nullstone to prevent magic use, the Iron Dungeon had been built half underground mostly with brick, iron, and stone.

It didn't take us long to reach the front gate. A single will-o-wisp arcanist stood at the door, a lantern on his hip. The lantern danced with green lights—a rare wisp. The man, dressed in half-leather and half-metal armor, tipped his helmet to us and then motioned us through.

I suspected he didn't recognize me, because the man mostly paid attention to Illia's forehead and eldrin. The fact that a god-arcanist's mark was on the chest instead of the forehead hadn't yet become common knowledge.

It didn't matter. I didn't need a parade to enter the dungeon.

The front door was a heavy slab of iron twisted to resemble hundreds of birds. Their feathers and bodies blended together, and in clear letters made from their legs, formed the words, "Iron Justice." I assumed it meant imprisonment, but I wasn't entirely sure.

I shoved the door open, though it took considerable effort, and then I stepped inside with my sister. The smell of sweat and fear permeated the area. The bricks would never be free of this stench, even if they were removed from the building.

Together, Illia and I strode to the first gate, which led into the main hallway. The jail keepers bowed deeply and opened the doors for us.

We walked the long hall, and I was surprised that Nicholin had nothing to say.

When I glanced over, I noticed he remained hidden in Illia's hair. Was he afraid? Or was he just anxious?

Then we came to a staircase that led down. Illia took the steps two at a time, and I followed behind her. Once in the actual dungeon, with the damp atmosphere and aroma of mold mixing with the fear, I knew there was nowhere left to go.

Sure enough, Master Zelfree stood in the long hall between jail cells.

*Everett.* Just like with the guildmaster, I tried to remember to use his first name, but it was difficult for me.

He was just as tall as I was, but he wore his exhaustion like a second shirt. His coat—long enough to reach his calves—was just as dark as the dungeon around us. Zelfree kept his hair cut short, and trimmed neatly on the sides, but nothing else about him seemed cared for. He carried scruff on his chin, and his hands were unsteady as he slipped them into his pockets.

His appearance worried me. It reminded me too much of how he had been when I had first met him, weighed down by several lifetimes' worth of mistakes and tragedy.

A blank star was on his forehead—the mark of a mimic arcanist.

His eldrin, Traces, stood on the stone floor next to his legs, her sleek gray fur somehow still shimmery, even in the shadows of the dungeon. Her eyes—one pink, one tan—scanned us as we approached.

Mimics were odd creatures, but I had grown to love Traces. She offered a purr as I drew near, her feline grace ever on display, even after a fierce battle.

"Volke, Illia," Master Zelfree said, his voice rusty.

"Zaxis bonded to the fenris wolf," I said, unable to stop myself from just blurting out the news.

Zelfree nodded once. "All right."

Then silence settled between us. I thought Zelfree would have been more excited, but the man didn't seem to have the energy.

In the far cell, the last one in the row, sat the Dread Pirate Calisto.

# Chapter 12

## Guilty Conscience

Calisto looked like he had been through the abyssal hells and back.

The man's copper hair, matted with dirt and sweat, clung to his head and face. I had never seen skin as pale and wan as his. Although he was muscular—practically built like a heroic statue—the man sat hunched on his cell bench, both elbows on his knees, giving him more of a fragile and exhausted appearance. When he took breaths, they were shallow and short.

I had no love for the man, but even I felt the dour aura he exuded. His fingers occasionally twitched, and I couldn't tell if that was due to the injuries Illia had given during the battle, or if it had resulted from the lack of care Calisto had been giving himself.

The arcanist mark on his forehead no longer glowed.

It was a faded etching of a seven-pointed star, once interwoven with a manticore. Calisto had been one of the few other people I had known to ever achieve a true form with their eldrin, and it was sad knowing that his eldrin was gone.

The keepers of the Iron Dungeon had allowed Calisto a pair

of rough trousers and a dirty tunic. That was it. No belt, no boots—what he had barely fit right.

Calisto kept his dead gaze on the floor. He might as well have been a corpse for all he reacted to us.

Before I could say anything, Zelfree stepped in front of Illia and me, blocking our view of the dread pirate.

"I've been speaking with Lynus for a long while," Zelfree muttered. He took a deep breath and then brushed back his short hair. "And he asked to speak to Illia again."

"What?" I balked. "Why?"

Illia folded her arms across her chest. Nicholin did the same, though his tiny ferret arms didn't convey the same kind of defensive posture that Illia exhibited.

"I apologize," Zelfree said. "I know you said you didn't want to see him much, Illia. If you'd rather leave, that's fine. No one is going to make you speak to him."

"Why does he want to speak to her again?" I asked.

"When I was speaking to him about the Second Ascension, Lynus mentioned something about rizzels. We got off on a tangent, and he asked to speak to Illia. He said he left some things unsaid."

Calisto had been Illia's tormenter since she had been a small child. He had taken her eye, her parents, and even when we had fought aboard his ship, the *Third Abyss*, he had taunted her into fighting. Would he be cruel to her now?

"I don't know if this is a good idea," I said.

Illia shook her head. "I've already spoken with him. There's nothing he can do to me now. He's lost his magic."

"You're not afraid he might try to goad you into something?"

"I can handle it." She gently touched her eyepatch. "I'm very familiar with his style." Then Illia lowered her hand. "Besides, I want to hear what he has to say."

I still didn't like it. What did Calisto have to say to her?

There was nothing to discuss. Was he going to apologize? A few words wouldn't change anything. They wouldn't bring back Illia's eye or resurrect her parents. What could Calisto possibly bring up that would matter?

But it wasn't my decision.

Illia hardened her expression and straightened her shoulders. Then she strode down the long corridor, the sound of her bootsteps echoing off the iron bars and stone bricks. Zelfree lingered behind, but I kept pace with her and accompanied her to the far back cell.

Calisto didn't look up.

There was a long moment where no one said anything. Fortunately, Nicholin never found himself at a loss for words.

"You called us here," he said with a slight squeak. He puffed up his chest. "What do you want? If you need help finding words, I've got a couple of choice ones specially for you."

Illia placed her hand on Nicholin's furry forehead. "It's okay. Just give him a minute."

"All right," he murmured. "I'll let him off easy. For you."

Despite the friendly gestures and soft-spoken words, Calisto still didn't bother to glance up. I almost wanted to yell at him—jerk him awake from his grim daydreams—but that wouldn't be helpful. Instead, I waited along with my sister.

When Calisto finally exhaled, I tensed. The ice in my veins gave me the same feeling I had in a fight.

"Why haven't you killed me?" Calisto asked, his voice rustier than Zelfree's.

He never really looked at us. His gaze was lifted, but he never seemed to focus on anything, not even the stone bricks of the wall.

Illia narrowed her eye. "That's why you asked me here?"

"I've given you all the information you wanted." Calisto shifted his weight around on the rickety jail bench. The wood board creaked under his frame. "I'm done with waiting."

"You've got places to go?" Nicholin quipped.

"I've got a Death Lord to meet."

According to legend, the Death Lords ruled over the third level of the abyssal hells. Only lost souls made their way to that level—souls who had failed to do anything meaningful with their life, or who had failed at their ultimate goals and duties. It was a place of misery, and the Death Lords were said to do all sorts of terrible things to the souls confined there.

If I remembered correctly... one of the Death Lords was named *Calisto*, which was probably how our Calisto had gotten his name. Pirates often took a new name when they took to the seas, and *Lynus* wasn't particularly imposing.

"Just end this already," Calisto muttered.

"Speaking with Zelfree didn't help?" Illia asked.

Calisto finally lifted his gaze to meet hers. The black marks under his eyes told a long, sleepless story. "What?"

"Speaking to Zelfree—to Everett—that didn't help? You didn't get everything you wanted off your chest?"

"What's it matter to you?" Calisto asked, curiosity in his rusty voice.

Illia took in a deep breath and then exhaled, her confidence coming with her next breath. Nicholin remained still and quiet, obviously giving her the space she needed to speak.

"You don't know me very well," Illia began, her words slow and careful, "but I've lived most of my life on a small island. Ever since... you took my eye... I had nightmares about being helpless, unable to do what was needed to save the people I loved. I thought it was because *you* still roamed the oceans."

Calisto listened intently, never looking away. Never even blinking.

"But I spoke with Master Zelfree many times." Illia closed her eye. "And I learned... he felt the same way. Not because he had lost an eye, but because he, too, had lost a lot in his life. His family. His friend. His lover. We've got a lot in common. Maybe *too* many things in common. And he helped me understand that strength doesn't come in the form of a single moment—or a single revenge kill. It comes from years of dedication, determination, and inner growth that has nothing to do with you."

With a mild amount of disinterest, Calisto shrugged. "Do I need to hear your monologue, lass? I just don't want to live anymore."

"Everett wants you to live," Illia stated, a slight amount of anger in her voice. "And that's not because he needs you to in order to feel forgiven, or because he feels he owes you something. It's because he knows you weren't given many chances in your life." She took another step closer to the bars of the jail cell. "He wants to do what's right. He wants *you* to atone for what you've done. He doesn't want to see you take the coward's way out."

Calisto half-chuckled and allowed his gaze to wander back to the brick floor. "I've bad news for you, lass. Either you kill me, and finally get some sort of revenge, or the stink of the dungeon will do it, and no one will feel very satisfied."

"You don't feel guilty about what you've done?" Illia asked, her voice barely a whisper.

Calisto didn't reply.

"You never think back to your villainy and regret your actions?"

Again, he said nothing.

"There aren't any words that linger in your thoughts and memories? Something you wish you could take back? You did everything without remorse?"

"And what if I did?" Calisto growled. He clenched his fists. "Could we cut to the chase, then?"

I wasn't sure what Illia wanted Calisto to say here. Would he admit to feeling guilty? I doubted it. I doubted he felt any sort of remorse whatsoever.

"Well, you can lie to me, but I know the truth." Illia stepped away from the jail cell. "When we last fought... I saw the look on your face. It was regret. It stuck with me." She rubbed her face, especially around her eye.

"You were seeing things, lass."

"I wasn't. And it made me realize that perhaps Everett was right."

Calisto shook his head, sweat dripping off the ends of his grimy hair. "I'm made of as much trash as the next guy."

"Everett wants to help you," Illia said as she walked away from the jailcell. "And I've made my peace. I won't be the one to kill you."

I turned and jogged to catch up with Illia as she strode away.

Calisto didn't reply. He returned his gaze to the floor in front of him, never straightening his posture. I doubted her words had much impact, but it was clear from his voice and gestures that he had been confused by Illia's declarations.

Even I was sort of confused.

"You sure about this?" I whispered.

She shot me a narrow glare, her lips pursed. "I said what I had to. It... didn't come out like I had practiced." She half-shrugged. "But I still got most of the words out. And I already discussed this with Master Zelfree."

"What did you discuss with me?" Zelfree asked as we drew near.

Illia and I stopped in our tracks.

I rubbed the back of my neck. "Nothing."

"Calisto was just asking for death," she casually said.

Zelfree nodded once. "I know. He's asked me to do it a few times."

That news didn't sit right with me. Was the man wracked by regret? Could he really help us face the Second Ascension? He wasn't even an arcanist anymore. What could he possibly do for us besides provide information?

"Volke," Zelfree said. "I'm sorry to trouble you with this."

"Don't worry. I know it's important to both you and Illia. If you believe Calisto can be useful—"

"Lynus."

I caught my breath, nodded once, and then started again. "If you think Lynus can be useful, then we'll keep him around. But if he even looks like he's going to be trouble—or if he threatens to harm any innocents—I'll take action."

No one said anything, but Zelfree eventually nodded.

"He won't cause problems." Zelfree motioned to the corridor. "I'm going to stay here and speak with him a bit longer."

"Don't stay too long." I exhaled, nearly choking on the *stink* that Calisto had mentioned. "I was hoping to speak to you about Zaxis."

"All right. Later tonight."

Illia walked by, her hair shaking with Nicholin's movements across her shoulders. "We should go, Volke. Let's have Zelfree handle the rest. We need to see the queen."

# CHAPTER 13

## THE LAMPLIGHTERS

Instead of teleporting around Thronehold, Illia and I walked out of the Justice District and headed for the Dragon District on foot. I wanted to see more of the city, and I needed time to think things over. With absent-minded energy, I fidgeted with the bone pendant on the necklace around my neck.

Guildmaster Eventide had crafted the pendant for me as a sign of respect. As a god-arcanist, I was set apart from the other arcanists of the Frith Guild, and I briefly wondered if she would make Zaxis the same kind of pendant. Did she have enough material?

All magical items were made from a combination of magics. First, the magic of the material being imbued. That was why so many mystic seekers hunted rare creatures. The feathers of a phoenix had different magical properties than the feathers of a grifter crow. Phoenixes had fire and healing, and the crows were most known for their minor illusions.

The second source of magic came from the arcanist. Their magic, added with the base material, could create wondrous items.

Eventide had used the piece of a shell bone from an atlas turtle for my pendant. Normally, arcanists couldn't imbue a creature part that had come from the same species as their eldrin —phoenix arcanists couldn't imbue phoenix feathers—but Eventide had used the bone of Gentel before she had achieved true form. And now, her true form magic had enhanced its protective magic to incredible heights.

Did she have more shell bone fragments? Would she have to find another?

I hoped Zaxis would get a similar pendant. It had saved my life before, and I assumed it would save me in the future.

"Are you okay?" Illia asked.

I slowly nodded as I stopped fidgeting with my pendant. Then I shoved my hands into my trouser pockets. "Sorry. I'm just lost in thought."

The twenty-three districts of Thronehold were all vast and filled with their own unique architecture, businesses, and people. The Education District was a completely different creature compared to the Moonlight District. I knew, because the moment Illia and I entered the Moonlight District, I started seeing men and women with little crescent moon tattoos on their necks. They wore flashy clothing—bright red or blue— with plenty of bare skin.

Karna had a tattoo like that on her neck. It was small, and some might not have noticed, but since she had told me what it meant, marking her a prostitute, I sometimes looked for it when I was in Thronehold. Not because I wanted to hire anyone with that tattoo, but because I wondered if those people were in similar situations to Karna.

The Moonlight District also had a theater, but to my dismay, it was now just a pile of rubble. Fire and fighting had decimated the building.

When Illia and I walked by the singer's house, a twinge of nostalgia struck me in the chest. Karna had such a wonderful voice. I remembered our first encounter, and how she had taken my guild pendant.

The displaced theater workers and actors were helping with the reconstruction, but it was mostly just them urging the horses to haul the carts full of rubble away from the demolished district. I would like to have Terrakona help. But first, I'd have to speak to Queen Ladislava. I wouldn't want to have my eldrin rearranging her city without consulting her first.

Illia grabbed the collar of my shirt and tugged at it. "You should be showing your mark more prominently."

I had kept my shirt and coat shut the entire walk. Perhaps Illia was right.

With hesitant movements, I unbuttoned my shirt and tugged it open a bit—enough to expose my god-arcanist mark. The giant twelve-pointed star and colossal world serpent were prominent enough that, even with just a few undone buttons, anyone could see it.

"I sometimes feel odd when people approach me," I said.

Illia rolled her eye. "You really need to get over that."

"It doesn't happen all that often anyway," Nicholin muttered from the safety of her hair. "People are too afraid. Or polite. Or something."

The clacking of hooves rang down the street. I glanced over as a carriage came slowly rolling down the Moonlight District. A lantern was branded on the side door, and I recognized it as the symbol of the Lamplighters Guild. The will-o-wisp arcanists of the guild were peacekeepers and helpers, and their presence obviously brightened the spirits of the denizens in the district.

And then the carriage drove by Illia and me, and I smiled at the driver. The man did a double-take, glancing over twice in rapid succession. He pulled on the reins, and the horses came to a halt.

"Oh, there you are!" The driver leapt from the driver's seat and hit the cobblestones of the road, practically on his knees.

"Warlord Volke Savan the World Serpent Arcanist. It's an honor."

I rubbed at the back of my neck, and half-smiled. "That's me."

Illia stood close to me. She crossed her arms and lifted an eyebrow. "Can we help you?"

The carriage driver, a middle-aged man with thinning gray hair and no arcanist mark, quickly stood. He was spry for a man his age and bowed deeply without much difficulty. "I'm so pleased I was the one to find you."

"Really?" I asked.

"Zaxis Ren has requested your presence at the Lamplighters Guild. We went straight to the Justice District—right where we were told you would be—but you had just left. Me and a few others have been searching for you."

"Why is he at the Lamplighters Guild?" I had told Zaxis to speak with Guildmaster Eventide. Why would he veer off and do something else?

"I'm not sure, Warlord. But I believe he was speaking with his brother."

"Lyell?" Illia asked.

The man nodded several times. "Yes, yes. The will-o-wisp arcanist."

I stepped close to the carriage. "All right. Take us to the guild."

"I can just port us over there," Illia said.

The man leapt in front of us and shook his head. "It would be my honor to drive you! Please, let me assist you, Warlord. Everyone in Thronehold knows they owe their lives to you. Some of the guilds are talking about building a monument to commemorate your victory over the accursed soul forge. Please let me do what I can to repay you."

The mere mention of the battle bothered me a bit. When I glanced around the city, I still saw the terrible devastation brought about by Theasin and his soul forge. Did the citizens really think I was their savior? Some part of me feared they'd blame me for the chaos. I didn't know why—there was no logic to it—but the fear lingered in my thoughts regardless.

"You can take us there," I said to the man. "I'd be happy if you did."

He bowed several more times before opening the door for me. I stepped into the carriage, and Illia did as well. Nicholin poked himself out of her wavy hair and puffed up his chest. "It's nice to be taken around town instead of having to do all the traveling myself."

With a chuckle, I sat back on the cushioned seat, and allowed the driver to take the carriage out of the Moonlight District.

---

Lamps all around the city were lit by the will-o-wisp arcanists of the Lamplighters Guild. Even the broken lamps were lit, their fire providing hope to the residents of Thronehold. It was a sign of normalcy, even amid the destruction and turmoil.

I respected the Lamplighters Guild. They weren't flashy, like the Frith Guild, nor did they have legendary swashbucklers among their ranks, but they provided stability and order, and that was an admirable cause.

The Lamplighters Guild House wasn't far. We exited the Moonlight District, crossed through two others, and found the headquarters near the edge of the Dragon District. This was where the unicorns and pegasi were housed, as well as barracks for the Sky Legionnaires and the Knights Draconic.

Unfortunately, almost everything in the Dragon District was a pile of ash, a heap of rubble, or a combination of the two. Some of the stone buildings had survived, like the Knights Hall and the Pegasi Aerie, but anything made of wood was completely gone. There were mountains of trash and debris, and the road snaked between them like a river.

Now I understood why Zaxis had stopped here. It was a location on the way to the castle...

He had probably thought of his brother, and decided he needed to speak to him.

Lyell had always been the kind to get into trouble. I had saved the kid from a plague-ridden white hart, after all.

So many years ago...

The carriage pulled up to the guild hall, a building mostly constructed of brick. I stepped out and then held the carriage door for Illia. She gave me a quick smile before teleporting from inside the carriage to the other side of me. The glitter and pop of her magic made me grin. She liked to show off.

That made me happy. Although she hadn't said much during our trek, I could tell that her conversation with Calisto hadn't shaken her at all. For the first time in a long time, Illia seemed truly at peace.

The carriage driver leapt off the vehicle and hurried to the front doors of the Lamplighters Guild. He opened them up and bowed again. "This way, Warlord. I'll show you straight to the main hall."

"Thank you," I muttered. "I really appreciate it."

"No problem. None whatsoever."

With giddy energy, the man hurried into the guild. Although the outside was still intact, the inside looked like it had seen its fair share of battles. Parts of the roof were missing, the tile floors were cracked, and the front desk had been shattered into a million splinters. I stepped over the destruction, my boots crunching on the wood.

"Yikes," Nicholin said as he glanced around, his nose twitching. "But at least it smells nice!"

Smells nice?

After a deep breath, I realized what he had been talking

about. There was a pleasant aroma of lavender and lemon. It smelled fresh and inviting.

"There's a flower fairy arcanist who has been helping with the reconstruction," the carriage driver said as he motioned for us to follow. "Those flower fairies manipulate aroma. They make everything smell pleasant, even through the ashes."

The smell of char and coal permeated the rest of the city. I wondered if the flower fairy was really lifting the spirits of everyone here. Who knew a simple manipulation could be so inspiring?

The carriage driver opened another door for us, and I walked through, surprised to see Zaxis and two other individuals in the main hall.

Zaxis stood in the center of the giant rectangular room, away from a massive pile of broken wood that had been stacked in the back. Several lanterns were lit and hanging from each wall, providing plenty of light and allowing me to see he had taken his armor off, leaving his shirt open.

Zaxis was clearly proud to display his god-arcanist mark.

Standing next to him was none other than Lyell, his younger brother. Lyell had a lantern on his hip with a little red will-o-wisp inside. The hue of his wisp matched the red of his hair. When they had been younger, Lyell and Zaxis had practically been twins, but that had ended years ago. Now Zaxis was muscular and intimidating, while Lyell had the physique of a librarian.

Still, their facial features, tanned skin, and green eyes marked them as close relatives.

The last man in the room was someone I had never met before. The right side of his face was scarred—gnarled, practically—and his right eye was pale as milk. He, too, had a lantern with a will-o-wisp inside, but his was white.

The mark on his forehead was a seven-pointed star with a wisp orb behind it.

"I see we have another god-arcanist joining us today," the man said as I approached. Then he crossed his arms. "Welcome, *Warlord*. Always nice to meet the city savior."

I wasn't really a fan of the way he had said my title, but I nodded in acknowledgement regardless. "Thank you. It's nice to see the Lamplighters Guild is still here."

"Yeah, someone has to clean up the city after all that fighting, right?" The man smiled, but the right side of his face didn't move correctly. He sort of... half smiled. "It would be a tragedy if we didn't have grunts to mop up."

Illia narrowed her eye at the man. "Who are you?"

Before anyone could get a word in, Lyell stepped forward. "Uh, well, our old guildmaster died during the battle. This is Deen Strenos, the *new* guildmaster of the Lamplighters Guild. He's a white will-o-wisp arcanist."

"I can see that," Illia muttered, her sarcasm apparent.

Zaxis placed a hand on his brother's shoulder and pulled him back. "Volke. I wanted you to come here for a reason."

"What's that?" I walked over and turned away from Guildmaster Strenos, not really wanting to engage him in any further conversation.

"During the fighting, a lot of mystical creatures came back to life."

"Yeah, I know. What's new?"

Zaxis stepped closer to me and then lowered his voice. "I think we might have a minor problem. The lamplighters have been reporting all sorts of strange things around the city. Some mystical creatures... They were buried deep, and they might be trying to reach the surface through the old sewers and tunnels."

"Really?" I crossed my arms, my thoughts immediately going to Luthair. "Are they still there? Why haven't the lamplighters helped them?"

"There's a lot of rubble. And some of the creatures might've been buried."

Lyell stood a bit closer and waved his hand at me. I nodded to the man, acknowledging his presence, but now wasn't the time for pleasant conversations and heart-felt reunions. What if Luthair *was* down underground?

I wasn't sure why he would be... But maybe...

"We have a problem," Guildmaster Strenos said. "And I suppose the only people who can clean up our current mess would be god-arcanists."

"What're you talking about?" I asked as I glanced over my shoulder.

"Some of the creatures buried in the city are none other than king basilisks that the old queen had ordered to be killed."

# CHAPTER 14

## KING BASILISKS

I held my breath, my heart pounding louder than I liked.

The late Queen Velleta had ordered all of the king basilisks killed. I knew all about it, especially because I had seen several of their corpses underground when visiting her castle. Their bones had decorated her dungeon and basement, like sick trophies.

And the soul forge had resurrected the corpses of mythical creatures all over the city. How had I not thought about the king basilisks before this point?

King basilisks were gigantic six-legged pseudo-dragons with abilities designed to instantly kill anyone they came across. Their venom was deadly—even a single drop would end most arcanists —and they were capable of turning people to stone.

The queen, a sovereign dragon arcanist, had feared them. That was why she had ordered their deaths. She had said their arcanists were only suited for assassination.

Ironically, Queen Velleta's actions had brought about the very fate she had feared most. The assassin, Akiva, a mighty king basilisk arcanist, had murdered her for ordering the death of his friends and family.

Everyone remained silent for a long while. Guildmaster Strenos, Lyell, Zaxis, Illia... Even Nicholin didn't have any commentary on the situation. The gravity of our circumstances weighed heavy.

"Well?" Strenos asked, breaking the silence and jarring me from my dark thoughts. "Can we rely on the legendary and wonderful god-arcanists to handle this?"

"Have you told Queen Ladislava about this yet?" I asked.

"I asked to speak with the queen, but she said she had *more pressing matters to attend to*." Strenos huffed and crossed his arms. The white will-o-wisp on his belt shifted around inside his lantern, seemingly agitated. "And I tried going to the Knights Draconic, but they're exhausted from the fighting and stretched thin. Most of them are helping with repairs to the city, even as we speak."

"And the Sky Legionnaires were mostly disbanded," Lyell added. He moved to stand a little closer to his guildmaster. "They had been helping King Cardozo, and—"

"The *false* king," Strenos corrected.

"Right. Sorry. But since they had been helping *him*, most of the Sky Legionnaires were either killed in battle, locked away in the dungeons, or exiled."

Zaxis turned to me, his gaze unflinching. I stared at him, wondering what he wanted from me. Did he think I would ignore the city when it was in trouble?

"I'm going to help," I said. "Why are you giving me that look?"

"I'm going to help, too," he stated.

Oh. It was then that I understood why he was so intent.

I held up a hand. "You should stay here. Or maybe go see the queen. She'll see you immediately. We both know it. Then you can tell her about the king basilisks."

"I'm a god-arcanist now. This is the kind of stuff I should be dealing with."

A part of me had known he'd throw that argument in my face. But I remembered the first few days of being the world serpent arcanist. I'd had to heal first. And I hadn't known what my powers were, and I'd had to go through the discovery process of being a new arcanist all over again. Granted, it had been faster and easier than when I had first bonded with Luthair, but...

"Zaxis," I said, my voice filled with more emotion than I wanted.

I didn't want to mention Forsythe's name, but I remembered how it had hurt to lose Luthair. And Zaxis needed to rest. He hadn't done that yet. It was like he was avoiding thinking about anything by filling every moment with something—speaking to his brother, dealing with the lamplighters, and now trying to fight king basilisks mere moments after becoming the fenris wolf arcanist.

Zaxis must've sensed my unspoken words because his gaze fell to the floor.

"You're right," he whispered. "I can't even evoke anything yet."

I placed a hand on his shoulder. "Just take your time."

Illia—silent but present—stepped close to Zaxis and took his hand. He glanced over and the two of them shared a quiet moment. For some reason, that relaxed Zaxis more.

"Well, *I* know how to evoke things," Nicholin said. He exhaled into the air and white flames wafted upward. It didn't cause any damage—he just belched out a tiny bit—but it was enough to light up the room for half a second. "*I'll* go with you!"

"Actually, I think I should take Fain with me," I said.

King basilisks were dangerous, but if I had someone invisible with me...

Not only that, but wendigo arcanists could manipulate flesh. King basilisks augmented flesh into stone with their eyesight, not their claws, so if it came to a fight, we'd have to blind them quickly. Fain could do it. He could be invisible and then seal their eyes shut.

Illia opened her mouth—like she was about to protest—but then she stopped herself. After a long moment, she nodded once. "Fain is a good choice. Maybe you should bring Hexa as well. I think she might be immune to the venom of king basilisks."

"Really?" I asked.

She nodded once. "And she heals quickly, because she's a hydra arcanist."

That wouldn't help her when it came to the stone, however.

Still... That was a good start. Perhaps I could speak with Yesna, or one of the other master arcanists in the city.

"Do you mind if I stay with Zaxis and his brother?" Illia whispered.

I shook my head. "I think it's a good idea. Just make sure he heads toward the queen and Eventide at some point. I swear, once I understand the situation with the king basilisks—or handle it myself—I'll be at the castle to help with everything."

"Okay."

I nodded to everyone and then turned on my heel, intent on gathering a team.

Would Master Zelfree be willing to help? I knew he wanted time with Calisto, but king basilisks were a more pressing issue. Traces could mimic one, and Zelfree could gain immunity to some of the deadliest of their abilities.

Before I reached the door out of the ruined room, Guildmaster Strenos grabbed my shoulder and held me back. I turned to face him, baffled by his touch. His milky white eye and gnarled face reminded me of Illia. Had he been attacked at some point? The man seemed mighty aggressive for a will-o-wisp arcanist. I could see him getting into a brawl or two.

"Can I help you?" I asked.

"I'm going to help with the king basilisks," Strenos said, finality in his tone.

I glanced down at his white will-o-wisp. Although I knew a good deal about red will-o-wisps, I wasn't familiar with the other colors. However, did it really matter? Will-o-wisps were in the lowest tier of mystical creatures, which meant their overall power was much weaker. The flames of a will-o-wisp were candles compared to the raging inferno a dragon could bring to the table.

What did Strenos hope to prove?

"I'll handle it," I said. "I need to start pulling my weight and cleaning up around here, right?"

Strenos sneered. Then he opened the door and motioned me out. "This is *my* city. You and the other god-arcanists gallivanted in, and you'll gallivant right out whenever you're done—or whenever you have to go fight the next big disaster—but I *live* here."

"King basilisks are dangerous."

"I didn't sign up with the Lamplighters Guild because I wanted to hide away whenever there's danger. I joined so I could help the city I love."

His harsh statements resonated with me. I almost smiled—it reminded me of why I had joined the Frith Guild. I had wanted to help everyone, especially those who couldn't fight back against the power of the darkness.

Maybe Strenos and I weren't that different.

"Fine," I said with a sigh. "Come with me. I want to gather a few other arcanists before we head underground."

---

It was easy to locate Hexa and Fain.

Hexa stood at the walls of the city, speaking with local scouts about Vethica's disappearance. The two of them had seemed inseparable before, and it didn't surprise me that Hexa was focused on this. And even if I hadn't known her general location, Hexa's hydra, Raisen, could be seen from most rooftops. He had gotten larger again. Disturbingly so. Now he had *six* heads, and his body was about the size of a small horse.

Hexa actually rode him around on the streets, even though he wasn't particularly fast.

And Fain was easy because he, too, was by the walls of the city, waiting for Adelgis to return. Plus, Adelgis just seemed to know when I needed people.

I swear, Adelgis had sent Fain to me, just because he had known I had wanted the man.

Master Zelfree was exactly where I had left him. He hadn't left the dungeons, not even for a short break. Fortunately, he agreed with me about the king basilisks. They were more important than Calisto.

I couldn't find Yesna or Devlin, however. I didn't want to spend too much time searching, either. If the king basilisks emerged from the underground and started storming through the streets, we'd have another pile of corpses on our hands.

We had to act quickly.

So, with Fain, Zelfree, and Hexa, I followed Strenos to a small stone building. It looked like it was just a single room—like an outhouse in the middle of the Education District—but Strenos pulled a key out from his belt and opened the door, revealing a set of stairs that led down into the sewers.

"The underground isn't usually connected," Strenos said as he tucked his key away. "But after the attack on Thronehold, a lot of the walls broke down. Some tunnels are blocked off, but others now connect to places they never should have. The sewers now seem to have access to the castle cellar and dungeon."

We all stared at the dark stairway that led into the ground.

I turned to Fain. He stood closest to me, his dark eyes on the path in front of us. His eldrin sat at his feet. Wraith, like all wendigo, looked like a wolf that had starved to death and then risen from the grave. His face was covered by a skull, his red eyes glowing underneath.

Normally, wendigo had antlers on their skulls, but Wraith's had been removed. Now he just had two nubs.

Fain ran a hand through his hair, exposing his black fingers. It seemed as though he had suffered severe frostbite—even his ears were black—but I knew it to be an odd side effect of bonding to a wendigo.

Strenos stared at Fain with a disgusted curl of his lip.

Fain didn't seem to care, though. Once his dark brown hair was swept back, he glanced over at me.

"You want me to take point?" he asked, his voice calm and quiet.

"That's the plan." I motioned to the stairs. "You walk ahead of us—invisible—and report back if you catch sight of any king basilisks. They're dangerous. Don't let them know you're nearby."

Hexa huffed and pushed Fain aside. "Will we be done with this soon?"

"That's the plan," I said.

"I want to get back to the search parties. I know Adelgis can find Vethica faster than I can, but..."

No one said anything. I wanted to tell her—*yes, other people are more suited to the task*—but I knew it wouldn't be received well. If Evianna were missing, I'd be looking for her, even if I were blind and missing a leg.

"What's the plan when we find them?" Hexa demanded, her patience and words short. "Kill them again?"

Her volume was just as bombastic as her gravity-defying hair. As she spoke—yelled, really—her cinnamon curls bounced with every syllable. Somehow, she had tied her frizzy mane into a ponytail and the puff went upward instead of hanging down her back.

Today she had her arms covered, hiding her otherwise prominent scars. Normally Hexa liked displaying her scars... But the weather was chilly. I didn't blame her for opting for more clothes.

"They won't remember anything," I said. "That's what happened with the other mystical creatures resurrected by the soul forge. They woke up without their memories, which means the king basilisks probably won't remember they were murdered by the late queen."

Strenos scoffed. "I'm sure someone will tell them. Or they'll figure it out eventually."

I waved away his comment. "My plan is to gather up the king basilisks *peacefully*, and then take them out of the city. Preferably to the nearest dock that could support them."

"Why?" Hexa asked, her tone on the verge of demanding.

Her hydra, Raisen, stood watch on the road, five of his six heads keeping watch while one head—the *king head*—paid close attention to the conversation. "Yeah," Raisen growled, his voice deep and unforgiving. "Why would you send king basilisks to the nearest port?"

"Because these basilisks originally hail from a small island off the coast. If we return them to the island, I'm sure we can find people who know how to care for them—or at least know where they can start nesting again."

Raisen, seemingly satisfied with my answer, leaned his king head away. Unlike the other five heads, which were serpent-like, with snake snouts and sharp scales, the king head had horns like a dragon's. According to Hexa, every fifth head a hydra grew was considered a king head. They were different than the others, somehow, though I wasn't entirely sure how.

"Do we really want more king basilisks in the world?" Strenos asked.

I shot him a glower. "Are you seriously advocating that we kill them? They probably don't even know where they are."

"There was a reason the old queen wanted them dead. They're lethal in every sense of the word, and if they decide they don't like us—or like your plan—they could just kill us." Strenos snapped his fingers. "Like that."

There wasn't anything I could say to negate his claims, but I hated his argument regardless. Just because they *could* kill us didn't mean they would. And it wasn't right to kill them just because we were afraid. What kind of mentality was that?

A part of me feared them, though. Technically, I had fought Akiva and his king basilisk, Nyre, outside Terrakona's lair. But Terrakona had been the one to deal with them, not me. This time, I didn't have his size and strength on my side. If something happened, I'd have to handle it all. And even if the venom wouldn't kill me—since it didn't kill Terrakona—I couldn't stand the thought of other people dying. I had to be strong. I had to handle this.

Master Zelfree pinched the bridge of his nose. Then he rubbed his eyes and stepped between us. "Listen. This isn't helping. Each basilisk is its own individual. I say we take it on a case-by-case basis. We'll approach and offer them an island paradise, but be prepared to fight if they become hostile."

Fain nodded along with Zelfree's words. "I agree with the Faceless. I don't think it's right to judge them preemptively—either good or bad. We should give them a chance to prove they're not hostile, and then we should help the ones we can."

"Don't call me that," Zelfree muttered under his breath.

Fain gave him a sideways glance. "I thought you said you didn't mind?"

"When we're talking in private—or at the guild. Not here. Not with *him*."

Although Zelfree hadn't made any motions to Strenos, I knew who he was talking about. Zelfree didn't want anyone to know much about his past, and he hated discussing details of any kind. I was surprised he ever let Fain call him *the Faceless*.

Zelfree hadn't been known by that name since his days as a pirate.

Hexa, apparently tired of the discussion, strode into the building. Raisen lumbered forward and then leaned toward the tiny building. Eventually, all six of his heads hissed in irritation.

"I won't fit," he growled, glaring at the narrow stairway as if it had insulted him.

Hexa glanced over her shoulder. "Then stand guard. Tell people they can't come down here until we return."

Raisen's king head nodded. The others hissed and grumbled irritations about being left behind.

"Wait, Hexa," Fain called out. He jogged forward and went down the steps first. "I have to take point, remember?"

His wendigo shrouded himself with invisibility and then hurried after Fain. Together, Fain and Wraith descended into the sewers of Thronehold.

I glanced around. Groups of people stood on the edge of the road, watching us with wide eyes. They muttered things between themselves, and the moment they noticed me staring, they hurried away.

Master Zelfree patted his shoulder. "Let's go, Traces."

His mimic—who had been standing behind his leg the entire time—leapt up onto his shoulder, her balance a little off since her tail had been cut short. Traces gripped Zelfree's long coat and then snuggled close to his neck.

"I'll know the instant we get close to the basilisks," Zelfree said. "Mimic magic allows me to sense things."

I nodded along with his words. "I know. That's one of the reasons I wanted you with me."

"*One* of the reasons?"

"Well, you think quick on your feet, and you know a lot about dangerous situations." I motioned to the stairway. "Besides Guildmaster Eventide, I think you're the first master arcanist I'd turn to in any given situation."

Zelfree didn't respond to my statement. He just stared for a moment, his gaze searching mine. Then he smiled, patted my shoulder, and headed into the sewers. "You should start calling her *Liet*," he chided.

That was all he said.

Strenos waited by the door. When I walked by, his eyes followed me, even the white one. His gaze felt cold, somehow. It was hard to describe. The man made me uneasy.

"I'll lock the door behind us," Strenos said.

"Raisen is here." I motioned to the hydra. "You don't need to worry about it."

"I don't want anything getting out. There are more mystical creatures in the sewers besides the king basilisks."

Without any reason to argue, I offered a shrug. "Fine. If you want to lock it, then do. But we shouldn't waste any more time. Let's go."

# CHAPTER 15

---

# UNDER THRONEHOLD

Thronehold was the largest city I knew, and by the size of the underground tunnels, the sewers were in equal proportion.

I walked down the many steps until I reached the bottom. Thick darkness infested the area like a fog, and the stagnant smell of rot irritated my nose. As a knightmare arcanist, I could see in the dark, but as a world serpent arcanist, the shadows made things difficult. I could evoke molten rock—it produced a fair amount of light—but then obsidian would start to form from my body.

Once everyone had gathered together, Strenos stepped forward. "C'mon, Cao-Cao," he said as he opened his lantern.

The white will-o-wisp flew out and danced around in the air. It was just three orbs of light, each barely the size of an egg. When they spun around together, it was almost hypnotic, and I remembered old tales I had read about how some mischievous will-o-wisps drowned people who failed their Trail of Worth in swamps.

The white light from the wisp grew brighter and brighter,

until finally we had plenty of light with which to make our way through the sewers.

The walls were twelve feet tall, and the ceiling arched. Everything was made of gray stone bricks, stacked neatly on top of each other, some even forming patterns. A lot of time and dedication had gone into the construction, and it was disheartening to see deep cracks spider webbing themselves across most of the supports.

This place wasn't safe. If we got into combat, I would have to keep an eye on our environment.

Hexa crossed her arms and looked away. "My grandpappy said will-o-wisps are bad luck—and with light like that, we're sure to be spotted."

Guildmaster Strenos shot her a sidelong glance. "Cao-Cao is plenty useful, rest assured. If anything spots us, he's going to dazzle them into confusion."

"You're taking a terrible risk if that's your plan," Zelfree stated. "Some mystical creatures go into a frenzy when they're dazzled by will-o-wisps."

"Who here is the expert on will-o-wisps? *You?* I think not. Trust me, I can handle this."

I wanted to side with Zelfree, but I decided to let this go. Strenos had made a whole speech about how his dedication to Thronehold ran deeper than these tunnels. His conviction in his abilities was likely genuine.

Fain stepped forward, still visible. His wendigo appeared and then walked up to his side, his skull-covered head held high. They both glanced at me, as if to ask if I was ready.

I gave them a nod.

The two wrapped themselves in a shroud of invisibility and headed forward. I waited to give them a chance to scout ahead.

The star on Zelfree's forehead shifted. One moment it was blank, and the next moment it contained a wolf with a skull mask and antlers. He had transformed himself into a wendigo arcanist, and before Traces could transform, she leapt off his shoulders. By the time she had hit the ground, she was a fully grown wendigo, complete with long antlers.

"I'll help him out," Zelfree muttered as he disappeared from sight.

When he chased after Fain, I didn't hear anything. Even when Traces followed him, there were no sounds.

"I wish I could do that," Hexa said under her breath.

"Tsk," Strenos said with a click of his tongue. "You say will-o-wisps are bad luck, but wendigo are terrible man-eating beasts. Anyone bonded with one is probably a criminal of the highest degree."

"Hey, you watch your month." Hexa stepped up close to Strenos and scoffed. "*Fain* has sworn himself to the world serpent arcanist. That makes him a knight." She wheeled around and glared. "Right, Volke?"

I nodded. "That's right. Fain is one of us, and you'll treat him with respect." I started my way down the stone tunnel. "Now, c'mon. We shouldn't waste time. After this, I need to speak to the queen, and I really shouldn't keep her waiting."

Hexa jogged to reach my side, but Strenos remained a few steps back, his white will-o-wisp providing a pleasant glow. We strode forward through the rotting sewers, my nose assaulted by the odors. Hexa held a hand over half her face, but never once complained.

"You allowed a wendigo arcanist to swear himself to you?" Strenos asked, his voice low so it didn't echo off the walls.

I glanced over my shoulder and replied, "That's right."

"Aren't you the first god-arcanist? Shouldn't you only accept the best of the best?"

"I'll accept whoever I think is worthy," I stated. "And Fain is more than worthy to fight the Second Ascension by my side."

Hexa nodded along with my words, a smile growing on her face. She fluffed her puffy ponytail as she said, "Yeah, even the

Frith Guild is dedicated to Volke and Terrakona. We're gonna end the arcane plague *and* anyone who thinks they can get away with murder and kidnapping."

Her angry statement, increasing in volume with each word, echoed down the long sewer tunnels. Vethica's disappearance still bothered her, obviously. I turned to face Hexa, my jaw clenched. While I appreciated the conviction, was now really the time?

Hexa rubbed the back of her neck and mouthed the words, *I'm sorry*.

Before I could take another step, I tensed. Slight vibration in the floor told me someone approached. Then that someone grabbed me by the collar of my shirt. I evoked magma into the palm of my hand—the molten rock oozing from the lines of my palm—but right as I was about to lash out, Zelfree's angry growl reached my ears.

"*Keep it down*," he said through gritted teeth. "This won't work if you're yelling."

I grabbed his wrist and nodded. "I know. We'll be quiet."

Zelfree released me and then disappeared into the tunnel.

Without any more words between us, we continued our way through the sewers. Cao-Cao floated alongside his arcanist, playfully zooming around Strenos's head and sometimes poking at his scarred cheek. To my surprise, Strenos didn't bat the creature away or even get upset. He occasionally brought a hand up and stroked the glowing orbs with a couple of fingers.

We stopped once we came to a four-way intersection.

"We waited," Fain whispered from the entrance of the left-most tunnel. "Which way?"

"There," Strenos said, motioning to the right. "My lamplighters said they saw some there. This tunnel leads to the Mining District, and the tunnels there now connect to the castle."

With a nod, we headed in the direction Guildmaster Strenos suggested.

The deeper we went, however, the more the odors shifted into something sulfuric. The smell of rotten eggs made me gag more than once, but after a few minutes, the worst of the scent faded as my body adjusted.

The gray brick walls slowly became large granite blocks as the tunnels grew to resemble more of an actual building. Signs for the trolleys were carved into the stones. I frowned when I noticed several busted stations and ruined trolley cars. The devastation of Thronehold had gone all the way to its roots.

I stopped and took a deep breath. Then I closed my eyes and allowed my tremor sense to provide me with information. Any kind of movement traveled straight into my mind, letting me know the locations of objects and people nearby. I felt Hexa and Strenos as they continued forward—I even felt Fain and Zelfree, though they tiptoed their way over the large granite slabs. I didn't sense much else, though. No mice or rats or even very many insects. They must have known enough to flee the moment an apex predator had moved in.

After another long exhale, I felt the rumble of creatures far larger than we were. I also felt the trembling of people... Dozens of people.

I rubbed my eyes, trying to picture their exact locations in relation to us. The tunnels under the Mining District were vast and numerous. And Strenos wasn't lying. I felt... the broken walls of several tunnels, each linking whole sections of the underground with other sections that were never meant to be open to the public.

"Zelfree, Fain," I called out. "Wait. I think... we're close to something. I feel—"

The ground quaked and rumbled, and I almost lost my footing. Hexa had to balance herself, and Strenos hit the ground on one knee, his wisp zipping around him in tight circles.

Could the will-o-wisps speak? I wondered why Cao-Cao said nothing.

"What was that?" Hexa asked.

The rumbling happened again, this time worse than before.

I kept my eyes shut and even placed my palm on the nearby wall. "It's a king basilisk. I can feel it moving."

Strenos got to both feet. When the quake happened a third time, he braced himself against the wall as well. "What're we going to do?"

"I think people are in danger. We have to hurry."

Zelfree and Fain appeared next to me.

"I saw something ahead," Fain muttered.

"More tunnels?"

"Worse than that. Statues of people. They look like miners and builders."

"There were also blood stains," Zelfree added, his tone grim.

Hexa rushed forward, running down the tunnel as fast as she could while it quaked.

"Wait!" I called out.

Rocks and dust were raining from the ceiling. The whole place seemed to be on the verge of crumbling. Fortunately, the archways built into the ceiling were firm and stable. We probably had time to handle the situation—but not much more.

Hexa either didn't hear me or didn't care. She left the light of the wisp and continued into the darkness. Perhaps she figured we would just follow.

"She's gotten reckless," Zelfree growled. "The girl has no patience for anything."

I pointed to the tunnel. "We need to go. Cut her off and tell her to calm down. The king basilisk is close."

Fain and Zelfree disappeared in the next instant, leaving me with Strenos and his wisp. I motioned for him to follow me, and we ran forward down the tunnel, my tremor sense giving me a general idea of where the massive beast was moving.

"How do you know where it is?" Strenos asked.

"I'm the world serpent arcanist," I said, not feeling the need for further explanation.

And none was needed, apparently. Strenos nodded once, a slight smirk on his face as we hurried to our destination. On the way there, my thoughts were haunted by the statues we passed. They were men and women, frozen in position, some of them mid-run. Their faces were contorted in fear or surprise. The shadows cast by the wisp's light made everything worse.

I turned away from them, my chest tight.

Was there a way to change them back?

Some of the statues had toppled over during the quaking, shattered into a million pieces.

I hoped there was some way to undo this.

It didn't take long for us to come across a ruined wall. The granite stones had cracked and then crumbled, creating a mountain of debris. More statues were nearby, some of them even clawing for the crack in the wall.

Hexa and Zelfree stood at the base of the rubble.

Strenos and I reached them as the rumbling intensified. When I sensed the movement of the king basilisk, I was shocked to feel it lumbering down a tunnel toward something else. It was beyond this cracked wall and pile of rubble—the massive basilisk was trying to catch something.

Something smaller than us.

"Zelfree, someone is in danger. I think it might be another mystical creature." I turned to Strenos. "Listen—there are people through this crack in the wall, and to the right. At least a dozen of them."

"Is the basilisk there?" Strenos asked.

"It left to chase something."

Strenos slowly nodded. Then he turned and climbed the rumble. Halfway up, he stopped and turned to his white wisp. "Stay with them."

"What about you?" Hexa asked. "You'll need light to guide those people."

"I still have an actual lantern," Strenos said, patting the device on his hip.

"Oh. All right. Hurry, then."

With Fain, Zelfree, and Hexa, I made my way up and over the rubble. We entered the ruined tunnel, and I noticed the arched ceilings were scraped and damaged. Cao-Cao floated close to me, but never in front of my face. He hovered in a semi-circle overhead. Together, we made our way forward.

Zelfree and Fain disappeared again. They rushed forward, not bothering to hide their steps. The quaking covered up most noises, even my heavy breathing, as I picked up my pace. Hexa shadowed my every step, never showing any signs of becoming winded.

Then the rumbling stopped.

I held my breath as I came to a standstill.

The vibrations in the ground...

The king basilisk was eating *something*.

With my hands balled into fists, I rushed forward. Hexa struggled to keep up.

There were two tunnels between us and the king basilisk. Once we passed the next two intersections, we'd be face-to-face with a legendary monster of death. How was I going to handle this? The beast had clearly turned innocent people to stone. If I didn't stop it now, more people were going to die.

Then I caught my breath.

More rumbling.

A second king basilisk was alive and well...

And it was heading for the first.

# CHAPTER 16

## TWO KING BASILISKS

Although the tunnels were a winding maze of darkness, my tremor sense provided everything I needed to assess the situation. Two king basilisks were in the next tunnel over. They were facing each other, both tensed, both gargantuan in size.

Neither were larger than Terrakona, but they were the size of fully grown sovereign dragons, which meant these beasts were adults.

Cao-Cao the white wisp lowered himself to the ground, so that the shine of his wispy body didn't extend far. I slowed my run, and Hexa followed my lead without a need for words between us. When we reached the T-intersection in the tunnel, I stopped and gazed at the floor.

This had been an old mining tunnel. The ground was packed dirt covered in rough tracks. Blood speckled the area—the king basilisk had eaten a smaller mystical creature before lumbering off toward the other basilisk.

"Which way?" Hexa whispered, glancing in both available directions.

I held a finger to my lips and pointed to the left.

A deep growl of words echoed down the massive tunnel, the gruff timber enough to shake loose dust from the walls and ceiling. "What have you done?"

I didn't recognize the voice, and I assumed it was one of the king basilisks.

"Everyone here must be put to *death*," another voice answered, this one louder and stronger than the first.

"Why? What has happened?"

Were they both males? They sounded male. Large, frightening, and filled with immense power. No other creatures could kill like king basilisks, and my worst fears were coming to fruition. But why did they want to kill everyone? They shouldn't have any memories.

Or were king basilisks filled with general bloodlust? Had the old queen been correct to fear them?

"The mortals here told me everything," one of the king basilisks said, the growl in his voice intensifying. "*They killed us. We were dead mere days ago. Trophies for a queen. This is a grave! Our grave. We must claw our way free.*"

Zelfree walked back and placed a hand on my shoulder. I turned as he allowed his invisibility to drop. He stood next to me with a hard gaze on the tunnel, his eyebrows knitted in concern.

Fain was still up ahead, but not far.

"You hear them," Zelfree muttered under his breath. "We need to do something. *Now.* Before they take revenge on the whole city."

I ran a hand through my hair, trying to think of what would be best. The basilisks had every right to be upset, but the one who had wronged them was long dead. Rampaging through the city wouldn't help anything now. What would Guildmaster Eventide do?

"Terrakona," I whispered.

**"Warlord."**

His instant telepathy with me was always a comfort.

Somehow, even in the depths of the underground, it was like Terrakona stood by my side.

"Will the king basilisks recognize me? Will they know a god-arcanist by my magic or presence?"

**"Mystical creatures are not made knowing there are god-creatures, but magic can sense magic. They will feel your power, but you must carry it with authority. Your might is a tool, but tools are only useful in the hands of the skilled."**

I shook my head, knowing Terrakona was right. This was my problem to handle—if I failed to persuade the king basilisks that they weren't in any danger, I'd have to fight and kill them before they further harmed the already devastated Thronehold.

"Wait here," I commanded Hexa. I pointed to the white wisp. "Stay out of sight." Then I exhaled. "If things start to turn violent, I'll distract the basilisks so Zelfree and Fain can blind them. After that, we go for a quick kill. We can't afford to hesitate."

Hexa and Zelfree nodded, and then Zelfree disappeared. Cao-Cao somehow dimmed himself, but not by much. He hid near the tracks, shielding the flames of his tiny body.

After a deep breath, I closed my eyes.

At first, I was worried about walking around with my eyes closed, relying only on my tremor sense for guidance. But as the light faded to absolute darkness, I was reminded of Luthair. The shadows had always been my shelter. Even without my powers as a knightmare arcanist, the darkness would protect me.

With my head held high, I rounded the corner and strode down the mining tunnel, Zelfree and Fain following closely. When the king basilisks turned to face me, their feet shook the ground, but the quaking didn't cause me to slip.

"An arcanist approaches," one of the basilisks hissed. "Come to bury us again."

I held up a hand, keeping my eyes closed. "Wait, please! I

don't wish to fight." I continued my approach, not allowing any fear or hesitation to show in either my words or stride. "My name is Volke Savan the Second World Serpent Arcanist. I've come here to help you."

When I was within twenty feet of the mighty beasts, I stopped. Heat raced through my veins, and I knew I could evoke magma at any second, but would that be enough? These creatures far outweighed me.

It didn't matter. I shook away the thoughts. I wouldn't allow myself to fail Thronehold.

The basilisks were almost too large for the tunnel. When the one closest to me turned, his body scraped along the walls and disturbed the foundation of the mines. Although I felt their movement—right down to their breathing—I couldn't see the color or luster of their scales.

The only king basilisk I had ever seen was Nyre, the eldrin to the assassin, Akiva. That basilisk had been gray, so I imagined these beasts were the same sheen and color.

"Help us?" the second basilisk asked, his voice low, but still loud.

"The mortals told us everything!" the other roared, his words increasing in anger. "Our arcanists are *dead*. Killed at the hands of your suspicious queen. Our bodies were mounted to the walls for decoration."

"I can explain." I motioned to our surroundings. "You aren't in the castle anymore. The queen who ordered your deaths is no longer with us. You're not in any danger. Please, calm yourself."

The closest king basilisk turned, his six legs stomping as he moved. Dirt kicked up everywhere, and I rubbed some off my cheek as the beast drew near.

"My name is Kezrik," the basilisk said, his tongue sliding out of his massive mouth as he spoke. "But I can remember nothing else... *Why*? Where is my arcanist?"

His hot breath washed over me like a wave across the beach. I shook my head, keeping my eyes closed—if I met his gaze, I could turn to stone.

"Your new life was given to you by a god-creature known as a soul forge. It died, just recently, but right before its death, the beast's magic resurrected nearby mystical creatures. I don't know why it didn't restore all your memories, but now that you're back, you can leave this place and return to your home."

I tried to sound diplomatic—controlled, authoritative—but I feared I was being too friendly. Should I have taken a harsher stance? Told them what to do and demanded they listen? No. They were confused and disoriented, and I'd rather have them as willing allies than fearful subjects who could turn at any moment.

"Where is my arcanist?" Kezrik asked.

After a short sigh, I replied, "Your arcanist is likely dead."

"Then I must take revenge." His breath became hotter, and it washed over me in quick, angry bursts. "*If the queen cannot pay, then her kingdom must! My arcanist...*" He dug his claws into the ground, tensing for combat. "To steal my memories of my arcanist is far worse than death. Now I must live, knowing my arcanist can never return."

The gigantic beast lifted two of its clawed hands and placed them against his scaled chest. "My arcanist... Their soul is part of me, yet I cannot remember... Such a terrible fate. Basilisks don't abandon their own. *We never abandon our own.*"

If the creature could breathe fire, I suspected the whole tunnel would be ablaze. His words were laced with hatred and shame.

Zelfree placed a hand on my shoulder, his grip tight. He whispered, "*Be careful.* Even smaller basilisks are known for their loyalty. Try to appeal to him in another way that involves his arcanist—something that involves hope."

At first, I wasn't sure what he meant, but then it came to me.

"Killing the people of Thronehold won't bring back your

arcanist," I said. Before the beast could respond, I added, "And I'm not even entirely sure your arcanist *is* dead. There's a chance they could still be alive, but you'll never figure that out if you wantonly destroy everything around you. Think about this— there's still a chance you could be reunited. But not if we fight."

The two basilisks breathed deeply. Then Kezrik turned his head to face the other.

"I think I've heard enough," the second basilisk said, his voice more a hiss. "What if this was how we died the first time? Believing the lies of people who weren't our arcanists? If our arcanists are alive, we'll find them soon enough if we make ourselves known."

I gritted my teeth, my pulse picking up with the heat of inevitable conflict.

"No, Thryce, the world serpent arcanist speaks sense," Kezrik said, much to my shock, his rumbling tone softening to something gentle. "If my arcanist lives, I must do everything in my power to find them."

"This arcanist didn't even deny we were killed. We must protect ourselves and ignore the rest."

"There's no need to act rash," I said, firm and confident. "I'm here to answer your questions. We can solve this together."

Thryce hissed. Then he stomped forward, like he was coming for me. Kezrik moved his colossal body to come between us. The tunnel was small—if one basilisk blocked the way, no one could get through. The two basilisks faced each other, their hearts pounding faster and faster. I felt the drum of their aggression through the soles of my feet.

When Kezrik snapped his fangs, Thryce replied with a guttural growl. Then Thryce slammed against Kezrik, shoving the other massive reptile against the walls of the tunnel. Everything shook, and I evoked molten rock, obsidian sprouting from my knuckles, elbows, and shoulders, but I kept the deadly heat in my palms.

Kezrik roared and then lunged. The two basilisks were titans in the small underground area. With each movement, they threatened to bury us all.

"*I don't trust him*," Thryce growled, his volume enough to hurt my ears. "He'll be the death of us!"

Kezrik thrashed his tail from side to side, his large body reminding me of an alligator's. "You forget—we are death made flesh. If we stand together, he can't face us both."

"You stand with *him*. An arcanist we don't know." Thryce slammed his tail into the wall, shaking the foundation of the tunnels. "You've already proven you won't stay loyal to your kind."

Zelfree cursed under his breath. "The other one will collapse this whole tunnel. The city above is in danger."

"*We're* in danger," Fain darkly muttered.

"Well... That, too."

Determined to keep the basilisks from killing each other, I tensed and stepped forward. "Thryce, Kezrik—*stop this*. There's no need for conflict! The city above can't handle another disaster! As the world serpent arcanist, *I won't allow it!*"

The two basilisks hissed and clawed at one another. I kept my eyes closed, but their movements and breaths were sharp in my mind.

**"I'm here for you, Warlord. Stand your ground."**

Terrakona's voice filled me with a moment of tranquility. I remembered he was with me—so were the others. We could handle this.

"I won't die again," Thryce roared.

He slashed his claws across Kezrik's face, gouging his flesh and splattering blood across the tunnel. Kezrik snapped his fangs and caught one of Thryce's legs. They thrashed about, slamming the wall and collapsing some of the tunnel around us.

"*Fain, Everett*—focus on Thryce!"

I thought they would have difficulty in the dark tunnel, but then a flood of light shone throughout the entire area. My eyes were closed, but I could see the brightness through my eyelids. The light was coming from behind us. When I glanced over my shoulder, and peeked at the source, I saw Cao-Cao flittering near the ceiling.

I had to shield my eyes and turn away. Cao-Cao was so bright, and so white, he put the sun to shame. And it wasn't just me he was blinding—the two basilisks were caught off guard. They both closed their deadly eyes and hissed at the little white will-o-wisp.

That was when Fain and Zelfree struck. The moment Thryce lowered his head and rubbed at his reptilian face, Fain leapt up and ran his hands over the creature's eyes. He could manipulate flesh, and it was an easy feat to melt Thryce's eyelids closed.

But king basilisks had four eyes.

Zelfree leapt up on the other side and used his flesh manipulation to effortlessly climb the monster. His fingers slid in between the scales, and he lifted himself to the beast's eyes, but that was when Thryce thrashed his head. He slammed Zelfree against the far wall, causing more rubble to crash to the ground.

Despite being crushed against a rock wall, Zelfree clung to the basilisk. He managed to seal one eye shut before letting go and tumbling across the ground, away from the basilisk.

With my eyes still closed, I rushed forward and went straight for Thryce. I threw some of my molten rock across his snout and face. My aim wasn't true—being blind affected my strike, even if I could see through the tremors in the ground.

Thryce screeched—my evocation still burned, after all. And that was when I had the beast's attention. Even with Cao-Cao's bright light blinding the creature, he headed for me. I tried to dodge to the right, but Thryce got lucky with a swipe of his claw. He struck me, and I hit the ground, back-first. Winded and dizzy, I almost didn't feel Hexa running to my side. She grabbed my upper arm, yanked me to my feet, and held me steady as the ground quaked.

"Let's do this," she said through gritted teeth.

"Subdue him," I commanded. "I think we can still talk some logic into him."

Hexa grumbled something, but she didn't argue.

Kezrik clawed Thrice, but that was when the king basilisks decided to use their deadly venom. Both of them oozed venom from their fangs, their saliva darkening with death itself. A single touch, and most would perish.

# CHAPTER 17

## DEFENDING THRONEHOLD

Cao-Cao kept his light bright, allowing everyone to fight the basilisks so long as they kept their back to the will-o-wisp. It also meant the king basilisks couldn't keep their eyes open for very long. Well, Thryce only had the one eye that wasn't sealed shut—and Kezrik had kept his four eyes shut before the light, obviously trying to shield us from his stone-gaze.

Hexa pulled a dagger from her belt, took a second to aim, and then threw the blade with expert accuracy. It would've struck Thryce in his one remaining eye, but Kezrik slammed his massive head against the other basilisk, knocking him back a step just before the blade struck. The dagger hit the side of Thryce's neck instead, and stuck between some of his scales, barely injuring him.

Hexa cursed under her breath as she reached for another dagger.

A moment later, the dagger vanished from Thryce's neck. I suspected either Fain of Zelfree had stolen the weapon to try to put out the basilisk's last eye.

Intent on subduing Thryce, I imagined vegetation growing

in this underground tunnel. My evocation came in two flavors—creation or destruction—and I evoked vines from my arms, much like magma. I felt them, but not like limbs. It was like my tremor sense, where the vibrations along the vegetation registered in my mind.

But to my surprise, I didn't *just* evoke vines from my body this time. I also evoked plants from the ground around us. The vines jutted out of the dirt in vast amounts more than my flesh, bursting from the ground.

I lashed the vines around Thryce's six legs.

If I could hold him down, perhaps we could talk some sense into the beast...

But Thryce screeched and vomited his deadly venom across the vines. The moment the venom touched the plants, they wilted and died. That was the danger of the basilisks—they were deadly beyond belief, capable of killing nearly anything with a single splash of their venom.

Not me. Terrakona had taken a dose of the venom, and hadn't died, which meant I probably wouldn't either. But I didn't want to test that theory.

Once free, Thryce thrashed his head, front legs, and tail. His head bashed into Kezrik's snout, splattering blood across the floor of the tunnel. It was acidic and burned some of the dirt, but since no one had been struck, I wasn't as concerned. Thryce's claws tore into the ground with the power of cannon fire, causing explosions of dust and rock chips to fill the air. His tail struck the wall, crushing a support beam and bringing down part of the ceiling. Chunks of stone rained down around us, some as large as a human head, with jagged edges sharp enough to gouge bone.

During the confusion—while everyone wiped away the dirt from their eyes—Thryce lunged forward. He charged past Kezrik, stormed down the tunnel, and knocked Hexa and me aside as he headed for Cao-Cao.

"No!" I shouted.

I waved my hand and manipulated the ground around us. The floor—mostly dirt—sucked down the beast's legs and then hardened into stone around his knees, locking him in place. But I hadn't anticipated the strength of the king basilisks. Thryce roared and strained with all his might. The stone encasing his front legs shattered like glass.

Before he could fully free himself, Cao-Cao blazed even brighter. He shone like the sun, forcing everyone to close their eyes or be blinded. He reminded me of Forsythe. The little wisp stood his ground against death incarnate to protect the people behind him.

Although I couldn't see the combat, I relied on my tremor sense to keep a visual in my mind's eye. Then I manipulated the dirt again.

Zelfree's voice echoed in the tunnel. "Volke! Careful—you could collapse the entire mine!"

But he didn't need to worry. At my will, a pillar of stone erupted from the ground, catching Thryce in the gut and carrying him into the air. The pillar was large enough to support the massive beast's weight, and I slammed Thryce's body against the ceiling of the tunnel, pinning him in place and preventing him from reaching the will-o-wisp.

I marveled for a moment, surprised at my level of control. My tremor sense... I felt the tunnel and the pressures it was under. Part of me understood where the ceiling was weak, and which arches and braces were coming apart, threatening to weaken the tunnel's stability. By pinning the basilisk to the ceiling, I had created another support beam for the tunnel, preventing it from crashing down on top of us.

And manipulating the ground with such precision also shocked me. My knightmare magic had come so slowly, and after years of training, but my world serpent magic seemed to be improving by leaps and bounds.

"Thryce, calm down," I shouted. "We don't have to fight!"

Blood wept from three of his four eyes, streaming over his reptilian face like red tears. With his tongue lashing, Thryce turned his attention to the bright white light of Cao-Cao. To my horror, Thryce sucked in his breath and then spat.

I hadn't realized king basilisk could spit their venom. The surprise cost me a single precious moment. I unleashed a wave of magma, hoping to evaporate the venom, but I just wasn't fast enough.

A wad of king basilisk venom sailed through the air and struck the white will-o-wisp.

All at once, the wisp's light disappeared.

A scream echoed down the tunnels, half a cry of pain, half a howl of pure despair. Strenos. It had to be.

I gritted my teeth, guilt lancing through my chest. Losing his eldrin after Thronehold was "safe" must have been a devastating feeling. And I was supposed to make sure the city was safe from disaster—I couldn't allow this. I couldn't fail Thronehold.

When Thryce inhaled a second time, I feared he would spit more of his deadly venom across the tunnel, but the temperature suddenly plummeted. Ice coated the ground, my stone pillar, and the ceiling of the tunnel. The ice frosted Thryce, covering his scales, jaw, and face. The rime prevented Thryce from moving well, and although it was clear he wanted to spit more venom, the ice kept him unable to fully open his mouth.

I reached out, willing another pillar of stone to rise and pin Thryce's head to the ceiling. My anger, and guilt, caused me to use more force than necessary. The pillar slammed into Thryce's head with the force of a battering ram, partially embedding his head in the ceiling and shattering several of his fangs.

A second coating of ice spread throughout the tunnel, gluing the king basilisk in place.

With my tremor sense, I felt the creature's breath slowing, and his heart beating at half the rate it had been previously. Thryce was still alive, but the chill of the ice evocation was slowing him down. At this rate, he would die if we just left him here.

Kezrik huffed and shook his massive head. "Please," he said, his voice a growl. "Spare him, world serpent arcanist. He doesn't deserve a second death."

"I won't be killing him," I muttered.

Even if Thryce had killed Cao-Cao, I didn't want any more death. Besides, I didn't feel Thyce was truly responsibility for this. Queen Vellata had ordered him killed for no reason. The Second Ascension had pulled him back from his eternal rest and wiped his memories in order to turn him into a weapon. He had every reason to be scared, confused, and angry. In his mind, he was just defending himself.

"Thank you."

"Kezrik, I need your help reaching him." I turned to face the other basilisk, but it was too dark to really see anything. "And if you know of any other king basilisks, we need to know their location so we can help them as well."

"Help them find their arcanists?"

"Of course. It's my goal to right the wrongs of the past and build a better future. But we won't be able to do that if we keep fighting amongst ourselves."

Kezrik didn't reply. He walked over, his six legs stomping as he went, but he stopped next to the stone pillars I had created to restrain Thryce. With deep inhales, Kezrik sniffed the ground. "You have powerful magic."

"I'm a god-arcanist."

The basilisk exhaled, his hot breath washing over me. "I've never seen a god-arcanist before..." Then Kezrik shook his head. "Or maybe I have... My memories have abandoned me. But I don't think... I've ever felt this amount of power before."

"The god creatures have not spawned for thousands of

years," I muttered. "They only returned in the last five or so. I doubt you ever met one."

Kezrik lowered his snout close to me, his breath laced with an acidic aroma. At first, I was fearful of his venom, but Kezrik didn't have an aggressive stance. He slowly moved his nose closer, and I lifted a hand to touch the cold scales of his body. With hesitant movements, I rubbed his smooth scales.

I had never touched a king basilisk before. They were among the mightiest and deadliest of mystical creatures, yet here I was, petting one on the snout. The thought caused my mouth to quirk into a smile.

A faint lantern light illuminated a far tunnel. Strenos hurried into our area, his lantern swinging in his sweaty hand as he huffed and puffed. His scarred face looked even more twisted when the flames of the lantern cast dark shadows over the wrinkles around his milky-white eye.

Several citizens of Thronehold followed behind him, trying to match his pace. Their wide eyes and shaking hands betrayed their fear. I didn't blame them. Being trapped in an underground tunnel with king basilisks lurking nearby would scare anyone, even the legendary swashbuckler arcanists of old.

Were they miners? They wore thick leathers, and each of them had faces smudged with dirt. Their boots reached their knees, and their gloves went to their elbows.

"Cao-Cao!" Strenos called out. "*Cao-Cao!*"

I lifted my hand off Kezrik and stepped forward. "Strenos... I—"

"What're you doing, Strenos?" Zelfree barked, cutting me off. "Get those people out of here! It's not safe."

Strenos slowly came to a stop. He was only twenty feet from us, and the lantern highlighted his knitted eyebrows and hard gaze. I stood at the edge of his light, and he glared at me.

"You let my eldrin die?" he asked, his voice strained.

I had never wanted that. Strenos had to know that. No one

had wanted the eldrin harmed. It was just a risk of dealing with deadly beasts.

"You call yourself a guildmaster?" Zelfree allowed his invisibility to drop and then stepped forward, well into the lantern light. "Get those people out of here! Then we'll talk about what happened."

The words barely seemed to penetrate Strenos's skull. He continued to glare at me, never allowing his gaze to wander. The citizens of Thronehold made their way closer, clearly drawn to Strenos's lantern light. There was nowhere else to go—they acted like moths, trying to stay as close as possible to the illumination.

A harsh crack from behind me caused me to break Streno's gaze and spin around. Thryce had managed to pull his head free of the column pinning it to the ceiling and had sucked in a deep breath, his mouth full of venom once again.

"Look out!" I cried.

With a wave of my hand, I evoked vines to grab the dozen citizens and move them aside. It wasn't a gentle movement—I lashed the denizens with vines and tossed them aside, trying to protect them from the venom as fast as I possibly could.

But I missed two.

Strenos and the miner closest to him.

When Thryce spat, his venom went toward the lantern light. With selfless passion, Strenos pushed the miner aside, saving the man from the king basilisk venom. Strenos's coat was doused in the vile liquid, but it hadn't yet soaked through and touched his skin. Strenos struggled to remove his clothing—his panic making all his movements erratic.

Before Thryce could attack again, Fain evoked more ice, frosting the king basilisk in another layer. Hexa threw another dagger, striking the side of the beast's head, cutting open a fresh wound and drawing its ire.

Kezrik hustled forward, knocking me over in order to shield Strenos and the miner. With his body over them, Kezrik waited.

Zelfree appeared out of nowhere and cut at Streno's coat with Hexa's dagger. Three slices, and the coat was off.

I raised a pillar to pin Thryce's mouth shut. Then for good measure, I caused the stone of the ceiling to flow over his head, sealing his head in the cavern roof. I left holes for him to breathe, however.

"Th-Thank you," the miner said to Strenos.

"The world serpent arcanist saved us," someone else in the tunnel muttered.

Another miner pulled off my vines. "We're safe now that the warlord is here!"

I stepped forward and waved them all to the far tunnel. "Please, everyone, listen! We need to get you out of here right away. These tunnels aren't safe. Don't worry—I'll handle everything here. It's more important that you leave. Once you're on the surface, you can write down any valuable information for me and the new queen."

The new miners did as I instructed, even the miner whom Strenos had saved.

But Strenos wasn't as happy to leave as the others. He kept his gaze on the floor as he moved, his lantern gripped firmly in his hand, his knuckles white. The mark on his forehead was bleeding, and I wondered what he was thinking.

Then again, perhaps I didn't want to know.

This situation already reminded me too much of Luthair.

---

Kezrik dragged Thryce out of the tunnels and out onto the streets of Thronehold.

Thryce's head was still encased in stone, and Fain and Zelfree had coated him in ice until he had resembled a miniature iceberg.

I was still wary about taking him above ground, but we needed to get him out of the city—and out of the fragile tunnels—before the king basilisk could do any more damage.

There were likely more king basilisks in the underground, but since none of them had shown themselves, I decided to first visit the queen. I'd bring Kezrik, so I could explain the situation, but I didn't know what I'd say, exactly. I wanted to tell her that the king basilisks were friendly, but Strenos was going to have a different story.

Once he explained his eldrin had been killed, I suspected Queen Ladislava would consider ordering the death of the king basilisks all over again.

The moment we got onto the streets, the nearby denizens ran to tell the Knights Draconic. Within minutes, unicorn arcanists surrounded us.

Knight Captain Alrick was among them, sitting upon his pale white unicorn, his uniform crisp. The symbol of the Argo Empire—a dragon and a rose—was etched into his full plate armor across the breastplate. He wore a shining helmet that glittered in the sunlight. Somehow, after the battle for the city had been won, this man had found himself a new suit of armor.

I wondered if it had been due to vanity, or because he had wanted to convey a sense of stability.

"What is the meaning of this?" Alrick asked, his voice breathless as he gazed upon the half-frozen Thryce and the mighty Kezrik.

"We need to speak with the queen," I muttered. "Will you take us to see her?"

# CHAPTER 18

## ACTING FERAL

Knight Captain Alrick held his reins tightly. His unicorn eldrin snorted and then glared at the half-frozen king basilisk. Because of the beast's giant body, we had to return to the streets through the ceiling of a shattered tunnel. I worried this area of Thronehold wouldn't be stable—especially with *two* gargantuan basilisks—and while I appreciated the knight captain coming to see us, I didn't want to stay long.

"The king basilisks..." Alrick's face, squarish in shape, hardened into the expression of an angry brick. "You went to handle these beasts on your own? Are you a *fool*?"

"They were a possible threat to everyone in the city." I motioned to the devastation around us. "Immediate action was required to keep the situation from escalating. I didn't want any more loss."

"You should have waited for the Knights Draconic. Unicorn arcanists are immune to the venom of the basilisks." He patted the neck of his eldrin.

Although Alrick was correct—unicorn arcanists had several

passive defenses, including poison immunity—we hadn't had time to wait and search. Not only that, but most of the Knights Draconic were busy in the city. When I glanced around, I noticed Alrick only had four other unicorn arcanists with him, and each could barely keep their eyes open.

They wouldn't have been a major asset in our fight with Thryce.

"We need to speak with the queen," I said again, ignoring the knight captain's chiding. "There may be more king basilisks, and I have to report to her about the fenris wolf."

Knight Captain Alrick's brick expression never left him. He tugged on the reins, and his unicorn complied with his movements. He turned to the other knights. "Secure the area. Don't allow anyone to get near these *creatures*." With a wave of his hand, he motioned to both Thryce and Kezrik.

"I'm going to stay here," Strenos said, his voice shaky. He rubbed at the scars on his face, his gaze distant and unseeing. The mark on his forehead disturbed me—cracked, faded, slightly bloody—and I tried not to stare. "I'll make sure the knights are informed about what happened," Strenos concluded.

Zelfree and Fain seemed to step out of thin air, allowing their invisibility to fade off them. "That's for the best," Zelfree said to the man. "Make sure the knights don't try to kill them."

Strenos didn't reply.

Part of me worried for the king basilisks, but I couldn't waste any more time. When the knight captain trotted by, he gestured for us to follow. I hurried after him, ready to speak to Queen Ladislava and get this all settled.

Hexa, Zelfree, and Fain all followed after me, each jogging to keep my pace. Alrick rode out ahead, the clop of his unicorn's hooves echoing through the destruction of the city around us. Occasionally, we passed the denizens of the district, and they cheered as we went by. I forced myself to wave back, even though my thoughts dwelled on Strenos's little will-o-wisp. Poor Cao-Cao had been doing everything in his power to help us.

"You handled yourself well back there," Zelfree said between huffs.

At first, I thought he was talking to me, but when I glanced over my shoulder, I noticed his attention was on Hexa. She remained silent, glaring at the street as we went through Thronehold.

I had never seen her so distracted.

We slowed our pace as we neared the castle. The Dragon District was quiet, with large roads and dozens of broken statues. Once we reached the gates around King Drake Castle, Hexa stopped. It was only then that she took a deep breath and replied with, "I'm not afraid of giant reptiles."

"That's obvious," Fain muttered, his words almost inaudible.

"I grew up in Regal Heights." Hexa huffed as she patted down her trousers. "We have to deal with all sorts of strange creatures. The canyons have hydra and—" She caught her breath and then glanced up, her eyes wide. "By the abyssal hells. *Why didn't I think of this earlier?*"

I faced her, my eyebrows knitted. "What's wrong?"

Hexa stepped forward and grabbed my shoulders. She stared into my eyes, a smile creeping onto her face. "Moonbeam thinks he's having trouble finding Vethica with his dreamwalking because the Second Ascension has an arcanist or a trinket that's hiding their thoughts and concealing their location."

"O-Okay..."

"But in Regal Heights, we had to track mystical creatures all the time." She shook me slightly. "We have real trackers. Their eldrin's magic helps them pick up physical trails and spot clues and smell the subtlest of scents, instead of just scrying for the target. They can find anything! Even midnight bats and white harts. *They could find people.* They could find Vethica!"

That was a lot of jumps and assumptions all in one statement. Yes, Adelgis was having a hard time finding people, but he was getting better and better each day he practiced his magic. And ever since he had removed the abyssal leech from his body, his magic had been growing stronger. He would likely find everyone we needed in a short amount of time.

But...

I hadn't thought about asking world-class trackers. And Regal Heights—the city in the canyon—was known for their strange methods of doing things. Perhaps *their* trackers would be the people we needed.

But Regal Heights was far from here. Would it be worth the time to travel there?

Perhaps we could find a lair of a god-creature along the way, or at least in that general direction. If we could, this would be a boon.

Fain stepped up close to us. He crossed his arms and tucked his black fingers into his armpits. "If we can find arcanists to track people, that would be preferred. Moonbeam needs his rest."

After a long exhale, I nodded.

"Hexa," I said. "Round up the Frith Guild and tell them about these trackers. Once I'm done with the queen, I'll come back, and we can discuss our next course of action."

She nodded once, her smile widening. "This is a perfect idea. I know it. I feel it in my bones."

"It seems like a good plan, but I need to handle a few things here first."

"But Vethica—"

I placed a hand on her arm and gritted my teeth. She seemed to sense my seriousness, because she didn't even finish her statement. Hexa just held her breath and stared at me.

"Gather the Frith Guild, and we'll discuss it later tonight." I released her arm and moved out of her grip. "Trust me. I want to find her as well, but we shouldn't do anything hasty." And we had so many problems to deal with. I had to stay organized.

The world was crumbling, but I wouldn't allow my thoughts to fall apart as well.

Hexa stepped away and bowed her head slightly. "Don't worry, Warlord. I'll handle this. I'll gather everyone and tell them everything I know about the trackers in Regal Heights."

She turned and hurried away before I could say anything further. There wasn't much to say, though. I had convinced myself this would be for the best. I had never seen Regal Heights, but Hexa had told us so much about it that I was actually excited to visit it.

Zelfree watched Hexa go and then turned to me with a lifted eyebrow. "The queen will likely try to keep us in Thronehold."

"Why?" Fain interjected. "You really think she'll try to command a god-arcanist?"

"Volke is still a neonate."

"So?"

"So, Volke has only been bonded to the world serpent for a few months. He's powerful, but an army or an adult dragon arcanist could potentially overpower him. Ladislava loves giving orders and hates taking them."

I nodded along with Zelfree's assessment. Ladislava was forceful. She had fought against her own countrymen for the crown, after all. She wasn't the type of person to sit around and allow everyone else to make decisions.

Zelfree held up a hand, getting animated in his speech. "Ladislava wants to control a god-arcanist. It'll solidify her power and offer more legitimacy to her rule. But Volke is getting more powerful by the day—and soon she won't have any advantage over him. Which is why she wanted someone loyal to her to bond with the fenris wolf. She wanted the power of a god-arcanist to command. And now that Zaxis has bonded with the wolf, her plan has failed."

"And she's going to get upset," Fain muttered, his eyes narrowed.

"Ladislava is likely going to pressure Volke or Zaxis into swearing themselves to her." Zelfree glanced over to me, and then returned his attention to Fain. "And since Volke already has knights and sworn allies, I'm pretty sure Ladislava is going to go after Zaxis. She might even make a scene of this—anything to get her ultimate goal."

My chest twisted a bit.

Ladislava was a sovereign dragon arcanist. From what I knew of them, they were autocrats—people who desired power over everything else. Zelfree's assessment of the situation made perfect sense.

"Tsk." Fain tensed as he glanced over.

I sometimes forgot he was older than I was, but when Fain became cold in attitude, I saw it. There was a harshness to his demeanor he usually hid.

"Maybe you should act a little bit more like Calisto in moments like this."

Zelfree clenched his fists at the mere mention of Calisto. He narrowed his eyes and shot Fain a sidelong glance. But he said nothing. He just waited—like he wanted to hear whatever explanation Fain had to offer.

"Calisto wouldn't let someone he barely knew control him," Fain muttered. He shook his head. "He always conducted himself with a feral attitude that put people on-edge. They never *tried* to mess with him, for fear he would snap."

"And that's what you think I should do?" I asked.

Fain stared at me for a long moment. Then he sighed, and his shoulders slumped. "Well, when I imagine you acting like Calisto... I almost laugh, to be honest. But yes. I think if you could pull it off, it would help you."

"Being *feral*?" I repeated, the word weird on the tip of my tongue. I never thought that would be considered a positive trait.

With a sigh, I turned to Master Zelfree, hoping he would recommend the exact opposite behavior. Unfortunately, Zelfree met my gaze with a look of sardonic amusement.

"He's not wrong," Zelfree muttered. "What he's trying to say is—you never want anyone to think you're passive, or otherwise within their control. You always want people to think, *I need to be on this man's good side.*"

"And you don't think Queen Ladislava thinks I'm passive?" I asked.

Before Zelfree or Fain could reply, Knight Captain Alrick barked out, "Come! The queen grows impatient."

The setting sun covered all of Thronehold in a crimson hue. A cold wind rushed down the road, but I shrugged off the chill, my mind on Zelfree and Fain's advice. I never wanted to be *passive*—I just wanted to be helpful and agreeable. Did that make me controllable? I hadn't thought of it like that.

But I shook my head, dispelling the confusion.

The traits of a great leader weren't the same traits as those of a great follower.

When I had been younger, my dream had been to *follow* the path of the swashbuckling hero arcanists of the past. I had to shake some of that mentality. It just... was harder than it seemed it would be.

Zelfree placed a hand on my shoulder and turned me toward the large gate and bridge to the castle. We had to step over trolley tracks and broken bits of carriage to make it to the front garden of the castle, but I barely took note of our surroundings.

"Terrakona?" I whispered, my voice carried away by the sunset wind.

**"Warlord?"**

"You... Everyone's afraid of you. And it's not just your size and your ancient magic. It's your demeanor. You're a child—a hatchling—but you speak and act... so powerfully." I lamely added the last bit because I lacked the words to describe what I meant.

**"I will never be controlled."** Terrakona's telepathy was filled with a sense of force. **"You and I are one—your commands are my true desire. But everyone else's words are mere suggestion."**

*Mere suggestion?*

As soon as Terrakona had said it, I knew that was what Zelfree and Fain were talking about. The Dread Pirate Calisto wasn't a man who took kindly to orders. Even the Second Ascension hadn't *ordered him around*—they had traded him trinkets and artifacts in order to gain his cooperation. But he had never been fully theirs, and everyone knew it.

Did I really need to embody that type of personality?

"Should I be more forceful?" I whispered as I walked around the fountains outside of King Drake Castle.

Fain followed close, his brow furrowed. He glanced over at me and frowned. "Are you speaking to yourself?"

With a forced half-smile, I shook my head. "No. I'm talking to Terrakona. He, uh—"

"No, don't worry about it." Fain shrugged and glanced away. "Moonbeam mutters to himself all the time. You just reminded me of him for a moment."

The way he spoke of Adelgis—and the way Hexa had spoken of Vethica—made me think of Evianna. We hadn't been separated long, but I already missed her. We should've gone to the castle together, as a sentimental reminder of when we had first met. I had "saved" her from a river not too far from here. The memory floated in my thoughts as we entered the castle courtyard.

Alrick and his unicorn stood by the large double doors. He turned and pushed open the doors, allowing us to enter at the same time.

The front room was massive. A large tapestry covered the near wall. It displayed a giant sovereign dragon fighting a leviathan, their colors bright and vibrant.

Castle servants hurried forward, their eyes down, their hands shaky. They fussed with Alrick, asking if he wanted anything to drink, or if they should clean his armor. A single servant went to Zelfree, and three hastily ran to my side, bowing several times, all muttering apologies for random details, including the state of the castle or the weather outside. I waved them away, needing nothing.

Knight Captain Alrick turned on his heel and led us toward the reception hall. His unicorn waited behind, practically guarding the front door. Its beautiful white coat practically sparkled in the light of the many lanterns.

The moment we entered the reception hall, regret blazed through me like a wildfire.

The giant room had two-story-tall windows that stretched from the floor to the ceiling—but they were cracked, some shattered completely. The many tables were toppled over, and the dozens of chairs were strewn about the area. The queen's servants were busy tidying the space, but it was just another clear reminder that war had come to Thronehold.

"You three shall wait here," Alrick said matter-of-factly, not even bothering to glance back at us. "Queen Ladislava will come to speak with you."

Zelfree and Fain stopped and waited.

But...

Perhaps this was a moment to be feral.

I continued walking along with Alrick. The clink of his armor rang through the ruined reception hall, and the stomp of my footfalls was right in sync. We reached the far door before Alrick even realized I was still following him. He touched the door handle and then glanced over his shoulder, his eyes widening.

"You can wait here," he said again.

"I don't have time to wait," I stated.

"Queen Ladislava is currently meeting with dragon arcanists from neighboring nations."

I glanced over at the man, keeping my face neutral. "I guess I'll be meeting them as well."

# CHAPTER 19

## THREE DRAGONS

Knight Captain Alrick walked with a stiff gait as we strode down a long hall, the crimson carpets muffling our steps. He said nothing. He didn't even look at me. Which was fine. I didn't need him to like me—I just needed him to fall in line.

Where was Zaxis? He clearly hadn't come to the castle yet. There was no sign of him or the fenris wolf. Where had they gone? Part of me hoped he was with Guildmaster Eventide.

Alrick and I reached a giant spiral staircase, and my thoughts, and my steps, came to a halt. The stairs circled around a bluish-black statue of a sovereign dragon—and while that was impressive, it didn't interest me. I had seen it before.

All I could think about was the previous knight captain...

Alrick went straight to the stairs, but he slowed and then glanced over his shoulder. "This way, Warlord. The queen is one floor up, entertaining her guests."

"Knight Captain Rendell died here," I muttered as I walked over to him. "I saw him and his black unicorn the night the city was attacked by the Second Ascension."

Alrick stiffened. Once we were together, he walked by my

side, occasionally smoothing his brown, bushy eyebrows. After a short exhale, he asked, "Rendell... Was he...? No. What I mean is, *how was he*? At the end?"

We took the steps at a slow rate, my thoughts dwelling on that terrible night. "Despite the death and destruction, Knight Captain Rendell stood his ground. He was strong and determined, even when he knew he had been infected with the plague."

Alrick listened intently, his breath held.

I closed my eyes, my tremor sense allowing me to climb the stairs without trouble. "Rendell held off the Second Ascension long enough for me to get Princess Evianna to safety... I didn't know Rendell for very long, but he left a powerful impression on me."

When I opened my eyes again, Alrick wasn't looking at me. His attention was on the steps forward, his fingers tracing the arcanist mark on his forehead.

The statue in the middle of the staircase was made of nullstone. The smooth surface of the sculpture gave the dragon a sleek glint, and I admired it for a brief moment. It reminded me of Rendell's black unicorn.

"Knight Captain Rendell helped train me," Alrick said, jarring me out of my thoughts. "He was stalwart. Brave." Alrick held himself a little taller. "Everyone in the Knights Draconic refers to him in whispered awe. He's a legend. Have you ever admired someone like that, Warlord?"

"Gregory Ruma," I muttered. Though I didn't elaborate.

"Rendell was the greatest man I've known. I was honored when Ladislava chose me for the position of knight captain, but how can I compare to a man like Rendell? He'll go down in history as a legend. I don't know if I can say the same for myself."

I didn't think that way. Maybe once I had, but not anymore. All my heroes—all the legends I admired—had been larger than life, but their deeds weren't beyond my grasp. Someday, I would be one of them, so long as I didn't falter in my path.

If I wanted to do my heroes proud, I had to rise to the challenge.

We reached the next floor before I could find any words for Alrick. He didn't seem to mind. He walked a little easier, his tension and irritation almost completely gone. He even offered me a tight smile as he motioned to the nearest door. "Here. This room is beneath the throne room. It has a pleasant view of the garden—and the dragons."

"Thank you," I said as I reached for the handle.

Alrick threw an arm in front of me. "Allow me. I'll announce you."

I stepped back, one eyebrow raised. "All right."

He opened the large door, pushing it inward and then stepping inside before me. After a deep breath, he said, "Queen Ladislava, the world serpent arcanist, Warlord Volke Savan, is here to speak to you."

I didn't wait for an offer to enter. I stepped into the large meeting room, surprised by the décor. A single table the size of a small boat was in the middle of the room, at least two dozen chairs positioned around the sides. A fur rug was under the table. It *used* to be a mystical creature, but I couldn't tell which. The ivory sheen of the fur rug betrayed its high quality. The light danced off each strand of fur. The darkness of the night outside was held at bay thanks to the magic in the chandelier.

The table was equally white, as though it had been carved from bone or antlers. The chairs were twisted white sculptures made of a wood-like material with black spots. Birch? Or perhaps something more magical.

Giant glass windows, most cracked, lined two of the walls. The back of the room was a balcony that overlooked the gardens, large enough for the three dragons to poke their heads into the room. All three dragons were basically three stories in height, each hunching down so that their heads were close to the room, their snouts in the castle itself.

I couldn't help but smile. Dragons were so powerful and majestic—I couldn't help but admire them. Queen Ladislava's sovereign dragon had black scales along his back and shoulders, but crimson red scales for his underbelly. His face was mighty, but scarred from several battles, the thin scales around his eyes marred.

The horns on his head were scuffed, giving them a well-used appearance.

The second dragon was a pyroclastic dragon. Unlike other dragons, who had scales and horns, pyroclastic dragons had skin made of hardened magma. This was the first time I had seen one in person, and I couldn't help but feel close to the beast. The dragon's fiery body reminded me of my own evocation. Would Terrakona like the pyroclastic dragon? He had once said he was lonely, because there were no other world serpents, but maybe a dragon would be close enough in power and size...

This pyroclastic dragon had cracks in his glowing skin, like rivers of lava. He shimmered with heat, as though surrounded by mirages. His eyes were small pools of fire, each their own pyre.

The last dragon...

"A celestial dragon," I said aloud, my voice barely above a whisper.

Celestial dragons barely had a physical form. They were creatures of pure magic, their bodies made of glittering starlight and darkness—a living night sky. From what I had read, celestial dragons were born whenever the corpse of a dragon was struck with star shards that fell from the sky. A rare occurrence, but one that had happened more than half a dozen times on the small island nation of Sellix.

Apparently, the old rulers of Sellix had had a sacred mountain where they had placed the bones of past sovereign dragons. These were the first celestial dragons—once they had been struck with star shards, they had lifted from the ground again, their starlight bodies a thing of wonder.

The celestial dragon didn't really have a face—its head was just the night sky, and its horns were wisps of partially physical magic.

"Warlord," Alrick said to me, stealing my attention. "You know Queen Ladislava." He motioned to the head of the table, where she sat. Then he pointed to the two men sitting at the long table. "But allow me to introduce you to King Kalasardo the Great Pyroclastic Dragon Arcanist of the Nuul Kingdom, and Emperor Barnett the Sixth Celestial Dragon Arcanist of Sellix."

I didn't have much time to stare at them. Queen Ladislava quickly stood from her chair. She wore her half-plate armor, each section stamped with the Argo Empire's dragon-and-rose emblem. Her silver armor incorporated the black scales from her dragon, a perfect mix of regal and threatening.

Her white hair had been painstakingly woven into an elaborate braid that swirled around her head, similar to a crown. Ladislava's bluish-purple eyes, narrowed in a glower, locked on to mine. Her indignant expression was quickly suppressed as she forced herself to smile.

"*Warlord*," she said, terse. "I wasn't expecting you."

I walked up to the opposite end of the table and swept my hair back. How would Calisto have acted in this situation? Feral, yes. But rude and threatening. That wasn't me. What about—if I had Zelfree's cunning and Calisto's fierce defiance? The thought made me smirk, but I quickly controlled my expression in order to face the dragon arcanists.

"Given the state of the world, I don't have time to waste," I said. "After I returned from the lair of the fenris wolf, I found the city was infested with king basilisks."

Both the other dragon arcanists stood from their chairs.

King Kalasardo was an interesting one. He wore phoenix

feathers on almost every portion of his outfit. The scarlet feathers lined his cape, and a grouping of down feathers had been used as a plume on the front of his vest. Pyroclastic dragons were known for their love of fire and flame, so it didn't surprise me that a pyroclastic dragon arcanist would take that to heart.

His cape, vest, shirt, and trousers were likely all magical trinkets.

"I thought king basilisks were extinct," Kalasardo said. He clutched the plume of down feathers. "Such beasts are beyond dangerous. They can't be allowed to roam the streets."

The other dragon arcanist—Emperor Barnett—said nothing. He glanced between me, Kalasardo, and the queen, his calculating gaze betraying his cunning. His expression reminded me of Adelgis. He maintained a neutral demeanor, and when his gaze met mine, it was as if it saw deeply beyond the conversation and to my soul. This dragon arcanist was icier than Adelgis, though.

He clearly wanted more information before he spoke.

Barnett was taller than most, but thin and lithe, like an island tree. He wore fine robes marked with star constellations so intricate and detailed, they were practically a map of the night sky. It gave him an otherworldly aura, like he was a man concerned with matters of the heavens, and not matters of the earth.

Ladislava pursed her lips. "I will send the Knights Draconic to handle the basilisks." She pointed to Alrick. "Remove their heads. Kill every last one of them."

Knight Captain Alrick opened his mouth, likely to explain the situation, but I didn't let him.

"That's not needed," I interjected. I placed a hand on the bone-white table. The queen's words were mere suggestion. "I handled two of the basilisks, and it's clear they're confused and disoriented. The basilisks can be subdued without killing them, and I'm going to leave that up to the Frith Guild to handle."

Queen Ladislava flinched as though my statement had been a slap in the face. She recovered before the other two dragon arcanists could notice, however. She stood her ground, tall and unmoving, her eyes never leaving mine.

When she went to speak, I interjected a second time.

"They may need the assistance of the Knights Draconic," I said. "Especially if the basilisks are to be removed from the city. I was hoping they would aid us."

"You won't kill them?" Kalasardo asked.

He was a little older than the other two in appearance, with darker brown hair coated in a light amount of soot. Perhaps a live phoenix was nearby? It made sense that perhaps the dragon arcanist would have an assistant or a knight who would be a phoenix arcanist.

Then again, the Nuul Kingdom was a land near volcanoes. Perhaps the soot was a specific look the king was going for.

I shook the thoughts away and then hardened my expression when I turned to face him. "I won't kill them, no. They don't deserve that."

"But their hides could be used for artifacts and trinkets. We could use them to fight the Second Ascension, as Queen Ladislava was saying."

"If we had king basilisk arcanists on our side, that would be far better than a single item," I stated, firm and unwavering. "We should be focused on the long-term and not fixated on short-term solutions."

Plus, any items we had could break. The Second Ascension had *decay dust*, a foul substance that broke weaker items. Or worse—the items could be taken and used against us.

"What if the basilisks bond with members of the Second Ascension?" Kalasardo turned to the queen, avoiding my harsh gaze. "We can't face an army of deadly assassins."

"*I'll* handle any king basilisks who side with the enemy," I stated, heat in my voice. That was the essence of a hero and leader. I'd handle the tasks the others were too frightened to face. "And I won't be party to genocide just because you're afraid of hypothetical outcomes."

Challenging the bravery of a dragon arcanist probably wasn't the best move, but it seemed to do the trick. Kalasardo straightened himself and held firm, like he wasn't about to be outmatched.

"Forgive me," he said. "I'm unaccustomed to working with a god-arcanist. Having you handle any basilisk defectors does ease my concerns."

The three dragons beyond the balcony tilted their heads, each of them leaning a bit closer. The breath of the pyroclastic dragon raised the temperature of the room, despite the large balcony that allowed fresh air to cycle through.

Ladislava cleared her throat and said, "Well, we can't be certain of all matters. What if the enemy has—"

"No," I interjected. "I'm certain. I'll handle all enemy basilisks. But if we work together now—and make them our allies—this whole discussion is moot. So I suggest we focus on the immediate. Unless you're saying you're incapable of handling this?"

I was probably being more aggressive than necessary, but now was the time for a show of force. Before we discussed Zaxis's fate, and whether or not he would stay here in the Argo Empire, I wanted them to know I wouldn't let my voice go unheard.

But every word I spoke bothered Ladislava. She reacted as though I were driving wood splinters under her fingernails. She clenched her fists, the corners of her lips twitching downward in a restrained frown.

"We're capable of handling a great many things," she said. "The question is whether or not it's an effective use of our time and resources."

"I've taken that into consideration."

That was it. The finality in my voice ended the discussion.

If Ladislava argued with me—in front of royal dragon arcanists from other nations—it would make her seem weak. She didn't want that. She had *just* taken the throne, and her position as queen was in question. Ladislava wanted as many allies as possible, and to seem in control. If word got out that we were arguing in the middle of a diplomatic meeting, confidence in her reign would surely plummet.

"Who is the other god-arcanist?" Emperor Barnett finally asked. "We saw the pillar of light in the distance. That was the sign the fenris wolf had bonded, was it not?"

I nodded once, curt and tense.

Kalasardo and Ladislava exchanged quick glances, and I wondered if they knew the symbology behind the pillars. Had they been confused? But Barnett had known?

The tall emperor kept his tone controlled and low, his robes held tightly by his side. He reminded me of a wizard from ancient tales. Even his arcanist mark seemed more mystical than others—tiny stars were woven around the larger one. "Did a member of the Argo Empire's royal family bond with the mighty fenris wolf?"

I shook my head. "The fenris wolf has chosen Zaxis Ren, a man from the Isle of Ruma."

My statement was met with icy silence. None of the dragon arcanists liked this news—I could tell by the harsh expressions they wore. Why? Had Ladislava promised a different outcome? If Zelfree's suspicions were correct, that was likely it.

"He and I will be in charge of helping Thronehold through this difficult situation with the basilisks." I offered a slight bow of my head. "Then Zaxis will present himself to the queen and thank her for her hospitality."

"But—" Ladislava began.

"The Frith Guild wants to make sure we thank our allies," I stated, cutting her off. "The Argo Empire has been instrumental in helping us combat the Second Ascension. Obviously, we're tremendously grateful, and all god-arcanists will remember it."

I stated everything as matter-of-factly as I could. If I controlled the narrative, the other two dragon arcanists would understand who was in charge.

Ladislava smirked and replied, "Of course. Yes. The Frith Guild and the Argo Empire are great allies."

She had said every word with hate. She wanted control of a god-arcanist, and the narrative I had woven wasn't that.

Both Kalasardo and Barnett nodded along with her words, accepting them as truth and then regarding me with slight bows. I had defied Ladislava's first command as queen and had made it clear she didn't control me. It seemed acting feral *was* beneficial —everyone seemed too scared to contradict me.

"The Knights Draconic will help us with the basilisks," I said, my tone a statement and not a question.

Ladislava glanced at Alrick, gave him a single nod, and then returned her glare to me. "Of course, Warlord."

"Perfect." I turned to leave when Ladislava held up a hand.

"Afterward, when Zaxis Ren comes to present himself, we will have diplomats and royalty from all our allied nations to greet him as the next god-arcanist." Ladislava continued with her false smile. "I went to great lengths to find someone who can help us unravel the mysteries surrounding the god-creatures. Apparently, the fenris wolf and the world serpent are epic rivals in history. I was hoping we could discuss that before any future decisions are made."

## CHAPTER 20

# THE FENRIS WOLF IN
# THRONEHOLD

Queen Ladislava walked around the bone-white table with quick and powerful strides. I waited, and then we walked to the door together, no words between us—no words even to the other dragon arcanists. They watched us go with intense gazes, but when I glanced over to them, they looked away, suddenly more interested in their dragon eldrin.

Alrick joined me and Ladislava as we exited.

Once in the giant hallway, out on the plush red carpets and away from the door, Ladislava turned on her heel to face me. "Warlord."

"Yes?"

I came to a stop and faced her, ready for whatever aggression she was going to throw my way. The tone of her voice and her wide stance told me she was itching for a fight. She had said she had hired researchers, but I suspected that was just a pretense for her to walk out into the hall with me.

She stared at me dead on, her bluish-purple eyes dark and intense. "This is *my* city. *My* nation. *My* rules."

Ladislava spoke every word through gritted teeth. She stepped a little closer, limiting the distance between us.

"And let me remind you of a few important facts," she said. "I've been trained to rule over a nation. I've studied tactics. I've developed my magic. I've spent dozens of years honing my abilities. *You're just a child.* A guild arcanist from a tiny island of no importance. You've barely stumbled out of your baby bed, and just because you've bonded with a god-creature doesn't mean you have the skills to govern. *I'll* make the decisions. You'll follow them."

The sheer venom in her words surprised me, but I kept my shock to myself, showing nothing on my face. I had known the queen would be upset. This was more than I had expected, however.

But feral animals didn't stand down just because another animal was barking at them.

I stepped closer—we were practically close enough to share body heat, but I didn't care. I glared straight into Ladislava's eyes. "You forgot a few facts, but that's common among people your age, so I'll forgive you."

I swear she stopped breathing, her rage overtaking all other senses as she met my gaze with an unblinking glower.

Before she could recover and escalate this further, I continued, "Since you can't remember, let me remind *you* of a few facts. There are hundreds of dragon arcanists in the world, but there are only a few god-arcanists. Whoever the god-arcanists side with will have a tremendous advantage in all things— politics, war, power. And that's because their magic is far greater than anyone else's. This is the new age of magic, and it won't be determined by people like you. It'll be determined by people like me, and Zaxis."

She opened her mouth, but I just kept talking.

"And let me remind you that the Second Ascension

assassinated the last queen while she was safe in her city, surrounded by her knights and legionnaires. How she was older and more powerful than you—with far more experience—without a city in ruin that demanded her attention. Do you really want to lose my support? Or the support of the clever arcanists of the Frith Guild? Over a simple dispute, like *who's calling the shots*? After all your years of training, I thought you'd be more diplomatic than this."

Queen Ladislava narrowed her eyes, no doubt calculating her next statement carefully.

"And the final thing you have forgotten is that you agreed to this arrangement. You promised the Argo Empire's support until the Second Ascension was defeated. The wolf might've bonded with someone you didn't want it to, but that's hardly a reason to back out of your agreement, wouldn't you say?"

Queen Ladislava swallowed her words as I turned and walked away. Knight Captain Alrick stood off to the side, his eyebrows near his hairline, his posture stiff. He didn't offer me any words as I strode by. I didn't say anything to him either. It felt awkward leaving the situation so tense and unresolved, but it felt right in this situation to state my position in an uncompromising way.

Hopefully this was the right choice. I had never done anything quite like it.

Before I reached the spiral staircase, a castle servant leapt up the steps and nearly crashed into me. He wore fine black trousers, a long white silk tunic, and a gold sash belt that glittered. I suspected he was some sort of herald or head of ceremonies. Who else would be wearing something like that? It was an ostentatious and attention-grabbing outfit.

The man fumbled when he spotted me, his eyes wide. Then he glanced over to Ladislava and hesitantly smiled. "My queen! The fenris wolf arcanist has arrived. He awaits you in the courtyard."

Ladislava squared her shoulders and patted her white braids

against her head, making sure every hair was perfectly in place. Then she exhaled, calming herself. With the poise required of a queen, she walked over to the staircase to join me, our argument seemingly a thing of the past. "Excellent. I'll gather my eldrin and meet the new god-arcanist in just a moment." She gave Alrick a sideways glance. "Tell my guests I'll be a moment longer."

Her knight captain bowed slightly and then returned to the pyroclastic and celestial dragon arcanists in the other room.

She went down the staircase with haste, though she never skipped any steps. I waited until she had gone halfway before starting my own descent.

**"Warlord?"**

Terrakona's telepathic voice filtered into my thoughts like a whisper. As I went down the steps, I shoved my hands in my trouser pockets and smirked. "I took everyone's advice. I think it worked."

**"Excellent. Your confidence is infectious."**

"Oh?" I asked. "You can feel it?"

**"Of course. And soon the world will feel it."**

The giant sovereign dragon statue in the center of the staircase was a mighty display of power, but when Terrakona spoke about the world changing, it reminded me that our mission was far greater than anything even the greatest of sovereign dragon arcanists had attempted in the past. It was exciting—even if a bit daunting—and I couldn't wait to rise to the occasion.

The castle's glowstones created a warm yellow light that filled the massive building, chasing away the shadows. The moon outside the window was full and bright—a pleasant sight.

**"Also... I found something while waiting for you by the walls."**

I stutter-stepped, almost tripping as I reached the bottom. "You found something? What do you mean?"

"A baby dryad. It emerged from the ground, and since I was nearby, I went to greet it."

"Oh." I continued through the castle and entered the main hallway leading to the entrance. "It's probably a result of the soul forge's power. Maybe someone buried a dead dryad outside the city." That was a sad thought, but at least the mystical creature would get another chance.

"No, Warlord. This is a new creature, born of the oaks in the nearby area. She is fresh and alight with curiosity."

The statement intrigued me. New creatures were born all the time, so I shouldn't have been surprised by a dryad. At the same time, I couldn't remember dryads being common to this area. I wondered why the new mystical creature had appeared now.

"Her name is Foil. May I keep her?"

I reached the entrance foyer—the massive room with the dragon and leviathan tapestries—and furrowed my brow. "What? N-No. She needs to find an arcanist. Why would you want to keep her?"

Terrakona's telepathic voice was filled with disappointment. "She is younger than me, and she is afraid. I want to protect her."

I rubbed at the back of my neck. Several castle servants rushed around, some even bowing and muttering greetings. I waved them away, my thoughts wrapped up in Terrakona's odd request. "Well," I said aloud, startling one of the servants. "I mean, you can protect her, sure. I don't want any harm to come to a young dryad. But you have to say goodbye once we find a place where she can hold a Trial of Worth."

Joy returned to Terrakona's communications. "Excellent."

The moment I stepped outside, I was met with a surprising sight. Hundreds of Thronehold citizens had gathered beyond the gates of the castle, watching from a safe distance, most with lanterns in hand. Vjorn stood in the middle of the castle courtyard, his massive wolf body and giant chains a thing of legend. The crowd pointed and whispered, their voices filled with a frightened urgency.

The courtyard was lit with more glowstones, like giant fireflies in a field of flowers.

Zaxis stood next to his god-creature, but he was dwarfed by the size of the fenris wolf. His brother, Lyell, hovered beside him, in the shadow of the wolf, his red head down, as if he were trying to shrink and disappear from sight.

A few unicorn arcanists stood around, each wearing their knightly full plate armor. Two of them held flags, four of them carried ornate lanterns, and one had a drum, no doubt as part of a ceremony.

I strode past them and went straight for Zaxis.

He stood with his arms crossed, his eyes narrowed. Once he spotted me, he frowned, and then motioned me over with a tilt of his head. I lifted an eyebrow as I approached, confused by his irritation.

"Is everything okay?" I asked once I was close.

"You won't believe what happened," Zaxis muttered. "One of the king basilisks already bonded."

I caught my breath, stunned. "What? When?"

"As I was coming over here, Eventide and I stopped to see the basilisks you had brought out of the underground. Not the one you left frozen—it was still contained—but the other one wandering around."

"Kezrik bonded already?" I asked.

"Is that its name? Kezrik? Well, yeah. *Apparently*. Everyone in the city is outraged. News of the basilisks is spreading faster than the wind. Even as I walked over here, everyone was demanding I use my god-arcanist magic to deal with the situation." Zaxis tensed and rotated his shoulders. Then he got closer to me and lowered his voice. "I can't seem to use my magic yet. Is that... normal?"

I nodded once. "But forget about that—tell me who bonded with Kezrik. I thought he was going to search for his old arcanist."

Lyell hesitantly stepped out of the shadows, his gaze down. "Warlord, uh, Volke. It was Guildmaster Strenos. The basilisk... It liked him, and the knights found records that confirmed its old arcanist was dead, so..."

Shock went straight through me. "Kezrik bonded with *Strenos*?" At least the new guildmaster of the Lamplighters Guild hadn't been taken out of commission so soon after his predecessor's death. But now he was a king basilisk arcanist? Unbelievable.

"How did he bond without going through a Trial of Worth?" Zaxis asked.

His brother just shrugged.

"That's what happens," I muttered. "All these creatures who were given a second life seem to have no memories—but they believe their Trial of Worth was already completed. I've seen it a few times now. They'll bond with almost anybody, so long as they have a passing appreciation for them."

From what I understood, Theasin Venrover had intended to use his soul forge to resurrect mystical creatures in order to create an arcanist army for the Second Ascension. He could fill the army with *anyone* if the Trials of Worth weren't required.

Zaxis ran a hand through his red hair. Then he patted the giant wolf by his side. Ice flaked off the creature's fur, frosting the ground with a bit of rime.

Vjorn snorted. More frost coated the area.

"So, where's the queen?" Zaxis asked, impatience in his voice. "We have things to do, and I don't want to have some sort of stupid ceremony for my bonding."

"I think everyone is expecting it." I eyed the distant crowds.

"What we should have is a funeral for Forsythe."

I held my breath, knowing that Zaxis was still quite angry

about what had happened. The way he spoke made me think he was also filled with guilt over the way things had transpired.

"I think you should take some time to rest," I muttered, quiet enough that only he could hear. "You've been through a lot."

He glared at me, his green eyes cold. "Look, what I need to do is keep busy. If I'm idle too long... my thoughts get weird. I want to work until I collapse, and only then will I rest."

"Maybe you should spend time with Illia. She'll keep you from thinking dark thoughts. Being alone only makes the pain worse."

It was obvious Zaxis hadn't thought about that. He held his breath for a moment, and then slowly nodded. "Yeah... Well, maybe later. Right now, we're working, right? Basilisks are around, and the queen has to be dealt with."

The courtyard rumbled with the movement of a large dragon. As if summoned by Zaxis's statement, Ladislava rode her eldrin around the outside of the castle, prominently on top of its massive head. The crowd cheered and pointed, obviously elated they had a new ruler to handle the problems of the city.

Her sovereign dragon wore a crown of glowstones, and a crest of silver around its neck—the metal glittered in the light.

It didn't take the queen long to reach us in the courtyard. She wore a smile like a dancer wore a gown—with ease and beauty. Part of me knew it was fake, though. She had been quite angry a few minutes earlier, but she didn't want the citizens of Thronehold to see.

The drummer played his instrument as the queen and her eldrin drew near. The crowd clapped along with the drumming. Once the massive dragon had stopped in the courtyard, the drummer stopped, and the citizens grew quiet.

"Ah, great fenris wolf arcanist," Ladislava said, loud enough for the crowds to hear. "It's a pleasure to finally meet you. Allow me to welcome you to the Argo Empire—not just as a guest, but as a close and trusted ally."

That was quick. No beating around the bush here. She wanted everyone to know we were "friends" as soon as possible.

Her dragon lowered his head, and Vjorn's fur raised in an instant, his hackles prominent. The wolf flashed his fangs, and the dragon hesitated, his golden eyes narrowed on the beast.

Queen Ladislava patted her eldrin and forced a short laugh. "What a fierce beast."

Zaxis patted the fenris wolf, and Vjorn calmed himself.

The dragon finished lowering his head, allowing the queen to step off and stand on the stones of the courtyard. She held her head high and smiled at everyone around. "Thank you for coming to see me right away," she said as she offered Zaxis a bow. "I'm pleased we have another god-arcanist on our side. The Second Ascension must be dealt with swiftly and without mercy."

"Yeah, I agree," Zaxis growled.

I gently elbowed him and motioned to our surroundings. "Be diplomatic," I whispered.

He sighed and half rolled his eyes. Then he said, "Thank you, Queen Ladislava. I'm honored to be here. Call me *the Hunter*—it's the title of the old fenris wolf arcanist, but it's mine now."

More murmurs spread through the crowd. I knew the sound well. Everyone wanted to spread the news of the god-arcanists, and things like ancient titles were fascinating news.

"Hunter Zaxis Ren," the queen said as she stood straight. "An apt name." She pointed to the city in the distance. "Perhaps that title could be put to the test. King basilisks in the underground need to be rounded up as soon as possible, and Warlord Volke Savan has said that the god-arcanists can handle such a dangerous matter."

Zaxis shot me a sideways glance.

I nodded to him, confident we could handle it.

Zaxis returned his attention to Ladislava. Then he smiled and smoothed his hair—a bit of his old pompous self returned to the surface. "Of course, Your Majesty. You can always rely on me, Zaxis Ren, to handle these dangerous situations. I've never turned away from a challenge. It's probably why I was chosen to become a god-arcanist."

I wanted to drag a hand down my face, but I stifled the urge. Sometimes Zaxis went too far. Then again, I was glad he had said it. It amused me to see the slight frown on Ladislava's face.

"Then you have my permission to traverse the city," Ladislava stated. "End this nightmare and quell the king basilisks. Preferably before daybreak."

# CHAPTER 21

## CITY-WIDE MAGIC

Ladislava gave the order like it had been her idea. I just bowed my head, my eyebrow quirked.

Before I could leave the moonlit courtyard with Zaxis, the mighty fenris wolf huffed. His icy breath coated the nearby bushes and the brick walkway. We all turned to face him, even Ladislava's sovereign dragon.

**"No introductions for your eldrin, *Hunter*?"** the wolf asked, turning his dark gaze to Zaxis.

There was a long stretch of silence as Zaxis slowly returned his attention to the queen. With another bow, he finally said, "Forgive me. I forgot to introduce my eldrin. This is Vjorn, the second fenris wolf." He stood straight and then ran his palm over the frosty fur of the wolf.

"It's an honor to meet you, mighty Vjorn," the queen said as she offered the creature a bow.

To my surprise, her dragon did the same. I wondered if it bothered them to do so, but I didn't ask. Now wasn't the time or place to push the queen any further.

Vjorn shook his body, rattling some of the chains. Those in

the crowds beyond the castle gates collectively gasped. Some even leapt away, practically slamming into the citizens around them. But Vjorn didn't offer any words. He regarded the queen with a dismissive snort.

"Sorry about that," Zaxis whispered to Vjorn. "I just…"

He didn't finish his sentence, but I knew what he felt. Zaxis still didn't consider himself the fenris wolf arcanist. It hadn't yet sunk into his mind. He still thought of Forsythe and his phoenix powers, no doubt.

Vjorn huffed and then nudged Zaxis with his massive snout. Zaxis almost toppled over, but he half-laughed as he playfully smacked the wolf. Then he headed for the front gate, the creature following close behind, Vjorn's gigantic paws leaving frosty footprints in his wake. The path was reinforced—likely to accommodate the weight of dragons—and nothing shook or broke as Vjorn walked across it.

Lyell hurried after his brother, mostly keeping out of sight. The will-o-wisp in his lantern seemed dim and barely offered any illumination. Was the little creature scared? Or perhaps it just didn't want to draw any attention.

A couple of the Knights Draconic opened the gates for us. The people of Thronehold moved away as Zaxis and I walked ahead. Vjorn and Lyell followed, no words exchanged between anyone. The crowds held their breath, as if fearing the worst.

It was dark, and the wind picked up, rushing down the ruined streets. I wondered if Hexa had gathered the Frith Guild, but at the same time, I knew some of them would be asleep.

Two unicorn arcanists mounted their eldrin and trotted after us. An escort? That wasn't necessary, but I wouldn't deny them, either. It was probably on the queen's orders.

The Frith Guild had gathered in the Education District. Specifically, everyone had met at Skarn University, a rather revered place of learning. I had been there before—to learn about the god-creatures. It made sense to meet there now, just in case there was any further information we had overlooked hiding in their libraries.

We walked the long, rubble-filled streets of the district, away from the crowds and merchants. The Education District didn't have many shops, just artificer labs, libraries, and the university. The clop of the unicorn hooves echoed between the tall buildings, a constant reminder that the Knights Draconic traveled with us.

"I wonder why they call it *Skarn* University," Lyell murmured as he rubbed his hands.

"It's named after the waste rock they dig up with the nullstone." I crossed my arms, tense and feeling partially exhausted. "The Argo Empire is known for its mining."

"I've never seen *skarn* before."

Neither had I.

With my brow furrowed, I stared at the bricks of the street. "Terrakona," I whispered. "Do you know what skarn looks like?"

**"I do, Warlord. It is a colorful stone, mixed with many minerals. It is not the glory of a rainbow, but the cast-off bits of other stones fused into one."**

I hadn't known that. It made me wonder why the university had used such an odd stone's name as their own.

As if answering my unspoken question, Zaxis said, "Skarn can have bits of all kinds of metal inside it. Copper, tin, nickel... I bet the university thought itself clever when they picked *that* rock. It's a rock that can have anything inside it—can *be* anything, with the right smith—like it's a metaphor for fresh, new students."

"You really think so?" Lyell asked, his voice louder and filled with awe. "I've lived here for years and never thought of it like that. That's pretty wise, which is weird, since it came from you."

Zaxis shot his younger brother a sidelong glance. Then he motioned to the god-arcanist mark on his chest. "Do you see this? I'm definitely wise."

"Being a god-arcanist doesn't make you wise," I muttered.

Zaxis shot me the same glower. "It doesn't mean I'm *not* wise." Then he glanced up at Vjorn. "Tell them. You picked me because I have plenty of wisdom and strength and skill and leadership."

**"You passed my Trial of Worth because you entered my lair and proved your sense of justice. It had little to do with wisdom."** The gargantuan wolf tilted his head to the side, reminding me of a dog with a curious expression. **"Though, I suppose wisdom is required for a hunter. Knowledge is not enough."**

Zaxis scoffed. "Not the ringing endorsement I wanted, but I suppose I'll take it."

"What would your woman say?" Lyell asked, smirking. "Remember what mother told us? *You know if a man's wise by how happy his wife is.*"

"Illia is plenty happy with me, thank you very much."

The comment got me chuckling. I wondered what Illia *would* say if she heard this conversation. Nicholin would have a quip, no doubt.

"Milords," one of the knights said from atop his unicorn eldrin. He urged his mount to move up in order to get closer. "Shouldn't we be discussing how to best handle the basilisk threat?" The man wore his plate armor, including his helmet, the visor down, obscuring his face. Only the hints of a mustache managed to poke through the holes of the helmet. "The queen asked that the matter be handled before daybreak."

"**We needn't worry about a threat in the tunnels beneath us,**" Vjorn said, laughter on the edge of his words. "**We have the world serpent arcanist with us. Those in the subterrain should be concocting plans to flee before it's too late.**"

"What do you mean?" I asked, coming to a halt.

Everyone else stopped as well. Lyell fussed with his hands, the unicorns trotted in circles around us, and Zaxis placed his hands on his hips. They glanced between me and the wolf, their gazes questioning.

Vjorn lowered his snout, so it was closer to me. He sniffed, and I was almost dragged toward him by the force of his inhale.

"**You control the terrain, do you not?**" Vjorn's fur stood on end, and he flashed his fangs. "**I have... little memory before I was born in my lair... But from what I can recall, I was jealous of the serpent's ability to move the land and trees. He was... so frighteningly powerful...**" Vjorn shook his head. "**Or perhaps those are nightmares. Figments of my rattled mind.**" He exhaled, and a winter's worth of frost covered the entire street, making everything slick, even under the hooves of the unicorns.

The Knights Draconic had to steady their steeds as the unicorns slipped and tumbled about. Their heavy armor didn't help matters, either.

With some concentration, I waved my hand and attempted to rearrange the ground, breaking up the ice, and moving the worked stone bricks aside so that the unicorns could regain their footing.

"Enough," I said. "Maybe the first world serpent arcanist could do that, but I'm not powerful enough."

"**You reek of the power,**" Vjorn said. He shook his head, clattering some of his rune-covered chains. "**Go to your eldrin. You're stronger when you're closer. Close your eyes and**

**concentrate. You can control the tunnels. This, I feel, is the truth."**

I caught my breath, unsure what to say. It was true—an arcanist's magic was better when close to their eldrin, but I had thought it only mattered with significant distances. Terrakona wasn't *that* far from me. He was just outside the city walls. Was that short distance enough to weaken my god-arcanist magic?

The moonlight gave me enough illumination to see the city's wall far down the road. If I went there, and summoned Terrakona, would I be able to handle the tunnel situation? If I could move the tunnels, and fix the structural damage to the city, I would be helping all of Thronehold. I could even trap the basilisks or guide them out to the surface all at once. No one would have to venture underground to get to them.

"Wait," Zaxis said, holding up his hands. "You're saying that Volke could just trap all the basilisks? Or bring them to the surface?"

His eldrin nodded.

"Then we should do it. And we can get the knights to quell the basilisks, since they're immune to poison, and maybe even get Hexa and a few others from the Frith Guild handling everything."

Lyell's eyes went wide. "I should go tell Guildmaster Strenos. He's a king basilisk arcanist now. He can help once all the mystical creatures are out of the underground."

Zaxis snapped his fingers. "Yeah. That's it." Then he turned to me. "You just have to reshape all the tunnels."

Oh, was that it?

*Just* reshape all the tunnels in a massive city? Did he know what kind of task that was? It seemed... extreme. I had never done anything like that.

"Terrakona," I whispered as I glanced away from the others. "Do you think we can handle that? Rearranging all the tunnels?"

"It might take time, but if you maintain concentration, I suspect we can."

His answer surprised me. It also filled me with a bit of confidence, as well as a real excitement at the thought of trying. What if I *could* manipulate the terrain of an entire city? What an invaluable power.

"Theasin was able to encompass the entire city, and the Scholar had only been bonded a short while longer than you. There is no reason to be surprised."

"I just hadn't thought of it," I muttered. But Terrakona was right. Theasin *had* used his magic to affect the entire city.

"You are a god-arcanist. Your magic is a vast ocean of untapped potential. If you fear the power within, or if you stifle your creativity by believing yourself weak, you will subconsciously hold yourself back from your true potential."

"Right," I murmured. "I'll be by your side in just a minute." Then I glanced over at Zaxis. "Okay, let's try this. I'm going to Terrakona. You get everyone in order."

He nodded once, smiling wide.

His brother hurried off down a nearby alleyway. His will-o-wisp lantern chased away the dark as he ran, and I watched him go for a few moments before I turned for the city wall. Part of me missed Evianna—she could allow me to see in the dark, after all, but I also wanted to tell her all about my experiences with Ladislava and the dragon arcanists. My exhaustion was taking hold, threatening to tether me to the ground like a pair of shackles, but I couldn't stop yet.

I ran down the road, leaping over rubble or even using my manipulation to push it aside as I went. Since it was night, most of Thronehold was asleep. I tried to keep my huffing quiet as I dashed down each street, but the Education District didn't have many dwellings, so I doubted it would be a problem.

When I made it to the wall, I smiled to myself. A crack in the massive structure made it easy for me to exit the city. I stepped over the shattered bricks and made it out onto a grass field. Terrakona approached from the north, his colossal body shaking the ground with each serpentine movement.

I stood and waited, catching my breath. Terrakona rushed to my side, the dirt and grass parting underneath him as he moved. When he reached my side, he stopped and then lowered his head. His tongue flicked out, and the runes on his flesh reminded me of the runes on Vjorn's chains. Were they related? I figured they had to be.

I placed a hand on Terrakona's nose. "We haven't time to waste. Are you ready?"

Terrakona's two colored eyes stared at me. Then his pupils narrowed into slits. **"All is ready, Warlord."**

With excitement coursing through my veins like lightning, I closed my eyes. That was when I focused. I calmed my breathing, counted my heartbeats, and then used my tremor sense to feel the surrounding area. The wall... the buildings... even a dozen field rabbits... I felt it all.

One exhale.

Two exhales.

The more I focused on the surroundings, the more I left my physical body. Terrakona's heartbeat was loud—almost distracting—but I added it to my focus, using it to count the time as I reached my magic into the city.

Nullstone...

I felt the nullstone underneath Thronehold. It didn't really affect me, but it still stung my magic when I reached out to cross it. With my teeth gritted, I kept expanding my senses, trying to feel every bit of the Education District. Then the Moonlight District. Then the Dragon District.

The buildings...

The horses...

The knights...

The broken trolleys...

I just kept feeling more and more. The images in my mind's eye were getting complicated and difficult to keep track of. It was like trying to memorize a hundred random numbers and also keep them in order. Feeling the many citizens, and the many mystical creatures, and also their heartbeats, their breaths, the shudders in the ground, and in the tunnels, and...

Then I felt the king basilisks. They were underground. In the broken tunnels.

Six more of them.

I almost lost my concentration when I found them. I was so happy, I wanted to cheer with Terrakona.

**"Relax,"** Terrakona telepathically said. **"Keep your thoughts on the moment. Keep your attention on the goal."**

I took a deep breath, and kept using my magic to sense all of Thronehold. There was so much information, I didn't know what to do with it all. So I just ignored it. Instead, I turned my focus to the tunnels. One by one, I closed and rearranged them, altering the pathways and strengthening areas that were threatening to collapse.

I closed tunnels. Routed the basilisks. Kept them moving as I rearranged the underground.

Terrakona's heart beat faster and faster. Time was flying. But I was doing it! I was fixing the tunnels. I just had to do a little more...

With all my might, I closed tunnels around the six basilisks, forcing them toward the surface. Some of the basilisks attacked the walls and the ground, like they were searching for me, but they'd never find the source of the manipulation. It amused me, and I smiled as I continued my work.

I was safe... far from them...

**"Stay focused,"** Terrakona gently warned.

My eyes scrunched together when the six got closer to the streets of Thronehold. If they were angry when they emerged...

The Knights Draconic were waiting nearby—and so were Vjorn and Guildmaster Strenos.

They were ready. I just had to rearrange the tunnels and push the basilisks up the last little bit. And then we would have them all.

# CHAPTER 22

## A NEW MORNING

Reshaping the underground was like traveling through a maze in my mind's eye.

I had never realized how interconnected the world truly was. When I moved the walls of one tunnel, the ground above was affected. When I strengthened the structural integrity of one street, three others were shifted. It was like walking to a dead end in the maze and needing to back up, constantly keeping the path I had taken in my thoughts, so that I didn't get lost.

Any changes I made would have effects beyond what I intended.

Stone by stone, brick by brick, I molded the structure of the tunnels, twisting and folding the earth to avoid collapse and disaster.

Five of the king basilisks were brought to the surface. The ones who had fought back in the beginning had long since given up. I felt their frantic heartbeats and panicked breaths. Their panic led to paralysis, and that worked for my purposes.

My goal wasn't to frighten them. I didn't want the basilisks to go to the surface and fight the Knights Draconic. So I did the last of the terrain alteration in slow and steady chunks, bringing them up with plenty of time to absorb what was happening.

Hopefully, the knights would have the tact to act with diplomacy.

The last basilisk, however...

It wasn't as cooperative. It thrashed and fought against my terrain manipulation, trying to dig its way out of the tunnels, or beating the walls with its massive body and tail. When I tried to trap it in place, the beast cut itself to use its acidic blood to help disintegrate rock and support columns.

It was fighting to stay away from my grasp, and it made it difficult to focus on the whole city when it was going berserk.

A part of me didn't want to bring the basilisk to the surface. Clearly, it was going to struggle. I couldn't have that.

So I focused on the others, and held my breath when they finally came into contact with the surface. For several tense moments, the knights, Vjorn, and Strenos faced off against five of the deadliest creatures around. They spoke, but my tremor sense wasn't powerful enough yet to follow the conversation. To my delight, no fights broke out. The heartbeats of everyone involved slowed and calmed.

They had done it. An agreement must've been reached.

**"Warlord. The last king basilisk..."**

I felt it. The beast thrashed and agitated the tunnels. Then the structure of the overhead streets broke. I gritted my teeth as I prevented the district from collapsing into the sinkhole, but it required all my attention. Now I no longer felt the other five basilisks, or the knights who were surrounding them. I had my focus solely on the sixth troublesome mystical creature.

It was the Justice District.

Several of the buildings were large and grandiose—heavy from the marble, stone, and iron used in their construction. After a deep breath where I exhaled to calm myself, I shifted the terrain so that the buildings wouldn't fully collapse. When the basilisk tried to climb up to the brick streets through a newly formed crack, I turned the rock beneath him to sand. Caught in quicksand, he sank into the ground, half of his body submerged. Then I used what rubble I could to bury him in a shallow pit.

The debris was heavy, but large enough that the beast had air. The king basilisk wouldn't be able to move, at least not for a little bit. If he used his blood again, he could probably escape, but I doubted he would bleed himself dry simply to escape.

Then he started melting some of the stone. What kind of lunacy was this? Was the basilisk that fearful? Or just that desperate.

To my surprise, Strenos and his basilisk eldrin, Kezrik, rushed to the district. I suspected the desperate basilisk was roaring—screaming as it used its own blood to free itself. Strenos and his new eldrin would be the only ones brave enough to face such a danger.

They rushed for the basilisk just as it was clawing its way out of my pit trap. The resulting combat was short—just a few blows, and the sixth basilisk collapsed to the ground.

It was probably from blood loss.

But the basilisk was so large and powerful that the force of those few blows caused another building to collapse. There was nothing I could do to stop it.

"Can we fix those?" I asked, my eyes still scrunched shut.

Terrakona growled, his voice deep and guttural. Then with his telepathic voice, he said, **"Such fine manipulation is probably beyond our current capabilities, Warlord."**

With a sigh, I finished repairing the tunnel structure beneath the Justice District. Then I fortified the remaining buildings that were still standing. I freed anyone trapped in rubble and made paths through the devastation to make it easier for people to evacuate. The Iron Dungeon was half collapsed, which made me worry about Calisto. And then I hated myself for *worrying* about his safety. I shook my head and eventually opened my eyes.

There hadn't been any casualties.

All six king basilisks were accounted for.

Then the dawn broke, and I laughed to myself. I had done it all in one night—and the whole city was better than before. Why hadn't I done this sooner? I wished Vjorn had suggested I use my magic before I had gone deep into the tunnels looking for basilisks to deal with personally.

"How long did that take?" I asked, glancing up at Terrakona.

He tilted his massive serpent head. **"Close to five hours."**

"Five?" I blinked back my surprise. "It didn't feel like that long."

**"I assure you—it was."**

With a sigh, I tried to walk over to him, but that was when one of my legs gave out. I half stumbled, and Terrakona brought his tail over to quickly steady me. I grabbed on to his scales, admiring the vibrant green.

That had... taken a lot more out of me than I had initially noticed.

From the moment I had bonded to Terrakona, magic had pulsed just beneath my skin, pushing to be released. The magic was still there, but quiet. For the first time, I had truly pushed my bond with Terrakona to its limit. Now it would take time to recover.

I held on to Terrakona, allowing myself to catch my breath.

Tiny sparks of magic radiating up from his body. I ran my fingers along his scales, admiring how hard they felt. The iridescent sheen glittered, even in the darkness. It was the glow of raw magic. His scales reminded me more and more of the scale I had used to imbue Forfend, my shield. I had used a scale of the first world serpent...

Terrakona's scales didn't yet radiate magic like the previous scale, but his were closer now. Sturdier. Filled with inner magic.

"Are you growing more powerful?" I whispered.

Terrakona lowered himself so that his chin rested on the

grass next to me. His nostrils flared as he inhaled, and his slit-pupils grew larger. **"I have gotten larger."** Then he shook and shifted. **"Do you want to see my dryad now, Warlord?"**

I stared into one of his glossy eyes, now recognizing his expression as amusement. With half a smile, I said, "Well, we did just saved the city. Don't you think we should go in and see everyone?"

**"I fear you might sleep afterward, and then it will be a long while before you meet her."**

He had a point. I would need to sleep.

"All right. Let's see her."

Terrakona slowly coiled himself around me, moving without much urgency, probably in an attempt to not spook the dryad. When he was done coiling, I was basically inside a house made of his scaled body—he encompassed me on all four sides. Then the dryad lifted herself from the dirt, emerging like a plant that had broken free of the seed.

Dryads were humanoid in shape, but made of tree bark, leaves, and branches.

The baby dryad stretched and yawned, her child-like face puffy with fat. Her green skin had the waxy sheen of a milkweed, and her body was clothed in orange leaves stitched together with vines.

Her eyes...

They weren't like mine or Terrakona's. They were open flowers, both pink and made of dozens of petals. At first, I was caught off guard, but I eventually relaxed when the dryad nervously fidgeted with her leaves.

She appeared to be the same size and shape as an eight-year-old. She halfway reminded me of Biyu, Captain Devlin's little cabin girl—except for the dryad's lush hair of vines, which flowed with her slight movement. That was rather unique and kept my attention.

"My name is Foil Merrell Scane," the little dryad said, her

voice soft and gentle, with the rustle of leaves on the edge of her words. She bowed low. "Just call me *Foil*. It's nice to meet you, Warlord!" She trembled a bit, never straightening herself to stand again.

"Hello," I awkwardly said right before yawning.

Since when did mystical creatures have full names? That was odd. But I didn't ask about it. The morning glow, and the brightness of the sun, put me at ease. It was like a long night had finally ended. I just wanted to rest.

"You can stand," I said, motioning for the dryad to get up. "Any friend of Terrakona's is a friend of mine."

The little dryad sank halfway into the dirt, her waist submerged. Then she straightened the rest of herself and "stared" at me with her flower eyes. "Terrakona said he would protect me until I'm ready to find an arcanist."

I nodded along with her words. "That's right."

"He said you gave him permission."

"Uh, I did."

"Thank you so much." Foil bowed again, her vine hair spilling onto the grass. "Terrakona said you were kind."

I rubbed at the back of my neck. "Don't mention it." Hardly seemed like I had done anything.

The rumble of something large drew my attention. Terrakona lifted his head high, his black crystal mane shimmering in the early morning light. For a brief moment, his mane was a blaze of glittering black fire, powerful, arcane, and occult.

**"Kezrik and his new arcanist approach."**

Foil dove beneath the ground, hiding from the newcomers. Terrakona uncoiled himself, much faster than he had moved before. Once I was free from the circle of his body, I forced myself to stand straight with a wide stance.

The cracked walls of Thronehold allowed me to easily see into the streets. Kezrik moved down the cobblestone road, his six legs slamming down with each step. Strenos rode on his back, the man's scarred face distinct enough that I could recognize it, even from afar.

I waited as the king basilisk lumbered his way over a broken position of the wall. Kezrik's gray scales on top shimmered in the light. His underbelly was a dark blue—like the depths of an ocean. It was beautiful—it reminded me of my home island.

Once they were close, Strenos slid off Kezrik's scaled back. He landed with a huff and then stood tall before striding over to me. The arcanist mark on his head was now a seven-pointed star with the king basilisk wrapped around it, each of the beast's six legs resting on a different point of the star, with the head resting on the final point at the top.

"Warlord," Strenos said with a huff.

I nodded once. "Guildmaster Strenos."

"I came to escort you to Skarn University. Guildmaster Eventide asked you to stay there with her." Strenos adjusted the belt around his trousers and then gave me the once over. "Why didn't you just move around the whole city before?"

"I... I didn't know I could," I said.

"You look like you've been to the abyssal hells and back."

I glanced down at my body. I felt okay—just exhausted—but I wasn't the steadiest. Using my magic for five whole hours had been a momentous task. Of course I'd be drained.

"Is everyone okay?" I asked.

Strenos crossed his arms. His milky white eye, no doubt blind, still moved in time with the other eye. He focused his gaze on me and frowned. "Besides my will-o-wisp, and the miners, there were no deaths."

I flinched when he said it, still frustrated at the loss.

Strenos relaxed a bit as he allowed his gaze to fall to the grass at my feet. "You needn't make that face."

I lifted an eyebrow. "But—"

"Do you know anything about will-o-wisps, Warlord?"

"I mean... I know of them generally. They're weaker mystical creatures. According to Theasin, among the weakest of all, actually. They're beings of fire, and I believe they're born from fable conditions, rather than through breeding."

Strenos answered me with a click of his tongue. "*Tch*. Not like that, *Warlord*. I meant do you know of their legends? Anything about them?"

I slowly shook my head.

"Well, will-o-wisps are guides, and they come in many colors. Red will-o-wisps are little mischief makers. They tend to lead people astray. They eventually help, but only after their games."

"Okay," I said.

"And purple will-o-wisps guide lost children back to their parents. And blue will-o-wisps help those who are lost in bad weather. But white will-o-wisps..." Strenos exhaled as he met my gaze. "They say white will-o-wisps guide you to great destiny. And perhaps—because Cao-Cao had been so adamant that I help with the basilisks..."

But Strenos never finished his thought. He didn't need to. Had his little wisp been taking him to Kezrik?

"And I see your knightmare mark," Strenos muttered as he turned away and faced the city. "I know you must've felt the same. So—don't lose sleep over what happened. You saved the city. *Twice*. In the span of two days. You've done more for Thronehold than any three people combined. I was glad I could help. And Cao-Cao... he would've felt the same."

His words stuck with me. I wanted to thank him, but my throat was tight, and I couldn't find the words. It meant the world to hear that he didn't blame me for what had happened. And that it might've been the turning point for something grand.

"Let's go," Strenos said. He walked over to his king basilisk eldrin. "We need to get you to Skarn University."

# CHAPTER 23

## UNIVERSITY LIVING

The moment I arrived at Skarn University, I was escorted to a dormitory and given the room all to myself. There were at least ten beds, but all were empty. I picked the nearest one, rested my head on the pillow, and immediately fell asleep.

When I opened my eyes again, it was night.

The stars twinkled out beyond the one window, filling the dark sky with glitter.

It reminded me of Luthair's cape. It was missing. *He* was missing. I had to find him. No matter what. But my exhaustion dragged me back to sleep.

The silver stars spun in the void far above, and my last thought before succumbing to sleep was... *Can Luthair see the stars?*

Sunshine woke me a second time. I rolled onto my side, confused by the light. How long had I been sleeping? I sat up, rubbing my eyes, surprised by the crust that had formed.

"Terrakona," I said aloud.

**"Warlord?"**

"How long have I been sleeping?" My stomach grumbled like it wanted a chance to answer.

**"You've been asleep for a whole day,"** my eldrin telepathically replied. **"But fear not. I protected the city while you slept. The citizens are safe, and they sing your praises. The king basilisks have been gathered by Hexa and Strenos and brought to a location beyond the walls. All is well."**

With a contented sigh, I smiled. "That's good to hear."

"What's good to hear?"

I flinched as I turned to face the person who had spoken.

It took me a moment to notice the white ferret with silver stripes. Good ol' Nicholin. His tail had grown out, and his silver stripes were more numerous. He seemed more mystical than ever before. Almost occult and otherworldly.

In the quiet comfort of Skarn University, it was nice to see Nicholin just sitting on a pillow. He reminded me of a fur scarf. His appearance was wondrous, sleek, and elegant beyond compare. It fit perfectly with our surroundings.

"You talk to yourself a lot, you know that?" Nicholin asked as he rubbed his face with a front paw. "In your sleep—even when you're awake. You might be touched in the head. Might be a good idea to get someone to help you with that."

I brushed back my messy hair. Magic burned through my veins, replenished after my long rest. An invigorating feeling blazed under my skin, making me feel like I could do anything. With a smile, I asked, "What're you doing here? Watching me talk to myself in my sleep? You might be a creeper. Might be a good idea to get someone to help you with that."

Nicholin leapt from the pillow and puffed his fur. With his blue eyes narrowed in a glare, he poked his nose at me. "Hm! I'll have you know that I'm on watch duty. That's right, the great and mighty Nicholin volunteered to keep you safe while you slept. I was told to report to Illia and Evianna *the moment* you awoke. Both of them are worried about you, ya know."

"You failed your mission then. You spent the first moments talking to me rather than reporting."

"Hm! Well, I have a problem, and you need to listen."

I slid off the small bed and stretched.

The mattress and sheets were made of cheap wool, but I didn't mind. My rest had been delightful. The dorm room was large enough for ten horses, but the beds were placed close together—I imagined that the student scholars would often bump into each other in the mornings. A single nightstand stood between each bed, a lantern resting atop them all.

A fireplace in the back of the room was lit, but the dying embers told me that wouldn't be the case for long. The stone walls, large glass window, and blue rug were all clean—too clean. It made me think university workers had been called to tidy up for my presence, and they had gone overboard.

"Were you listening?"

Nicholin teleported over to my mattress with a quick popping sound and a puff of glitter. He stood on my sheets, staring up at me, his nose twitching.

"I have a bone to pick with you."

I pointed to myself. "Me?"

"That's right. You could've told us you were going to use your magic to rearrange the tunnels! Before you started doing that, everyone was concocting ludicrous plans to deal with the basilisks. One of those plans was to use me as a lure! *Me.* Nicholin. The best friend of both the world serpent arcanist *and now* the fenris wolf arcanist!"

"The nerve of them," I quipped.

Nicholin squeaked as he waved his paws around. "Right? I'm no longer the eldrin to an apprentice arcanist. *I'm top of my class.* Elite. Special." He rubbed the fur on his chest. "You wouldn't have known what to do with yourself if I had died, right?"

I patted him on the head. "You're the most amazing rizzel I know."

He rubbed his head against my palm, but stopped a moment later. "I'm the *only* rizzel you know."

"Didn't you say you were going to tell Evianna and Illia that I've woken up? I'd like to speak with them."

Nicholin huffed and then dashed around my bed as though he needed to burn excess energy. "Fine!" He stopped on top of a pillow. "But we're gonna need to talk about priorities. I'm not a lure anymore, got it? Those days are done." He crossed his front arms into an "X."

"Sounds good to me."

After a few moments of clapping for himself, Nicholin teleported away, glitter fluttering all over the pillow. Once he was gone, I ran my hands over my body. I was still in the same clothing I'd had on a few days ago. I lifted the fabric of my shirt to my nose and sniffed—but only for half a second.

I wasn't really presentable.

It was embarrassing to think of Evianna seeing me like this.

Determined to impress, I walked out of the dorm, wandered down a stone brick hall, and opened a nearby door. A closet. I closed the door and went to the next, knowing a washroom would be nearby. The third room I checked confirmed my suspicion. It was a small washroom with a bowl of water and several towels.

I removed my shirt—the poor cloth would reek for days—and washed myself as best I could. It was only then that I noticed I had no boots. The cold stone floor of the washroom wasn't pleasant for my bare feet, but my evocation allowed me to heat myself a bit, even without a fireplace.

I still had my atlas turtle pendant, though. I touched it briefly and allowed it to rest against my bare chest. Where were my sword and shield? Were they back in the dorm? I'd have to look for them. They were *my* artifacts, the ones I had created—and the last keepsakes I had of Luthair.

Then I glanced around the room and found a small mirror near the far window. I was on the third story, and when I glanced outside, I watched the bustle of the broken city. Workers from near and far were already fixing up the Education District and the Justice District.

The mirror wasn't as kind. It showed me a vision of youth and recklessness. My chest had faint lines—almost scars. Arcanists typically healed fast, but the time a roc had skewered me with his talon had been rough. I ran my fingers along the lines on my body.

My sun-tanned skin was darker in some areas than others, depending on where my skin was actually exposed to the elements. It made me smile—I looked like the adventurers who would sometimes stop at port.

I was a lot more muscular than I remembered myself being. It surprised me a bit, and I ran a hand over my chest and stomach. The world serpent god-arcanist mark on my chest, shoulder, and ribs seemed more prominent.

It felt like forever since I had just stared at it.

"Volke?"

Evianna's voice brought me back to reality. I perked up and turned around, excited to see her and tell her all about the king basilisks, and my "discussions" with her distant cousin, Ladislava. I hoped she wouldn't be upset about how I had treated the queen.

I hurried out of the washroom and entered the hallway with a smile. Evianna was there searching for me, and I drank in the sight of her. Her wide expressive eyes, and the way her long white hair fluttered behind her as she moved, made her seem mystic. No other woman compared. Just seeing her made me feel at peace.

The instant she spotted me, Evianna stepped into the shadows of the hall and disappeared within the darkness. I waited, my arms out, and she appeared a second later right in front of me, practically already in my embrace.

She smelled like wildflowers and honey. Her soft hair felt amazing on my shoulder, and I ran my fingers through her locks. I held her close and stared into her eyes while I tried to find the words to tell her how happy I was to see her. Then someone pointedly coughed, and I realized we weren't alone.

Adelgis and Master Zelfree stood nearby.

"Don't mind me," Adelgis said with half a smile. "I like watching you two express your affection for each other."

I stared at him for a long moment. If *anyone else* had said that, I would've been disturbed, but this was Adelgis. He had an awkward way with words, and I knew he didn't mean to upset me.

Zelfree crossed his arms and narrowed his eyes. "Well, I *don't* like watching you. Wrap this up. *And put on a shirt.* We have business to conduct."

My stomach growled in disapproval as Evianna stepped to my side. She pointed at me and then motioned to my gut. "We need breakfast first. You can't expect Volke to just power through everything as if he's a magic item you can throw at the enemy!"

"He's been sleeping for an entire day. We have places to go. People to meet. Business to conduct." Zelfree glanced over to me, and then quickly looked away, like he didn't want to stare too long. "Fine. I'll tell the university staff to prepare something."

Adelgis smoothed his long robes. They were from Skarn University—they had the gemstone design woven into the chest, and they were a deep maroon in coloration. His long inky hair was twisted in a loose braid that hung over one shoulder.

"It would improve everyone's spirits if we ate breakfast

together." Adelgis glanced between me, Evianna, and Zelfree. "I could easily summon everyone to the instructors' dining hall."

"We don't need to eat together," Zelfree said with a groan. "Volke just needs something to sate his appetite so we can leave."

Evianna placed her hands on her hips. "I think breakfast is a fabulous idea. We haven't done something like that *in a long while*."

"Because it's not—"

"I think it's a good idea," I interjected.

For far too long we had been trying to catch up to the Second Ascension. Now we had stopped a major part of their plans and deprived them of Theasin's magic and support. If we were ever going to get any rest—and breakfasts with the arcanists from the Frith Guild—now was the time. Why was Zelfree in such a hurry to leave?

Evianna patted my shoulder. "See? The world serpent arcanist has spoken. We're having breakfast together." She snapped her fingers. "Moonbeam, let everyone know where to meet us."

With a nervous chuckle, Adelgis replied, "Of course, Princess Evianna."

Zelfree was less agreeable, though. After a long sigh, he walked down the hallway and approached me with a grim expression. I waited, fearing news of some new disaster. I rapidly cycled through all the things that could have gone wrong as I slept.

When he drew near, he lowered his voice to a gruff whisper. "Listen, I've spoken to the guildmaster, and to Hexa, and the others. Apparently, we'll be traveling to Regal Heights to look for specialty trackers."

I was surprised that Hexa had managed to convince Eventide to go to Regal Heights. I had mostly told Hexa to talk to Eventide to calm her down. But if Eventide had agreed... there had to be merit to this plan.

Zelfree met my gaze, bringing me back to reality. "But before we head straight there, I'd like to take a minor detour."

"For what?" I asked, lifting an eyebrow.

"I need to find some things that will help me deal with Lynus."

The way he worded the sentence... *that will help me deal with Lynus*... sounded unpleasant. I just stared at Zelfree, hoping he would elaborate. But he didn't. The man remained silent.

"We can take a detour," I said. "That's fine."

"That means you should eat *quickly*," Zelfree said, stressing the last word. "No weird games. No celebrations. Just breakfast with the guild, and then we're off."

He turned on his heel, intent to leave, but I held up a hand.

"What happened to Calis—I mean, Lynus? Was he hurt when the basilisk broke through the surface and entered the Justice District?"

Zelfree stopped and then shook his head. "He was okay. He's here in the university now."

"Here? Really? Why?"

"So I can keep an eye on him." Zelfree turned to me, his gaze icy. "Do you want me to do something different?"

What else could he do? I was at a loss. I just offered him a shrug. "That's fine. I just think... we shouldn't be dragging him around. He could be dangerous."

Zelfree scratched at his jawline and then smirked. "Well, once we've stopped at our detour, I think we won't need to worry about that. *Again*—eat quickly." This time, he stormed down the hall, not bothering to offer another word.

He had a cunning expression about him. Sometimes I forgot how knowledgeable and resourceful he was. Perhaps I should've questioned him further about his plans for Calisto. Had he changed his mind? Was he going to kill him now?

Evianna flung some of her white hair over her shoulder. Then she smiled and stared up at me with her bluish-purple eyes.

"It's been so long since we've had time to sit down and eat together."

"That's true." I patted my chest. "I need to find a shirt first."

With her cheeks pink, Evianna rolled her eyes. "You're fine the way you are. Master Zelfree doesn't know what he's talking about. Plus, we can see your god-arcanist mark."

Adelgis ambled over just as Evianna finished her statement. He stared at my mark for a prolonged moment before frowning. "I think... given the thoughts of the nearby arcanists... half of them would approve of you abandoning your shirt, and half of them would prefer you wear *even more* clothing. Like two coats. Or perhaps a blanket."

"I don't want to know any more details," I drawled.

Evianna clapped her hands together once and then moved between us. "I'm going to cook you something, Volke." Her smile widened. "Yes! Just me. For you. It'll be special."

I knitted my eyebrows together as I asked, "Do you know how to cook?"

"Yes. Of course." She rolled her eyes. "You know that."

Did I?

"I'm sure it'll be great," I said, not really certain of anything, but trying to be supportive.

With a giddy squeal, Evianna leapt into the shadows and moved away, the darkness slithering down the hall at a surprising speed. I watched her go, a smile tugging at my lips. No matter what she did, Evianna always put everything of herself into the task and seemed to thrive on challenges. She was alight with life, and that was one of the many things I loved about her.

"The king basilisks are going to be moved away from Thronehold," Adelgis said, jarring me out of my thoughts. "Everything has been arranged."

"That's good."

"The city has materials being brought in from all over from the Argo Empire in order to repair the damage from the battle."

"Also good."

"Odion's dreams aren't hidden from me. He's heading west. I'm not sure why."

"Has he... succumbed to the madness?"

"His twilight dragon has."

I dwelled on the news for a moment. Gregory Ruma had gone a long time without anyone knowing he was plague-ridden. His leviathan had hidden in the waters, and while the plague had driven Ruma insane, he had kept it to himself.

Would Odion be the same way? What was he doing out west?

Adelgis held up a finger. "And word of Zaxis's role as the fenris wolf arcanist has already spread to every street corner and alleyway."

I met his gaze. "Why are you reporting all this like it's a list or something?"

"Oh. Well, I thought you'd appreciate being updated." He bowed slightly. "Your thoughts are scattered, and I thought you'd like direction. That's all."

"I do appreciate it."

"Every god-arcanist needs their sworn arcanists nearby, and I figured my best role would be your advisor and confidant. A part of that duty would be keeping you apprised of everything you aren't able to observe yourself."

I nodded once. "All right. If you want... That would be helpful. Thank you, Adelgis. I mean it. You're always looking out for me."

"Of course. I feel like I owe you so much, and minor things like this are hardly anything."

"I haven't done much."

Adelgis's eyes widened. "You spared my sister when she came to assassinate you. And I managed to speak with her yesterday. Guildmaster Eventide allowed her to rebond with her white hart, so she's an arcanist again. But she's being held in nullstone until a proper punishment can be devised."

I had almost forgotten about the attempt Adelgis's sister had made on my life. It had been a wild fight—only because she had gotten the drop on me, and I didn't have the option of seriously harming her. I had promised Adelgis I would spare her, and I was glad to see it had worked out for him.

"Now I just have to find my other brothers." Adelgis sighed and turned away from me. "Then everything will be... better."

"I hope so," I muttered.

"Me, too." After a short moment, Adelgis waved his arm. "Come. Everyone is gathering for breakfast. And if we're going to find you new clothes, we should do so quickly."

Together, we walked down the halls of Skarn University. My thoughts remained on the future, but I was elated to hear that so many of our efforts in the city had ended in triumph.

## CHAPTER 24

# TOGETHER BREAKFAST

The only clothes at Skarn University were robes—a uniform for the students, and fine outer robes for the instructors. I took a set for an instructor of mystical creatures. Tiny images of creatures were stitched across the chest, collar, and sleeves, to the point where I was fascinated and kept glancing at my outfit. The small griffins, unicorns, leviathans, and phoenixes were as adorable as they were wondrous.

Once dressed, and with Adelgis in tow, I made my way to the instructors' longue and kitchen. The many halls of the university would typically be packed with scholars and students, but the entire university was surprisingly empty.

When I glanced out the cracked windows, though, I had my answer. Everyone was involved in reconstruction. The gardens around the university had been transformed into a menagerie for mystical creatures. All the creatures who had lost their arcanists, or the creatures who hadn't been taken by the Second Ascension, were staying at the university. The scholars cared for them, and the students gathered food and supplies.

I stared at the menagerie for a short while, hoping to spot Luthair's black cape. But no luck. He wasn't there.

Adelgis placed a hand on my shoulder, and I offered him a quick smile.

"I'm sure we'll find him," he said.

I nodded once. "Yeah. We'll find him." I said the words with a confidence I didn't feel.

After traveling down a long stairwell, we spotted Captain Devlin in the main hall. He leaned against the stone wall, a flask in one hand and a piece of parchment in the other. He was reading something as Adelgis and I approached but tucked the note away once we were close.

His eyes were half-lidded as he took a sip from his flask. His roc arcanist mark—the star with the massive bird—seemed fiercer than normal. It was hard to describe. And Devlin wore a hat or bandana most of the time, making it difficult to see his mark clearly. Perhaps this was the first time for me.

"You starin' at somethin'?" Devlin snapped.

He rubbed at his forehead and then dragged his hand along his chinstrap beard, smoothing the thin line of hair into place.

"Are you okay?" I asked. He seemed more agitated than normal.

Devlin huffed, took another drink, and then replied, "Life is like a boat that's taking on water—and every day, your bucket gets a little bit smaller."

"That's bleak," Adelgis stated. "Must you dwell on such dark thoughts?"

"I *thought* I had gotten away from it all. I had an *airship*. I had no alliances. No master. No authority I needed to answer to." Devlin motioned to the university. "Now look at me. On the ground again. Neck deep in water. And my bucket is a teacup."

Perhaps he was right, but I disagreed. "That's why you have friends and family, right? To help you with the pressures of a sinking ship?"

Devlin slowly turned to me, his eyes narrowed. "My pa used

to say, *kith and kin keep a man sailing.* Apparently, it's taken me centuries to hear it again, but this time from a god-arcanist." He took a swig of his drink. It smelled of powerful alcohol. "I'll learn the lesson at some point, I reckon."

"Are you joining us for breakfast?"

Devlin laughed and sarcastically saluted me with his flask. "Yessir, Warlord, sir."

He was a weird one. I nodded once as I walked by, sure he would join us later. Adelgis matched my pace, smiling. He didn't say anything, though. I assumed he'd tell me if Captain Devlin were in trouble. Maybe he was just drunk...

Adelgis pointed to a door, and I opened it, revealing a modest dining hall. Two long tables had been pushed together, and a dozen chairs were placed around. The room looked like it used to have two chandeliers, but now there was only one. The chain for the other hung from the ceiling without anything attached.

Bits of shattered glass littered the edges of the room.

Had the second chandelier shattered during the Battle of Thronehold? Most likely.

"Volke! There you are!"

There were so many people in the room, I didn't know who had called my name.

Hexa, Zaxis, and Illia sat together near one end of the table. Nicholin was the only eldrin there with them, his white fur brilliant and beautiful.

My brother, Ryker, Karna, and Fain sat near each other on the other end of the table. Wraith was likely invisible, and Karr—Karna's doppelgänger—sat in a chair next to her. He had taken the form of a young man in a purple outfit with a small top hat. Rather flamboyant. And Ryker's eldrin, the Mother of Shapeshifters, was just a tiny white mouse, sitting on the table.

I knew it was MOS because of her glowing red eyes. She was a creature of intense magic, and just a little creepy.

Hundreds of other mice were probably nearby... The other parts of her massive body that she had shapeshifted into rodents.

Zelfree and Yesna sat together near the middle—though Zelfree's arms were crossed, and his attention was on the ceiling. His mimic, Traces, sat on the table near him. Her tail was short. It had been sliced off during the Battle of Thronehold, and apparently, she couldn't heal it all the way.

Yesna carried two swords at her hips, but her siren eldrin was nowhere to be seen.

Atty and Evianna were standing near the kitchen door, obviously waiting for the food to finish cooking. Evianna's shadow shifted around her feet, indicating her knightmare was nearby. Atty's phoenix, Titania, stood nearby, her scarlet feathers shimmering. Titania perked her heron-like head up the moment she spotted me.

"Warlord," she said, her voice singsong. "It's a pleasure that you're joining us. I'm glad you made it back safely."

She said the last part with a hint of sorrow. She knew about Forsythe, obviously. Her brother.

"It's nice to see everyone," I said.

The room replied with jovial greetings, and a few people stood from their chairs and motioned me to their position at the table.

Fain stood and pointed to the chair at the head of the table —the one opposite Zaxis, who sat at the other end. I decided it was probably the most appropriate place for me to sit, so I did. When Adelgis went to join me, Fain pulled out a chair for him, his frostbitten hands a harsh contrast to the golden brown of the wooden furniture.

I wasn't the only one who had to wear university robes. Almost everyone in the room had opted for either a uniform robe of the students, or one of the many robes for the various instructors. Only Zelfree, Illia, and Zaxis had kept their old clothing, even though they were still stained with the remnants of battle.

Well, that wasn't true.

Zaxis had decided not to wear a shirt. He wore his trousers, but his salamander scale armor was nowhere to be seen. His guild pendant—the old one he had, that proclaimed he was a phoenix arcanist—was around his neck. And without his armor, it was easy to see how much more muscular he was than me.

I stared at Zaxis and met his gaze. He lifted an eyebrow, his expression questioning.

"No shirt?" I mouthed, not voicing my displeasure.

Zaxis scoffed as he motioned to the god-arcanist mark on his chest. The fierce fenris wolf was around his shoulder, the chains cascading down his arm and around his ribs. It was an impressive mark, but it still seemed odd to eat breakfast shirtless when everyone else was clothed.

Adelgis leaned over as I took a seat. "Zaxis thinks he needs to make it known he's a god-arcanist. He doesn't want to live in your shadow."

"That doesn't mean—"

"Volke!"

Evianna bounded over to me, interrupting the conversation. She wrapped her arms around my neck, and I gave her half a hug in return. Then she backed away and smiled.

"We have plenty of food for everyone. I didn't make much— just enough for you. The rest was made by some of the university staff and Atty."

I glanced over at Atty.

She was beautiful, as always. Her long golden blonde hair was woven together in an elegant braid, and the university robes were stunning on her. She smiled when she noticed I was staring, and I replied with a short wave.

Out of everyone in the Frith Guild, Atty confused me the most. We had grown close before the attack on the Isle of Ruma, but my time with her—as something a little more than friends—had revealed a new side of her I didn't know what to make of. Now she locked herself away from everyone and everything, barely interacting with the outside world. Did she even know about my relationship with Evianna?

I would have to speak to her. Maybe even convince her to abandon her obsession with having a true form phoenix.

I shook my head. "Wait, why is Atty cooking?"

"She said she needed a break from her magic training," Evianna said, keeping her voice low. Then she leaned in close to me. "It's a good thing the staff was here to help, because I don't think she knows what she's doing."

I gave her a sideways glance. "Do *you* know what you're doing?"

Evianna pursed her lips and glowered at me. "I've learned a few things, thank you very much!"

She had lived a life in the castle, a pampered princess. I didn't think it was unreasonable to assume she didn't know anything about the art of cooking.

From across the table, Nicholin playfully banged his paws on the table, shaking the plates and silverware. "King Nicholin requires food!"

Illia placed a hand on his head, stopping him from banging. "Don't be rude."

Nicholin disappeared with a pop and puff of glitter. Then he appeared on the other side of Zaxis. "We need sustenance, woman! It fuels our fight against our *enemies*!" He spoke every word like an actor on a stage.

Illia glared with her one eye, and her rizzel eldrin shrank a little. With a squeak, he said, "But... I'm basically rizzel royalty. What other rizzel is friends with *two* god-creatures?"

"Still," Illia muttered.

Nicholin lay down on the table. "All right."

Although Hexa sat close to Nicholin's antics, she didn't

seem interested. She played with a fork by her plate, twirling it and occasionally stabbing it into the wood of the table. She wore student robes, with the sleeves lifted, revealing her scars—the injuries given to her when she had bonded with her hydra.

I had never seen her so despondent. She looked like she would murder the table if it had been a living being.

While eating together was a great stress reliever, I was certain it wasn't doing anything for Hexa's mood. Vethica was still missing, and the longer we sat around and did nothing, the longer she was in danger. Unfortunately, we needed our strength, and once we'd had breakfast, we'd hurry to find our trackers.

I glanced over at Atty. "Is the food almost ready?"

She opened the kitchen door, peeked inside, and then smiled. "It seems that way. I'll help bring it out." After pushing some of her golden hair over her shoulder, Atty entered the steam-filled kitchen. Her phoenix hurried after, dropping soot as she moved.

Evianna stepped into the shadows and quickly slithered into the kitchen, no doubt looking to grab the food she had prepared. When Atty, Evianna, and the university workers appeared, they were all carrying trays of fine food—enough for thirty people, at least.

They had fresh bread, bowls of warm oatmeal, stacks of fresh fruit, and plenty of milk and water. I thought they would just place everything on the table, but they actually set the trays down on another table and proceeded to serve everyone. The university workers fluttered around as they gave Zaxis his food. Evianna handed me mine—it was just bread and oatmeal, like the rest, but the fruits had been sliced into little star shapes and placed throughout my food.

I liked it.

My face heated when I turned to her and said, "Thank you."

Evianna's cheeks were pink as she nodded and took the seat

next to me. Fain and Adelgis sat in the next chairs over, followed by Ryker, Karna, Zelfree and Yesna. Then there were empty chairs, and finally Hexa, Zaxis, and Illia.

It felt odd sitting so far from the others.

Fain glanced over and narrowed his eyes at Adelgis. "You all right, Moonbeam?"

"Hm?" Adelgis rubbed at his eyes. "Yes."

"Overwhelmed by the thoughts?"

"Actually, I've been trying a new technique for not listening to multiple people at once. I focus on a single question and think of all the possible answers."

Fain stirred his oatmeal and poured in some fresh milk. "Like what kind of questions?"

"Well, I was thinking... A person's life is worth more than a fish's life, right? If you had to kill one—a person or a fish—you would kill the fish, correct? Hypothetically, of course."

The question hit Fain like a wet rag to the face. He just stared at his meal, like he had been baffled into inaction.

Adelgis, either not noticing, or not caring, continued with, "But if the choice was either to kill one person or to kill *all* fish, you would then pick killing a single person, yes? If that's the case, what's the number of fish equal to a person's life? There has to be a number between *one* and *all*." Adelgis grabbed himself a lemon and slowly peeled off the waxy outside. "But it's difficult to determine the answer..."

"The answer is obviously *never kill the person*." Fain smoothed his student robes, obviously irritated with the flowing fabric. "That way, you don't have to do any calculations. It's easy."

"The world's delicate balance would be thrown into chaos if all the fish died."

Fain cracked his knuckles and then slowly glanced over at Adelgis. "You ever just think about spending a night with someone, locked in their arms? That's what most pirates think of when they're bored on a ship. Trust me—it's much more amusing than thinking about destroying the *delicate balance* of anything."

Adelgis sighed. He stared at his untouched food, frowning. "I suppose I could. But I'm not sure who I would imagine. And given the nature of the thought, and my association with memories and dreams, I feel like I would need to ask permission before I fantasized about a particular person."

I almost choked on a star-shaped strawberry.

Evianna leaned forward on the table and offered both Fain and Adelgis a glare. "*This isn't a proper breakfast discussion*," she growled under her voice. "Weren't either of you taught the rules of etiquette? Pleasant, non-personal conversations *only*."

"You got us in trouble, Moonbeam," Fain whispered as he took a small bite of oatmeal. Then he elbowed Adelgis. "And no one ever asks for permission, *ya gib*."

"Oh, I know." Adelgis frowned. "I know."

The conversations in the room mixed together, making it difficult to differentiate one voice from another. I didn't pay attention to any one person. I just ate my food, content for the moment to have the time with everyone. Whenever I glanced over to Evianna, she smiled.

"Do you like it?" she whispered.

I had barely tasted my food. My hunger had demanded I swallow everything whole—without wasting time to chew—and it didn't occur to me until most of it was gone. After Evianna's question, I forced myself to taste the creaminess of the oatmeal, and the juiciness of the fruit.

"It's good," I said. "Very good."

The shadow around Evianna fluttered, and I suspected her knightmare was just as happy as she was.

I was about to go back to just enjoying my food, but I decided to check in on everyone else. My brother wasn't a very confident man. I had only known him a short time—I hadn't even known he existed a few years ago—but since I was older, I felt responsible for his wellbeing.

He sat next to Karna, and the two of them spoke in hushed whispers.

While Karna was wearing university robes, like everyone else, hers were open somewhat in the front, revealing more of her skin than necessary. Nothing indecent, but it was noticeable when compared to Ryker, who wore his robes so tightly laced shut that they almost restricted his movement.

They were opposites in more than their clothing. Ryker's black hair was like mine. Karna's hair was spun gold, gleaming and beautiful. Ryker was tall, and Karna was shorter. Ryker was lean, but Karna had the athletic body of a dancer.

With a smile, Karna grazed a finger over the corner of Ryker's lips. His cheeks brightened to a blazing red, but he didn't flinch or move away from her. Karna just giggled as Ryker tried to hide his face with a napkin.

I was probably the only one paying attention to them. Everyone else was engaged in their own conversations—and Zelfree was still staring at the ceiling—so the moment was only captured in my memory.

"You should try shifting your shape while eating," Karna said in a sweet voice. She ran her knuckles over Ryker's cheek. "It's amazing, actually. People taste things differently. I think only doppelgängers and their arcanists would ever know that, truly. When I'm myself, strawberries are too sweet, but when I'm Zaxis, for example, they barely taste sweet at all."

"I-I don't know," Ryker mumbled. He ate more of his oatmeal like he was hoping it would save him from the conversation.

"You need to practice more."

Ryker nodded.

Karna sat a little closer to him, a sly smile creeping on her lips. "You made real progress last night. Just a little more, and you'll make a full transformation."

"*This breakfast is delicious,*" Ryker said, patting his stomach. "You should try." He lifted some fruit up for Karna, ignoring her statements.

I would've continued to listen, but that was when Atty returned with her eldrin.

She took a seat at the table near Zaxis, Illia, and Hexa. Her phoenix stayed close to her, just taking a seat on the floor near Atty's chair. With delicate movements, Atty ate her food. Zaxis pushed his empty bowl to the side and then leaned his elbows on the table.

"You should teach me your technique for combining augmentation and evocation," he said. "According to Vjorn, I have *two* things I can manipulate, and *two* types of evocation. If I can mix those together, I'll be one of the most powerful god-arcanists around."

I stopped eating, my curiosity piqued.

Atty nodded once. "I'd be more than happy to teach you. Now that I've done it multiple times, I think I have it down to an art. I've been... writing everything down." She glanced at her hands, and then returned her attention to Zaxis. "I think it's a good idea that everyone in the Frith Guild learn this technique."

Attempts to combine the manifestations of magic had been going on for centuries, but all such experiments had failed or resulted in disaster. To my knowledge, Atty was the first to successfully combine two branches of magic in a way that was practical to use. She hadn't even been trying for such a magic— she had just been obsessed with achieving her true form.

And gaining a true form eldrin was a deeply personal process, which I suspected was Atty's problem. It wasn't really *her* dream. It was her mother's.

Eldrin were living manifestations of magic, after all. They were forces, concepts, and ideas given living form. When an arcanist's soul was defined by the same telos as their eldrin's magic, their bond strengthened and let them touch the purest magic and bring back the smallest piece to let the eldrin become its ideal form.

But that was a vague concept that few understood. Atty was obviously frustrated by the limitation, and her desires didn't align with a phoenix's telos.

"We can learn that while we travel," Hexa snapped. She slammed her fork into the table. "Hurry up and eat. It's almost high noon. We should be on the road already."

Before anyone could comment one way or another, the door to the dining area opened. Everyone looked up as two more people joined us in the small room.

# CHAPTER 25

## TO REGAL HEIGHTS

Devlin and his little cabin girl, Biyu, walked into the dining room.

Biyu was only nine, at the most, but she held herself tall. Like Illia, she was scarred and missing an eye—a dread pirate had taken it from her as well. But unlike Illia, Biyu was bubbly enough to rival a hot spring, constantly talking and jumping from one person to the next.

The moment Biyu joined us at the table, she hurried over to the chair next to Master Zelfree. Her shoulder-length brown hair, silky and straight, flowed behind her whenever she moved. She also wore university robes, but they were too large for her and dragged along the floor. When she took a seat, she pulled a small book from the folds of her robes and placed it down in front of Zelfree.

"I drew more pictures," she said, pointing to the pages. "Do you want to see? I drew a chimera! You said that was your favorite, right?"

With a sigh, Zelfree sat up and glanced down at the book. "It's beautiful."

Biyu playfully pouted. "You barely looked."

"That's how beautiful it was," he said, monotone. "With merely a glance, I was blinded by brilliance."

Devlin stomped over to the table, placed a heavy hand on Zelfree's shoulder and then gripped hard. He practically yanked Zelfree from his chair when he turned the man to face him. "Be nice to Biyu."

"I'm being perfectly pleasant," Zelfree drawled.

"You need to pull yourself together. I don't know why you're so glum, but this isn't the time." Devlin leaned in close, his voice a growl I could barely hear. "Do it for the younger arcanists."

Zelfree grabbed the man's wrist and jerked his hand off his shoulder. "I'm just tired." Then he shot Zaxis a glare. Everyone turned to face Zaxis, as if expecting something to happen. "*Put on a damn shirt.* How many times do I have to tell you that? *Why* do I have to keep telling you that?" Zelfree stood from the table. "Curse the abyssal hells—kids can't keep their damn clothes on."

He stormed out of the room, even though Biyu was holding up her book, trying to show him another picture. Zelfree slammed the door as he went, leaving the friendly atmosphere suddenly chilled.

"He's so grumpy," Evianna muttered. "It's unbecoming of nobility."

I shook my head. "He isn't nobility."

"If he keeps associating with god-arcanists, he will be."

Her comment gave me pause. I had never thought of it like that. Was it true? It already seemed like it. The university workers were tripping over themselves to serve us food. The last time I'd been here—as just a knightmare arcanist—they had almost denied me access. I hadn't been worth much then, but now I was everything. Even more important than the queen.

Sometimes it was hard to remember that bonding with

Terrakona had changed everyone's perception of me and the people I associated with.

I stood from my chair, intent on speaking with Zelfree, when Hexa suddenly stood from her chair as well. We faced each other for a moment, but then she shoved away from the table and headed for the door.

"Master Zelfree has the right idea," she announced as she went. As she passed me, she said, "He's upset because he wants out of here, too, ya know." Then—just as dramatically as Zelfree—Hexa exited the room.

Zelfree wanted to leave?

He *had* made cryptic remarks about dealing with Calisto. I wondered if *that* was the reason he wanted to go. He wanted to make a detour as soon as possible.

Evianna stood, her shadow fluttering around. "I'm ready if you are." She glanced at the food on the table, then to me. "You need your strength, so remember to eat as much food as you can." She scooped up some fruits and held them close in her arms. "Just in case you need a snack later."

"You don't have to worry about me so much," I said as Evianna hurried to my side, her arms filled with apples, cranberries, and strawberries.

She shot me a glare.

That surprised me.

"I can worry all I want, Volke Savan. That's my right as your significant other."

I... didn't know what to say to that. "All right," I eventually muttered.

The others cleaned up their plates and continued chatting. I opted to leave the dining room. I wanted to speak with Zelfree, collect my sword and shield, and head for Terrakona.

When Evianna and I stepped into the hallway, we were met by an interesting sight.

My father, Jozé Blackwater, and my adoptive father, William

Savan, were standing by the hall window, both engaged in deep conversation. I perked up upon seeing them, my eyebrows lifting toward my hairline.

Words failed, however.

Both men turned to face me. Jozé smirked, and William smiled wide. My adoptive father held out his arms and motioned me over. "C'mon now, lad."

I walked over and gave him an embrace. Last time I'd seen him, he'd been in Fortuna, watching over my estate. He was a large man, his barrel chest wide and solid. I almost couldn't reach my arms around him.

His thick coat smelled of salt water. It reminded me of home.

"What're you doing here?" I asked.

William stepped back and rubbed at his smooth chin. "Eventide arranged everything. She requested arcanists to have me brought here. Teleported part of the trip. I see what Illia means about *freedom*."

I couldn't help but smile.

"Apparently," William muttered as he leaned close. "They were arcanists associated with a *celestial dragon arcanist*. Have you see those, lad? Out on the islands to the north? In my navy days, I thought I saw one once. Just once."

"I've seen one," I said. "I think one's around here. If you search the garden, you might see it."

"Is that right?"

Celestial dragons were rare creatures of might and magic, but they were reclusive. I wasn't surprised to hear that William would be happy to see one. They weren't combat dragons—just like sovereign dragons weren't known for fighting—but their ties to magic couldn't be overstated.

William patted my shoulder. "Everyone wants to be in your good graces. They were happy to jump to Eventide's requests. I can't believe how quickly I got here." Then his expression shifted to something more thoughtful. "It seemed important I get here quickly. Eventide was insistent. Do you know what she wants?"

I held my breath, wondering if I should say anything. Technically, we had several more god-creatures to find. Each of them would need an arcanist. Eventide had suggested William attempt to impress them, but I wasn't sure if I should say anything just yet. What if he said *no*? I didn't want to deal with that without Eventide by my side.

Jozé placed a hand on William's shoulder.

"Don't worry. Everything will be explained in time. You saw Zelfree—we should be leaving soon."

William nodded once. "Hmm."

My birth father was a tall man, but he walked with a slight limp. His leg wasn't what it should have been, and while he often had energy, he couldn't go far. He was a master artificer, though. He had made plenty of magical trinkets and artifacts, and he had even helped to maintain Devlin's old airship. Before the ship had been blown from the sky.

The arcanist mark on his forehead was a seven-pointed star with a phoenix wrapped around the points. But since arcanist marks didn't have colors, I didn't have an easy way to tell his was a *blue* phoenix, a slight variant of the normal red. Perhaps there was a trick, but I wasn't privy to it. Blue phoenixes couldn't heal, but their fire burned anything, even mystical creatures and arcanists normally immune to heat.

"William and I will be travelin' with you all," Jozé stated. He offered me half a smile. "Your guildmaster has strong feelings that we'll meet members of the Second Ascension on our journey."

"Oh?" I asked, my blood running cold in an instant.

"She says that if we end up killing their eldrin, I should use the parts for trinkets. Since those dastards started using decay dust, every battle has cost valuable items. We need to rebuild our arsenal."

I nodded along with his words. I had lost a lot of items...

"I'm glad you're both traveling with us," I said to them. Seeing them together made me feel strange, but happy.

Evianna stood a little straighter. "Yes. We're both glad."

"If you'll excuse us. Evianna and I are going to collect our gear and then head for Terrakona, out beyond the wall. I'll see everyone there."

---

It wasn't difficult to find my sword and shield—Retribution and Forfend. Zelfree had put them in a safe place within the university. The walk up and down the stairs had taken time, however. Everyone else had left by the time I made my way down to the streets.

The trek to the wall was a short one, but it was relaxing nonetheless. Evianna stayed close to my side, and the sun shone over the city, invigorating everyone and everything. While the stakes were still high, and there was much ahead, I didn't feel daunted. It was amazing what a little food and rest could do for my spirits.

Terrakona and Vjorn waited for us outside the ruined wall of the city, as did Guildmaster Eventide.

As well as some of the Knights Draconic.

And Queen Ladislava.

And Guildmaster Strenos.

And the pyroclastic dragon arcanist, King Kalasardo, and the celestial dragon arcanist, Emperor Barnett. Their eldrin stood a few hundred feet back, practically glaring at each other. Amusingly, both the rulers wore ceremonial armor. Kalasardo even held an ornate bow—his armor and weapon gilded and basically useless for war, but beautiful when in direct sunlight.

Barnett's armor was half plate over silk robes, combining the flowing freedom of cloth and the glittering wonder of silver plate over his shoulders and chest.

The two rulers stood out among everyone else. Their personal guard stood nearby, but there were only half a dozen knights. Both nations were small and considered vassal states to the Argo Empire, so it wasn't surprising they didn't have as many troops as the empire.

King Kalasardo and Emperor Barnett bowed when I strode over to meet everyone.

The large crowd of important individuals got me a little nervous, but I quickly shook away the feeling. I had dealt with several influential monarchs at this point. I could handle them.

And perhaps I would need to.

Ladislava moved with pent-up energy, her steps stiff and harsh. I could understand. Our rapid departure for Regal Heights had caught even *me* off guard. Ladislava had planned to bring all her vassals together for a celebration to honor Zaxis—and likely to plant her hooks in him.

Then it dawned on me.

Perhaps that was why Eventide wanted us to leave so early. To avoid this. And Ladislava. If we left on urgent business, to lands in the west, we could meet with other powerful arcanists *without* the ever-watchful gaze of Queen Ladislava, who was already trying to influence everything.

A caravan of carriages and horses was gathered around the broken gate, enough for most of the Frith Guild. Not everyone was going, however. Yesna, and Gillie the Grand Apothecary had agreed to stay and watch over everything in the city, as well as the apprentices and journeymen arcanists who were still in the city. Captain Devlin had agreed to help move the king basilisks away from the city. His massive roc would make it easy to watch over them from the sky.

Before anyone else could speak to me, Guildmaster Eventide

walked over. She smiled, but her expression lacked its usual cheer. The afternoon winds had picked up, and they brought dust and debris from the city as they howled over the walls. Eventide held her gray braid in place as she approached.

"Warlord," she said with a slight bow. "We're almost ready to depart. I was hoping to speak with you about the logistics."

"Sure," I said.

"I think it would be best if you, Zaxis, Ryker, Karna, Hexa, and Zelfree traveled as one unit." Eventide motioned to Terrakona. "The world serpent and fenris wolf can easily carry you all to Regal Heights. You'll reach the city long before any of us on horseback will."

I glanced around, confused by the selection. "Are you sure?"

"You, Zaxis, and Ryker need the most training."

She said the statement with no hesitation.

I replied with a curt nod.

"Ryker hasn't developed much of his magic, and Zaxis needs to learn his as quickly as possible." Eventide exhaled. Then she straightened her patchwork coat, fixing it after the breeze had rumpled it up. "Zelfree has done a good job helping you along, and I think he and Karna can still help Ryker. However..."

"He wants to bring Calisto," I said, knowing where this was going.

Eventide met my gaze, her smile long gone. "That's right. Can I trust you to watch him?"

"Why wouldn't you be able to trust me?"

"Forgive me. What I mean is—can I trust you to handle a situation where Calisto might try to harm you or anyone else in the Frith Guild? I need to know that *someone* won't hesitate. Zelfree obviously wants to help him, and I'm not sure that's possible, but I'm not about to stop him, either."

"I'll handle it," I said.

That was when Eventide's smile returned in full. The smile

lines around her eyes crinkled. "How do you feel about reading?"

I tilted my head slightly at the odd question. "What?"

"Reading. You can do that while riding a giant serpent, can't you?" She patted my shoulder. "Of course you can."

She motioned to a woman who stood nearby, but somewhat out of sight. She wasn't an arcanist—she had no mark on her forehead—and she wore the robes of Skarn University, so I assumed she was a scholar in training. The woman walked over with two large tomes.

"These are books the queen had gathered by the city's researchers," Eventide stated. She pointed to the thick pages and old bindings on the leather covers. "Apparently, these tomes have some information on the previous god-arcanists, but they're in the form of old tales, poems, and stories. It'll take some time to put the information all together into something useful."

"I can do that," I said, unable to hide the elation in my voice. I practically snatched the books right out of the woman's hands. "I'd love to." Then I frowned. "Did... the queen give these over willingly? She seemed upset the last time we spoke."

Eventide slowly lifted an eyebrow. "I have plenty of friends at Skarn University. Let's just say I *checked these out* before the queen did." She offered me a mischievous grin. "I don't plan to have ego hinder our efforts."

I huffed out a laugh. "I understand. Thank you."

Eventide chuckled and then bowed her head. "Thank you, Warlord. I'm counting on you to find trackers capable of locating the Second Ascension."

It was an important task, and I wasn't about to fail. No matter what, we'd find them, and stop them in their tracks. I held the books close, intent on traveling to Regal Heights as fast as Terrakona and Vjorn could handle.

Once Eventide had stepped aside, I headed for my eldrin. On the way, King Kalasardo stepped forward. He bowed deeply.

"Thank you, Warlord," he said. "You have the support of Nuul, my glorious kingdom. If ever you need our arcanists or knights, I shall provide them."

The emperor also stepped forward. "And you will have my magic. The island nation of Sellix is the home of celestial dragons and relickeepers—we are experts of the arcane, and while we prefer to keep to ourselves, you are welcome to cross our borders at any time."

I gave them both a slight bow of head. "Thank you. I appreciate the support."

"I was worried Queen Ladislava wouldn't be the best ruler for the Argo Empire, but with your support, I believe this will be a glorious age of prosperity." Kalasardo rubbed his golden armor and smiled. "May your travels be safe, and the Death Lords far from your door."

Barnett straightened himself. "Swift travels, Warlord."

I left the two of them, but I had more energy in my step. Meeting so many powerful arcanists was invigorating. And they had welcomed me into their nations without a second thought. I hoped I would prove them all right and show them what I was made of.

Zaxis was already next to his massive fenris wolf. Illia stood by his side. She wasn't coming along, so I suspected she was just there to wish him goodbye. They embraced for much longer than I had expected, and at a point, I had to turn away.

Ryker, Karna, Hexa, Zelfree, and Calisto stood by the world serpent. Raisen, the six-headed hydra, was also by the group, his large body low to the ground, like an alligator. He was bigger than a horse, but much slower. Terrakona could carry him, but I worried about the weight.

**"No need to worry,"** Terrakona said telepathically. **"I can carry the load."**

Karr, Karna's doppelgänger was also here. It was surprising, because I normally didn't see Karr around. He kept out of sight

—or looking like someone else—and I wondered why he was being so blatant.

Ryker's bizarre eldrin, the Mother of Shapeshifters, kept herself as a mouse. The other pieces of her body were nowhere to be seen. I suspected they might have been birds, which would travel easily alongside us. That was for the best. It would be weird to see the world serpent covered in white rodents as we traveled around the countryside.

Traces, in her little cat form, was easy to carry with us.

Calisto...

He stood near Zelfree, his copper hair bright in the afternoon light. He didn't look at anyone—he never met a single gaze—and wore nothing but simple boots, a tunic, and trousers. Had they given him the outfit after he had left the dungeon? They were a dull color and ripped at the hems.

A pair of manacles was all he had for his hands. They weren't made of nullstone—that wasn't needed—but they were solid steel.

If he tried to hurt anyone...

That was when I thought about Evianna. She wasn't one of the people traveling first to Regal Heights with the god-arcanists. I turned to her, my brow furrowed.

"It's all right," she said matter-of-factly. That was when she handed me a satchel. She had packed it at the university full of the fruits she had taken from the dining room. "I'll see you soon enough. You take care of yourself, maintain a noble demeanor, and make sure to remain confident in your skills."

"Thank you," I said as I hooked the satchel over one of my arms. The books were difficult to balance, but I managed. "Stay close to the group. Stay safe. Don't go anywhere by yourself."

She placed her hands on her hips. "I'm not *weak*. I can—"

"I can worry all I want," I interjected. "That's my right as your significant other."

Evianna opened her mouth like she was ready to go off on a

tirade, but then she swallowed her words. Her cheeks grew pink, and her mannerisms fluttered. Then she hugged me—only a moment—and hurried toward the other members of the Frith Guild, like she couldn't stay and speak to me anymore.

**"Warlord."**

"Yeah?" I turned on my heel and faced Terrakona. His giant serpent head created a pool of shadow, blocking out some of the afternoon sun.

**"Can I bring the dryad, Foil?"**

"Of course."

He lowered his head, his tongue flicking out. **"Thank you."**

I patted his snout, no words needed between us. Terrakona could be remarkably gentle for a creature that could eat five men whole in a single bite.

"Let's get everything together and head out," I muttered. "We have a lot of ground to cover."

From what I could remember, Regal Heights was at least 500 miles from Thronehold, and we would be traveling through some rocky terrain. It would be at least two weeks for those on horseback. How long would it take Terrakona and Vjorn? Likely less, but we would see.

# CHAPTER 26

# LEGEND OF THE TYPHON BEAST

Traveling atop Terrakona wasn't the most comfortable means of transportation, but it was better than horseback. I could fit myself in the crystal lattice of Terrakona's mane. My feet fit between some of the rock-like structures, as if they were meant to be footholds. The only problem was the sun. The lack of clouds left me without shade, and I sweated more than I had ever in my life. Shouldn't I have been immune to sweating? I supposed it was both the physical movement, and the unrelenting sun that did it.

Terrakona tore across the land, moving at speeds shocking for a creature his size. Watching the terrain gradually shift and feeling the roaring wind against my skin more than made up for any discomfort.

The others riding along with us were on Terrakona's back. They hung on to his scales as we traveled across the land, heading for the border of the Argo Empire. Terrakona was large enough that everyone could sit and relax, but they also didn't have any shade.

Everyone would be sweaty by the time night fell.

As I watched the world blur past, I noticed that Zelfree and

Hexa exchanged words frequently throughout our travels. Although I couldn't hear their words, Hexa seemed to calm down the longer we went, the burning rage and desperation fading to steely determination. Zelfree's sage advice always had that effect on me.

From my experience… grief, when shared, was lessened, and joy, when shared, was multiplied. Zelfree had gone through his fair share of loss. Almost everyone he had loved had died. If anyone could help Hexa calm herself—so she could focus on helping Vethica—it was Zelfree.

I had feared that Calisto would cause problems at some point during our travels, but he never did anything. He sat on Terrakona, barely holding on to the world serpent's scales, his gaze on the horizon in the distance. Without his manticore magic, was he even really a threat?

Karna and Ryker sat farther down Terrakona's back. They were close—talking in quiet voices—and always had something to discuss. Were they talking about Ryker's magic? I hoped so.

The islands of my birth were to the north, but Regal Heights was to the west, near the Rocky Wastes. The forests of the Argo Empire grew thinner and thinner as we traveled west, replaced with grassy fields and then foothills covered in rocks. Terrakona easily slithered across the ground. The earth moved aside for his massive body, and then reformed once Terrakona was gone.

The closer we got to the western canyons, the more the grass faded to stony earth. Regal Heights was a massive city built on the edge, and down the side, of a gigantic canyon. The crack in the ground was so wide, dragons could fly in it and their wings wouldn't touch the sides.

The canyon was called Hydra's Gorge, and for good reason. It was one of the few places in the world that hydras called home. They hid in caves around the gorge and gobbled up anything—or anyone—who wandered into them. The goats and canyon prawns were a hydra's preferred meal, but they could devour all sorts of things.

I had never been there before, and I couldn't wait to see it with my own eyes.

**"A massive canyon..."**

Terrakona's telepathy made me smile. "Are you excited, too?"

**"It seems familiar. Epic and catastrophic."**

I held my breath as we traveled, the wind whipping through my hair. When I was atop Terrakona's head, it was easy to see a great distance in every direction. I took in the sights while my thoughts mulled over his statement.

"You think the canyon exists because of a catastrophe?" I asked.

**"It may have been created by the last world serpent arcanist."** Terrakona growled, and I felt the reverberation from his throat travel up through the crystals of his mane. **"A battle may have happened there. Something legendary."**

While that sounded amazing—and I wished I knew for sure —I didn't have any way to tell.

Then it struck me.

I had used Evianna's satchel to hold the queen's books. There were old poems and stories within! Perhaps one was about a canyon. I decided to find out. With giddy energy, I yanked a book from the satchel on my shoulder and cracked it open to the first page.

I had plenty of time for reading...

———

I only found one tale about a battle, but it was so interesting, I read it a dozen times. It was a tale about the mighty *typhon beast*.

*The Thirty-Seventh Stratagem*
*Powerful was the typhon beast. Terrible was his desire for war.*

*Outrageous was his lust for magic. Lawless was his attitude toward nations.*

*Monster.*

*That was the title given to the typhon beast's master. He was a savage who did what he wanted, whenever he wanted. The typhon beast and the Monster had no court, no people, no great creation. Only destruction. Only pain. Only horror.*

*When arcanists approached the typhon beast, they pleaded with the Monster, and asked that he quell his fury. But the typhon beast and his master would not listen. The beast's hundred heads chattered among each other, causing madness in any who listened. And when the beast wasn't chattering, the beast's heads breathed fire worse than the volcanos. It was a fierce serpentine beast, alien and bizarre, capable of regrowing heads that were cut from its colossal body.*

*So the arcanists called upon the Warlord.*

*But the Monster had no love for reason or logic. When the Warlord approached, they argued ten days and ten nights. On the eleventh day, when they had no agreement, the typhon beast attacked without warning—a dastardly tactic.*

*A normal arcanist would have surely perished, but the Warlord fought the Monster, despite his crippling injury. Their battle devastated the land and changed the very region. But the typhon beast was deadly. No creature compared to his might—to his hundred heads.*

*But the beast had a weakness.*

*It was heavy and could not fly.*

*The Warlord knew this and used it against the typhon beast. During the final hours of their fight, when the typhon beast was slow with fatigue, the world serpent opened the ground wide, and the typhon beast fell. The Monster crashed to the bottom and had no hope of escaping.*

*And the typhon beast lived there until the end of his days.*

The tale intrigued me for multiple reasons. According to the tale, the typhon beast sounded like a hydra. Well, more powerful than a simple hydra, but similar nonetheless. Additionally, the first world serpent arcanist had apparently trapped the Monster and his eldrin in a canyon.

Was this a record of Hydra's Gorge? Was this how it had come into existence? It seemed that way. It would explain the presence of the hydras. They could be some sort of descendants of the typhon beast, or perhaps they had traveled to the canyon because the beast's body was somewhere within.

That was an interesting theory.

What if we found the old typhon beast, and used its body to create trinkets and artifacts? According to the tale, the typhon beast was frighteningly powerful.

"We have the runestone for the second typhon beast," I muttered to myself, thinking of the future.

**"That is true,"** Terrakona replied. **"The red jasper runestone will open the way to the typhon beast's lair."**

What if it appeared near the canyon?

I shook my head and rubbed at my temples. Who would we have bond with the beast? It was clearly a creature of chaos. Would someone like William be accepted? I somehow doubted it.

**"We should focus on the task at hand. Problems of the future will arrive when they arrive."**

"All right." I patted his crystal mane. "But it's something we should decide before we search for the lair. I don't want to enter the lair without someone we're confident in."

**"Understood."**

I glanced around, staring at the many passengers on Terrakona, including Raisen, the hydra. The giant reptile clung to Terrakona like a bear on a tree. His six heads were practically wrapped around Terrakona's side.

Raisen really didn't like to travel.

But he wasn't the one I was looking for.

"Where's your dryad?" I asked.

**"Here."**

The tiny girl-shaped plant poked her head out of Terrakona's mane. Her flower eyes were a little startling, but I quickly recovered. With a slight smile, I waved. She waved back. And then she disappeared back into the mane.

"How much longer?" I shielded my eyes from the sun and glanced to the horizon.

**"When darkness falls, we shall stop."**

"All right. Until then, I'm going to continue reading."

———

When the sun began its descent, Terrakona slowed his pace. It allowed Vjorn to catch up with us. Unlike Terrakona, who shaped the earth and dirt as he went, Vjorn had to run across the land, avoiding the obstacles. It didn't tire him, though. Vjorn had endless stamina that seemingly sprang from nowhere.

Terrakona finally came to a stop near a grouping of trees by the edge of a small creek. We could boil the water and eat some of our provisions for dinner, and the nearby field would provide us the room required to train.

The perfect spot.

Terrakona lowered his head, and I slid off his snout and landed on the ground. His tongue flicked out for a moment, and I chuckled as I patted the side of his serpentine head. The little dryad also tumbled out of his mane and landed in the dirt. As quick as a grasshopper in a field, she disappeared from sight, burrowing into the ground.

Everyone else dismounted and got to work setting up a temporary camp. We wouldn't be here long, but it was always nice to have a fire and bedrolls ready. Normally, Zaxis would set up the fire... But of course, he no longer could. Zaxis seemed to realize this once he reached for the kindling. He tossed one of the sticks away from the camp and stomped over to the creek, no doubt to get water instead.

I wished Illia had traveled with us. She would've calmed him down. Instead, I would just leave him alone, and hope that he worked through his frustrations before returning to the group.

The others milled about, their energy low after a day of travel. Zelfree led Calisto over to one of the nearby trees and had him sit. Then he removed the manacles—an odd choice, but I wasn't going to fight it. Zelfree was a competent man.

Ryker and Karna stood near each other, muttering about the local scenery.

With my manipulation, I rearranged the ground around us, smoothing out the terrain and making it more pleasant. I pushed the grass away from our eventual firepit, and scattered the rocks near the creek, leaving us with sand and soft dirt.

Ryker watched from a good twenty feet away, never blinking. He held MOS in his hand, her red mouse eyes examining my every movement. Her nose twitched when I made a pit for the fire and even surrounded it with clay and stone.

Within a matter of minutes, we had the perfect camp for our perfect spot.

"Impressive," Ryker said with a hint of awe.

I half-shrugged. "It wasn't *that* amazing. The story I just read claims the first world serpent arcanist created Hydra's Gorge in a single attack. This is nothing compared to that."

Hexa, who hadn't been paying much attention to anything, suddenly perked up. She jogged over to my new firepit and stood at the edge. With wide eyes, and her puffy hair free from its ponytail, she asked, "You really think so?"

Even Raisen lumbered over, his giant body leaving a furrow in the ground where his stomach slid across it. With my magic, I felt the disturbance in my perfectly made camp. For some reason, it bothered me. After he moved, I used my manipulation to fix it again, though it wasn't really necessary.

"Yeah, it seems that the gorge was made during a fight," I said. "A battle with the typhon beast because his god-arcanist was a lawless lunatic."

Hexa—back in her normal coat and trousers—rolled up her sleeves to show off her scars. Then she flexed a bit and pointed to the gnarly gouges. "All hydra arcanists get scars from their Trial of Worth, but in Regal Heights, we have these legends about how canyons are the scars of the land, and our scars are a reflection of the canyon. It ties us to our homeland."

I nodded along with her words. "Well, on the Isle of Ruma, we talk about canyons in the ocean. The schoolmaster taught us that the entrance to the abyssal hells is always found in a canyon. If you believe it's possible to reach the place, that is."

That was when Calisto lifted his head a bit, his eyes more alight with life than I had seen in the last four days. He glanced over to me as he leaned back on a birch tree. "Is that right?"

"It's a legend," I muttered. "And canyons on the ocean floor are impossible to get to unless you're an arcanist who can breathe underwater."

"Hydra's Gorge doesn't have any water," Hexa said, her attention on her scars as she traced some of the lines. "You probably can't actually get to the abyssal hells that way, though." Then she glanced up, an eyebrow raised. "Right?"

I shrugged. "I don't know. Like I said, it's just a legend. And some people don't even believe the place is a physical location."

"It's a physical location," Calisto cut in, his voice gruff. "Just like the Death Lords are real arcanists." He closed his eyes as he rested his head on the bark of the tree. "If one of you would just end me, rather than playing at this ridiculous parade of draggin' me from one city to the next, I'd finally get to meet one."

"Just do it yourself if you're that desperate," Hexa snapped. She took a seat next to the pit, shooting a glare in Calisto's direction. "Nobody cares about your wishes."

Calisto, unfazed by her taunts, just replied, "You don't get to meet Death Lords if you kill yourself, lass. So, one of you weak-spined arcanists needs to finish what you started. Then you won't need to listen to my wishes any longer."

"You don't deserve any mercy from us."

"You know who also isn't gettin' any mercy? That khepera arcanist the Second Ascension took. They might cut her up to study the extent of her *healing powers*."

"*What was that?*" Hexa stood and whirled around in one quick motion.

Raisen flared his scales, his six mouths open and venomous gases leaking from his fangs. When he stomped forward, he offered a chorus of growls.

Zelfree stepped between them, one hand up. "Stop. *Stop*, dammit. He's just goading you into fighting—it's what he wants." Zelfree walked over to Hexa and motioned to the firepit. "Sit down. Don't listen to him."

"We should just tie him up and gag him," Hexa said through gritted teeth.

Calisto chuckled, unafraid of her threats or venom. If he wanted death, Raisen would definitely serve it to him quickly.

"Who's the khepera arcanist to you, anyway? You've been upset by her disappearance for days." Calisto scratched at the stubble on his jaw. "She your lover?"

"*Yes*," Hexa stated, heat in her voice. "And if you say anything about her again—"

Zelfree narrowed his eyes into a glower.

"—*I'll make sure you live a very long time*," Hexa hastily concluded, obviously conflicted about her threats. She huffed and took a seat by the firepit. Raisen slammed down next to her, and five of his heads wrapped around her body in a protective circle, his snake-like necks easily coiling in a tight embrace. The venomous gas eventually dissipated.

Calisto's appearance hadn't improved from his time in the Iron Dungeon. He hadn't really groomed himself in a few days.

He slicked back his copper hair, crossed his arms and ankles, and just waited, returning to a lethargic state. Apparently, talk of the abyssal hells still excited him, but little else seemed to liven the man. Even death threats.

Probably for the best. At long as he didn't provoke someone into killing him, the trek would likely be without incident.

# CHAPTER 27

## RYKER'S TRANSFORMATION

The sky blazed orange, red, and purple as the sun set in the distance. Zaxis stood away from the group, watching as it happened. I didn't disturb him. His fenris wolf had lain amid a grouping of trees, his frosty fur blending in the harsh shadows, though he was too large to disappear from sight.

Ryker had gathered wood, and I lit it with my molten rock. It wasn't the best fire—everything was lopsided, and the wood was burning faster than normal—but it would have to do.

While Hexa, Zelfree, and Calisto stayed near the flames, I took my brother away from the group and out into the nearby field. For some reason, Karna accompanied us. Her doppelgänger—who I swear had been nearby just seconds ago—was now nowhere to be found. He was a trickster, all right.

Ryker held MOS in one hand, the cute little mouse staring up at him with beady red eyes. He patted her head and brushed her white fur.

"Are you ready?" I asked him once we were in the middle of the field.

Ryker shifted his weight from one foot to the other. Then he glanced over his shoulder at the others near the fire. "I'm not sure I want an audience."

"They're not going to pay attention to you," Karna said with a smile. She placed a delicate hand on his shoulder, and Ryker practically flinched. "You need to relax, or you'll never develop your magical abilities."

"W-Well, it's awkward having a dread pirate in our midst."

"Trust me—the pirate doesn't care about you." She walked her fingers up his perfectly smoothed shirt and then tugged on the collar. "He's too wrapped up in his own trauma to care what you're doing. This is the perfect time to practice."

"You talk like you know him."

Karna smirked. "Oh, I know him. Probably too well."

"A-Ah. Well, you did tell me you ran with questionable crowds at one point." Ryker fidgeted for a moment, and then glanced down at his uneven collar. He fixed it before saying, "Maybe you should talk to the pirate. And distract him."

"I guarantee that the only person who's going to distract him already is."

"Hexa?"

Karna half-laughed and then glanced over to the firepit. She subtly pointed. When I snuck a peep in that direction, I caught sight of Zelfree talking to Calisto. The pirate wasn't talking back —it wasn't a real conversation—but Zelfree was saying *something*, and he seemed enthusiastic about it, at least. Occasionally, Calisto turned his attention to him.

Hexa wasn't even looking at them. She held her hydra close, and warmed herself, and likely her spirits, by the lopsided fire.

"Zelfree knows him well," Ryker muttered. Then he sighed. "But still. It's difficult imagining my powers. What if I only *half* transform, and then I'm too nervous to *untransform*, so I'm stuck as a hideous monster?"

Karna slowly lifted a perfect eyebrow. Her hair gleamed in the sunset, practically merging with the dusk. She wore a loose tunic and flowing pants—not her normal, revealing outfit, which would probably not have helped with everyone's overall concentration.

"Let me help you," MOS said. Her voice was ancient and feminine, almost otherworldly. I always forgot what she sounded like until she spoke again—it was as if I heard her voice for the first time whenever we spoke.

Ryker patted her head again. "I don't know…"

"Perhaps if I am confident in my own skin, you will be confident in yours."

Her cryptic statement wasn't helping anything. What did she mean by that? And how was I supposed to help? I was about to suggest that Zelfree come over here, but a flock of birds stole my concentration.

Small birds—blue jays, all of them—flocked toward us from a distant grouping of trees. Their white underbellies and bright blue wings were slightly off color in the sunset lighting. They flew at surprising speeds, reaching us before I could comment on their bizarre beauty. Then the birds dove and circled, practically a whirlwind of feathers and beaks.

They landed on the field, and in an instant, merged together, shaping their bodies like warm clay around one another, growing larger with each additional bird. They lumped and clumped, forming a ball of flesh that writhed on its own. I had to hold my breath and steel myself as the mass of meat became more disturbing with each additional blue jay.

The Mother of Shapeshifters was a thing of nightmares. Her uneven body pulsated and undulated, her outside devoid of skin. It seemed like she was wet with blood, but like a newborn covered in vital fluid, not like someone with an injury.

Her glistening exterior caused my stomach to churn. I took a step away, trying not to flinch.

Then Ryker's mouse leapt into the ball, and a pair of eyes "surfaced" on the creature.

She was larger than an elephant and bloated enough to be filled with the blood of a hundred men. I preferred her as mice or birds or rats.

Karna kept her composure, but the corners of her mouth struggled to remain upright. Ryker stared at his own eldrin with a furrowed brow.

"Are you sure you should be like that?" he asked as he approached her massive fleshy body. "What if someone sees you?"

"I am safe with two god-arcanists," MOS replied, her ancient voice just as calm and confident as before. Now she was just louder.

"But aren't you... disgusted by what you look like?"

Karna tensed—only for a brief second. I wouldn't have noticed if I hadn't been looking in her direction. With subtle movements, she backed away from Ryker, her hands unsteady until she crossed them over her chest.

"Young arcanist," MOS said. "The realm of appearance is now yours to control. You needn't fear the judgment of others ever again. And even if the fear crept back into your thoughts, please remember that those who ridicule and mock your appearance are like frogs with brightly colored skin. They have given you a warning. They are vile and filled with poison. Not you."

Ryker slowly nodded along with her words, his gaze on the grass around his feet. For a long while, he said nothing. He just waited, his breath held. Then he swallowed hard and glanced up at the mass of flesh. "You... aren't afraid?"

"I am not."

"I wish... I had your confidence."

MOS jiggled a bit, still glistening in the sunset. "Then allow me to give you my confidence."

Everyone remained still and silent for a full ten seconds. I glanced over to Karna, hoping she would know what that meant.

She met my gaze with an identical expression. She clearly wouldn't have any answers for me.

When Ryker didn't reply, MOS's body contorted and changed. A small hand reached out from her bulbous body, its little fingers stretching out for Ryker. My chest tightened as I readied myself for something to happen. What was MOS doing?

Ryker, hesitant and fumbling, slowly reached his hand out to take MOS's. Her little fingers were half the size of his. When they connected, it was like Ryker was shaking hands with a child.

Then MOS yanked his hand, pulling him closer.

Ryker gasped and stumbled forward. MOS yanked harder, and Ryker shouted as he collided with the wet ball of muscle, membranes, and fatty tissue. I stepped forward, my hand on Retribution, wondering if I would have to cut MOS to help my brother.

Then... Ryker was absorbed into the Mother of Shapeshifters, like an insect sinking into tar.

"What in the name of my grandfather's diseased left foot was *that*?" Hexa called out from the firepit.

She and Zelfree hurried over, everything else forgotten after... whatever had just happened.

Then Zaxis and Vjorn turned their attention to the commotion, both obviously confused as to what was happening. They approached, but slowly, their gazes shifting to our surroundings, like we might be under attack.

Zelfree dashed over to MOS and frantically glanced around her. "Where is he?"

MOS shook and writhed, her body flattening and expanding, the muscle twisting in on itself.

"Wait," I said, my heart beating hard. "Let's... back up. Give her space."

MOS had never been malicious. Whatever was happening, I felt it must have been beneficial to Ryker. Somehow. I just didn't know how. Despite feeling like I had just been smacked in the face by a wet fish, I decided to wait for the moment.

Terrakona craned his head over all of us, his bright eyes observing the event.

The sun finally set, blanketing us in darkness. In that short moment, in which the world was darker than before, a chill came over the area. MOS twisted and grew into a distinct shape. Four legs erupted out of her body, followed by four serpentine necks with hydra heads. Flesh condensed into layers of purple black scales, each of which glowed with a radiant, raging power.

The heads roared and thrashed about, their voices out of sync and screeching at different times. I pulled Retribution from its sheath and hesitated, concerned, but still willing to trust MOS.

She contorted and puffed outward until finally she was an awkward hydra beast, twice the size of Raisen, and somehow with more muscle, longer fangs, and thicker scales. Her heads shrieked, brutal and savage. It was as if an ancient ancestor of the hydra had risen from the grave, awakened from a primordial era in which only power ruled.

Hexa stared with wide eyes, her eldrin close by her side, the same look of concern on all six of his reptile faces. After a short while, Hexa blinked away her shock. Then she approached, her steps slow but obvious. The four-headed monster hydra wobbled a bit, but didn't attack.

And then the new hydra collapsed to the ground. It burst into a hundred bats, each one black, furry, and with large wings. They chirped and flew off into the night, scattering like a flock of startled animals. I lifted my sword, shielding my eyes as they all rushed off toward a distant grouping of birch trees.

Ryker was left on the grass, shaken and stunned.

A single bat remained by his side. Its red eyes glowed enough to see in the dark, and it sat on Ryker's knee, its wings tucked in close to its body.

"Wow," Karna said, a nervous laugh in her voice. "I wasn't expecting that."

Hexa motioned to the bats. "Did any of you *see* that? The transformation? The bats afterward? That was... That was unbelievable. I've never seen anything like it."

For a long moment, Zelfree just stared at the field of grass around us. With a sigh, and a slump of his shoulders, he turned back toward the firepit. "Eh. I've seen weirder."

He wandered back to his spot in camp and took a seat, like nothing had even happened. Calisto, who had just watched from afar, barely seemed interested in the bizarre event that had just taken place.

Ryker trembled. He was covered in... viscous fluid. It clung to his shirt, his black hair, his tanned skin—everything. He looked like he had been dragged through a barrel of saliva.

"Are you okay?" I asked as I jogged over.

He managed to nod once. "I... Uh..."

I knelt next to him and almost put a hand on his shoulder, but I decided against it when I saw that a glob of clear liquid jelly was there.

"I was one with her," Ryker finally managed to say. "We. Us. Together. And, uh, I was also a hydra. I think."

Karna sauntered over, swaying her hips as she went. "Mighty impressive for someone who can't seem to master transforming."

"I barely did anything." Ryker turned his gaze down to the bat. "It was all... MOS... She just did it. And, uh, together, we were..."

"You wanted confidence," MOS said, her voice small again, but still laced with age. "I had hoped you would will us to transform, but if you need my will, I will control the situation."

"I..."

"Together, we can mimic the magic of nearby mystical creatures. And improve them. My magic is vast—not like the god-creatures, but unique. I am descended from the progenitor behemoth, and am capable of great things."

I sheathed my sword, unsure what to do with the information. That seemed like a useful ability. If Ryker could get the confidence to use it more than not at all. Normally, mimics only mirrored the creature they transformed into. MOS could gain *more* power, it seemed. And Ryker could fight with her?

Like a fleshy... knightmare...

Or a muscly reaper.

Either way, if he could master it, that could come in handy. Ryker could win most one-on-one fights. Well, not with a god-arcanist, but likely any others.

Karna knelt and wiped the bizarre fluid off Ryker's clothing. He flinched at her first touch but calmed afterward and allowed her to work.

"It's disgusting," he muttered. "You don't have to do that."

She offered a smile. "The correct thing to say is *thank you*."

Ryker's face reddened and then he whispered, "Thank you, Karna. I'm sorry for—"

"No. Just *thank you*. You don't need to say anything else."

# CHAPTER 28

## ZAXIS'S MAGIC

After the sun went down, Ryker and MOS stayed in the grassy field. I watched them for a short while—as did Karna—just in case something else went weird. Nothing horrific happened, but Ryker discovered an odd ability.

MOS, as a bat, turned back into flesh and then "merged" with Ryker, adding to his muscle. It was a small change and confined to just one arm, but he could notice a difference in his strength. While I remembered what it felt like to fight merged with Luthair, *this* kind of merging seemed abstract and foreign to me. It was like MOS was... moldable flesh. She could be anything.

And now that she was bonded with Ryker, she could grow in power. Could they become *anything*? People? Mystical creatures? I was interested to see her limitations, but that would have to come in time, and with plenty of practice.

Ryker ripped off MOS's tiny amount of flesh and added it to his other arm. The malleable tissue became muscle. Then he was a bit stronger—with the other arm. It was disturbing to watch him peel her away again and try another location, but I didn't want to comment. Ryker didn't take those kinds of observations well.

"Your eldrin is powerful," I said as Ryker slowly peeled her off his bicep.

He chuckled and gave me a sideways glance. "Not as powerful as yours."

I didn't know how to respond to that, so I just shrugged. "You should still be excited. I would be."

"Hm."

Karna walked between us, her movements dancer-like. She did a little twirl and placed a hand on Ryker's shoulder. "Volkie, you don't have to worry anymore. I'll watch Ryker. You should go see your new wolf friend, hm? He seems lost over there."

We all glanced over to find Zaxis standing by the edge of the creek. He hadn't spoken to anyone since we had arrived, and he had kept his eyes to the ground after Ryker's jarring transformation. What was he waiting for?

"Is *lost* the right word?" Ryker whispered. "It doesn't seem right."

Karna touched a finger to her bottom lip. "Did I say *lost*? I meant *pouty*." She crossed her arms and shook her head. "It's not a good look for him."

"I'll handle it," I said.

No one protested as I walked out of the field and returned to our camp. Ryker and Karna remained behind, no doubt to train more. Or perhaps talk. Karna had definitely taken a liking to my brother, and I debated with myself whether or not I should give her a speech about treating him right. Ryker was technically an adult, but he was still my little brother. On the other hand, I barely knew him, and he could take care of himself.

I still hadn't come to a conclusion.

I walked by the fire and stopped to check if the hastily made flame was still properly contained. Spending so many years with phoenix arcanists, as well as learning my new powers, had given me a healthy respect for fire. There were no embers outside the pit, no logs being left out of the flame. Hexa and her hydra were already asleep at the edge of the fire's glow. She was curled up on Raisen, despite his prickly scales. How did she do that? I swear, she could sleep on a bed of broken glass without much difficulty.

Zelfree and Calisto sat at the base of a tree, neither talking nor moving, even as I approached. But when I went to walk by, Calisto lifted his head and gave me the once over. With keen eyes, he seemed to take note of my sword and shield.

"Everything okay over here?" I asked, staring at Zelfree.

He returned my gaze with narrowed eyes. "In the morning, we need to head northwest. Just a short distance." Zelfree didn't even bother to answer my question.

"Very well." I lifted an eyebrow. "Is that all? Your detour won't take us too long, will it?"

"Only half a day's travel, at the most."

"Where are we going?"

"Have you ever heard of the *Rocky Wastes*?" His tone had shifted to something serious and cold.

I nodded once. "I've heard of it. Luthair told me about a time he and Mathis chased a criminal into the wastes. It apparently didn't end well for anyone."

"That's because it's dangerous. I was hoping we could travel to the edge, and then you and I—and Terrakona—could travel into the interior, beyond the Shrieking Peaks."

My knowledge of the territory wasn't vast. All I knew was that the Rocky Wastes were a desolate land. Barely any plants grew there, and no nations claimed it as their own. The only people who traveled there were mystic seekers—arcanists hired by nobles and royals to catch rare mystical creatures and bring them to civilization. Or sometimes relocate them.

And occasionally kill them for trinket and artifact parts.

"What's there?" I asked. "Why visit at all?"

Zelfree shot Calisto a quick glance. They exchanged neutral

expressions. Then Calisto huffed and turned away. "I don't know what you're scheming, Everett, but stop this charade. It sickens me. Every minute I'm here is like a dagger shoved straight into my damn kidney. I keep hoping I'll bleed out, but you never let me."

"I'll tell you all about what we're looking for when we get to the Rocky Wastes," Zelfree said to me, never acknowledging Calisto's comments.

"Fair enough."

I left them and headed toward the creek. Terrakona shifted his massive serpentine body, and I glanced over my shoulder to watch him positioning himself in a tight coil. If anyone came through the area, they would surely notice his towering body, but hopefully, it wouldn't frighten them too much.

And I also hoped the Second Ascension wasn't waiting in the shadows, ready to attack with some new weapon that we had yet to deal with. I shivered as I thought of terrible possibilities.

The sooner we ended them, the better I would sleep at night.

Zaxis waited at the water's edge, his hands in his pockets. He wore a button-up shirt, but it wasn't buttoned at all. His god-arcanist mark was impressive, but was it worth suffering through the chill? Or perhaps he didn't feel it, since his new powers seemed to be drawn from the heart of an endless winter.

I stood next to him and awkwardly folded my arms and then unfolded them. "It's a nice evening." That wasn't the best opening, but I wanted to keep it casual, in case Zaxis was dwelling on dark thoughts. "So, you want to practice your magic?"

Zaxis didn't say anything. He stared at the quiet waters flowing in the creek, his face set in a hard neutral expression, like he was clenching his jaw just barely. I wasn't sure how to interpret that.

"It can be difficult at first," I said. I tapped my hands

together, trying to remember my first few days. "I was feeling really alone, and isolated, and I thought of Luthair nonstop."

Still, Zaxis didn't say anything to me.

"But, uh, I got better the more I learned all my new powers. Oh! And there's something important you should know. You have two versions of your evocation, manipulation, augmentation, and aura."

"I know that," he drawled. "I helped you train, remember?"

"Er, right. Sorry. I was just... excited to tell you. Well, I think, given what happened in the fenris wolf's lair—"

"Volke."

Zaxis's interjection caught me off guard. I stopped my speech and turned to face him. "Yeah?"

"I think I'd rather do this on my own."

"*What* on your own?" I asked, glancing around.

"Learn my magic. I want to do that on my own."

The sky sparkled with stars overhead, giving us enough light to see clearly. The moon reflected in the small amounts of water, and the shimmer of the tiny ripples was like a poem of nature. I wished I could enjoy it more.

"I don't think that's a good idea," I finally said. "I already went through the most difficult parts—learning about god-creatures, and how to use the magic—and I think you'll learn it faster if I just teach you."

Zaxis glanced over, his eyes narrowed. "There're only supposed to be twelve of us, right?"

"God-arcanists? Yeah."

"And each creature is unique and special and powerful in its own regard?"

I nodded once, already knowing where he was going with this.

"Then I should discover my own powers," he stated. "*You* did. Which means I can, too."

I rotated my shoulders and then sighed. "This isn't a competition. We're on the same side. Let me help you."

"Listen—some things are better if they're learned on your own, okay?" Zaxis growled something under his breath, his whole body tenser than before. He turned away, unable to look at me. "Nobody teaches you how to make love, do they? *You just do that on your own.*"

I rubbed at my hot face. "Th-This is different, and you know it. We're supposed to be a team! We're fighting the Second Ascension *together*. How am I supposed to know what your capabilities are on the battlefield if you just train off in secret?"

"It doesn't have to be *in secret*." Zaxis wheeled on me, his hands still in his pockets, but his arms stiff. "I just want to do it without your help, okay? *I want to do it on my own, just like you.* You can watch, but I don't want any *advice* or *insight* or you *telling me how it is.* I just want... to figure it out."

Someone stomped over, their footfalls registering with my tremor sense long before I had heard them. I turned and spotted Hexa walking over, a deep frown on her face. When had she woken? Had she heard Zaxis and I fighting?

My tremor sense came easier now... I hadn't even realized I had been using it.

Hexa stormed over to Zaxis's side and punched him in the shoulder. Hard. He didn't flinch or grimace. He just turned away with a huff.

"Hey," Hexa said. "When someone offers you a hand, you take it, shake it, and move on with your life! Pride doesn't help anyone, okay? That's what Vethica says all the time, and she's right."

Zaxis shook his head. "This isn't just about pride."

"We don't have time for whatever this is, then! We need to find Vethica—we need to stop the Second Ascension—and we have to do it as fast as possible."

A deathly chill washed over the area, creating an icy fog that blanketed the creek and nearby field. A shiver ran the length of my spine, and I felt Vjorn moving as he shifted through the cold clouds that had wrapped around us. With silent steps, he made his way closer, until he was fifteen feet away, still hidden by the mist. I wouldn't have known he was there if it hadn't been for my magic.

"**Hunter,**" Vjorn said, a growl in his voice. "**Shall I remove these two?**"

A sudden mix of anger and concern radiated from Terrakona. Waves of heat clashed against the mist, and the air crackled as the potent magics clashed.

I shook my head. "Whoa, whoa. It's not like that. I won't force Zaxis to train with me. Everyone, calm down."

Hexa scoffed and stepped away. "I think you're being damn selfish." When Zaxis didn't reply, she stomped off into the fog, heedless of where the fenris wolf was hiding.

A moment later, Terrakona evoked magma and heat enough that the fog burned away in an instant. The bright glow of embers from his mouth were enough to draw everyone's attention. Vjorn was revealed, his wolf form by the river, his eyes narrowed in a glare at Terrakona.

My eldrin wasn't prone to violence, but he was making it clear that he didn't appreciate threats. I suspected Terrakona would attack without hesitation if I were actually in danger, and for that, I appreciated his presence.

I exhaled. What was I supposed to say to Zaxis? I understood his desire to do things on his own. I had wanted the same after I had lost my eldrin. Our magics didn't seem to overlap—except when it came to power. Vjorn seemed fierce, and I was sure Zaxis would be able to wield the full devastation of a blizzard one day.

"Well, just let me watch you train, okay?" I asked.

Zaxis snorted.

"Hey."

He glanced over. "What?"

"I'll let you crush me in a sandpit or something, like I did to you. Ya know, to make it even between us."

After a short moment, Zaxis cracked a smile. "Oh, yeah? What if I bury you in snow?"

"That works."

He chuckled, and I felt better afterward. One of the things that concerned me was the cryptic statement the queen had made. She had said there were tales of rivalry between the fenris wolf and the world serpent. Was it because of the god-creatures, or was it because of the previous god-arcanists and their personalities?

I hoped Zaxis and I would be great partners in this. He was with Illia, my sister, and we came from the same island. We often butted heads, but whenever I needed him, Zaxis was there. He was a good and loyal friend, someone I would be happy to call brother. Why wouldn't we be good allies? It was in the stars, surely.

"Give me a bit," Zaxis whispered, his attention once again on the water. "I'll train in the morning. Until then, I just want to think about... things."

"All right."

I patted him once on the shoulder and then awkwardly ambled away, not sure what else to say. Zaxis didn't acknowledge me. That was fine. He seemed better now than before. Much better.

---

We took turns for guard duty throughout the night.

Zelfree went first.

Then Zaxis.

Then me.

Everyone else slept peacefully. Well, not *everyone*. When I woke for my shift, I noticed Calisto sitting next to the fire, awake enough that the flames reflected in the glossiness of his eyes. I left him alone, though, and went to sit near Terrakona. My tremor sense would tell me if anyone was approaching, even in the dead of night.

The evening chill wasn't too bad. A comfortable breeze swept over the area, carrying dust and dryness. Nothing like island weather.

Although Terrakona was on the edge of sleep, he telepathically spoke to me.

**"The Children of Balastar are reckless,"** he said, his voice distant.

"Oh, yeah?" I sat on the ground and flipped through the books that Eventide had given me. "There are a few mentions of the god-arcanists' names in these poems. One of them is about Balastar."

**"You are a child of his line..."**

"Hm." I kept my lantern close, but the shutters mostly closed, so that I wouldn't wake the others.

Balastar had been the first fenris wolf arcanist. Apparently, I was distantly related to him. *Distantly.* Everything I had heard about him was that he had been reckless and wouldn't be swayed from his path. Sort of like Zaxis. He was a Child of Balastar, as well.

I wanted to find more information about Luvi, the first world serpent arcanist. I had met him. Well, not really. I had met his illusion. He seemed intelligent, and kind, but also determined, just in a different sense. He had set up a fortress just to give me a message, because he had known that one day I might need it.

Luvi's planning and long-term strategies amazed me.

But as I flipped through the books, it was obvious all the old tales and poems written about them were from before the appearance of the apoch dragon. Most of the stories spoke of the Warlord and the Hunter and the Scholar as though they were still alive, or wandering the world, or building a family somewhere. But I knew that wasn't the case.

All the first god-arcanists were dead.

Five of them had died to fighting each other, and the rest had died when the apoch dragon had appeared. It had killed them all—because it had been time for the age of god-arcanists to end.

Not everyone knew that. The god-arcanists had lived so long ago, that most things about them were long forgotten, or now just myths and legends.

I liked solving the mysteries of their lives. I wanted to know more—I wanted to understand my eventual fate. In a way, I had signed my own death warrant when I had bonded with Terrakona. But did it have to be at the hands of the dragon? Was there no other way? Sometimes I wondered.

Calisto stood. I felt the shift of his weight across the dirt.

With a chill in my veins, I closed my book and also stood. It was dark, and the flicker of the distant fire was easy to see, but once Calisto walked off—into the shadows of the night—my eyes couldn't make out his form. Fortunately, they didn't need to, but I still worried about his motives.

I strode through the shadows and followed Calisto at a distance.

Everyone else was asleep. What was he up to?

Then he stopped at the creek. I waited, wondering if he would do something. After a few minutes, I decided to approach. I didn't want to linger in the darkness like a craven stalker.

Calisto slowly turned to face me when I approached, his hands in the pockets of his trousers. He seemed tense—his stance wide—and I placed my hand on the hilt of my blade.

"Has the Warlord come to check up on me?" he sarcastically asked. "Good news. You caught me gettin' into trouble."

# CHAPTER 29

## CALISTO'S SECRETS

"What're you doing, Calisto?" I asked as I quickly glanced around the area.

It was just us. The splash of the gentle creek added a quiet backdrop, but otherwise, the music of the night echoed between the trees. Chirping crickets, an owl, and the hum of wind reminded me this was a peaceful area, even if Calisto's presence tainted that feeling.

"I told you what I was doin'," Calisto said, irritation in his voice.

Even though he wasn't bonded to a manticore anymore, Calisto was still a large man. If it came to a fight, he could still hold his own. His lack of magic would be his undoing, but what if he fatally stabbed someone? I couldn't take any risks.

I kept my hand on the hilt of Retribution. "I'm not playing games. I'm keeping a close eye on you."

"I bet."

His dark delivery didn't sit right with me. Nothing about him seemed right. It felt off—like he wasn't himself. I wished I had Adelgis's ability to read minds. What was Calisto thinking?

I could guess.

"Listen," I said, keeping my voice low. "I'm not going to let you hurt anyone. Especially not Zelfree. So if you think you can force my hand—force me to kill you—by hurting someone, you've got everything wrong. I can lock you away in a cell of stone anywhere we go."

To my surprise, Calisto smirked. He narrowed his eyes as he asked, "What makes you think I'm gonna hurt Everett?"

"You always do."

For a prolonged moment, Calisto said nothing. He just stared—no reaction to my comment—but the tension between us couldn't be any thicker.

"You don't need to worry this time," Calisto drawled. "I'm not gonna hurt Everett."

"He killed Hellion," I stated. "You're telling me you're not thinking about revenge or—"

Calisto snorted, cutting me off. "He didn't kill Hellion."

"Yes, he did." I forced a laugh. "I was *there*. I know you're still suffering from the shock of everything, but once you get your wits back, Master Zelfree and Illia are at the top of your list for revenge. *Admit it.*"

Calisto's icy gaze drifted to the ground. He stared for a long while at the dirt by the creek. "Everett didn't bring Hellion to a fight between gods. I did." Calisto clicked his tongue and smiled —but it had no mirth behind it. It was a dead smile, no life whatsoever. "Everett didn't train Hellion to never surrender, no matter the circumstance... I did."

I caught my breath, unsettled by the cold statements.

"*I* brought Hellion to thugs with deadly intentions. *I* didn't fight with Hellion, even though I knew I should have. *I* sold myself and my crew for magical power, even when Hellion said it wrong."

Calisto took in a ragged breath as he returned his gaze to meet mine.

"Illia might've killed my man, Markus, but *I* was his captain.

*I* disregarded his feelings. *I* made all the wrong choices. *I* wasn't there for those who relied on me—for those who trusted me."

I had no words. What was I supposed to say? He was wrong? He wasn't.

"I..." Calisto ran a shaky hand over his chin, his voice becoming quiet. "I don't deserve to live. And we both know it."

I wanted to agree with him, but I had promised Zelfree I wouldn't just kill the man. But it felt odd to hear Calisto lay out his sins in order, and then decide he didn't deserve to be forgiven. Most people never wanted to admit they did anything wrong.

Calisto grabbed the collar of my shirt, tearing me from my thoughts. I tightened my grip on Retribution, a second away from unsheathing it. Calisto jerked me forward. And with his other hand, he grabbed the hilt of my sword, like he would attempt to take it from me.

I grabbed his arm with my free hand, but Calisto never followed through. He just waited, staring at me, the two of us locked in a tense stance.

Calisto narrowed his eyes and smirked. "No one would blame you," he whispered. *"Tell them I tried to take your sword.* They'd believe it. I stole your blade once before—and we all know it's deadly, even in the hands of a man without an eldrin."

His heart beat faster than before. I felt it through the slight tremors in the ground. My chest twisted with indecision, my breath held in my throat.

He was right. No one would blame me if I cut him down.

Calisto tightened his grip on the collar of my shirt. "Everett's a fool. He cares about *Lynus*, but I'm not that man anymore. But you... You hate me. I know it. Just end this. Run me through—*I would've done it to you, if I'd gotten the chance.*"

I gritted my teeth and then used my manipulation to rearrange the terrain. I shifted the ground around Calisto's feet, throwing him off-balance. When he stumbled, I hit him in the gut with the hilt of my blade. He slammed to the ground, and before he could stand, I twisted the dirt into a quicksand trap. Once half his body was submerged, I hardened everything into stone, trapping him.

His heart raced faster than before, but Calisto never fought back. He just waited—one leg and arm half trapped in rock, and his waist locked to the ground, like he had been laced there.

Calisto glanced up at me. "Well?"

"I'm not going to kill you." I sheathed my blade. "I told you I wouldn't."

He exhaled and tilted his head back until his copper hair rested in the mud near the creek. "Damn you to the abyssal hells. *Is everyone here a wagon wheel?*"

"I think you're afraid," I said.

That statement silenced Calisto. He didn't move. He just remained semi-trapped by the rock, his gaze on the stars overhead. "Death doesn't scare me."

"I didn't say you were afraid of dying. I think... you're afraid of living." I stepped closer and sighed. "You could've *actually* tried to take my sword, but instead, you stopped. You're afraid, aren't you? You're afraid you're too weak to take it from me. Without your manticore magic, you're slower, and not as powerful. And I think that frightens you."

Calisto didn't reply.

"I think all the terrible things in your life scare you as well. But you always thought you'd escape the consequences through death. You never planned on living beyond the battle at Thronehold. You were tired then—you had nothing to live for. And now you're just saddled with regrets, and it'd be easier to leave it all behind."

Calisto snorted and laughed once. "Yeah, well, you're right, lad. Ya got me. I want death because it's easier. For me. For you. For everyone. *Do it already.*"

"Zelfree thinks he has a way to help you," I said with a sigh. "So we're going to do that first."

"Everett's insane. He thinks he can *kill Calisto* but *leave Lynus alive*." Calisto chuckled to himself, his gaze stuck on the sky. "We both know that's not possible. And every minute that I live is torture."

"Well... consider the torture your punishment for failing Hellion and Markus."

Calisto tensed, his heart still beating fast, even if he didn't betray that fact through his expression. He had no words for a reply, just stunned silence. I wondered if he was dwelling on that —and a small part of me hoped his life *was* a torture. He *did* deserve it.

I waved my hand and manipulated the ground to release Calisto. Even after I freed him, he remained on the ground, lying on his back. He seemed more tired than ever—no energy for anything.

"Let's go back to the firepit," I said as I offered him my hand.

He didn't say anything. He didn't even move.

I waited, my hand outstretched. At first, I thought he wouldn't move, but to my surprise, Calisto tensed, lifted a hand, and allowed me to help him to his feet. He staggered a bit, but eventually, he stood straight and sighed.

Without any words between us, we headed to the firepit. Calisto was covered in dirt, and his hair had some leaves in it, but otherwise, he looked normal. Or at least, as normal as he could look.

When he sat by the small fire, he did so with slow movements.

I grabbed my books and returned to the pit, intent on reading, but close by, just in case Calisto wanted to talk. I still didn't care for the man, but for Zelfree's sake, I would try to keep him from sliding too far into the despair.

The rest of the evening passed without incident.

In the morning, I manipulated the creek to extinguish our fire.

Manipulating water was the destructive side of my manipulation. According to Terrakona, water eroded everything in its path. Rivers sliced through mountains, tsunamis devastated islands, and floods crippled civilizations—ruining crop soil and forever changing the landscape.

Water manipulation was powerful, and while rearranging a lake, river, or bay *could* be helpful, it was mostly a tool for carving away life. People could live on land, but they couldn't breathe underwater. Water was a quick killer, even if everyone needed it to live.

Although I hadn't given it much thought, I leaned more toward mastering land manipulation. Once I mastered it, though, I would lose the ability to manipulate the water...

But then my ability to change the terrain would be beyond powerful.

The others packed their blankets, bedrolls, and tools. Zaxis packed his things on the back of Vjorn. Zelfree managed to throw a couple of bags onto Terrakona.

Ryker and MOS were the only ones not participating. My brother stood off to the side, using a piece of MOS's flesh to practice his magic. He grafted it to one arm, and then ripped it off to place it on his neck.

Hexa half watched, her eyebrows close to her hairline. "That's freakish."

Ryker nervously laughed. "Uh, yeah, well... It's a little odd, I admit."

"Freakish," Raisen muttered, his six heads all frowning. His reptilian tail lashed back and forth. "I don't like it."

"Don't listen to them." Karna sauntered over and placed her hands on Ryker's shoulders. "You might become one of our greatest fighters."

"That would be a plot twist," Calisto said with a snort and a laugh.

Karna fluffed her blonde hair and shot him a glare. "You're *talkative* this morning. Have a good night?" She glanced between Calisto and Zelfree.

"Better than your best night with the *flesh-blob arcanist*," Calisto quipped.

Hexa and her hydra turned their anger on Calisto in one swift moment. She stormed over and shoved him toward Terrakona. "No more commentary for you. Get on the serpent. We're leaving."

Calisto chuckled—adding to Hexa's anger—but he complied with her demands by sauntering over to Terrakona. For some reason, he *did* seem to be in a better mood, but it wasn't by much.

I wondered if Zelfree had spoken with him, or if our conversation last night had shifted Calisto's perception of the situation. But I didn't waste much time dwelling on the matter. There were more important things to think about.

Once Zaxis had finished packing, he grabbed his salamander scale armor from a pack and stared at it. For a long while, he just touched the scales, his fingers grazing over the bindings. Then he stuffed the armor away and opted to just wear his trousers and unbuttoned shirt.

I walked over, my arms crossed. "Hey, uh, before we leave, aren't you going to practice your magic?"

Zaxis grimaced as he turned to face me. With a frown, he said, "It can wait. Until we stop again."

His fenris wolf snorted. Frost went everywhere. It melted as quickly as it came. I shivered once, and then the chill was gone.

"You said you'd practice in the morning," I said. "I think it's important that—"

Zaxis gritted his teeth. "*Fine*. I'll try. Just... stand back."

I did as he wanted and took a few steps back. When I glanced over my shoulder, I realized everyone else had stopped their packing just to watch. All six of Raisen's heads stared with bright golden eyes. Traces leapt up to Zelfree's shoulder, and the two of them watched with scrutinizing gazes.

Karna, MOS, and Ryker waited by Terrakona, observing from a safe distance. Hexa kept close to Calisto, like she was guarding him—ready to silence him if he got too uppity again.

Now with everyone's attention squarely on him, Zaxis walked out onto the grass and sighed. He swung his arms loosely at his sides, and then rotated his shoulders, likely warming up. I waited with bated breath, wondering what he would do. He would likely evoke ice, but since the fenris wolf had illusions in his lair, I thought it was possible Zaxis could evoke that as well.

Or perhaps the illusions were a manipulation? A manipulation of perception? I didn't know, and the curiosity was killing me.

Zaxis lifted his hand, and everyone tensed. The heart rate of everyone nearby sped up, the excitement as thick as smoke.

But for a long moment, Zaxis didn't do anything. He just kept his hand up.

It reminded me of when I had first tried to evoke terrors as a knightmare arcanist. Maybe he was struggling to evoke anything?

"Don't worry, it'll happen," I said.

Zaxis shot me a glare. "*I said I could do this on my own.*"

"I know. I was just talking aloud."

He grumbled something as he returned his focus to his magic. For another long minute—which passed in silence—Zaxis kept his hand up in place.

Right as it seemed everyone was about to return to their packing, Zaxis waved his hand in an arc.

He evoked a tiny gush of icy wind, akin to a cold fart.

Calisto laughed and shook his head. Hexa immediately shot him a glare, but it didn't faze him.

With a shrug, Calisto said, "It'll be amusing to watch you all fight the Autarch."

The mere mention of the *Autarch* got everyone's attention, even Zaxis's.

Technically, I had seen the Autarch. But only once. I had been immobilized, and unable to say anything. The Autarch and his gold kirin had issued orders to members of the Second Ascension. No one had questioned his decisions or judgments—they had gone along with his orders as though they had been binding law.

"You know the Autarch?" Hexa asked, her brow furrowed.

Calisto glanced down at her, a hint of amusement in his expression. "That's right."

"And you've seen him fight? You know we can't beat him?"

"I've never seen him fight." Calisto shrugged. "But I don't need to. The man has more trinkets and artifacts than people have rice in their lunch bowl. His eldrin—that damn gold kirin—empowers creatures bonded to him, and last I heard, he went straight to the abyssal kraken's lair in order to get his *own* god-creature. It was supposed to be his second, but *the Warlord* beat him to the real prize."

I held my breath, my gut twisting into knots.

That must've been the light I had seen in the sky. The one out in the ocean. *The abyssal kraken.* According to legend, it dwelled in the abyssal hells. Had the Autarch gone to the depths and back? Beyond the first, second, and third abyss? It seemed... impossible.

I closed my eyes, my thoughts buzzing. The god-creatures spawned in a specific order, but apparently, they had started appearing at the height of the arcane plague, which meant several already had lairs around the world.

Which number was the abyssal kraken?

The first was the world serpent.

The second was the soul forge.

The third was the fenris wolf.

The fourth was the sky titan.

The fifth was the garuda bird.

And the sixth... was the abyssal kraken.

That meant *six* of the twelve god-creatures had already spawned. And the Autarch had bonded with the kraken? We had to make sure the others didn't fall to the Second Ascension.

"We don't know if the abyssal kraken bonded with the Autarch," Zelfree said to the group. He motioned everyone over to Terrakona. "And it's best not to dwell on it. We should head out—we can practice more magic later."

The news of the Autarch had obviously unsettled everyone. They worked slower this time, putting everything away with little enthusiasm. I didn't blame them.

Someday we would face off against the Autarch.

It was inevitable.

## CHAPTER 30

## ZELFREE'S DETOUR

Terrakona took us across land much faster than any horse.

We headed in the direction of the Rocky Wastes, making great time. I sat in Terrakona's mane again, allowing the wind to style my hair. We quickly left the trees behind and found ourselves crossing rolling hills of grass and sand. Vjorn raced alongside Terrakona as much as he could, but occasionally, he slowed a bit. He was still young, after all.

At one point, Vjorn's ears perked, and he leapt at a wild sheep that had wandered far from its herd. Hexa pointed and laughed, one of the few times she did so on the entire trek. I chuckled as well. It had been amusing to see a legendary god-creature act like a puppy and pounce on an unsuspecting sheep. And the sheep's reaction upon seeing the massive predator bearing down on it... The poor little guy had evacuated his bowels at record-breaking speed.

Then I remembered Terrakona's speech to me—how the god-creatures didn't need to eat, because ambient magic sustained them. They *could* eat, but it wasn't required. Which was good, because their massive forms would require hundreds of sheep a day to maintain if they were normal animals.

A flock of birds followed us at a distance.

The Mother of Shapeshifters.

I tried not to look at her. If I stared too long, even at the birds, I remembered my brother's transformation, and then my stomach flipped. That had been an event that would haunt my dreams for weeks to come.

Red rocks appeared amid the grass. A few at first, then by the dozens. As the sun began to set, we reached the edge of an unusual desert—the sand was as scarlet as rubies. The twisting of the dunes created blazing crimson swirls as far as the eye could see.

Speckles of white poked through the scarlet sands. They were bones.

Black trees, devoid of leaves, dotted the landscape. They were dead.

I had seen the Amber Dunes, and that desert had been one of unforgiving heat, but this one... This desert felt different. This was a desolate wasteland. There were no lizards or cacti, and the winds kept the area chill.

I didn't like it.

Terrakona stopped at the edge of the red sands and then hissed. His voice was loud enough to disturb the nearby dunes.

"Terrakona?" I asked as I patted his head. "Is everything okay?"

**"Corruption is here,"** Terrakona telepathically said. **"Something taints the land."**

"Do we need to be worried? Is something here?"

**"Listen to the magic. The arcane plague dwells here."**

I caught my breath and waited. The winds brought ice and a foul scent. Although I wasn't *certain* it was the plague, I felt a terrible sting in the air.

"This is the Rocky Wastes," I muttered.

**"A horrible place."**

Zelfree slid off the back of the world serpent, careful to bring Calisto with him, and then motioned for the others to follow suit. Karna leapt off, elegant and graceful. When Ryker almost slipped, she half-caught him and steadied him on his feet.

Traces remained on the world serpent. She curled into a little ball and yawned. Then she turned back and licked at her shorter tail.

Vjorn and Zaxis arrived a few seconds later. Just like Terrakona, Vjorn stopped at the edge of the sand and lifted his massive head. The chains around his body clinked as he shifted his weight between his four paws.

**"The corruption is here,"** the fenris wolf growled.

Zaxis leapt off his eldrin and landed hard. Then he strode over to Zelfree and exchanged a few words. It was only after their conversation that Zelfree left Calisto.

Once ready, Zelfree climbed back on top of Terrakona and then pointed into the Rocky Wastes. Although Terrakona was hesitant, he moved forward as soon as I urged him. The red sand moved aside as the world serpent advanced, just like any other terrain.

The bones and dead trees littered throughout the sands gave me pause. I kept my attention on our surroundings, concerned about the plague. It couldn't affect me or Terrakona, but what about Zelfree? Traces couldn't transform into a world serpent. And if there were no other mystical creatures nearby, she couldn't transform into anything. They'd be vulnerable in an attack.

As Terrakona slipped through the sands, I turned around. "What're we looking for?"

"There's a collection of black boulders out in the sands," Zelfree said, pointing. "Berry bushes grow on top of the rocks. *That's* what we're looking for."

"All right."

Sand made it difficult to feel vibrations. The shifting of the desert was a hum in my mind, disturbing my ability to "feel" everything around us. Terrakona glanced from side to side occasionally, especially when there was a slight pulse of movement below the surface of the desert.

**"There are creatures nearby,"** he telepathically said.

I gritted my teeth, confused by their presence.

Zelfree clung to Terrakona's back, his attention on the horizon. He called up to me, "There are *falak* and *ghouls* nearby. At least three of each." His mimic magic allowed him to sense nearby mystical creatures.

But falak and ghouls?

Well, the falak made sense. They were giant desert snakes—gold in color, and with double tails. Their mouths could open wide enough to swallow someone whole. From what I had read, they hid underground, waiting for a chance to strike from the sand.

But the presence of *ghouls* didn't make much sense to me.

Very little was known about how they came into existence, but I had never read about ghouls being in the desert before. From what I understood, they dwelled in dark forests, far from sight, and often near small villages with large graveyards.

There weren't any forests for miles, and no towns or villages were located in the Rocky Wastes.

A loud scream dragged me back to the present. Terrakona stopped and flared his scales. I stood and held Retribution close. But I didn't see anyone. The second scream—just as loud and prominent as the one before—traveled over the desert, carried by the winds.

"What is that?" I asked aloud.

Zelfree pointed to a few rocks that were circular in shape with a hole in the middle. "The Shrieking Peaks," he said. Then he pointed to a few mountains in the distance, each one made out of the circular rocks. "Whenever wind goes through the hole in the rocks, it creates that screeching noise."

Terrakona and I waited.

Sure enough, the moment the wind went through the rocks, another scream sounded across the desert. It was an unnerving sound—like a young woman caught in terror—and I didn't care for the rocks at all. Why were they here?

**"What a disturbing noise,"** Terrakona said. **"When you become more powerful, I vote you come here and rearrange these peaks, Warlord."**

I patted Terrakona. "Yeah. After this is all over... That's what we're going to do."

Terrakona resumed our journey, even as the distant peaks screamed and wailed. Part of me wondered if someone was out in the desert, actually crying out. No one would ever know. Everyone would just assume it was the Shrieking Peaks. What a sad way to die.

Just as the sun started to disappear in the distance, filling the sky with as much red as the desert sand, I spotted the black rocks. Plants grew atop them, and for a brief moment, I thought I recognized what they were.

Charberries.

A charberry tree grew on the Isle of Ruma, atop the Pillar, which was a stone in the middle of the island. Phoenixes loved charberries. But these were bushes? Clearly, they weren't charberries, even if they grew atop rocks, just like the charberry tree.

"What are those?" I asked, calling down to Zelfree.

"They're sinberries." Zelfree sat straighter, and Traces leapt to his shoulder. "Head straight over to the rocks. We don't want to step on the sand. We'll climb off and gather as many berries as we can."

Terrakona snorted as he headed straight for the rocks and

bushes. I held on to his crystal mane, my brow furrowed. I had never heard of *sinberries.* Did they only grow in the Rocky Wastes? And only on these rocks? Or could they be found in other areas?

It didn't take us long to reach the rocks. When we drew near, I realized the "rocks" were more like boulders. They were the size of a two-story house, and wide enough for a full barn to rest on top of them. The sun was still setting as I leapt off Terrakona and landed on the nearest black boulder.

Then I almost slipped. The rock wasn't rough or coarse—it was as smooth as glass. And the bushes growing on top just had their roots wrapped around the sides, holding them in place. What were the roots even feasting on? What sustained these sinberry bushes?

Zelfree and Traces also leapt onto the nearest boulder, but only after Terrakona lifted his midsection so they could reach.

"Don't touch the berries with your bare hands," Zelfree said as he approached one of the massive bushes. "These berries are born of corrupted magic."

I frowned and glanced around, searching for a source of the corruption. But I didn't see anything. "What happened to the wastes?" I asked. "Why are they like this?"

Zelfree stared at the bushes for a moment. Then he replied with, "I've heard several legends, but they're just tales. Corrupted star shards fell here. A battle between Death Lords took place here. The king of these lands killed himself and placed a curse on the very soil. Take your pick—whichever sounds the spookiest."

I chuckled as I turned to him. "The spookiest, huh?"

"This place isn't to be taken lightly. Everything is out to mess with you."

I nodded once, taking his warning to heart. Then I stared at the boulder beneath my feet, the dull glitter of magic more sickly than stunning.

The nearby bushes were over seven feet tall. Hundreds of

berries grew on the branches in clusters. They reminded me of raspberries—they were small, had the shape of mini-grapes, and each one looked fuzzy.

They were an odd mix of dark red and purple, similar to bruised flesh. They also smelled of oil—a disgusting combination.

I tucked my hands into my sleeves before I reached for one. "Why are we collecting corrupted magic?"

Zelfree pulled off his coat and used it like a basket. He gathered dozens of berries at a quick rate, his sleeves dotted with red and purple juice. "Sinberries taste disgusting, smell terrible, and are difficult to swallow."

"Yum," I sarcastically said. "I can't wait to dig in."

"Don't be a fool." Zelfree shot me a glare. "If you eat these, you'll lose your memories."

I froze mid-pick. With a single berry held in my sleeve, I turned to him. "*What?*"

"The memory loss is only temporary," Zelfree said with a sigh as he threw a dozen more berries onto his coat. "Once they've gone through your body, your memories come right back. But it's still disorientating."

"Why are we gathering these?"

"I got the idea while we were in Thronehold." Zelfree plucked a few more berries, but his rate had slowed. "All the mystical creatures who were resurrected don't remember anything. Their mannerisms and behavior reminded me of the sinberries. I had seen them for sale in port once. I used them on someone—it doesn't matter who—but long story short, it wasn't a useful tactic for gathering information. After that, I never really thought of them ever again. Until now."

I stopped and faced him. "That doesn't explain why we're gathering them."

Zelfree also stopped, his eyes narrowed. "They're for Lynus."

The moment he said that, everything made sense.

Zelfree wanted to *erase* Calisto by taking away Lynus's memories. If Lynus never remembered he was a dread pirate, would that really allow him to escape the horrors of that past? I had never thought about it.

"So, what?" I asked. "You're just going to make Calisto eat sinberries for the rest of his life?" I glanced around, the red desert all around us. "How often can we come out here? How long will the berries last after we pick them?"

Zelfree chuckled as he grabbed a few more berries. "Get serious. I'm not about to feed these berries to him every day. I'm..." He stopped and stared at a single berry, glaring at it like it was the source of all his problems. "I'm going to make something permanent."

"How?"

"I don't know yet. The Second Ascension made their decay dust, didn't they? That dust is used up in order to get a permanent effect. What if... I made something with the sinberries? Something that would *permanently* steal someone's memories?"

This seemed like an extreme solution to Calisto's problem. Would it even work? And what would happen afterward? Would Calisto be free of any consequences because he couldn't remember any of his crimes? Was that even fair?

I didn't know.

I had told Zelfree he could do what he wanted, but I had never imagined *this* would be the path we took.

"What if this doesn't work?" I asked.

"Then I'll think of something else," Zelfree muttered as he gathered a couple more berries. "I always do."

"Do you think this is right?"

Zelfree offered me a sideways glance. "I'm not really a guy who follows all the rules."

I rubbed at the back of my neck. "Is that something you should be teaching one of your apprentices?"

"You're not my apprentice anymore." Zelfree finished up his picking and then scooped up his coat. "I'd say you were my equal, but that's not really true, is it?" He stood straight and lifted an eyebrow. "Are you saying I shouldn't do this? If the Warlord tells me I can't, then I won't."

I held my breath for a moment. Then I shook my head. "No. I wasn't saying that. I just... I wonder if this is right."

"I want to help him, but I don't have many options. He's... He's not making things easy."

While I hated Calisto, I understood Zelfree's frustration. Zelfree didn't have any options outside of death. And losing one's memories was *similar* to death, wasn't it? It seemed like a philosophical question I didn't have the appropriate answer to.

In truth, some of my apprehension came from the fact that I had seen the mystical creatures in Thronehold. They had been missing their memories. They had wandered the ruined roads, confused and alone.

"Terrakona," I whispered. "You don't think that can work on me, right?"

**"I would assume you are immune to corruption."**

But he didn't say for sure.

Another scream filled the air, followed by manic laughter.

The shrieks no longer bothered me, but the mirth sent chills down my spine.

A plague-ridden creature was nearby.

# CHAPTER 31

## ARRIVAL AT REGAL HEIGHTS

I pulled Retribution from its sheath and held Forfend on my arm. With my sword and shield at the ready, I tensed and glanced around. The glass-smooth rocks were a problem, and with my manipulation, I changed the slick surface into something that would give me a bit of traction. Small bumps appeared along the surface of the rocks, allowing my boots to catch.

"Smart move," Zelfree murmured as he glanced around.

The blank star on his forehead shifted and changed. A ghoul appeared in his mark—it was an undead person with skin hanging off their body in odd ways. Traces shifted and transformed, morphing into a disgusting ghoul at the same time as Zelfree's mark changed. She smelled of rot, and her skeletal face lacked the muscle and flesh to close her jaw.

Then Zelfree shrouded himself with invisibility, disappearing from my sight, but not my tremor sense.

Ghouls were sneaky creatures. They shambled and moved slowly, but they had deadly claws, and the ability to remain hidden. I never much cared for them, but I was glad Zelfree had an option for combat.

More laughter—this time, closer than before.

That was when the falak finally showed itself. A golden snake burst out of the red dune, its scales shimmering in the dying sunlight. Normally, falak were quite beautiful. There were several legends of rulers who had harvested their golden scales to make into ceremonial armor.

But not this one.

Ants and beetles swarmed out of the falak's scales, spilling out of it like blood weeping from an injury. The thousands of insects scurried across the surface of the giant snake, its golden scales marred with bloodstains.

The beast's eyes hung out of its skull on thin strips of flesh. They dangled around, smacking against the side of the monster's head whenever it moved. The falak didn't seem to care. It laughed constantly, like it couldn't even pause to take a deep breath.

The insects even spilled out of its mouth.

Was the snake filled with bugs? It seemed like it.

The monster rushed us, larger than I had thought it would be. It wasn't as big as Terrakona, but it could easily smash our two-story boulder. Instead of letting it get close, I manipulated the sands and tried to trap the creature.

I managed to change *some* of the ground, but not fast enough. It evaded my manipulation and slammed into the side of the black boulder.

Terrakona moved at frightening speeds. He whipped around the rock and bit down on the falak, crushing part of its body. Insects exploded outward, some with wings. They buzzed around the area, filling the sky with a harsh hiss.

I evoked magma from the creases of my palms and threw it through the air. It burned up a chunk of the bugs and then struck the laughing falak. The molten rock melted the creature's scales and went straight into its body.

"*Such beautiful burning*," the falak said, chuckling. "Soon,

I'll be *one* with... your magic... *and I'll be all powerful!*" The lunacy in his words bothered me, but I had fought too many plague-ridden creatures to be unnerved.

I closed my eyes and focused.

When I had been in Thronehold, I had changed the whole city. I needed to do that now.

With my attention on the combat, I sensed so much more. Terrakona's breathing. Zelfree's movements. Traces's attempt to use her ghoul-claws on the snake whenever it got close enough.

With a few small movements of my hands, I hardened the red sand into crimson stone. Then I twisted the stone, crushing it around the body of the falak. At first, I couldn't. The creature was too large, and its fortitude was too great. But each time it exhaled, I managed to crush it with the rocks a little more, like a python slowly squeezing its prey.

Terrakona bit the falak over and over, and the beast gasped out.

Was it immune to venom? It had to be.

But it wasn't immune to being filled with holes. Terrakona's fangs ripped through the creature, and when the falak went to bite back, his fangs weren't up to the challenge of the world serpent's scales.

The moment I finished crushing the snake, I opened my eyes. Curse the abyssal hells. I took in the brutality, and shock rendered me still.

Half the creature was squished between the red rocks I had created, and the other half was on the desert sand, writhing around, surrounded by flies, beetles, and ants. If I had started the fight this way, it would've been over much sooner.

Despite being crushed in half, the beast still laughed.

"You're nothing," the falak hissed. "*Your magic will...* eventually fail... and you, too, will become maggots..."

After its last words, the monster exhaled, and finally died. Goosebumps ran across my skin. The longer it took to solve the problem of the plague, the more innocent creatures and arcanists would needlessly die.

I had to get stronger.

Zelfree allowed his invisibility to fall away. He hadn't even left the boulder. "That was easier than I thought it'd be," he quipped.

With a smirk, I replied, "Next time, I'll give you a chance to fight before I handle everything."

"Don't worry, kid. My ego isn't wrapped up in being *the best at stabbing things.*" He glanced around as night finally fell over us. "Now stop patting yourself on the back and look over there. You see the ghouls?"

I followed his finger as he pointed to an area in the middle of the Rocky Wastes.

A trio of ghouls stood in the dunes, all three of them watching us with skull faces. They didn't move toward us, or even call out and wave. And the moment they realized we were staring, the three of them disappeared with their invisibility.

Had they been watching us?

"Why are there ghouls out here?"

Zelfree shrugged. "I don't know. But it gets me worried."

"Why?"

"Who infected the falak with the plague?"

I stared at the spot where the creatures had disappeared. "You think the ghouls did?"

"Someone did. That falak was fully grown, which means it was likely brought here, or its arcanist was killed nearby. It's like someone wanted to infect this area. And since no one lives here, no one would find out, if you catch my drift."

I slowly nodded with his words, wondering if the ghouls belonged to the Second Ascension.

"We should find out," I said.

Zelfree half smiled. "Can you find them out in the sands?"

"It's harder to sense them. But they're small and shambling.

They won't be able to evade us long." I motioned for Terrakona, and he moved his head close to the boulder and allowed me to get on. "We'll be right back."

Zelfree nodded once. "We only need one."

With speed and purpose, Terrakona rushed out into the desert. I held on to his crystal mane, my thoughts calm, but my blood icy. I had little mercy for anyone in the Second Ascension. They all needed to die.

**"Ghouls are not creatures of the desert. They leave blatant tracks."**

Sure enough, when I turned my attention to the dunes, I found deep footprints, some of which were lines, like the creature had to drag its leg across the sand. That made everything easier. Terrakona followed the short trail straight to our three ghouls. Their invisibility had ended—ghouls couldn't really move and maintain the magic—and that was unfortunate for them.

"Zelfree said we only need one," I whispered.

Terrakona roared and then crunched two of the ghouls with his fangs, ending them instantly. They were much too small, and too weak, to resist even a young world serpent.

These ghouls... They weren't powerful or old. It was difficult to tell the age of undead mystical creatures, since many had the appearance of corpses, but it was clear by the way the last ghoul shuddered and fell over in fright that it wasn't an adult of its kind.

Terrakona slithered around the remaining ghoul, circling until the undead beast was trapped. The ghoul couldn't bury itself in the sand or fly off. There was nowhere to run. Despite that, the creature hissed and swung its claws. It couldn't hurt Terrakona, though.

"If you want to live, you'll tell us who sent you here," I said.

The ghoul swung its claws again.

I patted Terrakona on the side of the head. We didn't need to speak. Terrakona understood what to do. Trees and vines sprouted from his scales, and they lashed out at the ghoul, wrapping his fleshy body in restraints.

Ghouls were always disgusting. A ghoul was a human skeleton with half its muscles and skin, and three times the amount of rot. Its fingers were practically bone claws, and normally, they'd be dangerous, but there was nothing the creature could do to us.

"I'm going to give you one last chance," I said.

The ghoul slowly stopped struggling. It went limp in Terrakona's vines, hanging like a lifeless mannequin. "You will regret killing my brothers," the ghoul whispered. "The Keeper of Corpses is far more powerful than you realize."

The Keeper of Corpses?

My eyebrows knitted together as I asked, "Who's that?"

But the ghoul didn't answer.

Terrakona shook the ghoul using his vines. The skeletal creature clacked together, rattled to its core. Then it said, "Kill me if you must. I will never betray my father."

For a long moment, I dwelled on the statement. I wasn't sure what it meant. I had never heard of *the Keeper of Corpses* before. Was it a person? Or a mystical creature?

"Tell me one thing," I said. "Do you work for the Second Ascension?"

The ghoul flopped its fleshy head from one side to the other. "My father serves... the sky titan."

The sky titan... A god-arcanist. Was it the Autarch? Or someone else? I held my breath, my chest tight. Would I have to face off against another god-arcanist so soon? It was probably better this way. The longer we waited, the more powerful they would become.

I placed a hand on Terrakona's head. "Let the ghoul go."

**"It will report to the sky titan arcanist. The Second Ascension will know we're here. I should destroy it."**

I thought over the options, and then I shook my head. "I want them to know I'm here."

**"Warlord?"**

"We need to find them as soon as possible. If they reveal themselves to us, it'll be easier to end this whole war."

**"It's risky to call the attention of your enemies."**

He was right, but I was tired of hiding. If I wanted to find Vethica—and Luthair—and face off against the Autarch, I couldn't be the one hiding.

"We'll focus on mastering some of our magic," I whispered as Terrakona released the ghoul. "Even if I just master one trick or ability, I'll have an advantage."

**"As you wish."**

The ghoul hurried into the red desert, across the Rocky Wastes. I watched it go, hoping the sky titan arcanist would come to find me. I'd let them meet their end.

---

We returned to the others with hundreds of sinberries.

Zelfree kept them wrapped in his coat, away from the others. When Karna and Ryker inquired about the stop, Zelfree said he had just needed to collect materials for an imbuing project. He didn't explain anything further, and no one pushed the issue.

We didn't travel for long before Terrakona found us a quiet meadow near a single tree. We prepared food, but everyone ate very little. To my surprise, Calisto ate some bread and water—more than he had in a few days. He didn't speak much, though. For that, I was grateful.

Then we set up camp, and once again took turns standing watch.

The evening flew by so quickly, it felt like the dawn came within a few minutes.

I sat atop Terrakona, and he slept while I watched Ryker and

MOS practice their bizarre transformation. And I wasn't the only one. Hexa, Raisen, and Karna watched from afar, occasionally offering encouragement.

I suspected that Zaxis preferred that. He trained on the other side of the camp, waving his arms in an attempt to learn his evocation. Every time he couldn't manifest ice, he grew frustrated. By the time he waved his arm the tenth time, he swung it with the intensity of battle. He practically punched the air, like he wanted to punish it.

When I had struggled, Terrakona had encouraged me, but Vjorn didn't move from his place in the shade. His massive wolf form was positioned between Zaxis and the others, blocking most of their view. It was probably intentional.

Zaxis swung out his arm an eleventh time.

Some frost burst across the ground.

Zaxis's first steps of evocation were already more powerful than Fain's icy evocation. Fain's hoarfrost required time to build up, and it was a thin sheet of snow that eventually coated everything. Zaxis's burst of frost was enough to kill the grass and freeze the dirt. It was a large arc of winter, blasting outward for a full twenty feet in front of him.

Seemingly fueled by confidence, Zaxis chuckled. He waved his arm out a twelfth time, and *more* frost rushed over the meadow, killing more vegetation and creating a smooth icy surface.

I watched with fascination, wondering if he would develop his magic faster than I had. I doubted it—but I still wondered. Zaxis seemed motivated by revenge. The plague had forced him to lose his eldrin. Luthair had sacrificed himself for me, and that display of love and honor had left me feeling worried.

What if I couldn't save the people I loved?

In the end, Luthair's gift had inspired me to give all of myself to protect the ones I loved.

But Zaxis seemed determined to bring icy justice to everyone who had created and spread the arcane plague. Was that helping him learn faster? I feared it would eventually hinder his progress.

Zaxis exhaled, and his breath appeared as a misty fog. Then he stepped forward and evoked more ice, but this time more controlled. A small burst of frost.

Then he removed his boots and stepped out onto the frozen ground. He didn't slip or slide. He strode out onto the ice, and evoked the winter winds again and again, smaller each time, more precise. The more he practiced, the more he seemed absorbed in his thoughts.

He never spoke to Vjorn.

He never called out to show everyone else how much progress he had made.

Zaxis just worked on his magic. Another burst of ice. And then another.

Finally, he stopped. He stepped away from the ice on the ground and stared at everything, like an artist admiring their own work.

I caught my breath, my chest tight.

Zaxis had created a picture with his frost on the ground—he had created a massive image of a bird, its wings spread wide. When the morning sun caught the edges of the icy crystals, the bird sparkled.

It was quite beautiful.

---

The third day's travel was faster than the last two. The landscape was flat, and Terrakona sped across the ground at surprising speeds. Vjorn ran alongside us, with Zaxis clinging to the scruff of his black fur. Zaxis smiled as they ran, the wind whipping through his red hair. He looked like an ember on the back of the fenris wolf.

Near the end of the day, we found the beginning of Hydra's

Gorge. It was a crack in the ground that went for two hundred miles. At some points, it was multiple miles deep. Was this the place where the first world serpent arcanist had fought the Monster?

The moment I laid eyes on the gorge, I knew it was true.

It was a scar on the land made of gold, red, and black rocks. The striped coloration of the canyon gave it a unique, almost sickly appearance. The gorge was wider and narrower at certain places—in the distance, it seemed like the gorge was fifteen miles wide, and at other places, just half a mile.

The most interesting feature was Regal Heights.

The city was built in and around Hydra's Gorge. Bridges went from one side to the other, and buildings were carved straight into the striped stone, on the side of the canyon wall. To my surprise, most of the bridges and walkways were made of metal, covered in furs. They were linked together in an odd design that allowed them to sway and move, but not fall apart.

Why not use wood? Or rope?

Why cover them in fur?

My sense of adventure went up with my excitement to see Hexa's hometown.

"There it is!" she yelled from Terrakona's back. "Regal Heights! I can't believe it! We got here so fast!"

Everyone craned their heads to get a better look. Terrakona and I had the best view. The sunset set the whole gorge ablaze with color. The striped rocks looked like tigers hidden in the canyon, and we headed straight for the main walkways of the city without any obstacles in our path.

# CHAPTER 32

# HEXA'S TRIBE

The gold, red, and black cliffs of the gorge were magnificent.

Windows, doors, and walkways were built into the stone—houses defying gravity. If someone fell off a balcony or bridge, they would surely plummet to their death. Railings and fences lined everything, however. Wrought-iron was used everywhere, from the handrails to the support for the windows —even a few fountains were lined with metal.

The buildings on the very top of Hydra's Gorge were like mini fortresses. The stone bricks were massive, and impressively sturdy. Large awnings were built over the canyon, creating artificial shade for everyone dwelling down below.

And there were caves!

So many caves. People walked in and out of them by the dozens, and I suspected there was a whole underground pathway I couldn't yet see or feel with my tremor sense.

Hexa clung to Terrakona, smiling so wide, I was sure the people on the Isle of Ruma could see it.

"It's been so long," she said. "I had almost forgotten how beautiful it is."

Zelfree let out a long exhale. "The people here are... pushy."

"I've met a few hydra arcanists from here," Karna muttered as she brushed her blonde hair with her fingers. "Most of them were pigs, but a few weren't so bad. They always paid well."

Hexa shot her a quick glare. "Well, you'll both see. Regal Heights is amazing."

All six of Raisen's heads roared, but it was short. He struggled to maintain his balance on Terrakona and kept his heads down, practically wrapping around Terrakona's body. "I can't wait," the king head said. "I can barely remember the place of my birth."

"You'll love it." Hexa ran her hand over her hydra's many heads. "And there are so many hydras here—I can't wait for you to meet some of the older ones."

Calisto said nothing amid the excitement. Unlike earlier, when he had seemed more his normal self, he had returned to a state of cold regret. I wondered if Zelfree had told him his plan or not.

Terrakona stopped near the outskirts of the city. A small wall had been built out of the gold, red, and black rocks, but it was only five feet tall. Terrakona could've easily slithered over the barrier, but he politely lowered his head near the gate so I could step off.

The people of Regal Heights watched us dismount Terrakona with wide eyes and murmured words. The second thing I noticed was their outfits. They were... minimal.

Everyone wore sandals, some with spines on the soles, no doubt to help them keep their balance or to grip otherwise smooth stone. And their fabric was thin, but it was at least brightly colored. Red, orange, and yellow had been spun into the cloth, giving everyone a fiery appearance. Sleeves weren't popular, apparently. Everyone's arms were exposed.

So were their backs, and most of their legs, and sometimes their stomachs.

It seemed most people opted for less covering, and more metal accessories than other places I had visited in the past. The women wore several necklaces, and the men had piercings in their ears.

The gold, silver, and copper glittered in the light, catching my eye anytime I turned and glanced around.

But while the citizens wore reds and yellows, the guards wore deep blues and purples. They were the only ones with their shoulders covered, and that was with leather armor. They held rifles, but also crossbows and daggers.

A hydra with ten heads was stitched into the purple of their overshirts.

One guard hesitantly stepped forward, his rifle held close. He stared up at Terrakona, his mouth half open in awe. He had been tanned by the sun, and his cinnamon hair reminded me so much of Hexa, I thought they might be related.

"W-Welcome to Regal Heights," the man said.

Even *he* wore sandals.

Compared to the people of Regal Heights, I looked like I was prepared for winter.

"I'm Warlord Volke Savan, the World Serpent Arcanist." I was about to add the reason for our trip, but the guard grew visibly flustered and shifted his weight around.

"We've heard of the god-arcanists," he quickly said, almost stumbling over his words in his haste. "What an honor to have you visit Regal Heights. Your eldrin is so... so big!"

Terrakona tilted his head slightly, his two-colored eyes locked on the guard.

The man avoided staring at Terrakona's gaze directly. He continued with, "You must meet with the minister. And the city founder. And our guard captain. They will all want to compare the size of their eldrin to yours." The man wagged a finger at the world serpent. "We never thought you would visit us. After word of what happened in Thronehold reached us, we figured it would be *years* before any god-arcanist came this way."

The man just kept going.

Even his speech patterns reminded me of Hexa. When she got excited, there was no stopping her.

Fortunately, both Zaxis and Hexa walked over, cutting the man off mid-speech.

To my surprise, Zaxis had removed his shirt completely. He wore trousers, his boots, and his guild pendant, and that was it. There was no reason for him to be embarrassed—not only was he muscled, but the random Regal Heights citizens around us didn't wear much clothing—but it still seemed weird for him to throw off his shirt.

I almost wanted to do the same thing, just to make sure everyone knew I was a god-arcanist as well. But I reined in my annoyance and instead unbuttoned most of my shirt to show off my god-arcanist mark. That would do.

"Here is it," Hexa declared. "The most beautiful place ever."

The guard snapped his ankles together and then bowed. "Hexa d'Tenni! It's a pleasure to see you return home."

"You don't have to be so formal." Hexa waved away his comment. "It's just me."

Another man walked out of the city gates, his clothing just as blue and purple as the guards'. Unlike the others, though, he proudly displayed an arcanist mark on his forehead. It was a seven-pointed star with an eight-headed hydra wrapped around the design.

The man had scars down his chest, and along his right shoulder, much like Hexa had on her arms. He didn't wear as much armor, and I suspected that was to make sure his hydra scars were clearly displayed.

"If it isn't Hexa," the man said. He was a lean fellow, with long arms and legs, and plenty of wiry muscle. "I thought we'd never see you again. Aren't you off gallivanting around the ocean, trying to get yourself killed by pirates or drowned in a deadly storm?" When he smiled, it seemed genuine and welcoming. I already liked the man.

Hexa fluffed her mane-like hair. "Is that you, Garrett? Still jealous?" She turned to me and half-shrugged. "This is Garrett Akiona. He got his hydra a few years before me, and he's been insufferable ever since."

The man, Garrett, just laughed. His hair had been cut short and trim—it reminded me of the style preferred by most warriors. "You look like an islander. I almost didn't recognize you."

I had always wondered what had driven Hexa from her homeland. She had never told me why, exactly, she had joined the Frith Guild. Illia would probably know, but I had never gotten the full story. Part of me wondered if she had grown tired of the sandals and revealing clothing.

Raisen stomped over, his tail swishing back and forth, kicking up dirt. When he noticed Garrett, his many eyes went wide, and then he hurried his pace. Like a giant dog, Raisen rushed the man and nearly toppled him over.

"Okay, okay," Garrett muttered as he shoved the hydra away. "You've clearly never learned any manners. I'm your superior, ya know. You have to respect me. That's the rules."

Hexa scoffed and rolled her eyes, but she smiled the entire time.

When Garrett turned to me, all mirth stopped, however. He straightened himself and offered a deep and formal bow. "God-arcanists. I apologize—we had no idea you were coming, or else we would've set up a celebration. Since we can't do that, allow us to offer hospitality. I was sent by my father to escort you to our city hall. If you'll come with me, I'll make sure you don't get lost."

Zaxis folded his arms over his chest. "What about our eldrin?"

Everyone glanced over at Terrakona and Vjorn.

While Regal Heights seemed sturdy and well-built, it definitely wasn't *huge*. Terrakona's weight alone would snap most of the bridges.

"Terrakona will wait here," I said.

Zaxis huffed and then stared at his fenris wolf. The mighty beast snorted and then sat down, his eyes piercing and filled with irritation. The guards must've sensed it as well, because they all took several steps back.

"Vjorn will also wait here, but he doesn't like it," Zaxis muttered. Then he shot Garrett a glare. "Sowe should make this quick."

"Can I get the pleasure of your name first, god-arcanist?" Garrett asked, bowing his head.

"I'm *the Hunter,* Zaxis Ren, the Fenris Wolf Arcanist."

"Yes. Of course. It's a pleasure. Please, this way."

Ryker, Karna, Zelfree, Raisen, and Calisto waited back with the god-creatures, none of them stepping forward to meet the city's minister. Hexa, on the other hand, took a place by my side and walked with us into the city. Garrett gave her an odd glance, but when Zaxis and I didn't protest, he must've decided to let the whole thing go.

The four of us walked into Regal Heights through the gate in their small stone wall.

The pathways immediately went straight to the cliffside. The buildings and houses were constructed right on the edge. The surrounding plains were used for farming and ranching. Goats wandered the vast rolling hills, gobbling up the grass with a mighty appetite. Corn grew in tall stalks in the north fields, while squash sprouted from the vine in the fields across the gorge.

Actually...

The gorge seemed to divide a great many things.

On one side, the fortress houses were tall and sturdy, each

with large crossbows mounted on the roofs. Some of the were so large, I thought they were meant for a siege. On the other side of the gorge, the houses were built longer and wider, with more fountains, wrought-iron decorations, and stained glass. It was the prettier side of Hydra's Gorge, while still remaining fortified and secure.

Garrett guided us down a long walkway, announcing our presence.

"Make way! The god-arcanists have arrived. Make way for Volke Savan, the World Serpent Arcanist!"

Zaxis clicked his tongue in disappointment, but he never said anything. While word of *my* accomplishments had spread across the land, to many nations, I was certain no one even knew the fenris wolf arcanist even existed.

It wouldn't be long before they knew, though.

To my surprise, the denizens of Regal Heights cheered our presence. Some men threw strips of colored cloth, and some women bowed low and deep. The walkways were large enough for five people to stand shoulder to shoulder, but that wasn't wide enough for huge crowds. Everyone gathered near the edges or piled into nearby houses and leaned out the windows, all to get a better look at us.

"Thank you, Warlord," someone shouted from a window.

Another person added, "He's so young! I never knew."

"Praise the world serpent arcanist!"

Zaxis rubbed at his upper arm, his jaw clenched. Several individuals pointed to the mark on his chest, and then pointed to mine, obviously comparing. They understood, even if they didn't know what to call Zaxis just yet.

Garrett stopped when he reached one of the long metal bridges covered in fur. He turned around and motioned the citizens to back away. Most of them listened, but a pair of young women lingered close, both whispering and giggling to themselves. Their smiles and stares caused my face to grow red and hot.

Unlike the guards, and the nearby residents, the two girls wore clothing of white and silver. Well, there wasn't much clothing. No sleeves. No trousers. Just flowing long skirts—open on the sides, showing their legs—and shirts that exposed their stomachs. They had no scars, but black tattoos had been inked onto their shoulders and biceps. The markings reminded me of reptile scales.

Their reddish-brown hair—a darker shade of cinnamon, really—was so curly that it bounced with their movements.

Garrett motioned to the bridge, but before he could guide us across, the two women stepped forward.

"You're so handsome," the first woman said to Zaxis, her cheeks pink.

The second girl smacked the other's arm and laughed with enough nervous energy that I was almost nervous along with her. "*I'm so sorry.* My sister is so *brazen* sometimes. I'm Randi, and this is my sister, Feyla."

Zaxis—unfazed by the compliment—merely crossed his arms over his bare chest and lifted an eyebrow. "I only have eyes for one woman."

His forceful statement had Feyla practically swooning. Her face lit up pink, and she placed a hand over her mouth as she cooed.

"What a man," Feyla whispered to her sister, but it was quite easy to hear.

Hexa, who stood a bit behind us, rolled her eyes. "Never mind them."

Garrett stomped over. He pushed the two women off to the side and pointed to one of the buildings on the side of the cliff. "Don't you two have work to do?" Then, in a low and harsh voice, he said, "*You're making a mockery of all of Regal Heights.*"

Randi, her face much redder than her sister's, sighed. "We

came over to tell the god-arcanists that we're the caretakers of hydras. We wanted to speak to their eldrin." She bowed deeply as she faced me. "Please, world serpent arcanist, forgive my sister's *rude* behavior. We meant no disrespect."

Before I could answer, Zaxis half-shrugged. "You can speak to our eldrin, but don't get too close. They're more powerful than any hydra you've met."

Feyla fanned herself. "Did you hear that?" she whispered. "So powerful."

Randi shielded her face, so embarrassed, she looked like she wanted to throw herself into the gorge. "Th-Thank you, god-arcanists. We'll be on our way."

I waved as they left, amused by their flustered mannerisms.

Hexa watched them go with narrowed eyes. "I can't believe they let those two become hydra keepers."

"Forgive them, Warlord," Garrett said to me. "It's not every day someone of your standing comes to Regal Heights. We rarely get any visitors, actually. Outside of merchants."

"Don't worry about it." I motioned to the bridge. "But I did have a quick question. Why all the furs? I don't understand."

Garrett smiled—it came easily to the man. He walked over and pointed at the metal chain link and plates that made up the flexible bridge. "When the sun beats down on the metal, it gets quite hot. The fur prevents some of that heat buildup. It also keeps the walkways from getting slick. You see, the furs are from the canyon rabbits, and they're slightly magical."

"Like star moths," I chimed in.

Garrett nodded once. "Yes. Well, the canyon rabbits have fur that's not only soft, but it shrugs off water and small bits of dirt, keeping itself clean, no matter the weather. It's the perfect material for our walkways. Not only will it clean itself, basically, but it'll provide a soft cushion for the walk. Metal is unforgiving."

I thought over his explanation and then glanced back at the

bridge. It was an interesting design. I loved it. But where were the canyon rabbits?

"Let's go," Zaxis snapped. "We have work to do."

Garrett jumped to the bridge and led us across. Zaxis and I went slow, and Hexa almost ran into us a couple times.

In the middle of the bridge, I glanced over the railing, wondering if I could see the bottom. I couldn't. A thick fog lingered at the bottom of Hydra's Gorge, and it was too far for me to sense anything with my magic.

"Where did the fog come from?" I asked. There wasn't much water nearby.

"Ghostwood grows down there." Garrett once again stopped and pointed. "An entire forest is at the bottom of the canyon. Fog gushes from the faces that appear in ghostwood bark."

"I know," I said. "I've seen it before."

Garrett perked up, smiling wider than before. "Have you? Then you know that the fog is permanent. We can't do much about it."

We walked the rest of the bridge and made it to the other side of the canyon without incident. I wasn't that afraid of heights, but I had worried something would happen. Could I manipulate the canyon walls in time to prevent a fall? I wondered...

We reached the other side, where a group of children and one schoolteacher waited to get a good look at us. The teacher wore clothing that was colored green.

Were the colors associated with professions? It seemed the majority of individuals wore yellow, orange, and red. Were they farmers and ranchers? And the blue and purples were guards... White for those who cared for the hydras...

"Hello, god-arcanist," the teacher said, her voice shaky. She was a little older than Randi and Feyla, but not by much. She had no arcanist mark, and when she bowed, it was deep enough that I thought her forehead would touch the rocks.

"Hello," I said. "It's a pleasure to be here."

Zaxis huffed.

One of the children—perhaps age six—stepped forward and pointed. "You're powerful?"

I wanted to reply, but Zaxis cut in with, "Of course we are."

"But where are your scars?"

Zaxis caught his breath. It seemed he might not have an answer, but then he smirked, his eyes growing hard and cold. "Sometimes they're on the inside, kid."

Once again, Garrett moved forward and scolded the teacher. Then he shooed the children away. "No more questions. *I'm trying to impress the god-arcanists.*" His loud whispering wasn't fooling anyone, and it almost made me chuckle.

The teacher took her class of students, no more than twelve, and guided them across the bridge. The sun was finally setting all the way, and evening settled over the cliffside city. Garrett hurried his steps after that, taking us to the "fancier" part of Regal Heights.

"Here we are," he said as he gestured to the next castle-like home. "City hall. My father is eagerly awaiting your arrival."

# CHAPTER 33

## POWERFUL ARCANISTS

City hall was taller than the other buildings and came complete with a horse-sized mirror housed in a central tower. There was no sunlight, but the reflection of the evening sky was enough to make it seem wondrous.

The rest of city hall was beautiful as well. Pictures of gargoyles, hydras, and falaks were etched into the bricks that made up the front of the building. Great care had gone into each placement. No mystical creature was ever next to the same one, and the level of detail in the carvings surprised me. The gargoyles were in different poses, and all the hydras had a different number of heads.

I wondered how long it had taken to etch the thousands of bricks required to make this place.

Hexa placed her fists on her hips and smiled. "Do you see this? Amazing."

Zaxis half-smiled. "I like it."

Garrett opened the large double doors for us to enter. "Normally, city hall isn't open to the public in the evening, but my father wants to see you both right away. Please forgive the lack of attendants." He shoved the doors into place so they wouldn't close right away. "Usually, there would be guards who held this for you."

I ignored his apologies and continued into the fortress-like building. The thick and sturdy walls had fewer windows than I would've expected. Lanterns and glowstones hung from the ceiling of every room and hallway, their illumination highlighting our path, but leaving the rest of the building in shadow.

As Garrett hurried into the main hall, Hexa quickened her step to join him. She whispered something, and they both smiled. Zaxis leaned in closer to me.

"Is it just me, or is this place *smaller* than you expected?"

I shrugged. "Well, it's not the size of Thronehold or Fortuna."

"I don't think it's even as large as Ellios."

Comparisons were hard to make. Thronehold and Fortuna were gigantic. Ellios was a mountain city that mainly served as a place of study. They had a massive university and a famous library, both of which attracted many artificers and scholars.

Regal Heights was different. It was difficult to judge how many people lived here, due to the unique construction. I had seen less than a hundred buildings, but I *felt* the caves beneath city hall. Hundreds of people were below us. How many people were here in total?

"Are you disappointed?" I asked.

Zaxis shook his head. Then he thought about it a moment longer. "It just feels... so casual."

I almost laughed. Regal Heights reminded me a bit of the Isle of Ruma. It was separated, with its own culture, and unique mystical creatures. The mirror on top of city hall probably had its own legend and history that was taught in school, just like the Pillar was taught on Ruma.

"You wanted this place to be rigid and formal?" I lifted an eyebrow. "I never like acting sophisticated."

Zaxis glared at me. "Of course *you* don't. I, however, was taught all sorts of etiquette, and now I'm a god-arcanist." He swept his hair back. "I was born to mingle in formal environments. Yet the first place we visit now that I'm the fenris wolf arcanist is a city that feels like we're walking through a *tavern*. Everyone knows everyone else. It's small and narrow. Podunk."

I smacked his shoulder, trying to make it look like a friendly gesture, but at the same time, I hissed, "*What's wrong with you?* Hexa loves this place. Don't let her hear you say that."

"*You* had the Argo Empire and the arcanists of Fortuna swearing themselves to you the moment you became the world serpent arcanist." Zaxis exhaled and rotated his shoulders. "I just figured *I* would be the one to speak to the hydra arcanists of Regal Heights."

"Why?"

"Why *not*?" Zaxis gave me a sideways glance. "Shouldn't I be doing the same thing you are?"

Zaxis was a friend. More importantly he was a peer, someone I could turn to for advice without looking weak. And we had been through so much together—as a team. I didn't really care if vassals swore to Zaxis instead of me, so long as they joined our cause.

Then again, I was more experienced. In all things. Magic. Negotiating with rulers. Leadership. And it would be a stretch to call Zaxis *diplomatic* on his best day. It made sense for me to take the lead in our operations. Eventide had even said as much.

But I knew Zaxis's frustrations. And he had just lost Forsythe. Perhaps, if he convinced the arcanists of Regal Heights to join us, it would feel like a *win* for him. Something he could claim *he* had done.

"You're right," I finally whispered. "You should speak to them about joining our cause."

Zaxis frowned. "You mean that? You don't care?"

"You, Illia, and Hexa have all been close. I think you'll be received better than I would. Hexa will sing your praises."

As if she had heard her name, Hexa stopped in the middle of the long hallway and turned around. She glanced between me and Zaxis and then pointed to the last door at the far end of the hall. "Stop clucking, ya two hens. We're here."

Garrett walked forward and grabbed the handle of the wooden door. Then he waited so that Zaxis and I could reach his side. Once together, he ushered us inside.

A cold blast of wind greeted us as we entered. Just like in Thronehold, where the queen had rooms that were each missing a wall so her eldrin could participate in a meeting, the main office in city hall was missing the roof.

I glanced up and smiled, delighting in the endless beauty of the night sky. Small glowstones were built into the walls, their gentle glow soft enough that they barely offered any light. Obviously, this room wasn't meant for late night meetings.

A massive table sat in the middle of the room, completely made of stone. The chairs around the sides—they, too, were made of stone. As were the bookshelves by the walls, and the desk near the door, and all the side tables. Cushions were tied to the seats, but otherwise, everything was gold, red, and black rock, matching the unique colors of the gorge.

And then I understood why.

A gargoyle stood at the back of the room, ten feet at the shoulder, his head covered in stone antler-horns. The gargoyle had reddish skin, black wings, and golden stone claws. The beast's tail was long and ended in a point.

When the gargoyle spread his wings, I was surprised to see a smaller, second set. And the creature's eyes appeared to be liquid silver—shimmering and filled with powerful magic. At first, I fought the instinctive urge to draw my sword, since the only gargoyle I had fought had been plague-ridden. But I kept that thought to myself. Every gargoyle I had seen since the plague-ridden one had been friendly.

"May I introduce Warlord Volke Savan, the World Serpent Arcanist," Garrett said, drawing my focus back to the room. "And we also have Zaxis Ren, the Fenris Wolf Arcanist."

I hadn't even noticed the two other arcanists in the room. Both men. Both... older. They reminded me of Eventide right away. Most arcanists didn't have gray hairs, but these men had.

The first man to step forward had darkly tanned skin, a wild amount of gray hair—curly and mane-like—and scars down his face, gnarling his mouth to the point that he couldn't smile properly. The man was also missing an eye, like Illia, but unlike my sister, he didn't wear an eyepatch. His piercing one-eyed gaze could have made the dead feel uncomfortable.

The mark on his forehead was a seven-pointed star and a ten-headed hydra.

His wrinkled face resembled a sixty-year-old man, but he held himself like he was thirty, and his muscles would've made a man in his twenties envious. His leather armor didn't fully cover him. Instead, he showed off his scars, much like everyone else in Regal Heights.

The second man in the room was the gargoyle arcanist.

The arcanist mark on his head... It glowed white with inner power. His gargoyle was true form.

A part of me already liked him.

The man's gray hair was thinning, leaving him somewhat bald. His beard, however, was pulling double duty to make up for the scalp. His beard went all the way down to the top of his stomach.

Would it have been inappropriate to ask about how his gargoyle had become true form? Or what had happened to spark the change? I wanted to ask, but it was likely inappropriate.

"This is our city's founder." Garrett motioned to the one-eyed hydra arcanist. "Brom d'Tenni."

Brom smirked. He had a confident stance, and a strong jaw. Impressive for someone who looked as old as he did. But why had he visibly aged? Someday, I would ask Eventide.

Garrett then motioned to the true form gargoyle arcanist. "And this is my father, the current minister of Regal Heights, Vinder Akiona."

The city's founder wasn't the ruler? That was odd. But perhaps there was a different system of rulership here. The title of *minister* implied the position had been granted. Had Brom gotten injured and then passed the duty of ruling Regal Heights to someone else? Or perhaps since Vinder was a true form arcanist, the denizens of Regal Heights had thought him more suitable for rulership.

Then Garrett bowed several times and excused himself. He exited out the door, leaving me, Zaxis, and Hexa to deal with the two older men.

Eventide wasn't here this time.

Zaxis and I would have to make a good impression on our own. I held myself with confidence, knowing I had gotten through worse. This wasn't like my birthday, where every nearby guildmaster and minor ruler had come to greet me, but it was still important. Hydra arcanists were powerful.

The stone chairs around the table melted into the floor, leaving their cushions behind. I lifted an eyebrow, confused by the moving furniture.

Hexa snorted and chuckled as she walked over to Brom. She hugged the man—both of them squeezing tightly. Then she stood by the table and smiled, all teeth. A new chair formed out of the ground, picking up a cushion, and then moving over to Hexa so she could sit.

I glanced over at Vinder, who sat at the head of the imposing table.

Gargoyle arcanists were capable of manipulating stone.

I walked to the table with Zaxis by my side. Two more chairs sprang from the floor, each under cushions, before rushing over to us so that we could sit.

Brom cleared his throat. He didn't take a seat. Instead, he stood at the head of the table, by Vinder. With a gruff and forceful voice, he said, "Welcome, god-arcanists. It's a pleasure."

Zaxis and I muttered greetings, and then Hexa interjected herself into the conversation, like she couldn't hold back any longer.

"We're here to speak to some trackers," she blurted out. "We need to find the arcanists who attacked Thronehold. We traveled here on the world serpent so that we could get searching *right away*."

Well, that was very diplomatic.

"Hmpf," Brom huffed. "Is that all?"

"Yeah."

"*No*," Zaxis immediately answered afterward, startling Hexa. Zaxis stood from his chair. "We're not just here to *find* the Second Ascension—we're going to *destroy* them. We need capable arcanists to help us when the time comes."

Brom and Vinder exchanged knowing glances. They had an entire conversation in silence, but I felt their heart rates increase. Was it from excitement? Or fear? I wasn't sure.

"We heard of the battle that devastated Thronehold," Brom said. He walked around the other side of the table, never taking a seat. He examined both Zaxis and me with his one eye. "Such combat is the thing of legends."

Zaxis sneered. "And your point?"

"My point is that you came here lookin' for more warriors, is that it? Cannon fodder?" Brom snorted. "We know about everyone swearing themselves to the world serpent arcanist, promising they'll support him in a battle."

"Hexa says the arcanists of Regal Heights know no fear."

Zaxis crossed his arms. "I didn't think you'd hesitate when the trumpets called you to war."

"*Did I say I was afraid, boy*?" Brom slammed his hand on the table, and the stone cracked. His strength was surprising.

I balled my hands into fists and stood. This was exactly what I had feared. Zaxis was too used to seeing problems as obstacles and then just powering through. We were complete strangers to these people, known only by reputation. They had every reason to be cautious, and if Zaxis pushed too hard, they would just dig in their heels. Building an alliance required more than just power. It first required respect, and we had to show that.

"We didn't mean any disrespect," I said.

Zaxis waved me away. "I'll take care of this."

Vinder's massive gargoyle stepped forward, silencing the room. His stone claws clicked on the rough-rock floor. He stood behind Vinder's chair, his silver eyes observing everyone in the room.

Vinder pulled at his long beard, his face wrinkled with hard lines. He wasn't as muscular as Brom, but he wasn't a desk-bound scholar, either. "We suspected you might ask us to join you." The timbre of his voice carried a sense of authority and confidence.

"The world is in peril," Zaxis said. "If you're as powerful as Hexa claims, we *need* your might."

"You god-arcanists are younger than I expected. You must know that I can't leave my people just because darkness is on the horizon. Sometimes, an arcanist must stay and protect what he loves. You understand, don't you?"

Zaxis held his breath. For a prolonged moment, no one said anything. But then Zaxis found his words. "If we fail to stop the Second Ascension, you won't have a home to defend. Those are the stakes before us—this isn't a distant storm you can ignore. This is a world-destroying earthquake that will crumble every structure."

Powerful words. I subtly glanced over, impressed that Zaxis could just throw out statements like that with little prep.

Or perhaps he had been practicing it since we had arrived. He had said he wanted them to swear to him.

"Quit the act, Vinder," Brom muttered. "Just tell the god-arcanists our demands, and let's be done with it. I hate the dance of politics. *Such a waste of time.*"

"You have demands?" I asked.

Vinder's gargoyle exhaled, some stone dust on his breath. When he flapped his wings, it scattered to the corners of the room.

"The arcane plague has lingered in the gorge for over a decade," Vinder stated, his calm tone never wavering. "We purge whatever plague-ridden hydras we find, but it's never enough. Something—or should I say, *someone*—has been wandering the tunnels in the gorge. They're looking for something, but the gorge is a tricky place, filled with magic."

That intrigued me. Perhaps the typhon beast really had died here. If that was the case, was someone looking for its body? The Second Ascension had used the remains of the apoch dragon to craft their deadly weapons. If they found the typhon beast, they'd be able to make more.

"You're god-arcanists," Brom said, cutting in. He touched the scars on his face—much like Illia's unconscious tic. "Rid Hydra's Gorge of the plague once and for all, and then Regal Heights will swear to aid you in battle."

Excitement caused me to smile.

Not only did I hate the arcane plague, but this environment was perfect for me. We were in a giant canyon with tunnels and caves everywhere. If I could control them like I had in Throuehold, this problem was already solved.

I'd crush everything in the tunnels that wasn't supposed to be there. I wouldn't even need to fight anything personally.

"Deal," I said. "I'll handle it before I head to bed this evening."

The confident statement drew the attention of both Vinder and Brom. Again, they exchanged quick glances, but this time, they frowned and shook their heads.

"*Tonight?*" Brom balked.

I replied with a curt nod. "I'm a god-arcanist, after all."

Zaxis turned to me, his eyes narrowed. When I met his gaze, *he* gave me an entire unspoken conversation. His anger was apparent, but I wasn't entirely sure what he wanted me to do. At this moment, his magic was weak. He could barely use his evocation. Did *he* want to handle the problem to prove himself to the arcanists of Regal Heights?

"*I'll* do it," Zaxis suddenly said, confirming my suspicions. Then he hesitated a moment and added, "But, uh, it'll take a day. Or two. Maybe a week. *But I'll do it.*"

Vinder narrowed his eyes as he mulled over the statement. "Even completing this task in a week is an impressive feat."

"True," Brom said with a huff. In a low voice, he added, "But I would've preferred it handled in one night."

"I don't care which one of you does it," Vinder stated matter-of-factly, motioning to Zaxis and me. "All that matters is that Regal Heights is safe. Those are the conditions of us swearing to you."

## CHAPTER 34

---

## AGGRESSIVE HOSPITALITY

As Vinder made his declaration, I tried to decide if it was worth pushing Zaxis to let me handle the situation. The plague wasn't an immediate threat to Regal Heights, and we had to wait here for the other members of the Frith Guild anyway. Spending a week so that Zaxis could learn his magic and handle the plague-ridden hydras wouldn't be a waste. This could work.

I stared at the true form gargoyle while Zaxis walked around the table and bowed to Brom and Vinder. The gargoyle stared at me, and I wondered what he was thinking. He hadn't said anything the entire meeting.

Luthair would've been silent and imposing as well.

"I'll show you how to get into the hydra tunnels," Brom said. He clapped his hands together once, and then pointed to the hydra mark on his forehead. "But you need to be careful. Hydras are feisty."

Hexa leapt from her seat and jogged over to Zaxis's side. "He's seen Raisen. He knows what to expect."

"Good." Brom snorted.

Then Hexa motioned to the door. "Do you mind if I ask

around to see if a tracker will help us?" She didn't even wait for an answer. She inched her way closer to the door, even as she spoke.

Vinder laughed and waved her away. "Off with you, Hexa. Hire whoever you wish. Tell them it's on my orders."

She smiled and shot straight for the door.

"Wait," Brom called out.

Hexa froze with her hand on the handle. Then she turned around, stiff and with nervous energy. "Yes?"

"Show me some of your magic, girl."

The command came as a relief to Hexa. She smiled, exhaled, and then waved her hands around. Toxic gas spewed from her palms, yellowish and purple. When it neared us, the gargoyle flapped his wings, kicking up wind and sending the gas out the open roof.

Brom chuckled and then waved her off. "All right, all right. You've passed the test. At least your precious Frith Guild hasn't failed you."

"I told you they wouldn't," she said.

"I know ya did. I just wanted to make sure."

Hexa smiled as both Vinder and Brom offered her proud grins.

Then, despite the late hour, Hexa rushed from the room with boundless energy. No matter what was happening, she always charged forward. Would Hexa wake the mystic seekers just to speak with them?

Of course she would.

"*Now* I'll show you the route to the tunnels," Brom said. He walked over to Zaxis and placed a grizzled hand on his shoulder. They were the same height—and had the same muscular physique. Brom tightened his grip on Zaxis as he said, "Ya know, you look like what I imagined a god-arcanist to be."

Zaxis smirked. "Really? You didn't imagine more scars?"

With a chuckle, Brom shrugged. "Ah. You got me. I

imagined *vastly* more scars. But you *smooth-skinned island boys* don't really know what it means to mark yourself with visible courage."

Zaxis gritted his teeth and forced a smile. "Well, I'm about to show you what we *island boys* can do."

Bold words for someone who couldn't yet wield his magic.

To my surprise, Vinder got up from his chair. Then the table "melted" into the floor, leaving the room wide open as the stone rearranged itself. He walked straight over to me, his stride strong and confident.

"Warlord," he said as he neared. Then he tugged on his beard. "I couldn't help but notice that bracelet you wear. A Warrior's Mark, yes? From the Kingdom of Javin?"

I glanced down at my wrist. I had almost forgotten I still wore Odion's gift. With a sigh, I rubbed at the thin bracelet. "Yes. It was given to me by the king."

"Hm. I met King Odion, the Twilight Dragon Arcanist."

I glanced up, my heart in my throat. "When?"

"Just yesterday." Vinder glowered at me. He wasn't as tall as I was, but he stood proud, which I respected. "He seemed a bit uneven. King Odion mentioned you a few times. He said he was on a secret mission on your behalf."

I swallowed hard, my mouth dry. "No. Odion... He's plague-ridden. I haven't seen him since... Not since the lair of the fenris wolf."

Vinder placed his hands behind his back and stood a little straighter. "I gave the king the supplies he asked for. But then he left. He wasn't here in Regal Heights for longer than a few hours. I never saw his eldrin."

None of this was good news. Coupled with the fact that the Second Ascension was infecting the Rocky Wastes, there could be plague-ridden creatures all over this area.

"I knew something was off about him," Vinder muttered. "I'm glad to hear he wasn't *actually* sent here by you."

I shook my head. "I apologize. I... I knew he was plague ridden, but we were looking for a cure. He ran off during that search. If I had been more vigilant, perhaps he wouldn't be out here."

"Arcanists driven mad by the plague do unspeakable things. I suggest you and the mighty fenris wolf arcanist handle this before King Odion does something we'll all regret."

I had seen the arcane plague from every angle. I had seen arcanists driven mad. I had seen *dread form* mystical creatures. I had seen creatures attempt to stop the change—who were frightened to die. All of it. All the horrors in all the situations.

Including my own, when I had been infected.

If anyone knew how the plague affected people, it was I. We couldn't let Odion spread this disease. Although, arcanists typically had six months before losing themselves completely to the plague's insanity, I wasn't sure if also having a corrupted eldrin altered the clock. Besides, Odion hadn't seemed completely stable after Zaxis had defeated him.

"I'll handle the king," I said. "Don't worry. If he's nearby, I won't allow him to hurt the people of Regal Heights."

Vinder's true form gargoyle wandered close. His heavy steps betrayed his massive weight. I suspected he was more than a thousand pounds. But he wasn't aggressive or intimidating. He stood near his arcanist, watching intently and listening carefully.

And staring at the gargoyle gave me an idea. If Zaxis needed a couple of days to handle the plague problem, perhaps I would have time to master my own magic.

And gargoyles had similar powers to my terrain manipulation...

"Um, Minister Vinder?" I asked.

The man cringed and then frowned. "Just *Vinder*. We rarely use titles like that here."

"Right. Well, I was wondering if you could show me some of

your magic? As in, some of the training you did with your gargoyle eldrin. I think it would be useful for me."

The gargoyle shook his head, his stone antlers pointed and heavy. I worried he would accidentally stab something.

"You're interested in my mark, aren't you?" Vinder motioned to his glowing, white arcanist mark. "This isn't something that comes easily."

"I know." I rubbed at my own forehead, my eyes closed. "My knightmare... The change was amazing. It felt like... touching magic itself."

When I opened my eyes again, Vinder's expression was one of shock. He was frozen, mid-tug of his beard. Then he recovered and let out a deep chuckle that originated from his gut. "I see you know all about it, then. You're filled with surprises. The mystic seekers here told me stories of you, but I didn't want to believe them. Clearly, I should have. You're talented."

My face heated a bit, but then I nodded. "Despite my talent, we still need help. The Second Ascension evades us. We need a way to find them."

"I'll make sure you get trackers," Vinder said. "And I'll train you myself when the sun crests over the distant ridge." He grabbed my shoulder and held me close. "I need to see your legendary magic firsthand."

---

Regal Heights had magnificent views unrivaled by any other city in which I had stayed. Vinder provided us with a wing in one of the fancy fortresses. It overlooked the gorge. Glancing out a window felt like we were up in the clouds. The plummet to the floor of the canyon had to be thousands of feet, but the fog obscured my ability to see the bottom.

Comfortable winds rushed through Hydra's Gorge, keeping

it cool and fresh. Fireplaces throughout the fortress kept the interior cozy.

The others made themselves at home the moment they arrived. Ryker and his eldrin took one room, Karna and her doppelgänger took another, and Zelfree and Calisto stayed in one of the large lounges.

Hexa and Zaxis never returned to the fortress. That made sense. Hexa lived here. No doubt she was seeing family. And Zaxis was likely with Brom, examining the hydra tunnels. He was a god-arcanist now, and I wouldn't have to worry about his safety as much as I did the others'.

I missed everyone else, though. Evianna, Illia, Adelgis—everyone else. Having breakfast with them felt like it had happened a lifetime ago, and I wanted to discuss my theory about the typhon beast with someone.

After a long exhale, I walked to the window in my gigantic room and rested my elbows on the sill. The bed was inviting—it had thirty pillows piled high near the headboard, each a different color and each stitched with a hydra. Blue, gold, red, silver, green, magenta... The theme was *everything*.

I did appreciate the hydra designs.

"If I rip up one pillow, two more will appear," I quipped.

To myself.

Since I was alone.

**"Warlord?"**

Terrakona's telepathy startled me. I knew he was always around, but this time, I hadn't been expecting it. After I calmed my nerves, I straightened myself and smiled.

"Terrakona? Is everything okay?"

**"The gorge is beautiful."**

I glanced back out the window. The evening sky provided enough moonlight to give the canyon a mystical glow. It was an endless crag—a scar on the earth. The many homes and fortresses built into the rock made it seem inviting, even if it had been created to kill a monster.

"We're going to be here for a little while," I whispered as I rested back on the sill. "I was thinking... Maybe we could search the gorge. Just you and me."

**"What're we looking for?"**

"The remains of the typhon beast. Maybe with our tremor sense, we can find something." I had never heard of *typhon beast* trinkets before, so I doubted anyone had found the corpse. "I think it could help us."

**"You claimed the typhon beast was a villain in all the stories. Something feared and depraved."**

I nodded along with his words. "Well, yeah. But that means its body would probably make powerful weapons. And if it's the king of all hydras, perhaps it might even have powerful amounts of healing."

**"Perhaps."**

"Do you think this is a bad idea?"

**"No, Warlord. We should check the gorge."**

My thoughts filled with adventure and wanderlust. I couldn't wait. There was so much left to see and discover, the excitement almost fueled me with enough energy to stay up all night. But I couldn't do that. I needed my rest.

Tomorrow would be an important day of training with Minister Vinder and his true form gargoyle.

---

I woke to the sound of someone knocking on the door.

After a long stretch, I pushed away several red and blue pillows, and then rolled off the side of the massive mattress. I had no shirt— just my trousers—and decided to head to the door straight away.

When I opened the heavy wooden door, I was greeted by a

man wearing a light brown outfit of flowing cloth. His beard was impressive—though not as prominent as Vinder's—and it was striped with white and black. The man's tanned skin was unscarred, and his forehead had no arcanist mark. He had plenty of muscles, though. Enough to rip a book in half.

"Mornin', Warlord," the man said with a grunt. He carried an empty burlap sack, and even showed it to me when I stared. "I'm here to keep the place lookin' presentable."

He shuffled into my room and immediately set to work making the bed and straightening the place up. I watched him work for just a moment, a little baffled by his aggressive hospitality.

"Was the bed soft?" the man asked.

I nodded once.

"The pillows to your likin'?"

"Yes," I muttered.

"The fire good? Enough wood? You were warm all night?"

"Everything was fine. You needn't worry."

The man grabbed my pillows and fluffed them with a few powerful punches, like he was punishing them for existing. I lifted an eyebrow and held back a smile. While I had dealt with plenty of servants at this point, Regal Heights was a... *unique* experience.

The man shuffled over to a small table by one of the windows. He glared at a plate covered by a pile of small biscuits. "You didn't eat none of this."

I'd had no idea that was there. Had the biscuits been in the room since last night? Perhaps I had been distracted by the view.

"I, uh, wasn't in the mood for them," I said with a shrug.

The man opened the window, grabbed the plate, and then tossed the biscuits out of the room.

"Heh. I'll tell the cook to make somethin' heartier."

I caught my breath, shocked he had thrown out so much food. On the other hand, the biscuits were likely stale at this point. But still. He had *thrown* them out the *window*. I just hoped whatever was at the bottom of the gorge wasn't offended.

Then again, I supposed the chamber pots were thrown out the same way…

The bottom of the gorge was likely a disaster area.

I grabbed my shirt, pushed my arms through the sleeves, and then quickly stepped into my boots. "I'll be heading out." Before I left, I grabbed Retribution and Forfend. "Don't worry too much about the room. Everything was great."

The man grumbled something under his breath, his tone discontent and grumpy in equal parts.

When I stepped out into the drafty hall, I shivered a bit. After a controlled exhale, I clenched my fists and started a bit of my magma evocation. Warmth flooded me. With a smirk, I headed down the hallway, to the stone stairs, and then out to the roof of the fortress. It was the only way to get outside—all walkways into the town started from the roof and went to one of the many bridges.

Unlike the roofs on my home island, or even in Thronehold, the roofs of Regal Heights were mini gardens. Fountains, potted plants, and even trees decorated the rooftops of the fortress houses. Benches and silk awnings created perfect mini paradises for socializing.

Once in the middle of the roof, under the shade of an ironwood tree, I knelt and closed my eyes. My tremor sense worked wonders in a city made almost entirely of rock and steel. I grazed my fingers across the top of the stone roof and felt the vibrations of the many people all around me.

The longer I concentrated, the more I saw.

Our fortress home was large enough to accommodate fifty people. Room after room after room, each filled with a mountain of pillows and blankets. Living in a city of rock meant cushions were a valuable resource, it seemed.

The tunnels below the fortress led to pathways throughout

the gorge. Long staircases connected to carved-out caverns filled with merchants and quiet shops. Blacksmiths, shoemakers, and other louder professions were located in buildings near the top of the canyon. The smoke of their industry was taken by the constant breeze, keeping the entire city beautiful and fresh.

Deeper down...

Below the city...

I felt the hydra caves.

Mother hydras—three in total—watched over eggs. Inside each egg rested an infant hydra, their tiny heartbeats just strong enough for me to sense with my magic.

The hydra keepers tended to the gigantic creatures, making sure they had everything they needed. They even spoke with the hydras, but I couldn't yet understand their words. The vibrations of their speech were all I could detect.

Someone walked onto the roof of the fortress, drawing my attention back to my immediate surroundings. I stood, opened my eyes, and reoriented myself.

Vinder stood at the top of the stone stairway, his hands behind his back. His gargoyle was nowhere to be seen, and I suspected it was inside. From what I remembered, gargoyles preferred to be active during the night.

"Are you ready to start training?" Vinder asked. He glanced at the sky, his gaze locked on the bright blues of the early morning.

"Well..." I rubbed at the back of my neck. Technically, I hadn't eaten yet.

"There's always an excuse not to do something, boy."

His statement lit a fire in my belly. "All right. I'm ready. Let's do this."

# CHAPTER 35

## MASTERING WORLD SERPENT MAGIC

Vinder led me to the edge of Hydra's Gorge just outside of the city. The harsh drop-off was intimidating. I didn't have a fear of heights, but I imagined I'd have a difficult time if I tumbled over and fell into the canyon.

Vinder ran a hand over his balding head. The cloudless sky —while beautiful—offered us no protection from the sun. Thankfully, the breeze was merciful. I kept my shirt open, and it fluttered behind me, much like a cape. Vinder took a position at the edge of the cliff, his foot half off the rocks.

I waited and watched, curious to hear his advice.

"How far along are you in your magic?" he asked.

I shook my head. "Not too far. I want to get stronger. Quickly."

"It takes time."

"I don't really have time."

Vinder exhaled. He thought for a long while, allowing the winds to wash over us.

Then he asked, "Who has been training you? Who would call themselves a *master* in front of a god?"

"Uh..." No one had ever put it like that before. "Master

Zelfree has always been my mentor. He might not have the magic of a god-arcanist, but he's gone through a lot in his life, and he's never failed to help me reach new heights."

"*Everett* Zelfree?" Vinder huffed and scoffed all in one dismissive breath. "He's here, too, isn't he? I should've known. That weasel gives the entire Frith Guild a bad name. He's a shadowy type—no love for honor or tradition."

I clenched my jaw, anger coming a little faster to me than I had expected. "Everett is a good friend of mine, and someone I'd trust with my life."

"Huh. So even gods can make mistakes."

While I *had* respect for Vinder, it was quickly diminishing. Last night, Vinder had conducted himself like a thoughtful man. Brom had been the impulsive and judgmental one. Now it seemed I had been mistaken. They were both reckless.

It seemed people were prone to doubt me, or even judge harshly if ever I did anything they disagreed with.

But I wouldn't let that stand anymore.

Vinder knelt and grazed his fingers along the ground. Then rocks jutted outward, forming a narrow rock walkway. *Very* narrow. Wide enough for one foot, and nothing else. Vinder kicked off his sandals and then stepped out onto the thin bit of rock. If it broke, he would tumble thousands of feet into the fog below.

My stomach twisted with worry for his safety, but then I remembered his harsh words, and my anxiety lessened.

Vinder glanced up to the sky as he gently tugged on his beard. "When I was first learning to use my manipulation, they said I needed to be able to use it without thinking. It had to *come to me* like breathing."

I crossed my arms. "Okay. But do you have to do the lesson standing on the rock like that? I mean, if the winds pick up, it could be difficult to keep your balance."

Vinder didn't acknowledge me. He kept his attention on the clear weather.

Then he took a step forward. I caught my breath, ready to lunge and manipulate the damn stone myself.

Thankfully, it wasn't needed. Stone flowed forward, the cliffside moving along with his stride so his foot landed on solid stone. Walking as if he were on a proper bridge, Vinder strode forward, the rocks moving to meet his every step. He manipulated the stone through his feet, drawing the rock from the cliffs to build a bridge.

"It takes concentration to use your magic," Vinder said as he glanced over his shoulder at me. "And perfect *unbroken* concentration requires practice. It's something you can train yourself in while your eldrin grows older and more powerful."

Part of me still worried about his safety, but I pushed the feeling aside. Zelfree had given me similar advice. Arcanists who could maintain concentration, even in the most difficult of situations, were true warriors.

"You can manipulate stone, you said?" Vinder asked.

"All terrain, actually."

"Huh." He pointed to the narrow stones under his feet. "Can you manipulate this? Even while I'm standing on it? Even while it's under my control?"

"Probably, yeah."

"I'd like to see you try."

I nervously laughed. Then I glanced around, like he was putting on a tough act for an audience. But no one was here. Even Terrakona remained by the city gates, coiled up tight and sleeping, like a scaled mountain. It was just me and Vinder on the side of a cliff.

After all the alliances I had made, I was basically a king in every way except title. If I manipulated the stone and sent him to his death at the bottom of the gorge, I'd start a war. No doubt in my mind.

"I don't think that's a good idea," I said. "I'm a god-arcanist. This might be an appropriate training exercise for other gargoyle arcanists, but not for me."

Vinder chuckled. "A little cocky, are we?"

I wanted to say the same damn thing to him, but I wasn't sure how he'd handle it. Now I definitely wanted to prove him wrong—even if he had true form gargoyle magic, he wouldn't compare to my might.

"When you fall," I said, my voice strained, "I promise I'll do my best to catch you."

Vinder's smile tightened into a smirk. "This is a contest of concentration, not just power. And I'm not about to lose to an apprentice of Everett."

I held my arms out. "You just tell me when to start, and I'll shatter all your delusions."

I almost wished we had an audience. It would save me a lot of trouble to just prove a whole group of people wrong all at once.

Vinder seemed to think this whole exchange was amusing. His heart rate picked up, either from excitement or fear, I wasn't sure. He didn't answer, though. Was he reconsidering his challenge? That was smart.

Then Vinder tensed. He shifted his weight on his feet, his thin stone bridge widening. I knew he was going to attack long before he did. The cliffside shifted and pulsed with his magic, rearranging at an impressive speed. The stone under my feet sank and then twisted, wrapping around my ankles in one swift action.

That was a clever opening move. But it wasn't good enough.

Then Vinder sharpened the rocks all around me, obviously preparing them for an attack. If they jutted upward, they could stab straight through me, especially since I wore no armor. A solid plan.

Finally, Vinder slanted the entire edge of the cliff, trapping me on a slide that pointed toward the bottom of the canyon. If he released my ankles—which I suspected was his next move—I would tumble down the slant, rolling over the sharp stones, shredding every inch of me.

That was when I understood his whole "lesson."

This was all meant as shock and awe, with a bit of temporary pain slapped on to damage my concentration. I suspected most new arcanists would grow more fearful with each one of Vinder's tricks, to the point that they wouldn't be able to use their magic properly. Vinder probably dealt with those apprentice arcanists all the time.

Once upon a time, I had been an apprentice—and these tricks probably would've worked then—but that wasn't me anymore.

Vinder released my ankles, his smirk never fading. He really thought he had won.

Before I tumbled across Vinder's sharp rocks, I took control of the situation. Vinder was capable of manipulating stone, but I ruled it. My magic blasted his aside and flowed into the earth, making it mine. Vinder flinched. Having someone override your manipulation created a painful backlash. And while he was reeling, I set to work.

I fixed the slant of the rock, so that I stood on flat ground.

I smoothed the sharp rocks, eliminating them in an instant.

And then I turned half the cliffside into a waterfall of sand. The red, black, and gold stones practically exploded as I transformed the terrain into something completely new. Vinder's narrow bridge disappeared, practically blowing away in the wind.

As Vinder fell, his face twisted in a stupefied expression. His shocked howl rang through the gorge, and the way he frantically flapped his arms was priceless. Gargoyle arcanists couldn't manipulate sand.

Although it was satisfying to just instantly end the fight, I knew I couldn't kill him. When I evoked vegetation, vines and leaves sprouted straight from my skin. My magic seeded into the ground, and as I closed my eyes to help my concentration, the vines sprouted out the side of the cliff and grabbed Vinder before he fell more than a few feet.

He gasped, his voice echoing down the vast chasm.

Then I waved my hand and rearranged the entire environment. The rocks shifted, the cliff twisted, and in a matter of moments, I created a *real* bridge from one side to the other, completely made out of the beautiful rocks that made up the gorge.

Then I used the vines and the vegetation to lift Vinder up to the new walkway. With my magic still in full force, I fixed the sand, placed the canyon back how it had been, and allowed my plant evocation to wither and die. The vines and leaves fell off, dead and wilted.

Then I took a deep breath and opened my eyes.

Vinder stood in the middle of the bridge, right where I had left him.

"Sorry about that," I said, motioning to the edge of the bridge. "I didn't want to rearrange the canyon too much, in case I damaged the foundation of your buildings. Hopefully, you didn't fall too far."

Vinder slowly ran a shaky hand down his long beard. "Well, there ya go." He glanced over the edge and stared at the fog down below. "I wasn't expecting that. Not at all."

"I held back," I said, not to gloat, but just to make sure he understood. "I've been trying to master city-wide techniques, and this is just small scale now. I, uh, didn't mean to offend—I thought maybe you had some advice that would help me, since you managed to achieve true form with your gargoyle."

Vinder turned to stare at me, his eyes narrowed in a scrutinizing gaze. It was like he was seeing me for the first time. With half a smile, he said, "City-wide magic?"

I nodded once.

"That was how you were going to handle all the hydras at once, wasn't it?"

"That's right."

Vinder laughed. "Well, don't I look foolish."

I glanced around, reminding myself that we were alone. "I don't think anyone else saw."

Vinder openly and earnestly laughed. He patted his gut a few times as he did so, like he was trying to stomp down his mirth. "Boy, do you hear yourself? I don't care if I look foolish in front of Brom and the others. I just looked like a fool in front of a god-arcanist. *The* world serpent arcanist."

I chuckled because I hadn't thought of it like that. "Oh. Right. Well, if it makes you feel better, I don't mind. Just... keep the comments about Everett to yourself."

Vinder stopped laughing and straightened his back. He exhaled. "I apologize. The bluster wasn't my true feelings. I try to fluster new arcanists when I train them, to teach about patience and control. Nothing gets an apprentice angrier than insulting his master, let me tell you."

I crossed my arms and smiled. "You just said that to get me angry?" He obviously didn't know how often it actually happened. Everett had a long history. "Well, that makes me feel a bit better."

Vinder walked over and clasped my shoulder. "Listen. I don't have much advice for you. *My* magic can't affect the whole city. And my connection with my gargoyle, Hudson, runs deep, yes, but I've never been able to tell people what *exactly* happened between us."

Although it was disappointing to hear he couldn't articulate how he had achieved true form, I understood the feeling. Perhaps he had achieved it in the heat of the moment, like I had when I had been fighting the Second Ascension.

"Are you close with Liet Eventide?" Vinder asked.

"I am," I said. "Why?"

Vinder smiled a little wider. "She's a wonderful woman. As wise as she is beautiful."

I lifted both my eyebrows, words failing me.

Vinder shook my shoulder. "I haven't seen her in years, but I know her well. *She'll* give you better advice than I could. This, I know."

I didn't have the heart to tell him that Eventide didn't have any more advice for me. She had admitted that I had outgrown the guild—and by association, her. But I had suggested we grow and expand the Frith Guild to something great and grand.

"Eventide—I mean, *Liet*—and I are building a bigger and better guild," I said as I turned my attention to the gorge. "Together. She's helped me every step of my journey, and I trust her completely. Perhaps, once this is over, the arcanists of Regal Heights might join us."

"In your new guild?" Vinder asked.

I nodded.

He removed his hand from my shoulder and stood by my side. "An interesting proposal." He placed both his hands behind his back. "If you and the fenris wolf arcanist solve the problems of Regal Heights, I'm sure something could be arranged. I know I would want to join—and so would Brom."

I gave him a sideways glance. "You would leave the city?"

Vinder sighed. "Well, I used to adventure across the lands, but things got complicated. I stopped to raise a family, and I just never started again." He smiled. "But now most of my children are grown—and fate has reunited me with the Frith Guild, and Liet herself... I probably shouldn't ignore the call to battle."

"We would love to have you."

"Not with my current skills." Vinder scoffed and slapped his own knees. "I was defeated *instantly*. I need to get back in shape." He leaned back and rotated his hips, stretching a little, his body cracking more than dried leaves underfoot. "I wouldn't want Liet to see me struggling so much."

The winds refreshed me, and for the first time since waking up, I felt calm and at home. Vinder *was* a wise leader, just as I had suspected. And he respected both Liet and Everett, which was excellent for what I was trying to accomplish. Having a true form gargoyle arcanist with us would be perfect.

I wanted to ask him all about his magics—and about the true form power he had with his gargoyle—but that was when I felt the hurried footfalls of someone running toward us. I glanced over my shoulder and caught sight of Hexa. She ran along the side of the cliff, straight to our position.

She seemed upset.

I stepped around Vinder and headed to the other side of the stone bridge. I met Hexa just as she reached our location.

"Is everything okay?" I asked.

She huffed and exhaled, and even had to brush back her curly hair. "*Volke*," she said through heavy breaths. "We have a problem. This isn't going to work."

I stepped close, my eyebrows knitted. "What's wrong? What do you mean?"

"I spoke to all the mystic seekers and trackers, and they all said same thing." She leaned forward and placed her hands on top of her knees. "They can't help us. They said Thronehold is too far away and Vethica has been gone too long, and since the city is under construction, there won't be anything for them to follow."

She scrunched her eyes closed, her whole body tense.

"It'll be okay," I said. "We'll find her."

Hexa suddenly stood straight and yelled, "*How*? How are we going to do it?"

I kept my tone calm as I replied, "We don't need to track *Vethica*. We need to track the Second Ascension."

She didn't understand. Hexa just stared for a long moment.

Then I had an idea. "Go and ask them if they can track ghouls."

The beasts in the Rocky Wastes were close. And the wastes were devoid of people. All evidence of their travel would be intact. A tracker was certain to be able to follow their shambling trail.

"Ghouls?" Hexa asked.

I nodded once. "Yes. And ask any of them if they're familiar with the Rocky Wastes. I think we can use them to find people from the Second Ascension, all right?"

Hexa's eyes grew wider. "Really?"

"Would I lie to you?"

She shook her head. Before I could reply, she threw her arms around me and hugged me tightly. I was a little shocked—Hexa had never seemed to like me much—but I was glad she was feeling better. I returned the embrace and patted her back.

"I'll go speak with them," she said as she shoved me away. "Thank you!"

Then she was off again.

Hexa didn't really like to wait around, that was for sure.

## CHAPTER 36

# HYDRA'S GORGE

I stood on the edge of the gorge, staring down at the fog. The afternoon sun shone straight into the canyon, but the mist didn't dissipate. The ghostwood produced it no matter the weather—or heat.

Vinder had returned to city hall for the day. I suspected—given his hasty exit—that he was embarrassed by his performance. At the same time, he seemed determined to improve his game. Perhaps my effortless victory had fueled his desire to adventure away from the quiet canyon city.

Alone, and staring down into the vast gorge, I decided to explore.

Well, Brom and Vinder had indicated that someone was hiding in the gorge. Perhaps I wasn't alone... But I wasn't going to ask anyone in the Frith Guild to go with me. I had wanted to explore with Terrakona, but perhaps later I would go fetch him. Our telepathy meant he was always with me regardless.

Everyone else was busy either finding a mystic seeker, preparing for the arrival of the Frith Guild, or taking the time to rest. I had time to myself, and I wanted to investigate the bottom of the gorge.

I shifted forward, my feet half on the cliff and half off. Then I manipulated the cliff so that it lowered, the stones shifting into a platform and sliding down into the gorge. I controlled the speed of descent, keeping the rocks together, careful not to disturb the foundation of anything nearby.

The trip down was long. Much longer than I had expected.

It grew darker and darker, and the moment I dropped below the fog, a chill rushed over my skin. I warmed myself with my evocation, creating just a bit of heat to ward off the cold. Once my rock reached the bottom of the gorge, I gagged.

A rank odor of decay filled my nose, throat, and lungs. I choked on it, rocked by the rot and stink of gas.

How many biscuits and chamber pots had they thrown down here?

It reminded me of the Endless Mire. On the far edge of the mire, away from my hometown, a deadly gas would often seep up from the ground. It smelled of burnt matches, and if someone inhaled it too long, they would faint—or even die.

Something similar was happening here.

My nostrils were on fire, but that was fine. As the world serpent arcanist, I didn't need to breathe. I had learned that long ago, when first fighting alongside Terrakona. So, instead of taking in a breath, I stopped inhaling altogether.

Then I stepped forward. My boots crunched on *something*, but I didn't have the courage to pick it up. The darkness of the fog obscured my sight, but my tremor sense gave me all the details I needed to wander the gorge.

I trekked forward, not needing to breathe, unconcerned with the gases and scents. The ghostwood trees grew in irregular shapes, some of them twisted and misshapen. They grew on the ground, in small patches of dirt and debris. Some managed to grow over the rocks, their roots reaching in every direction.

Some of the roots were wrapped around massive skeletons.

Dead mystical creatures—and people—littered the entire

bottom of the gorge. Most of them weren't whole. They had, for lack of a better term, splattered across the floor of the gorge.

As I walked, several more bones crunched beneath my feet. The sheer number of corpses made me wonder how many people had accidentally fallen and how many had intentionally jumped. I shook away those depressing thoughts and continued.

Dragon bones littered one portion of the gorge, and I wondered what had happened there. A mass murder? Perhaps. It must have occurred centuries ago—the bones lacked all flesh and were covered in spider webs.

Finally, I entered a cave. The deadly gas became thick—worse than outside.

One corpse, half-hidden in the mist, caught my attention. The skeleton wore the robes of a scholar, its bone hands wrapped tightly around a satchel. I knelt and opened the pack, wondering what was so important that the individual had kept it close, even in death.

Maps and letters. All detailing rumors of the typhon beast.

One letter was personal, however. It read:

*Dearest Papa,*

*If you get lonely while you adventure, please look at this drawing. I made it myself. It has you, me, Mama, and my favorite chicken, Cho-Cho. It's the best drawing I've ever done. Someday, I'll make maps as good as you.*

*Love,*
    *Emlie*

.   .   .

The drawing at the bottom of the parchment was so cute, and innocent, I couldn't look at it long. My chest hurt, and part of me wondered how long Emlie had waited up, long into the night, hoping to hear from her father. The parchment itself was yellowed and disgusting and breaking apart at the edges. Whoever this was—a mystic seeker, obviously—had likely died from the gas in the air. Had he even known he had been dying? Probably not.

The man's maps and documents were about things I already knew. I carefully tucked them back into his satchel and gently placed it back in his hands. Then I stood and resumed my walk.

A few hundred feet into my travel, I knew I needed to sense more of my surroundings. Although I didn't want to touch the ground, I knelt and placed the tips of my fingers against the rocks.

Then I closed my eyes.

Hydra's Gorge... was gigantic. I scrunched my eyes closed and gritted my teeth. Tunnels and caves were all around me. Some went deep. Some were dead ends. Others were small mazes. The longer I searched with my tremor sense, the more I understood that Hydra's Gorge wasn't something that a normal person could fully map.

No wonder no one had found the typhon beast's corpse, even after all this time. Someone would need to be able to fly or mold stone just to get this deep into the gorge. The rare arcanists capable of that likely hadn't recognized the gas or hadn't even had the means to protect themselves from it. And even if someone managed to get down into the gorge, *and* was immune to the poison, they would still have to navigate thousands of miles of nonsensical tunnels with no clear sign of where the corpse was.

My world serpent magic was a different story, however. I was immune to all the ill effects, and could find my way without trouble. If I had parchment and ink, I might be able to detail most of the nearby tunnels, including where they led.

The fog swirled around me, carrying death. But I ignored it.

I smiled to myself, my eyes still closed.

My ability to sense things had improved so much that I could now "see" spider silk. It was an interesting development.

Then I sensed something strange. More bones. They were gargantuan—at least the size of a great whale. But there was no way whale bones could be this far inland. I kept my focus on the sensations and visualized the entire creature. The bones were half in the rock, and half outside, like stones had crushed them at one point.

Was it several creatures? There were many skulls.

Or were these... the remains of the typhon beast?

I opened my eyes and stood straight. The excitement of discovering something amazing removed all discomfort. I rushed forward, my imagination filling with fantastical visions of the fallen god.

The bones were down one of the many tunnels in Hydra's Gorge. Perhaps the labyrinth would've confused others, but not me. I entered the caves, unafraid of the darkness, and made my way through the winding pathways. The void of black reminded me of Luthair, and it was like having him by my side as I hurried toward the mysterious bones.

The deeper into the ground I went, the worse the terrain became. At one point, I had to drop down a narrow pit, but I did so by using a rock slab, just like I had used to lower myself into the canyon. When I reached the bottom, I ran forward.

My legs hurt by the end of my journey. Then I finally arrived.

The bones...

I held up a hand and created molten magma from the creases of my palms. The light provided me enough illumination to examine the bones with my eyes.

Curse the abyssal hells.

It was the typhon beast. It couldn't have been anything else.

Even in death, the beast inspired a sense of primal terror. Its dozens of necks were wrapped around each other, creating a horrific knot of spines and skulls. Each head was bigger than a full-grown elephant and crowned with horns that looked sharp enough to split stone.

The beast had six legs, just like the king basilisks. Its claws would make even the fiercest dragon feel inferior. The entire skeleton radiated magic the same way a furnace gave off heat.

Purple lightning skittered across the bones, and sparks of flame flared among the teeth. These were the remains of a fully mature god-creature. If this monster were alive, it probably could have ripped Terrakona apart with just two heads.

According to legend, it could breathe fire, cause madness, and even devour entire armies all at once.

Supposedly, the bones of its arcanist were nearby, but I didn't even bother looking. Instead, I headed straight for the chest and found that it was half-crushed by a gigantic slab of rock.

I stared for a long while, wondering what had happened. Then it came to me. The typhon beast had probably been digging its way out of the gorge—tunneling away so that it could free itself from this dark pit. But then the canyon had collapsed on top of it.

No one had found this corpse in millennia. While most of the flesh had rotted away—likely consumed by insects and fungus—the bones were still intact. I walked over and examined some of the fangs. Each one was razor sharp and pointed like a stiletto. They were the size of my torso, some even longer than that.

The typhon beast had a hundred heads.

The most fearsome and devastating hydra of them all.

As I stepped over multiple heads, and then the shoulders, I

drew closer to the rocks of the gorge. I was going to manipulate them away, so that I could excavate the typhon beast and haul its body to the surface, but...

The rocks around the beast didn't answer to my magic.

Confused, I pressed my palm hard against the stones of the gorge and attempted to flood the area with my manipulation. But it still didn't work. Nothing moved. Nothing answered my commands.

For a brief moment, panic struck me. But then I found the reason. At the edge of my light, almost out of view, was a door.

A circular door—the entrance to a lair.

My chest twisted as I rushed over. I almost couldn't believe my eyes. The door had all the markings of the typhon beast—a hundred-headed monster breathing fire. Somehow, or for some reason, the *second* typhon beast had spawned right where the last one had died.

Giddy excitement flooded my thoughts. Not only had I found the remains of a powerful creature—one we could turn into trinkets and artifacts—but I had found the next lair for us to venture into.

But not until we had someone to bond with the typhon beast.

I stepped away from the circular door, my heart pounding.

"Terrakona?" I whispered, my voice echoing all around me.

**"Warlord?"**

"I found the lair of the typhon beast. I'll be back to town in a few hours. I need to gather all these bones."

**"As you wish."**

---

It took all day to lift parts of the typhon beast and some of the dead dragons, out of the gorge. I did it by myself, using just my terrain manipulation, in order to practice my magic.

And to keep the location of the typhon beast's lair a secret. I wouldn't tell anyone about it until I could speak with Eventide and the others.

I couldn't get the entire corpse, though. Since some of the bones were stuck in the wall of the lair, they couldn't be moved. Fortunately, the beast was colossal. We had plenty of fangs, claws, and horns to go around. Perhaps we could make sets of armor, or even weapons for a small army.

The people of Regal Heights, especially Brom and Vinder, wanted to examine the bones first, however. I let them—I didn't see the harm—and they seemed fascinated when I told them the tales of the creature.

Brom especially.

In fact, Brom nearly insisted on confiscating the bones due to them being found in territory claimed by Regal Heights. I had put my foot down before that idea could gain too much traction. This wasn't a game, and since I had been the one to locate, and excavate, the corpse, it was mine.

But I knew the importance of diplomacy. I wanted to be respectful of Regal Heights' sovereign rights, so I gifted them some of the bones. Brom and Vinder seemed pleased with this arrangement, which was the outcome I had wanted.

Once the sun had set, I returned to the fortress they had lent me and went straight to the wing with my bedroom. My room had been tidied while I had been away. A tray of meat pies had been placed by the side of my bed, giving the room a beautiful aroma of cooked goat.

But I didn't want to eat alone. Once I had washed, I met the others in a cozy dining room positioned near one of the large windows that overlooked the canyon.

I arrived first, but the burly servant man—the one who had thrown the biscuits from the window—entered right after me. He straightened all the chairs around the large circular table, and even wiped down the stone bricks of the serving counters. He grunted something about grease as he cleared the bottom of the fireplace, and then lifted the fur rug off the floor and dragged it out.

He... wasn't a sociable man.

I took a seat at the wooden table. A bowl of fruit and several trays of tarts and biscuits had already been placed around for people to snack on. I wondered who had made everything—the baked goods were flaky and delicious.

Zaxis entered a moment later.

He glanced up, spotted me, and then obviously gave the door a second glance, like he wanted to leave.

"Everything okay?" I asked.

Zaxis exhaled. He still wore no shirt, but at this point, I was used to it. "Everything is fine." His words were curt and icy.

"Did you find the plague-ridden hydras?"

"Brom knows where one is." Zaxis walked over to the table, yanked a chair out, and then sat. "I just need to develop my magic a bit more, that's all."

"If you need help finding the others, I can assist."

Zaxis shot me a glare. "No. *I* need to do this." He grabbed himself a tart and turned it in circles in his hand. The top of the tart was decorated with blackberries, and each glistened with a honey glaze. "But... thank you," he muttered. "I appreciate it."

"I can sense things in the ground," I said. "Just keep it in mind. I know you want to impress the arcanists of Regal Heights, but I could just sense the location and tell you—no one has to know I did it."

Zaxis glanced up at me, his green eyes softer than before. "Really?"

I nodded and shrugged. "I don't see why not."

He scratched at his eyebrow as he went back to staring at his food. "Well... All right. Yeah. Maybe. I'd prefer that."

The door opened before we could finish our conversation. Ryker entered wearing a long gold robe. It was an outfit of Regal

Heights—no sleeves, and plenty of skin showing. The robes were puffy around the legs and hips, but tighter around his chest. Claw-shaped holes and cutouts had been woven into the outfit, like it had been shredded by a monster. It was *stylish*, I supposed.

Ryker took a seat at the table and grabbed himself some fruit. When no one said anything, he half-smiled and muttered, "I, uh, transformed into a better hydra today."

"And you were able to use its magic?" I asked.

He immediately nodded. "Yes. It was incredible. And the hydra arcanists were impressed, and they began showing me some techniques."

"Hexa, too?"

"She wasn't with us," Ryker said. Then he pointed to his hair—it had been trimmed at the sides, and swirls had been cut near the temples. "A nice man in town gave me these clothes and styled my hair, though. I think he was related to Hexa."

Zaxis huffed and chuckled. "Half the people here are related to Hexa in some way, apparently."

"Really?" I asked.

Ryker nodded and then scooted his chair closer to mine. "One family had seven children married to seven other kids of another family," he whispered. "That's only two families, in case that's confusing. They just... All the kids. Married each other."

"Uh-huh. What does that have to do with Hexa?"

"People have bizarre marriage relations, is what I was trying to say." Ryker moved away and poked at his fruit. "Nice people, though. They, uh, aren't afraid to speak their minds. Or push things around."

"Or throw things out a window," I said.

Ryker's eyes widened as he nodded. "Yes."

A mouse leapt out of his pocket and scurried over to the tarts. With tiny hands, the rodent version of MOS grabbed a tart and dragged it back over to Ryker's seat. Then she nibbled at the edges, her red eyes watching me.

I turned my attention to the door, but it didn't open a third time. "Where's Karna?" I asked.

Ryker's face reddened a bit. "Uh, well, she said she wanted to speak with the girls in the local... inn."

The moment he said that, I understood. "Oh." I grabbed a pear from the bowl on the table and took a bite. After chewing and swallowing, I added, "She used to hire people for Captain Devlin's airship. She always tried to hire people who... didn't have many options in life, if that makes sense."

"Really?" Ryker smiled to himself. "That's kind of her. When I asked about her intentions, she refused to say."

"She likes to keep a lot of things hidden."

"I know." Ryker patted his little mouse eldrin. "Smart, if you ask me."

It was one of the reasons I had never really connected with Karna. I never felt right with her—like she was always hiding something important. It made me uneasy. "You like hiding things?" I asked.

My brother shook his head. Then he hesitated and nodded once. "I, well, I don't like to talk about myself around people I don't know. What if they're nefarious? Or dastardly? It's better to keep my cards hidden. There's less of a chance I'll be taken advantage of."

I hid a smile by taking another bite of my pear. Once I had swallowed, I said, "I think you and Karna have a lot more in common than I originally thought."

Zaxis smirked. Then he met Ryker's eyes. "Volke let her get away—don't make the same mistake."

Ryker's face reddened further, and I thought he might explode.

"That's not what happened," I muttered.

"Oh, it is." Zaxis turned his attention to the table. "I

remember the way she looked at you. It was getting to the point that it made *everyone* uncomfortable." Then he glanced back at Ryker. "She can make herself look like anyone. C'mon. It doesn't get much better than that."

That didn't help with Ryker's blushing situation.

"Karna wouldn't appreciate you talking about her like that." I leaned back in my chair, remembering the night we went had gone to the gala together. She had been... "She really doesn't like it when people are after her for purely physical reasons."

Ryker ran a hand down his face, took in a calming breath, and then stood from the table. "Well, I think I'll finish the rest of my food in my room. Thank you. Both of you."

He left without another word. Not even a *good night*. I wondered if we had offended him.

"She really doesn't like people admiring her body?" Zaxis suddenly asked me, shock in his voice. "Have you seen her? The way she dresses? And acts?"

"You know how mystical creatures have Trials of Worth?"

He lifted an eyebrow.

I replied with a shrug. "Think of it like that. She uses her physical, uh, *beauty*, to test people, I think."

That seemed to quiet Zaxis. He ate a few more bites, silent in all other regards. He and Karna never really interacted much, and I didn't think they would get along, but maybe they would now.

Or maybe not. Zaxis had a lot to learn in a short amount of time, and I suspected he didn't have the patience to speak to Karna for longer than a few minutes. But perhaps he would think of her differently.

"I'm gonna head back to my room," Zaxis said as he stood from the table. "If anyone from the Frith Guild arrives, come tell me right away, all right?"

I nodded.

Then he left. He had barely eaten.

Was I just offending everyone this evening?

When the door opened again, I expected to see Zaxis returning to question me about something. Instead, Calisto entered, and I caught my breath.

I had forgotten he was traveling with us.

Calisto stepped into the dining room, followed closely by Zelfree.

Just like Ryker, Calisto had been given new clothing. Unlike Ryker, however, Calisto's outfit actually fit. I realized now that Ryker's clothing looked like robes because he didn't have the physique for it. They were meant for someone muscular—like Calisto.

His arms were exposed, as was part of his back. When he took a seat at the table, I caught sight of a dragon tattoo on his back, and it reminded me briefly of Zelfree. I had seen a similar tattoo on his back when we had gone to the hot spring together.

Calisto's gold outfit had been crafted from fine materials, but he constantly picked and pulled at it, obviously uncomfortable. No matter how he shifted his weight, he couldn't stop grabbing and shifting his clothing.

Zelfree wore his long coat and shirt, but he walked around the table with the energy of a slug. It had been a long day.

"Good job finding the remains of the typhon beast," he said as he took a seat between me and Calisto. "Considering the strength of your sword and shield, whatever we make with those bones will be devastating. If they're like apoch dragon bones, we can make everything from armor to weapons."

"Are you going to start making trinkets?" I asked.

Zelfree shook his head. He ran a hand through his short black hair, ruffling it a bit. "I'm waiting for your father. He's the expert. Once he arrives, I'm sure we'll have plenty of materials with which to make all sorts of weapons and armor."

"Have you done anything with your berries?"

The question caused Zelfree to tense. Calisto glanced over, his sunken eyes now alight with interest.

"I'm waiting for your father for that as well."

"Ah," I muttered. "Sorry."

Zelfree stood from the table. With a serious tone and glare, he asked, "Can you watch *him* while I speak to Brom? I just need a minute to speak with him in private."

Although I didn't want to be left alone with Calisto, I agreed to the request with a nod. Zelfree had been watching him nonstop—he probably needed a break. This entire situation was his fault, though, not mine. If it had been up to me, we would've killed the man and been done with it.

Alone with Calisto, I gave him a sideways glance. He met my gaze with a glower. Neither of us spoke. Hating the silence, I sighed and tried to grasp at something to speak about.

"Have you ever been to Regal Heights?"

Calisto kicked his feet up on the table and placed one ankle over the other. With his arms crossed over his chest, he sneered. No reply. He almost seemed angered by the question, but I wasn't entirely sure. His eyes were sunken, and his complexion wan, no doubt from lack of sleep.

"The weather is nice," I said.

"Ya know what I hate more than the fact I'm still alive?" Calisto suddenly asked.

I lifted an eyebrow. "What?"

"This fake conversation between us."

"Well, first off, it's not *fake*. It was just..."

"Don't talk to me about the *town* or the *weather*. You don't care. I don't care. Stop pretending we're old chums. We don't know anything about each other, and this phony cordial attitude gets under my skin more than open animosity."

One thing I did appreciate about Calisto—he didn't really hide his feelings on a subject. What you saw was what you got. And while I didn't want him here, at least I knew how he felt about it. No sneakiness. No conniving plots. He hated me and everyone here for not killing him.

"That's not true," I said, thinking over everything he had stated.

Calisto frowned. "What's not true? Your farce of a cordial attitude?"

"That we don't know each other. I know a lot about you, actually."

With a scoff and a smirk, Calisto leaned his head back on the chair. "Everett been tellin' you fantastical stories?"

"Sometimes... But I also saw your memories. And Zelfree's memories. Of things you two probably wouldn't want me to see."

The comment didn't sit well with the dread pirate. He tensed, his amusement gone in an instant. With controlled breaths, he asked, "You really think you know me just because you've seen a few things?"

I shook my head. "I know enough. You're a dread pirate now, but it wasn't always like that. It just came from a long life of suffering at the hands of cruel people." I stared at the table, my chest tightening as I thought back to my own life. "I understand the feeling somewhat..."

He said nothing.

I continued regardless. "When I was younger, I was angry at my whole island for the way they treated Illia, William, and me. I thought it was unfair. I thought *the world* was unfair. It was only after I got away that I realized how small that island was. How small those people were. Cruel people plant the seeds of cruelty in others. But you don't need to be like them."

Calisto laughed once. After a long exhale, he said, "Everyone is cruel, lad. Some just show it more than others. Maybe once you've seen more of humanity, you'll finally see the real truth."

He liked to act as though he knew everything about the world. It was starting to grate at my patience.

"Is that why killing is so easy for you?" I asked, anger seeping into my words. "You think everyone is disgusting and callous, so what does it matter if they die?"

"That's right," Calisto stated, icy and confident. He sat forward, putting his feet back on the floor. "Some of the men I've killed were real monsters. Vile beasts who tore down everyone and everything they got their claws on. And all the other people I killed in between—they probably deserved it. Human depravity knows no limits."

"Not everyone is like that," I said.

Calisto shook his head. "Oh, yeah? Look around you, lad. Pirates, dastards, and lords of scum as far as the eye can see." He waved his hand through the air, like a mock introduction. "Your companions are a pathetic lot. My old crewmate, the wendigo arcanist. Killed a few men, he has. Then there's that slimy airship captain smuggling goods for others. And Theasin's spawn—the caretaker for that damn abyssal leech, and the provider of information." He shot me a glare. "I could keep goin'."

"Fain is actively building a better life, Devlin doesn't do that anymore, and Adelgis was tricked into helping his father. None of them are *lords of scum*." I stood from my chair. "Do you ever think it's just *you*? That *you're* the one who's vile and depraved?"

Calisto also stood from his chair, his hate cold compared to my hot anger.

At first, he didn't say much. He just forced himself to exhale, his hands unsteady. Then he turned away from me as he licked the edge of his teeth, like he was searching for just the right words, but they weren't coming.

Finally, he said, "Captain Redbeard tore people apart. Children. The elderly. And not just physically. He was sick. He hurt the others on our ship. He hurt... me. And Hellion. Sometimes I... I still have nightmares." Calisto glanced back at me. "And he was just one of many. I told people about it. *Hero arcanists* who claimed they would *deal with it*. But no one did anything. Because deep down, no one cares. So, I handled the problem, and all it cost was a river of blood."

"You're not listening," I said, slow and precise. "The people of my home island were unfair to me, my father, and the rest of my family—*but I'm not them*. I chose not to be. But you... You cut my sister's eye from her face, killed countless men, and sank dozens of ships. *You're* Captain Redbeard."

"You're right," Calisto said through clenched teeth. "But you're not listenin' either, lad. *I already told you I was trash.* Kill me. I deserve it. Just like Captain Redbeard did." He shook his head. "But I'm also sayin' that everyone will show their true colors eventually. Even you, one day. You'll see. You're fighting the Autarch now, but what happens when you kill him, and you're the most powerful god-arcanist of them all? Then *you'll* be the tyrant, killin' everyone who opposes your rule."

"That's not true."

"There's darkness in the hearts of all men. All you need is an excuse, and you'll show yours, too."

I pushed my chair aside—too hard. It slammed to the floor with a clatter.

Calisto didn't flinch. He stood there, probably waiting for me to strike him down.

After a deep breath to bleed away some of my anger, I said, "You said it was Fain, Devlin, and Adelgis who were pathetic... but it's just you. Your fear and anger control everything in your life. Just like every other vile person you've ever met. They tore you down. And the sad part is—you let them."

Calisto said nothing. He didn't even react.

"Most people aren't as weak as you are," I said, finality in my tone. "If you were stronger, you wouldn't have become everything you say you hate."

I didn't have any more words for him. I hoped Calisto knew I was right, though. I hoped he saw that he had given in to darkness because he was a coward.

But I didn't say it. If Calisto hadn't figured that out now, he never would. We just stared at each other for a prolonged moment, silence stretching out into a full minute.

The door opened again, and to my relief, it was Zelfree. I walked away from the table, giving Zelfree a quick nod as I left.

I didn't know how Calisto was going to take any of that, but what did it matter? Apparently, he was just going to forget it all anyway.

At least I had gotten to say my piece.

# CHAPTER 37

## ENDING THE PLAGUE

I slept through the night without any dreams.

When I awoke, it was to the sound of birds. They were *golden wrens*, apparently. Small birds with glittering feathers that flew the length of the canyon. With their company, I got out of my bed—wading through the pillows—and got dressed. With my sword and shield, I went straight from my fortress home to the entrance of the hydra tunnels.

I didn't need a guide, or anyone in town to show me around. With my tremor sense, I felt everything nearby, right down to the small cats that lived in the narrow alley between stone buildings.

Zaxis and Vjorn were near the entrance of a large tunnel on the outskirts of town. When I focused my magical senses, I felt the presence of a plague-ridden hydra in the back of the tunnel. I knew it was twisted by the plague because of the way it moved, and the vibrations it let out.

The creature was laughing. Its manic insanity was too much to contain. No normal creature did that. In my mind, and in my heart, I knew it was a corrupted beast.

**"Warlord?"**

"Yes, Terrakona?" I asked as I made my way down a long flight of stairs.

Some of the women in town offered waves and giggles, but I didn't have time for them. I waved back—to be polite—but continued on my way.

**"I have something to show you."**

"Can it wait until later tonight? I'm going to help Zaxis with the hydras first."

**"Of course,"** Terrakona replied. His telepathy seemed more playful than normal. **"I think you'll like the surprise."**

I smiled to myself as I finally made my way around a large home built into the stone of the gorge. "It's a surprise now?"

**"Somewhat."**

His fascination and amusement made me smile. I liked that about him, and sometimes wondered if it was just a reflection of *me* at some level, since eldrin usually grew to be more like their arcanists.

But I didn't have time to dwell on that.

I traveled through the red, black, and gold tunnels until I reached an area with wrought-iron gates. A sign had been constructed, warning people away from the area. The gate was large enough for horses to ride through, and I had to shove it with some force before it opened. Then I stepped through and hurried forward.

There were dozens of tunnels that led in multiple directions. Lanterns hung from chains on the ceiling, most filled with glowstones, which required no fuel to remain lit. The entire environment was an interesting series of walkways and air vents. Some of the tunnels even went straight up and were built with ladders.

Zaxis and Vjorn weren't too far inside. They waited in the main tunnel, near a wide cavern. The mighty wolf sat next to his arcanist, the frost in the tunnels a gentle whisper of winter. Small ice crystals had formed over the rocks in the tunnel.

**"Warlord,"** the fenris wolf growled. **"The Hunter told you he would handle this on his own."**

Zaxis held up a hand. "It's okay, Vjorn. Volke is just here to tell us where the plague-ridden beasts are. He's not going to help."

Vjorn snorted a bit of snow and then glared at me.

I shoved my hands into my pockets as I walked over. With a forced smile, I nodded to one of the many tunnels that broke off from the main thoroughfare. "The plague-ridden hydra is down that way."

Zaxis—shirtless and wearing only a pair of trousers—rotated his shoulders and headed in that direction. "Perfect. That's all I needed."

I kept pace, but after a few steps, he turned on his heel and glared at me.

"What're you doing?" he snapped.

"You said I could watch," I replied. "Remember?"

He huffed and then turned back around. "Fine." With anger in his steps, he strode down the tunnel, his gaze hard-set on the path directly ahead. I stayed by his side, keeping my focus on my tremor sense.

Vjorn walked behind us, his steps surprisingly quiet. His cold presence was never forgotten, however. I frequently exhaled, my breath always visible. I could've warmed myself, but I didn't want to use any visible magic while Zaxis was nearby, lest he think I was trying to help him.

When we arrived at another intersection, I pointed in the correct direction. I loved Regal Heights. With my new ability, it was an easy location to control and navigate. I made a mental note about how I should change my estate back in Fortuna to include more underground tunnels.

With a smile, I realized most locations would be easy for me to rearrange.

Except for something in the sky...

But there weren't many of those, so I didn't give the thought any more attention.

The tunnel we entered had no lanterns. They had been ripped from the ceiling and smashed across the floor, the glowstones stolen. The uninviting darkness was filled with a distant chorus of chuckles. Our plague-ridden hydra was nearby.

It felt wrong to be restricted by shadows. The darkness had always been my ally, and now that it had robbed me of my sight, it felt like a betrayal, cutting at my confidence. I shook the thought away. The shadows also reminded me of Luthair, and for that, I was grateful.

"Do you want me to use my molten rock?" I asked.

"No," Zaxis glanced back at the fenris wolf. "Vjorn, can you bring us one of the lanterns from the previous tunnel?"

The wolf grunted as it struggled to turn around. The massive beast *could* fit in this area, but his shoulders basically rubbed against the ceiling. These tunnels had obviously been dug so that full-grown hydras would have plenty of room to move about. Vjorn barely fit, and he was in essence a puppy.

Vjorn moved with an awkward shuffle until he managed to bite one of the chains and rip it out of the rock. Then Vjorn brought it back, the light hanging from the fangs of his massive mouth.

"Thank you," Zaxis muttered. He stepped forward, but at the same time, he said, "I don't want you to help at all, got it? I can handle everything."

"When we're fighting the Second Ascension, I intend to help you."

"That's fine. I don't care then."

"What makes this different?" I asked with half a smile.

Zaxis smacked my shoulder. "You asked me to help you all the time when we fought those dastards, even as a phoenix arcanist. So, ya know, I can ask for your help then. You already set that precedent."

I hit his shoulder right back. "Are you serious? I also asked you to help me train! Don't you remember that? I asked you to help with my magma, and with my ability to manipulate the terrain! So why won't you let me help you here?"

For the first time in a long while, Zaxis's face reddened. He seemed to mull over my statements, and then he said, "Well, that was different. I didn't help you *all* the time. There was that one time that Atty helped."

"Still! I asked for your help. I couldn't have become this strong without you."

Zaxis glanced over, his steps slowing. "Really?"

I glowered at him. "I swear—sometimes you don't think things all the way through."

He snorted. "Illia says that all the time."

But then I felt the monster hydra stop its laughter. The beast turned in our direction, no doubt hearing the echo of our boisterous conversation.

"It's coming," I whispered, all mirth gone from my voice.

Zaxis cracked his knuckles. "That's fine. Let that animal meet its end."

A rumble of appreciation came from Vjorn. I suspected he liked all the talk of death and destruction. The god-creature was winter given flesh.

The plague-ridden hydra stomped down the tunnel, its four clawed feet scraping across the rock floor. With each step, I felt its considerable weight. Hell, even the *tunnels* felt the weight. Stones and dust rained down from the ceiling, filling the icy air with debris.

"What do we have here?" one voice said. Its twisted cadence betrayed its madness.

A second—similar—voice answered, "A pair of arcanists."

"*So magical,*" another voice said, laughter in its words.

"Let's eat them," the first replied in delight.

"Let's make them suffer," the second growled.

The third laughed so loud, the sound reverberated off the walls. "*We'll use their blood to paint our scales.*"

When the hydra stepped into the light, I pulled out my sword and tensed.

The creature had six long serpentine necks, and six massive heads. One had horns—three sets of twisted, gnarled horns, obviously its king's head. The eyes of the king's head were dead fish eyes bulging from their sockets, but the other heads...

Their faces looked as if they were melting off their skulls. Their scales and flesh and blood wept off and splattered across the stone floor, creating a gory mess as the hydra dragged its giant body through the tunnel. The faces were contorted into odd smiles, each disturbingly "happy" despite falling apart.

Toxic gas gushed from three of the six heads, creating a cloud of protection. Hydras were deadly opponents, and the plague-ridden monstrosity was nothing to be sneered at. Its scales were pointed outward, creating a spiky and rough texture.

The monster's feet were misshapen. Each foot had additional claws growing out of the elbows and ankles. Random bits of bone protruded from the beast's body, each leaking vile liquid. No doubt venom.

"Come to play?" the king head asked

"*Play, play, play,*" another head said with a giggle.

Zaxis stepped forward and motioned me back. "I'll handle this."

I stepped to the side, my focus on the monster. If Zaxis needed help, I would step in, but otherwise, I'd let him try his hand.

Zaxis didn't waste any time. He evoked ice across the stone floor. It came out in a fierce burst, coating everything for a good twenty feet. The hydra hissed and laughed at the same time, like the entire battle was a joke. Then it exhaled a lake's worth of gas from all six of its heads.

"Zaxis!" I called out.

Vjorn roared, his breath strong enough to push back the cloud of toxic mist. A terrible chill filled the tunnels. Ice crystals sprouted from the ceiling and floor, creating stalactites and stalagmites everywhere.

Zaxis rushed forward, never touching the mist. At first, he went to punch the beast, but he hesitated. Instead of throwing a jab, he reached out with his hand and grazed his fingers along the scales of the hydra's chest.

Frost burst to life across the monster where Zaxis had touched it. Then the icy crystals spread and spread, like a disease all its own, freezing the hydra's flesh.

The six heads lashed out at him. Blood splattered across Zaxis from multiple angles as the heads rushed to grab him. Fortunately, he was immune to the plague due to being a god-arcanist. But it didn't make it any less disgusting.

The five melting heads bit at him, but Zaxis rolled away. The ice on their flesh slowed their movements.

Not the king's head, though. Just like Hexa had said—the king's head was much more intelligent than the rest. It lunged at Zaxis just as he was getting back to his feet. The beast thrashed its head and gored Zaxis with its horns. Three slashed across Zaxis's chest, cutting him deep, but not fatally.

I almost rushed forward, but Vjorn had it handled.

The massive wolf dropped the lantern on the floor, lunged forward, and then chomped his jaw down on the hydra's king head. Despite the three sets of horns, Vjorn cracked through the beast's skull, squishing it between his massive fangs.

When Vjorn exhaled, a blizzard's worth of frost rushed over the hydra.

The beast could barely move. Its legs shook and its faces no longer melted—they were all too frozen. Zaxis staggered backward, his hands on his injuries. He stared at the blood weeping from the gouges and cursed under his breath.

**"It's weak,"** Vjorn said, cold and hateful.

Zaxis nodded once. "Rip out its heart."

The fenris wolf replied with an eager growl. He rushed the massive hydra, his maw open. With a powerful bite, the wolf went for the creature's chest. The five remaining heads bit at the wolf. Their fangs tangled in Vjorn's frosty fur. The chains around the wolf clattered against them, the magical metal so strong, it shattered some of the hydra's teeth.

With sharp claws, the wolf dug into the hydra and tore it limb from limb. Vjorn bit into the creature, breaking the hydra's rib cage and crushing organs.

I watched, rapt with fascination. It was almost like Vjorn wanted the beast to suffer.

Zaxis also watched, his gaze intense. He smirked, obviously delighted by the gore and mayhem. Plague-ridden creatures were vile, yes, but I never remembered delighting in their destruction like this.

Vjorn never stopped. He ripped out the heart, then the lungs, then the intestines. Even though the hydra wasn't moving, the wolf ripped the heads off one by one, and then each of the legs.

"Do you think this is necessary?" I asked.

Zaxis shrugged. "No. But it's satisfying." The slashes on his chest had almost healed completely. He rubbed at them and frowned. "Are there any more nearby?"

"Yeah. Two others."

"Let's head to them."

"And fight them like this?" I asked. "Are you sure? I don't think you've mastered your magic enough to handle the creatures. You had Vjorn do most of the work."

Zaxis huffed and then shot me a glare. "I watched you fight from the back of Terrakona at his tree lair. Terrakona fought Akiva all by himself. You weren't doing anything."

I sheathed my sword. "We *had* to fight them. This is training for you. It's different. Why not get a different kind of weapon? A sword or a pistol or a crossbow or a spear—something other than your knuckles. Being a pugilist clearly won't work with your new style of magic."

"With what?" Zaxis snapped.

"We have the bones of the typhon beast, remember?" I motioned to my sword. "I made my sword from the bones of the apoch dragon. Maybe you can do something similar? The typhon beast was devastating."

Zaxis glanced down at his hands and frowned. "I... I don't really know much about imbuing."

"Neither do I." I rubbed at the back of my neck. "Why don't we wait for my father? He'll know what to do. Maybe... Maybe we can work on the weapons together. Our god-arcanist magic should make something incredible, right?"

The idea seemed to resonate with him. Zaxis eventually exhaled and nodded. Then he relaxed a bit and said, "Thank you. For... always being the voice of reason."

I smiled. "Don't worry about it. Let's just focus on the future, all right?"

Once that was settled, I used my molten rock to destroy the last of the hydra corpse. I didn't want the plague spreading inadvertently.

# CHAPTER 38

## ARTIFACT CREATION

There was so much to do, and just not enough time.

When I returned to my fortress home, I discovered that Hexa had left a note with the servants. She said she had left to investigate the Rocky Wastes and the ghouls along with a "talented tracker." I wished she had gotten me before she had left—I would've preferred to travel with her. Hexa was a hydra arcanist, though. And the tracker was probably skilled. She would probably be okay.

So I decided to wait for the Frith Guild to arrive. I needed to speak with my father.

For the next few days, all I did was train my magic at the side of the canyon. Zaxis also practiced his magic, but not on the plague-ridden hydras. He went to a place far outside town and used his ice on a small forest filled with thin trees. I went to see him occasionally, but not too often. He was still bothered by my presence, but every day, it lessened.

I was surprised how often he assumed I did everything on my own. I had to remind him that the Frith Guild always supported me through everything.

It was one of the many reasons I loved it so much.

Terrakona's "surprise" was just his dryad. He showed me Foil several times, and how her skin and vines changed color to match the environment.

Then he showed me a second dryad, which was a little shocking. Dryads weren't common to Thronehold, but they were positively unheard of out here.

Where were these dryads coming from? Terrakona didn't know, Foil didn't know, and neither did any of the arcanists in town. Even the new dryad didn't seem to know why he was here. He hadn't been following Terrakona—he had just *appeared*.

Adelgis would know what to do.

So, again, I waited. We'd solve the dryad mystery later.

---

On the fourteenth day, I still hadn't heard from Hexa, which worried me.

If we had to hire another set of trackers to find *her*, this was going to become ridiculous. I had ordered her not to engage the Second Ascension, but this was Hexa. In some ways, she was even more impulsive than Zaxis. She very well might attack on her own.

Despite that, I went to my place on the side of the gorge, hoping to practice the finer points of my magic, when I felt the approach of horses and carriages. The thought of the Frith Guild put me in a better mood. I traveled along the edge of Hydra's Gorge, hopping from one fortress rooftop to the next, heading straight for the walls.

Sure enough, the remainder of the Frith Guild arrived at the edge of town. Everyone appeared ragged from the long trek across scrublands, but that didn't slow them much. Terrakona was already by the wall and greeted them by poking his nose at the horses—which whinnied in fright, though I knew Terrakona wouldn't hurt them.

I ran out the city gates, past the guards.

Illia and Nicholin teleported to my side in a puff of glitter and pop of displaced air. Evianna shifted through the darkness and rose out of the shadows on my other side, her white hair pulled back in a curly ponytail. She grabbed my arm and held me tightly.

"Have you missed us?" Nicholin asked.

I smiled as I shielded my eyes from the sun. "Definitely. Zaxis isn't as much fun without his rizzel brother."

Nicholin puffed his chest out and slicked back the white fur on his head. "Oh, I know. I need to train Zaxis on how to manipulate people's emotions—it's the strongest magic of them all."

"Augmenting their happiness," Illia quipped. "That's the strongest magic of all."

"*Mass Mood Control Aura*, actually." Nicholin snickered into his paws. "I wonder if there's a mystical creature like that..."

Evianna rolled her eyes. "These two have been making weird jokes like this the entire trek."

I glanced down at her. "Really? Even Illia?"

"It's gotten tiring." Evianna smoothed her fine leather shirt down her side. "When I traveled with Oma, and all her servants of the Argo Empire, we had our own carriages, so we could have alone time, if we wanted. Not on this venture. I wanted to fill my ears with cotton."

"She's a grump sometimes," Nicholin commented.

I shot him a glare.

He half-hid in Illia's wavy hair.

"I'm going to explore the city." Illia took a few steps toward the city gates. Then she stopped and turned to me. "Did you want to show us around?"

"I have to speak to my father, unfortunately, or else I would."

Illia smiled and then motioned to Evianna. "Come on. Let's leave the Warlord to all his duties."

Evianna hesitated for a long moment. She squeezed my arm and stared at me, as if asking what I wanted without putting it to words. I just gestured to Illia. I'd spend time with Evianna later tonight, no doubt.

With my blessing, Evianna dove into the darkness and emerged near Illia. The two of them whispered things to each other as they headed into Regal Heights. I wondered what they were discussing...

But then Fain and Adelgis approached. To my surprise, Fain wore clothing brighter than most. A tall red hat, a long crimson cloak, and trousers just as scarlet as any phoenix. He seemed like an actor in a fancy play rather than the sullen man I knew.

With his frostbitten fingers, he tilted his hat on his head. It was pointed like a classic wizard's cap. "Volke," he said as he offered a slight bow. "My liege."

I half-smiled. "Fain. You look... different."

"Adelgis said I looked good in red." Fain shrugged. "We stopped at this market on the way, and a woman with several outrageous outfits gave me this. Even Wraith thinks it looks good."

His invisible wendigo muttered, "It's flashy."

Adelgis, on the other hand, wore his normal scholar robes. His long black hair was tied back, keeping it from twirling in the wind. He was leaner than I remembered, practically disappearing in his clothing.

"Warlord," Adelgis said with a smile. "I'm glad everything has been working out here. It seems... Zaxis has learned some of his magic, and that King Odion passed by..."

I nodded once. Before I could add anything, Adelgis's eyebrows knitted in concern.

"Hexa isn't here?" he asked. "You let her track the ghouls on her own?"

Fain pulled up the brim of his wizard hat and glanced between us. "Not everyone can read thoughts."

"Hexa is out searching for signs of the Second Ascension," Adelgis said. "She hasn't returned. Not yet. I'll... have to find her. For my own peace of mind."

"All right. Shouldn't be hard for you."

Then Adelgis pointed at the carriage in the middle of the caravan. It was made of wood infused in nullstone, which gave it a blackish appearance. "Eventide wants you to look at everything we brought with us."

"What did you bring?" I asked, staring at the carriage. The steel bars over the doors and windows made me think it was a treasure chest on wheels. Something pirates would want to get their hands on.

"Star shards. And pieces of mystical creatures." Adelgis perked up a bit, his eyes widening. "Oh, my. Well, I guess nothing we found compares to the bones of the *typhon beast*. What a discovery. I'm surprised you managed it."

I slowly turned to face him. "What? Why?"

"Oh, I didn't mean it as an insult. Just... that you did it. That's all."

For some reason, I didn't entirely believe him. But I didn't dwell on it. I turned away and headed for the bizarre nullstone carriage, wondering how many star shards Eventide had brought with her.

Before I reached the vehicle, however, I spotted my father, Jozé. Master Zelfree was speaking with him by one of the back carts. I figured they were discussing the sinberries, so I opted to ignore them and continued to Eventide. She stood near the grouping of horses, her gaze distant and directed at the ground. Her thoughts had taken her far from this place, and she didn't even react when I walked up to her.

She wore her tricorn cap and signature coat made of several mystical creature parts. The phoenix feathers twirled in the wind, and I wondered if Zaxis would be upset when he saw them.

"Liet?" I asked, remembering to use her first name.

She slowly smiled as she glanced up. "Volke. I'm glad you came to greet me."

"I have a few things I need to discuss with you."

Although I had a million topics I wanted to cover, I knew I couldn't just blurt them all out. Thankfully, she motioned to the black wood carriage. She used a key on the door and opened it for me. I stepped up and then in, surprised by the many boxes piled inside. There was enough room on one bench for two people to sit, and Eventide took a seat next to me.

The suffocating presence of nullstone bothered me a bit, but it didn't prevent me from accessing my magic. I suspected it prevented Eventide from using hers, though.

Being so far from Gentel had surely weakened her, but the nullstone would still feel uncomfortable.

The red velvet of the seats was a nice change from the stone around Regal Heights. The many pillows weren't as soft as I had hoped they would be. The inside of the nullstone carriage was lit by the small slivers of light that filtered through the bars and curtains over the windows.

"Enjoyed your time in Regal Heights?" Eventide asked.

I lifted both my eyebrows. "Well, I guess. I've spent most of my time just yelling at people."

Eventide chortled. "Brom and Vinder give you a hard time?"

"Only once with Vinder. Most of the time, it's Zaxis. Or Calisto." I leaned my head back on the velvet cushions. "People are difficult."

"You didn't argue with Brom?"

I shook my head.

A small smile crept onto Eventide's lips. "Vinder was probably giving you a hard time. The man does a good job of pretending. He's told me before that the true colors of a person are revealed when they're angry."

"Oh?" I asked, thinking that over.

Eventide slowly nodded, her smile staying in place. "It makes him a bit rough at first, but he's a good man."

I didn't want to talk about his comment regarding her, so I kept that to myself. Instead, I shifted the focus of the conversation. "I've managed to improve my magic a little bit. I, uh, went deep into Hydra's Gorge and found several interesting things."

"Bones," Eventide said.

I gave her a quizzical glance. "Someone told you?"

She shook her head. "I'm known for my educated guesses."

"Then... I have something else to tell you. I found the lair of the typhon beast. It's at the bottom of the gorge."

Now it was Eventide's turn to be shocked. She lifted the front of her tricorn cap. "Really?"

"The bones are from the first typhon beast. I thought it was interesting they were both together. Do you know why that would be?"

"No. The other lairs didn't seem to be where the first god-creatures died. This gorge might just be magically tied to the creature somehow."

I quickly nodded, excitement taking over my thoughts for a moment. "I read a few passages that implied the hydras of this gorge are descended from the typhon beast. And that the gorge was created to kill it. So maybe there is a powerful connection?"

"Interesting." Eventide turned her attention to the boxes that sat across from us. Just like the carriage, they were made of black wood—the kind cured in nullstone. "I have something for you, Warlord. I brought these supplies from Thronehold so we could craft outside of the queen's gaze."

"What's in the boxes?"

"Mystical creature parts."

Intrigued by the statement, I scooted to the edge of the seat and reached for a box. I opened one up and glanced inside. The sight surprised me. I held my breath as I reached inside and pulled out pegasi feathers and a unicorn horn.

"Where did you get these?" I whispered.

"They're the parts of creatures who died during the Battle of Thronehold." Eventide pointed to another box. "Except that one. That comes from Guildmaster Strenos. Apparently, he likes you."

"*Strenos*?" I balked. "The Lamplighter Guildmaster? I'm pretty sure he hates me." I looked over the glorious white feathers, wondering what we could do with them.

"Strenos spoke highly of you after you left. And his king basilisk wanted you to have some material to craft with. They gave us some scales—and a few vials of king basilisk venom."

I glanced over at her, my brow furrowed. "One drop of that could kill someone."

"They're locked up tight, I assure you."

Excited to see what else we had, I opened another box. Black and red scales shone in the small amount of light within the carriage. "Are these sovereign dragon scales?"

"That's right," Eventide muttered. "From the false king's eldrin."

"I see... And we didn't manage to get any of the soul forge because the Second Ascension took it away, right?"

"Correct. It's unfortunate."

I grabbed a third box and opened it up. My heart skipped a beat for a moment when I came across a cracked white mask, a pair of eyeballs, and bloodstained lion claws. The mask was emotionless—two straight-line eyes and a straight-line mouth—but I knew who it had belonged to.

Hellion, Calisto's true form manticore.

I closed the box, my hands shaky. I would have to make sure Calisto never saw this. No matter how much I hated the man, no one deserved to see their beloved eldrin carved to pieces.

"I figured we could take the time to outfit more of the Frith Guild," Eventide said. She pointed to a chest behind some of the boxes. "We have plenty of star shards—several hundred. If we use them properly, everyone should have *something* powerful for when we face the Second Ascension."

"Do you think this will be enough?" I asked.

"If you actually found bones of the typhon beast, I think we'll stand a chance."

I sat back in the seat next to her, my thoughts dwelling on the Autarch. He had *so* many trinkets and artifacts. And the bones of the apoch dragon were powerful. Would our supply really compare?

"Who do you think we should bring in front of the new typhon beast?" I asked.

"William has traveled with us." Eventide crossed her arms. "I don't know if the beast will take him, but I think it's worth a try."

I nodded once. "Yes. I think that's a good idea. Whenever we decide to open the lair, William should be right there, waiting."

"We have time to prepare, don't worry." Eventide pointed to the boxes. "In the meantime, I think you and your father should go through these. If you can learn more of your imbuing, your magic will make the most powerful trinkets and artifacts."

Yes—the few times I had experimented with imbuing using god-magic, I had produced results most artificers believed impossible.

"All right," I muttered. "I'll speak to my father about it."

## CHAPTER 39

## A SWORD OF LEGEND

Master Zelfree was with my father most of the day. Jozé was a talented artificer, after all. If anyone was going to help Zelfree create something out of the sinberries, it would be Jozé.

While I waited, I decided to return to my room. There were several things to contemplate—like what kind of magical items to create—and I wanted to read over some of the books again in the hopes of finding more information about the typhon beast.

When I neared my room, however, I sensed someone within. I stood in the hallway, just outside the door, wondering who would do such a thing. There were a few obvious options, but the paranoid part of me feared it was someone from the Second Ascension, here to attempt an assassination.

Then again, I had a right to be paranoid. Having your throat slit open during your birthday party had that effect.

I placed my hand on the handle of the door. The person within moved around, their footsteps nervous and hesitant. When I suspected their back was to the door, I opened the door a tiny amount and glanced inside.

Evianna's white hair betrayed her identity long before I saw her face. She stared out one of the windows, her attention fixed on the glass, her back to the door. Relief washed over me, but before I stepped inside, she said something to the window, talking to herself as though she were alone.

"Why does it always get wrinkled?" she asked.

Then she smoothed her clothing.

Which wasn't her normal leather armor and riding pants. She wore an outfit from Regal Heights—her arms exposed, her trousers flowing, and sandals that were laced up to her knees. The outfit left most of her back exposed, revealing her smooth tan skin. There were several other gaps that hinted at more. The people of Regal Heights had definitely embraced liberating clothing.

And if I were being honest, I agreed with Evianna's decision to wear the local clothing. She was beautiful no matter what she did, but this was a celebration of her form more than the clothing's.

Evianna patted her shirt in place and huffed. Then she leaned in closer to the glass and fidgeted with her hair, lining up each strand so that it was perfectly set in place. Once satisfied, she slowly—and carefully—backed up until she reached the bed. She sat at the edge of the mattress, rested back on the pillows, and crossed her legs, taking great care not to disturb her clothing or her hair.

She then uncrossed her legs. After a moment, she rolled to her side and stretched out, as if posing for an oil painting. With a sigh, she rested back onto the pile of pillows and positioned herself into something more casual, but slightly seductive.

"No... That's not right," she whispered to herself.

She shifted so that she was on her stomach, her legs kicked up behind her, her ankles crossed. Then she sighed and rested her face on the blankets.

"Too childish," she muttered, her voice muffled.

Was she just... waiting for me?

I decided to make my presence known—but instead of telling her I had been here the entire time, I closed the door quietly and reentered, louder than before.

Evianna had already repositioned herself so that she was lying across two pillows, her chin in her hands. Her cheeks were pink, but she covered that with her fingers.

"Oh, Volke," she said. "I was just taking a nap." She slowly slid off the mattress, once again making careful movements so as not to disturb her hair or clothing too much. "I must look a mess. Silly me."

I walked over and wrapped my arms around her. She smelled like *her*—some sort of floral scent that I had come to recognize as gorgeous. "Hello, beautiful," I muttered into her hair.

She tightened her grip around me, her whole body somehow warmer than a few seconds ago. "*Volke*." Then she pushed away and rubbed at her red cheeks. "You've never done that before."

"Done what?" I asked, confused.

"Said *beautiful* like it was my name." Evianna turned away, her neck, ears, and shoulders pink. "I mean, it's just... That's so..."

I rubbed at the back of my neck. It seemed like she had enjoyed it—I made a mental note to do it more often.

"Were you searching for me?" Evianna asked as she turned back around to face me.

I shook my head. "Well, actually, I was hoping to do some reading before I went to speak with my father. There're a lot of things I need to ask him about item creation."

Evianna pursed her lips, killing her smile.

"Is something wrong?" I asked with a nervous chuckle.

She placed her hands on her hips. "Illia was telling me about how Zaxis always goes looking for her whenever he doesn't know where she is. Whenever they have to spend days apart, the first thing he does when they reunite is take her into his arms and go somewhere to be alone."

I lifted an eyebrow. They were comparing Zaxis and me as companions? It struck me as a little unfair, since Zaxis and I never really discussed the matter. And we never would. For many reasons.

Evianna brought her hands together and fidgeted with her fingers. "Women like it when their partner wants to be with them above all other things. I understand you have important work to do, but I'd like to feel important, too."

"You *are* important," I said.

Evianna huffed. "No, I mean, I want you to show me. Or say it in a way that's romantic. Like how you called me beautiful." She sighed as she motioned to me. "You should come in, tell me how much you missed me, and how you couldn't focus without me around, and how you never want to be parted again. That type of thing."

That seemed extreme. But I understood the sentiment. It sounded like the love from the many tales I had read when I had been younger—the truest love, so deep and passionate, words could never do it justice.

"Okay," I muttered as I glanced around. "Well..."

I walked over to the stack of books and grabbed a few.

Evianna crossed her arms. "Are you listening, Volke Savan? Most women wouldn't bother to tell you this, I'll have you know. I'm doing you a favor by being open and frank, and you're just—"

I walked over to her and *also* scooped her up into my arms. Her eyes widened as I carried her the short distance to the bed. All at once, her cheeks returned to their red state as I climbed onto the mattress and rested on the pillows, Evianna still in my arms.

She wasn't that heavy. Evianna was surprisingly light, actually. She stared at me like she couldn't believe what had just happened, but it wasn't as impressive as her expression made it out to be.

With her held close, I rested back on the bed and opened one of the books. This way, we could be together—in each other's arms—while I read all the important information I needed to.

But she obviously wanted me to say something passionate and intimate. What would I utter that would please her? I thought back to the many poems I had read and tried to imitate their flowery language.

I pulled her close and grazed my lips across the shell of her ear. "Life away from you is akin to living in the desert without water," I whispered, my voice husky. "Evianna—your presence is a cup of cool water, and my thirst can never be quenched."

It felt mildly embarrassing saying such over the top statements, but the feeling was lessened by Evianna's wistful sigh. She snuggled against my chest, even going so far as to open my shirt more and caress me with her fingertips.

"Have you ever said that to anyone else?" she asked.

I shook my head. "Never."

Evianna snuggled closer, smiling wide enough that I felt it against my skin. My stomach twisted into a few knots. Her skin was soft, and the weight of her on me was pleasant.

And her warmth... the way my skin tingled where it touched hers, I suddenly understood those old poems of love and longing. All that mattered in this moment was Evianna. She was the light that defined my world, the moon shining at night.

"Also," Evianna added, "you need to use that husky voice more often. Just... all the time. But only when we're alone."

My face grew hot as I flipped the pages of the book to the place I had left off. "R-Right," I muttered. "I'll try to remember that."

"So, what're we going to read about?"

"The typhon beast. He's one of the god-creatures."

Evianna thought for a moment before replying, "It sounds crazed."

"Apparently, it was." I pointed to the section in the book. "It says here the typhon beast and the Monster were fiends."

"Hmm."

An idea occurred to me, and I hugged Evianna tighter. "I found the corpse of the typhon beast in the chasm."

Evianna perked up. "Really?"

"It's a fortune to make an emperor envious, worth more than the entire Argo Empire at its height." I kissed the top of Evianna's forehead. "And it's worth nothing compared to the treasure in my arms."

She squeezed me tighter, her face growing hot. "Volke..."

Evianna settled in to read, and I held her close as we flipped through the pages of the book. It didn't take long to catch her up on everything I had learned.

---

Once night had fallen, I left Evianna and headed out to see my father. Well, I didn't leave until I had told Evianna how much it pained me to have to leave. And in truth, I didn't like being apart from her, but we did have other responsibilities. Evianna needed to practice her magic, and I needed to help construct trinkets and artifacts.

We would see each other again. Soon.

The moment I focused on my tremor sense, I located my father in the same fortress building. Normally, I couldn't identify an individual just from their footfalls, but Jozé was different. He walked with a distinct limp.

I made my way through the kitchen and navigated a series of small libraries. I finally found my father in a large study next to a giant window that overlooked the canyon. His blue phoenix, Tine, sat on the sill, her sapphire feathers rustling in the evening air. Soot and embers trickled into the air and wafted into the canyon.

My father had cleared one of the bookshelves and organized all the mystical creature body parts by type and size. The books that *had* been on the shelf were piled in the corner of the study, some flopped on the ground, their pages crinkled. It made me a little sad to stare at the mountain of discarded tomes.

I glanced over at the mystical creature bits.

Hellion's face mask and the sovereign dragon scales intrigued me the most. I stared at them a long while, wondering about the possibilities. True form manticores used their face masks to hide their paralyzing faces... Not that I had seen more than one.

"Volke," Jozé said, startled. He narrowed his eyes, and then hesitantly smiled. "I didn't think you'd come to see me this late."

I walked over to him. He braced most of his weight against a large stone desk, the top of which was swirled with red, black, and golden stone. It was a beautiful design—I thought the colors and shapes were supposed to create an abstract hydra, but Jozé had blankets thrown across the top of the desk, half hiding the artwork.

Sinberries were piled high on the blankets, along with a fine black powder. At first, I thought it was gunpowder used for pistols and rifles, but when I got closer, I felt the horrible suffocating sensation I often felt with nullstone.

That was... decay dust. A horrible weapon created by the Second Ascension to destroy trinkets.

"What're you doing?" I asked.

Jozé glanced between the materials. "Hm. I'm trying to help Zelfree create a... well... a *potion*, for lack of a better word."

"You're going to combine decay dust and these berries?" I asked.

He nodded once. Then he held up a finger. "This dust is actually rather clever. It somehow uses the bones of the apoch dragon to leech away magic. That's how it destroys trinkets, by breaking away the bonds the star shards create."

Although I didn't know much about imbuing, I did know that star shards were required to make any item. They were an adhesive—a type of glue that held arcanist magic in an object. Without the star shards, the magic wouldn't remain. So if the decay dust *destroyed* the glue of the star shards...

"How will that help you make a potion?" I asked.

"I don't know yet." Jozé glared at the dust. "A part of the imbuing process requires you to focus on your magic and make it part of the object. Your thoughts, and focus, and concentration, can shift the magical purpose of the item. *Someone* imbued this decay dust, which is an impressive feat. I think they imbued it with the property to *cling to things*. If I can use that, and the berries, maybe I could make a potion where the essence of the berries will cling to a person's mind, breaking away the memories, much like the apoch dragon bones break magic."

I listened to his explanation, trying to absorb every little detail. Imbuing items was typically an involved process. I had done it a few times now, but when I had created my shield, Forfend, I had been under duress and nearly messed it up.

I had fixed it...

Made it better.

"Jozé?" I asked.

He turned to me. The scruff on his chin reminded me that I needed to shave as well. "What is it?"

"You said the apoch dragon bones caused the decay dust to unravel the magic of trinkets, right?"

"That's right."

"My sword is made of the bones of the apoch dragon. Do you think I could somehow improve it? Make it so that it can do that as well?"

"Cancel out magic?" he asked.

I nodded along with his words. "I mean... I've been thinking a lot about our equipment ever since Eventide said we would need to create things. I want to have a weapon that can't be taken from me."

"Hm." Jozé half-smiled. "You can attune items to a user, but that doesn't usually work well with weapons like swords. Anyone can swing it around, even if it's not attuned. Except..." He rubbed at his jaw, his gaze drifting. "You evoke magma, don't you? Maybe we can use that to our advantage."

I nodded. "But I made this sword with my knightmare magic."

"Huh. Let me see."

I pulled Retribution from its sheath and handed it over. Jozé knew it better than anyone—he had been the one to craft its shape and edge. He had also made the sheath and even helped me fix my shield, Forfend. I trusted him to help me now, even with more complicated changes.

Jozé ran his fingers down the sword before letting out a sigh. "If I had known I was using parts of a god-creature when I made this, I would've done it differently. And knightmare magic was not the best choice for the apoch dragon bones, at least not by itself."

"Why's that? I thought knightmare magic made great weapons."

"It does. But your knightmare imbuing fortified the physical weapon and focused the bone's properties into the metal. The magic wasn't potent enough to awaken the full potential of the bones. There's room for improvement."

"Can you alter it?"

"So, more magic can be imbued into an artifact, but..." Jozé frowned. "It requires increasingly more star shards. At a certain point, the object can't handle it. Apoch dragon bones might be the exception, though. They do seem to absorb all sorts of magic..."

"So, you think it can be improved with my god-arcanist magic?"

Jozé rotated his shoulder. "I do. But let me think on it a bit, boy. I need to solve the problem with the berries first, then we can move on to this." He waved his hand at the bookshelf of mystical creature parts. "And don't even get me started about these other bits. Eventide said I need to be workin' with you and Zaxis."

"Why us?"

"Your god-arcanist powers should be imbued into every piece of equipment we make." Then he patted my shoulder. "Plus, it's good practice. If we make a hundred suits of armor, I guarantee you'll be well on your way to mastering your imbuing."

I mulled over the thought. And then I recalled my ability to choose between creation and destruction magic. Was that the case with imbuing? Probably. But I wouldn't really understand until I had practiced a few times, like my father wanted.

"Zaxis is a brand-new god-arcanist," I muttered. "I think he'll need more time before he can imbue anything."

Jozé snorted and half-laughed. "Probably. I keep forgetting how young you all are." He turned to Tine, who had fallen asleep on the sill. "It feels like three lifetimes ago that I became an arcanist... You *children* and your new eldrin. Nothing makes me feel old like you all."

"Well, can I help you with your work?" I glanced at the bookshelf, and then the desk, and then the floor. "I can help separate the parts, or maybe talk with you about what we need for armor and weapons."

"Don't you need to sleep?" Jozé asked, hesitation in his voice.

"I'm excited to help with this. And I can sleep in later."

Jozé didn't protest. He motioned to the bookshelf, giving me all the access I wanted to the items.

"Volke."

I turned to find Jozé offering me a cunning smile.

"I will make you one promise," he said. "I promise that when I'm done with Retribution, it will be a sword without equal."

# CHAPTER 40

## TRACKER EXTRAORDINAIRE

When I returned to my room in the massive fortress overlooking Hydra's Gorge, Evianna was waiting for me. It was almost sunrise, and my eyelids were heavier than a pair of bricks, but when I noticed her, the fatigue vanished.

She sat on the edge of my bed, her knightmare, Layshl, standing next to her. Her knightmare was mostly leather scale armor with a cape that resembled wings. When she had first been born from the body of the slain queen, Layshl had been missing pieces, but now she seemed more complete.

But not entirely whole. Parts of her legs and shoulders were still missing, but overall, she was fuller. That was how I could judge her age—knightmares got more pieces of armor as they grew older.

"Evianna?" I asked.

She and Layshl both glanced in my direction.

"Volke?" Evianna asked. She stood and walked over. "You were gone for so long..."

"Sorry. I figured you would go to bed if you got tired."

Evianna glanced at the pile of pillows on my bed. "Well, I

slept for a little bit, but I was mostly waiting for you." Then she walked over to me and wrapped her arms around me in a tight hug. "I wanted to stay with you. Illia and Zaxis sleep in the same room."

I held my breath, the conversation taking a quick turn I hadn't expected.

"My family would think that terribly improper," Evianna stated matter-of-factly. "But I thought it would be nice... Just for one evening. Sleeping together. *Only*."

"I'd like that," I said, my own experiences limited. Technically, I had slept next to Karna a few times, but that hadn't been the same.

Things were strict for people of Evianna's social standing. It would hurt Evianna's standing among her peers, not to mention be a sign of disrespect from me to her, if anything happened before we were married.

"I won't, uh, do anything to tarnish your name."

Evianna glanced up at me with a smirk. "Oh, I know. You're *Volke*—your self-control is without equal. I'd never fear for my purity in your presence." She pressed her cheek on my chest. "But it will be nice when you won't need that restraint with me anymore."

That wasn't what I had expected. I swallowed down my surprise and held her close. I wanted to enjoy the closeness a little while longer—at least until my thoughts stopped buzzing —but Evianna broke away from me and headed for the door a moment later.

"I'll see you tomorrow night," she said in a playful tone.

With a slight giggle, she hurried into the hallway.

Layshl, however, didn't follow. She lingered in my room, a silent suit of armor. When I turned my attention to her, she glided over, her whole body nothing but shadow. Her head was a cowl—a type of hood—but nothing was inside. She was hollow, with no facial expressions for me to read.

Layshl swished her wing cape behind her. "Volke," she said, her voice low and serious.

"Yes?" I asked. We normally didn't have many conversations. "Is everything okay?"

"Knightmares don't need rest. I'll be up all night. Watching."

I lifted an eyebrow.

"If you try anything improper with my arcanist, I'll be there."

"I'm not—I mean, *obviously*, I'm not going to harm Evianna. You don't need to worry."

She pointed at me. "I just needed to voice my warning." Then Layshl lowered her hollow gauntlet hand. "I care about her, and I won't allow anything to happen that isn't supposed to." When Layshl glided past me, she muttered, "Have a pleasant rest, Warlord."

I allowed her to leave without any more commentary. What was there to argue about? I appreciated that Layshl would watch her arcanist, even if I thought it was unneeded in this case. I'd be a gentleman—just like all the hero swashbuckler arcanists I admired.

After a long exhale, I headed over to my bed, but I was more awake than ever. Evianna's statement about being with me had left me... energized. No other woman had made me feel that way. I threw myself on the mattress and slid into the pillows, pleased that some of them still smelled like her.

---

When I woke, it was to someone shaking me.

I sat up, my heart thumping against my ribcage. It was in the middle of the afternoon, and the gorge was alight with bright, unabated sunshine. I rubbed at my eyes, and then flinched when I realized there were *three* people in my bedroom.

First, the burly servant man.

He had clearly let everyone in, and once he realized I was awake, he grumped something about my uneaten food and shuffled out, like it was *my* fault he was inconvenienced.

Second was Hexa. She stood by my bed, half leaning on my mattress. She had been the one to shake me awake. I turned to face her, surprised by her garb. She didn't have her normal seafaring clothing, and had instead opted to wear a purple robe, much like the guards of the city. Her thin pieces of leather armor were positioned on her shoulders and not her arms, to better showcase her scars.

"Volke," she said. "Get up! We have good news."

I slid off my mattress wearing only my trousers. Hexa didn't seem to notice or care. She just grabbed my arm and tugged me toward the door.

"We should hurry," Hexa said.

I yanked my arm from her grip and shook my head. "What's going on?"

The third person in my room was an unknown. She was... tall. At least seven feet, which made her one of the tallest people I had ever known. Her bony frame and thin face made her seem more like a pole than a person, though.

The mark on her forehead was a seven-pointed star with a dog wrapped around the points. A single headed dog. Not a cerberus or orthrus arcanist—since cerberus dogs had three heads, and orthrus dogs had two.

No... I knew what she was.

The woman was a *laelaps* arcanist. Laelaps were golden hunting dogs! They were known for always tracking down their prey, no matter the circumstance. Laelaps dogs weren't known for anything else, though. Most considered them weak combatants, but mystic seekers loved to have laelaps arcanists among their ranks.

The woman didn't wear the open outfits of Regal Heights.

She wore a long tunic, and thick leather trousers, as well as a long cloak.

And then I finally noticed her eldrin. The laelaps sat behind her, half hidden behind the folds of her cape-like cloak. The dog's golden fur shone like metal, and his blue eyes were as bright as the cloudless sky.

The tall woman's hair, cut short, was a bright blonde that rivaled the color of her eldrin. Her green eyes reminded me of Zaxis—she stared at me with the same angry intensity he often did.

"You woke the Warlord to report directly to him?" the woman asked. "This hardly seems right..."

Hexa dismissively waved away her comment. "I know him. We're friends." She grabbed my arm a second time. "C'mon, Volke! You're not going to believe what we found. Vika here is a laelaps arcanist, and she found a ghoul trail in the Rocky Wastes, and we need to follow it, okay? It leads to something. Like an encampment, I'm not sure."

Vika, the towering woman, waved once and frowned. In a quiet voice, she muttered, "I would've liked to introduce myself, but this is fine, I suppose..."

I allowed Hexa to yank me toward the door, but I stumbled as I tried to grab my boots. With a quick yank, I freed myself a second time just so I could fully prepare and dress. "Calm down. We'll get there. Let me get everything I need."

Vika walked around me and headed for the door. Her long stride made it easy—she was out of the room in a matter of seconds.

Her laelaps—the golden dog—was about twice the size of Nicholin. It bounded after her, always staying within a few feet. A loyal beast.

"Vika is a tracker extraordinaire," Hexa said as she hovered around the door to my room. "She found tracks in the sand, and even claw marks on a rock or something. I don't even know. And then her dog sniffed out the undead smell, and they led us straight to the location. *It was amazing.*"

I nodded along with her story, all while dressing myself. "Excellent. And you found an encampment of the Second Ascension?"

"They're underground. We couldn't find a way in, but Vika was *certain* they were there."

Underground?

I couldn't help but smile.

This couldn't have been any more perfect. With my abilities, there would be no hiding.

"The only thing is..." Hexa stopped herself and exhaled. "I think they know that *we* know. If you get what I'm saying." She turned on her heel and faced me. "Which is why we need to hurry. What if they try to escape? We have to go before they get too far."

"Terrakona can take us there," I said.

"Good! I'll gather a few more people, and then we should leave!"

---

I didn't want to take any chances. We couldn't bring *everyone*, but I tried to bring as many people as possible on the back of Terrakona. Well, at least everyone who would be useful in a fight.

Zelfree, Vika, Evianna, Fain, Adelgis, and Hexa rode with me. Adelgis wasn't a combatant at all, but his unusual abilities would help us locate the dastards. Fain was useful for many reasons, and Zelfree was invaluable. Evianna, obviously, was my trusted companion. I wouldn't want to travel without her.

Zaxis and Vjorn ran with us as well. Illia rode with him, her hands twisted into the fur of the mighty fenris wolf. Nicholin clung to her shoulders, his white and silver fur glittering in the afternoon light.

The Rocky Wastes were only a day away, but we were moving so fast, the journey seemed even shorter. We didn't stop when night fell. We powered through the evening, traveling across the land until we reached the crimson sands of the barren wasteland.

Dawn brought with it a new wave of energy, and the others must have felt it as well. Hexa and her hydra were practically bursting at the seams, ready to leap off Terrakona and charge into a horde of arcanists.

Vika pointed to the desert dunes in the distance. "That way, Warlord. They're at the far end of that sandy valley."

Terrakona lunged in that direction before I could say a word. I held on to his crystal mane, mentally preparing myself for a fight. We'd have to capture at least two or three of the dastards, though. We needed someone to question.

In a matter of minutes, Terrakona crossed the valley and came to a halt. He lowered his head, and I leapt off. Evianna was at my side in an instant, rising out of the darkness already merged with her knightmare.

I knelt and closed my eyes, hoping to find the lair of the Second Ascension. The sands made it difficult to sense much, however.

Vika hesitantly, and awkwardly, dismounted Terrakona. She stumbled away from him afterward, like Terrakona would lash out and bite her at any moment. When he flicked out his rune-covered tongue, she flinched.

Once confident she wouldn't be eaten, Vika clapped her hands. "Archnie," she said. "Help the Warlord find our targets."

Her laelaps eldrin dashed across the sands of the Rocky Wastes, as if finally let loose from an eternity of imprisonment. Laelaps were majestic dogs. Archnie reminded me of a long-furred hound. His ears flopped as he ran, and the wind rippled his golden fur. According to legend, laelaps dogs were so proficient at hunting, they didn't run in packs or stay in groups. They were solitary creatures who rarely teamed up with others.

Vika didn't look like she had been born in Regal Heights. Had she just been passing through? Or was she working there on her own? It would match the legends—a loner hunter with her one dog.

The laelaps ran over to a large boulder and growled at the side. I stood and joined the canine, confused by his anger.

"What's here?"

"An illusion," the laelaps, Archnie, said through his fangs.

"You can see through illusions?"

"No. I just smell the winds of the underground wafting out of this stone, and I know it cannot be."

I placed my hand on the illusionary boulder. It felt solid under my touch, and when I pushed, I thought I sensed the resistance of stone.

Powerful illusions manipulated the mind just as much as they did light. I pushed my hand against empty air, but my mind was subconsciously being influenced to treat the rock as real. Any resistance I felt was just my arm locking up. It was a much simpler version of the illusions in the fenris wolf's lair.

Vjorn walked over, each step across the hot sands cooling the ambient temperature. The giant wolf was hundreds of times larger than Archnie, the dog. Still, when he drew close, he lowered his nose so that he could sniff at the laelaps. The two even briefly wagged their tails.

Then Vjorn turned his keen eyes to the boulder. With icy breath, he said, **"The tiny dog is correct. Foul winds blow up from under the illusion."**

Zaxis leapt off his eldrin and landed hard on the sand. When he stood, he brushed himself off. "Can't *I* make illusions? Isn't that another one of my evocations? Can I do something about this?"

**"The power to evoke does not mean the power to take away."**

Zaxis gave his god-creature a sidelong glance. "Yeah. I know that. I just mean, can't I do something about this?"

**"The illusion will trick your mind into thinking it's real. You must either find a way around it or find a way to dispel it."**

I glanced down at Retribution, my thoughts returning to my father. He had said the apoch dragon's bones absorbed magic. If my sword had had that ability, perhaps I could've dispelled the rock. Instead, I had to find a way around.

Fortunately, my world serpent magic was enough.

"Stand back," I commanded the others.

Everyone did as I had asked. Then I waved my hand and manipulated the ground around the boulder, shifting everything away. The boulder remained hovering in place, but when the sand moved, I found a tunnel in the ground. With a smile, I made a new entrance to the underground hideaway.

"There," I said, pointing to the new set of stairs I had created from rough rock. "That's our way in."

Adelgis slid off Terrakona's scales and ambled over. With a frown, he said, "We're too late."

"What's wrong?" I asked.

"I couldn't sense anything underground. Something about this place... messes with my magic... But now that you made an entrance, I can tell there's no one down there."

I caught my breath, my chest tight. "*What?*"

Adelgis shook his head. "They've gotten away." Then he glanced at the boulder. "I think that illusion is a trinket. A clever use of their undetectable magical items."

The hot winds fanned my frustration. I ran both my hands through my hair, hating the sand caught in my sweat and locks. That was when Hexa stomped over, her fury much greater than mine.

"Can you tell where they went?" she demanded. "They must be nearby!"

Adelgis frowned. "I can't ever seem to sense them when they're far off. Something is wrong. It's like they know how to hide from all magic. Or that…"

"Or that *what*?"

He furrowed his brow as he said, "I think their abyssal leech arcanist is doing something to manipulate magic. He's preventing it from finding people. He probably… created a trinket or artifact that hides things."

The abyssal leech arcanist…

Whoever he was, he was the last of his kind, apparently. Adelgis had nursed a tiny abyssal leech in his body, and given it to his dastardly father, who had gone straight to the Second Ascension and presented the rare beast for their use. They were considered so vile, they had been hunted to extinction.

Well, except the last one.

Normally, I would consider hunting a species to extinction to be wrong, but abyssal leeches needed to infest magical beings as part of their life cycles and almost always killed their hosts. And their ability to manipulate magic often resulted in cataclysm. It was likely for the best that they were mostly gone.

"You can sense things through the abyssal leech magic?" I asked Archnie.

The little dog shook his head, his ears flopping as he did so. "No. My sense of smell, hearing and sight are all enhanced by my magic. The boulder doesn't smell like a boulder, and these sands are laced with the flakes of undead skin. Whatever magic prevents divination and detection hasn't covered the smells and signs of habitation."

Then Hexa had been right. A talented tracker had managed to get around the magical protections the Second Ascension was using.

Hexa shoved past everyone and stomped over to the new

opening I had created. Without another word, she flew down the steps, clearly intent on seeing everything for herself. I followed after her. Although I knew Adelgis was right—I didn't feel anyone underground—they had to have left in a hurry. Maybe we could find clues to their whereabouts.

# CHAPTER 41

## LETTERS TO THE AUTARCH

The underground hideaway was larger and nicer than I had imagined.

Straight stone walls, tile floors, and furniture made of rare redwood. The space was giant, with several pillars created to support the roof. Glowstone lanterns hung from ornate chains, and several chests of dried foods were stored in the back. The makeshift pantry was enough to remind me that I was hungry.

There were three rooms off the main one.

A bedroom with ten plush, full-sized beds.

A washroom with a clean pool of water.

A kitchen with a crack in the ceiling that allowed for ventilation. Sunshine didn't shine through the crack, though, which meant it wasn't a straight shot to the surface. It was likely a long winding thing that led somewhere distant.

I walked over to one of the elegant chairs positioned around a table. The redwood had been carved into the shape of a tree.

"How did they get such fancy pieces of furniture down here?" I asked aloud. "Even if they had the coin, why would they waste it on a hideaway in the middle of the Rocky Wastes?"

Zaxis stepped off the last stair and scoffed. "Are you thick? The boulder on the surface was an illusion. *These* are illusions." He waved to the furniture. "I mean, they probably have a chair and a table, but not *this*. They're probably made of stone, and someone in their group thought they'd made everything look fancy."

I gritted my teeth, my eyes locked on the chair.

Hexa smashed her way through the room. She shoved the table over, and then threw the dried meat from the shelf in the pantry. She didn't say anything to anyone. She just kicked over more chairs and rushed into the bedroom, her focus singular.

I briefly considered sinking Hexa into the stone until she calmed down.

Hexa had always been as blunt and forceful as a battle-axe, but with Vethica missing, Hexa seemed to have abandoned all restraint and forethought. Her attitude was starting to wear. I really wanted to examine this place without smashing it to pieces. What if she destroyed useful information?

But since sealing her feet in place would cause more trouble than the momentary satisfaction was worth, I pushed the thought from my mind.

Evianna entered the hideout with a dagger in her hand. Once she glanced around, she put it away, a slight smile on her face. "Zaxis, you said these were illusions? They're so pretty."

Again, Zaxis scoffed. "Wait until you see *me* evoke some illusions. I'm going to blow all of this out of the water." He waved a hand through the air. "I'll be unparalleled."

"Uh-huh."

"Wait," I muttered.

Zaxis lifted an eyebrow. "Don't bother disagreeing with me. I'm a god-arcanist. You'll see."

"No. Listen. I'm not talking about you." I pointed to the illusioned chair. "Without star shards, magic fades away eventually. That's how evocation works. Like how your ice melts, or how Evianna's terrors eventually disappear."

The others listened to my explanation, but they hadn't thought through to my point.

I held up both arms. "It means the Second Ascension is *really* close. Whatever illusions are here were probably set up this morning or something."

Zaxis's winter winds and ice wouldn't last forever. A few hours, max. Which probably meant the same time limit for the illusions.

Vika walked down the stairway. She had to duck in order to avoid bumping her head as she went. Her laelaps dog dashed down the steps and then into the main room. He sniffed everything, his tail wagging faster than most insects fluttered their wings.

A few moments later, Hexa blasted out of the bedroom and went for the other area. She threw blankets around, shoved over furniture, and growled dark words the entire time. Her irritation was bleeding into my own. If Evianna were missing, I'd have probably been doing the same thing.

"Maybe focus your aggression," I said. "Instead of taking it out on the furniture."

"We need to catch them!" Hexa stormed back into the main room. Then she pointed to Vika. "If they really are close by, could you find them?"

"I can *try*," Vika said.

Her dog eldrin lifted his snout. "The scents linger. If we go now, before the winds shift, we might be able to follow them."

Hexa didn't need any more information. She leapt for the stairs, rushing to the surface. Vika went up after her, as did her laelaps dog, but I remained behind.

"Terrakona," I muttered aloud.

**"Warlord?"**

"Take the others wherever Vika tells you. I'm going to stay here and search around."

**"As you wish."**

Zaxis exited the hideaway, but Evianna stayed behind. She walked over to my side and then motioned to the stairs. "Aren't we going to leave?"

"I'm going to stay here," I said.

"Why?"

"Because if these illusions aren't created by trinkets, they'll eventually fade. And I want to search the place then."

Evianna crossed her arms over her chest. "Fine. Then I'll stay with you."

I half-smiled. "I'm sure I'll be safe here."

"I want to make sure you are with my own two eyes."

"All right." I glanced around the wrecked room, irritated by Hexa's whirlwind search tactics. "Let's look around while we wait."

---

It didn't take long for the illusions to fade. In less than an hour, the entire hideaway was a shabby hole meant for rats and fleas. There weren't any insects or rodents, but the old straw in the mattresses, the dirt coating all the furniture, and the moth-eaten blankets made me think this was a poorhouse.

The illusions had given the place a sense of elegance, but now...

I almost felt sorry for the members of the Second Ascension.

Evianna walked around the hideaway with a permanent sneer. She half-touched the dirty furniture, obviously afraid of smudging her clothes. Her knightmare shifted through the darkness, searching everything on the ground.

None of my magic helped me with anything in the hideaway, so I had to rely on my sight and common sense. I decided to search the beds, thinking that if they had lived here, they would surely have treated their beds as their personal spaces. One by one, I went through the terrible mattresses and ratty blankets.

When the illusions had been in place, I hadn't found anything, but now that they were gone, I immediately stumbled upon a letter. The parchment was perfectly folded, and the ink neatly laid. Whoever had written the letter had spent years at school.

It read:

*Dearest Nia,*

*I'm finally doing it. I'm going to become an arcanist. I've fulfilled my obligations with the Second Ascension, and they have mystical creatures who will bond with anyone, no Trial of Worth required. They said I'm going to become a charybdis arcanist.*

I stopped halfway through the letter, my teeth gritted. The charybdis was a mystical creature that had once been extinct. I had seen them resurrected in Thronehold, alongside all the other creatures. The Autarch was planning on handing them out, apparently.

In some ways, I detested the rank and file of the Second Ascension more than I did their leaders. The lowlifes who served the Autarch were generally people who had, for one reason or another, failed the Trials of Worth required to bond with a mystical creature. They were the kind of people who believed they were *owed* power and magic without wanting to improve themselves to earn it.

Or maybe... they were just too cowardly to admit they needed to improve.

Either way, the mentality didn't sit well with me.

The Second Ascension had gained its following by promising people a chance at bonding with powerful mystical creatures—without the need to go through a Trial of Worth. Of course people jumped at the chance, not caring what it would mean for everyone else so long as they got what they wanted.

With a sigh, I continued reading the letter.

*We walked around the Rocky Wastes today. My heels were nearly raw through new boots, and I eventually had to rest for a fortnight later on. While I rested, I saw a hill catch fire, the flames so massive, they could be seen from Thronehold. The sky titan extinguished the pyre in an instant. Its incredible power is a wonder to behold.*

*I don't know if I'll be able to mail this letter. We aren't supposed to let anyone know where we're staying. If I make it to a town, and no one recognizes me, maybe I'll have time to contact the couriers. If I don't, I'll deliver this letter to you personally, so that you know I was thinking of you.*

*Best,*
  *Toni*

Toni, huh?

I sighed as I folded the letter and placed it back on the ragged mattress. While it was interesting that he was going to become an arcanist, it wasn't relevant. I needed something *more*—something I could use.

Determined to find something, I went to the next few beds.

To my surprise, several of the Second Ascension members had letters stuffed between the sheets, each of them preparing for a day when they would reach a courier. Several wrote to their loved ones, and one wrote to her mother...

But nothing was of any importance.

I left the sleeping quarters and headed for the main room. The table and desk were suspicious pieces of furniture, and I searched them thoroughly. The desk yielded another letter. At first, I was going to throw it out, but I stopped when I saw who it was addressed to.

*To the Destined Ruler and Great Autarch, Cane Helvetti,*

The Autarch?

Cane Helvetti?

I had never seen his name before. Of course he had a name... I just hadn't thought about it. In my mind, he was just *the Autarch*. But it was silly to think a mother had given the name Autarch to her child. It seemed odd that he had a normal name that someone would call him.

The handwriting was curly and elegant. Each letter had its own little flourish, as though the letter had been written with great care. I read the letter with all my focus and concentration, hoping I would glean some sort of hidden information.

*Lith and I have done everything you've asked. And as you suspected, no one can tell that I'm a god-arcanist. I've walked through several settlements now, and the arcanist mark on my forehead is all they ever see.*

. . .

*You said I should win the hearts of those who follow me, but I don't know yet how I'll do that. Akiva suggested I write letters, since the others make a habit of writing their loved ones, and then I would appear normal, but I don't have anyone to write to.*

*I've written this letter to conform with expectations, even though I know I can never send it to you.*

*I miss my home in the woods. Sometimes, the bustle of these large cities bothers me. Thank you for sending Akiva to protect me. Nothing ever rattles him. I feel safer with him around, even if I'm the god-arcanist and he isn't. Traveling with him has been enlightening.*

*Best wishes,*
*Orwyn Tellia*

Orwyn?

Her name stuck with me. I knew her. I had met her near the excavation site—the place where the Second Ascension had dug up the apoch dragon.

Orwyn was a *kirin arcanist*...

Not a gold kirin, like the Autarch, but a silver kirin. The silver variants were the standard. They allowed their arcanists to bond with one additional creature, which meant Orwyn hadn't needed to give up her kirin to become a god-arcanist.

And kirins could empower the magic of the other creature bonded to their arcanist. Which meant Orwyn would have powerful abilities, even though she was a new god-arcanist, just like Zaxis.

She was either the sky titan arcanist, or the garuda bird arcanist, at least from my estimates, and based on the runestones the Second Ascension had had in their possession. And since the ghoul in the desert had said he served the sky titan arcanist, I could make a few important conclusions.

The sky titan arcanist was none other than Orwyn.

But the letter gave me little other information. It was addressed to the Autarch, but it didn't list his current location, or his schedule, or a list of his fears—nothing useful.

Evianna hurried to my side once she realized I was reading a letter. She leaned close, read the contents herself, and then snatched the letter away. With her eyebrows knitted, she read the letter a second time.

"Is everything okay?"

"I've seen this name before," Evianna whispered. "When I was studying in the castle... Cane Helvetti."

"The Autarch?"

"I didn't know Cane Helvetti was the Autarch. I learned he was an apothecary. He healed people." Evianna fidgeted with the edges of the letter, slowly frowning. "Even Artificer Theasin Venrover praised Helvetti's ability to heal individuals. It seems odd *he* would be the Autarch."

I took the letter back and reread it one more time. "Why is it odd? You said he was talented."

"He's a healer. I imagined the Autarch to be... a barbarian. Or a berserker. Or a violent brigand."

None of that had occurred to me. I knew the Autarch was a blackheart, but he couldn't have been a madman. No—not when he had so many people supporting him. Not when a gold kirin had decided to bond with him. He was probably a man like Theasin.

A plotter.

A planner.

A manipulator.

Although we had never formally met, I already knew the kind of man the Autarch was. His thirst for power would never be quenched. He would always want more, and he would do anything to get it.

Perhaps Helvetti *had* been an apothecary, but when he had taken the mantle of the Autarch, he had abandoned that.

Evianna glared at the signature at the end. "That Orwyn girl sounds too nice to be a stooge of the Autarch. Or perhaps too dimwitted. Is she talking about *Akiva the King Basilisk Arcanist?* The assassin who murdered my Oma? The fiend doesn't deserve any praise."

I nodded once. This meant Orwyn had some powerful allies.

Akiva, an assassin without rival.

The Keeper of Corpses, some unknown entity with ghouls at his command.

The sky titan, a god-creature I knew little about.

Brand new charybdis arcanists, all eager to gain power for themselves.

I would have to steel myself to the reality of another battle. If this god-arcanist was nearby—even if just on the same landmass —I would have to track her down. She couldn't be allowed to continue spreading the arcane plague, and if anyone would know where the Autarch was, it was her.

Which meant she'd probably know where to find Vethica.

And also where I might find Luthair.

# CHAPTER 42

## A HUNTER'S CELEBRATION

After finishing my search of the hideaway, I exited back to the Rocky Wastes. I hadn't found much, but the letters were enlightening. Orwyn was the sky titan arcanist, and the Autarch was the abyssal kraken arcanist. We knew the name of a few of our foes, and if Gravekeeper William managed to bond with the typhon beast, we would still have the advantage in numbers.

Where was the garuda bird?

I would have to focus on that later.

Terrakona, along with Hexa and the others, returned to the hideaway emptyhanded. I wasn't surprised. The Second Ascension seemed to have all sorts of tricks up their sleeves, including teleportation. They always managed to show up in all the wrong places, seemingly from nowhere.

We returned to Regal Heights, everyone cold and quiet. It was frustrating to have the Second Ascension so close, yet somehow they had escaped us. Had they teleported this time? Had they used some other trick to evade us?

I wished I knew.

Vika, from the back of my world serpent, called up to me.

"Warlord, I think it would be best if Archnie and I searched on our own."

"What?" Hexa barked. She turned to the woman with a harsh glare. "I want to be there! I *need* to find them."

"You're too manic, and traveling with a group was what got us caught. If I had found the hideaway, and reported the location in secret, the Second Ascension wouldn't have been warned we were coming. They escaped because they had a few days to flee."

Hexa's plan to run down the enemy was causing problems. Subtlety was sometimes needed.

"All right," I called down to Vika. "You should go alone. Just report to me whenever you find anything substantial."

My decision obviously bothered Hexa. She cursed under her breath and turned away, her body tense. I felt for her, but this was the best way to find our enemies.

---

Regal Heights was half-decorated when we returned. At first, I thought they were having some sort of festival for cats. Small four-legged animals were on display in every window and on every roof, some wooden carvings, some parchment puppets. But then I realized the decorations were actually *wolves*, not cats. Their hasty construction made it difficult to identify the animal from afar, but I noticed the fangs and claws once I had stepped off Terrakona and walked into the city.

The bridges were wrapped in strings with little wolf figurines, and the tops of the fortresses were lined with lanterns that included wolf shadow-box lights. They made me smile as I made my way down the long walkways built into the side of the gorge walls.

The hydra arcanists brought their massive eldrin to the edge of the canyon. Whenever the hydras roared, their multiple voices bounced down the gorge, echoing like a song.

While I was still irritated that we hadn't found the Second Ascension, the jovial attitude of most of the citizens of Regal Heights actually brightened my mood. The guards bowed to me as I went deeper into the city. The other members of the Frith Guild hung around near the wall, speaking to Hexa—likely cheering her up—and then explaining the situation to the others.

My mind was on other problems. I made my way down the narrow walkways until I eventually came upon Vinder and his true form gargoyle.

The man stood at the end of a long metal bridge, one hand behind his back, one hand stroking his long beard. His glowing arcanist mark was more prominent as the sun set, and I offered the man a smile as I approached.

"What's going on?" I asked.

Vinder met my gaze. "Apparently, the fenris wolf arcanist *just* bonded to his mighty eldrin."

I nodded once. "About three weeks ago, yes."

"And he was never really celebrated."

"That's... also true."

"Brom thought it a good idea to spread the cheer." Vinder waved an arm out, motioning to the many decorations around the gorge. "And I can't ever stop Brom from doing something once he sets his mind to it, you understand. Tonight, we'll entertain the Hunter and toast to his glorious future."

The thought of celebrating while our enemies ran free didn't sit right with me, but at the same time, this was probably good for Zaxis. I imagined him swimming in the praise. Perhaps it would improve his outlook on life.

"All right," I said. "Do, uh, I need to do anything?"

"No, no. I just wanted to make sure you *knew*."

I narrowed my eyes, wondering where this was going. Vinder

had said the last word with a slow cadence, as if it was a coded message for only my ears.

Just to make sure, I leaned forward and whispered, "If I'm supposed to do something, you have to let me know. I'm not the greatest at events like this."

Vinder stopped stroking his beard. "I'm hoping to tell the members of the Frith Guild—especially Liet. Everyone should be in attendance, you see."

"Oh. Right." I stepped away and then around him. "I'll make sure everyone knows. Don't worry. We'll be there."

That seemed to satisfy Vinder.

There wasn't much time left in the day, so I hurried to my fortress home in order to prep for the festivities. After all that traveling to the Rocky Wastes, I wasn't really in the mood to socialize, but I couldn't miss Zaxis's celebration. The whole city had done everything in its power to prepare, even though the citizens had been given little notice, which also fueled my desire to join in.

When I reached my room, however, I stopped and glanced at the books. My curiosity got the better of me. I grabbed the tomes and flipped through to a page that had mentioned the sky titan. I wanted to know more, especially now that I knew Orwyn was the sky titan arcanist.

I still had time...

It would only take a few minutes.

---

The books had many stories related to the sky titan, but each one was more confusing than the last. Apparently, no one had ever *seen* the beast. The old tales and poems all said the same thing— the sky titan was invisible.

The clearest story spoke of the sky titan like a spooky bogeyman lurking around every corner. It read:

· · ·

*A Vision of Air*

*Titans are powerful mystical creatures, but the most powerful of these living constructs is none other than the god of their kind, the sky titan. When I went to see the god-arcanist, the Falcon, I thought there had been a mistake. His massive eldrin was nowhere to be seen.*

*The Falcon had devastated an entire town by the sea, his control of the weather so frightening that there were no survivors. Yet, when I spoke to the Falcon, his eldrin was nowhere to be found. When I inquired, he claimed the titan was all around us, waiting for but a mere whisper of words to attack.*

*I have concluded that the sky titan is nothing but a vision of air. It has no body, no face, no physical form at all. Which probably explained the Falcon's arrogant demeanor. No blunt force or melee tactics would work against it.*

From what I had read, Luvi and the first world serpent had been master tacticians and strategists. Luvi had won all major battles, typically in interesting and grand ways, like how he had defeated the typhon beast by creating a gorge.

But there were no records of him facing off against the sky titan, which worried me. How was I supposed to fight a creature made of air? An *invisible* creature made of air? And it was immune to physical attacks?

It seemed impossible to defeat a creature with those characteristics.

I set the book down on the edge of the bed. "No, it's not

impossible," I muttered to myself, my thoughts grappling with the problem. "I just need to think about this. Air and wind are powerful forces, but..."

**"The celebrations are starting, Warlord."**

Terrakona's gentle voice brought me back to the present. I glanced up, like I would see him, but instead, I just stared at the ceiling. "I'll be right there."

**"Can I bring my dryads?"**

"Uh, yeah. Of course. I don't see why not."

Terrakona didn't say anything, but I felt a telepathic warmth —a sort of smile or emotional feeling of contentedness. It translated straight to me, and I found myself grinning as I fitted my boots into place.

With my mind still filled with facts about arcanists, the Autarch, and the other god-creatures, I headed out of my room and wandered through the fortress. The pulse of music and cheering traveled through the stones of the floor and walls. It wasn't beautiful or soothing or relaxing—it was the beat of drums, the clash of metal, and the harsh whistle of intensity.

The music of Regal Heights was bombastic, and I thought, surely, they were using cannons as musical instruments. Despite the rowdiness, the beating of the drums was in time with the whistles and clashes, creating a song that matched the heat of war.

I strode out to the gorge walkways, surprised by the thousands of people celebrating. They danced with the war music, most individuals opting for little clothing, despite the evening winds. I tried not to stare. My home island had been more obsessed with clothing than Regal Heights, and I wasn't sure what the etiquette here was.

With my arms crossed, I traveled through the crowds, looking for members of the Frith Guild.

The people of Regal Heights stepped out of my path

whenever they recognized me. A few ran forward with drinks and food, each offering me the most exquisite items the canyon had to offer.

I took bites of delicious shrimp, canyon rabbits, and diamond potatoes, but nothing compared to the mixed berry juice. I drank several cups as I made my way around the city.

Several children ran over and asked me all sorts of questions, but the music prevented me from hearing much. I tried to answer, but I often just offered a shrug and continued forward.

Back in Thronehold and Fortuna, everything had been different. Their celebrations and parties had had a rigid form and schedule. There was a guest list, and rules, and strict etiquette. Regal Heights had none of that. *Everyone* was celebrating. The party extended into houses, shops, and even the blacksmith's. While everyone paid me respect, they weren't so concerned with my status that they treated me like a gilded statue.

It felt invigorating.

The embers of impressive pyres fluttered into the night sky, like a hundred fireflies taking to the stars. If I could have painted the sight, I would've. It was a picture I wanted to see every day.

Unfortunately, sensing anything with tremors was like trying to stare directly into the sun. I thought I would have trouble locating the Frith Guild, but that wasn't the case. Most of its members were gathered around Terrakona, just outside the walls of the city.

Except Zaxis.

He and Vjorn were on the less-fancy side of Hydra's Gorge, entertaining most of the hydra caretakers and guards. The mystical creatures were gathered around the fenris wolf, all taking in the might of the giant canine.

When I made it to Terrakona, I noticed that a few key individuals were missing. Hexa, Eventide, Zelfree, Calisto, and Jozé were nowhere to be found. I understood why my father would be absent—he had said many times that the pain in his leg prohibited him from just wandering around. Zelfree and Calisto made sense. And Hexa was probably with her friends and family.

But Eventide? I didn't know why she was missing. Then again, I hadn't seen Vinder anywhere, either. Perhaps they had gone somewhere to catch up?

Fain and Adelgis were playing with the two dryads Terrakona had gathered. They, along with Wraith and Felicity, spoke to the little plant-people. Watching the ethereal whelk spin in the air and gently reach out little tentacles was adorable when the vines of the dryads reached back.

Karna, Evianna, and Ryker sat around a bonfire cooking themselves pieces of rabbit. Evianna clearly hadn't seen me. She laughed with the others, pointing to her long searing stick, obviously delighted by the fire. Had she ever cooked something like this before? Evianna seemed so happy to try.

I was about to walk over, when Atty walked up to me. She wore thin robes of sky blue, tied with a beautiful golden sash. I had never seen her wear it before, but it looked nice, and it complemented her blonde hair.

"Volke," she said with a smile. "Can I speak with you?"

The loud music required us to stand close together just to have a basic conversation. "Of course."

"Zaxis has been avoiding me." Atty grabbed a few strands of her hair and fidgeted with them, her gaze on the distant rocks. "Even tonight, he left me in the middle of a conversation. I was wondering if he spoke to you about it."

A part of me didn't know what to say. I had a lot of other problems on my mind—Zaxis hadn't brought up anything about Atty. "I think everything is fine," I said. "Sometimes Zaxis is moody."

"Yes, but he's never been this way with me. We've fought over things, but Zaxis doesn't... He doesn't avoid me. We've trained together for years, and when I offered to help him with his training now, he became indignant."

"Well, he just lost Forsythe, and he probably doesn't want to see you and Titania together. Once he's not so fragile about the subject, I'm sure he'll train with you. Everyone wants to learn how you mastered your combination technique." Then I stepped around her, determined to head to the pyre and joke around with Evianna, Ryker, and Karna.

Atty held up a shaky hand.

I stopped and turned to her, confused. Atty said nothing.

The many bonfires kept the area lit, but Atty had her gaze on the ground, shielding most of her expression from me. I waited, the awkward tension rising with each moment that she remained silent.

"Is something wrong?" I asked, my voice almost lost to the drumbeats.

She shook her head. "I..." After a calming inhale, Atty continued, "I feel as though everyone is avoiding me."

I glanced around, looking for her phoenix eldrin, but I didn't see her. "Where's Titania?"

"I left her with Jozé. He asked to speak with her, and perhaps use a few of her feathers for trinkets."

A part of me wanted to tell her that she had done this to herself. Atty rarely did anything with anyone. Atty had always been reserved, but in the last few months, she had cut everyone off and isolated herself, focusing on her personal ambitions while the rest of us had been putting everything we had into combating the Second Ascension.

Now Atty was lonely, and confused as to why everyone was avoiding her? But her trembling hands and shadowed face stopped me from commenting.

I motioned to the bonfire. "Come join us. We have a few stories to tell. Have you heard what happens when Ryker and his eldrin transform together?" I chuckled just thinking about it. "It was shocking."

"The music is so loud. I was hoping to step away from the

festivities, to gather my thoughts, but everyone was busy."

An awkward moment passed between us as I realized what she was asking.

But I *had* wanted to speak with her.

"We can take a stroll down the side of the gorge," I said, pointing away from the city. "I don't know if we'll ever escape the music."

Atty smiled. "The people in Thronehold can hear this."

"On the Isle of Ruma, too."

She chuckled as she walked to my side. Together, we headed away from the festivities at a leisurely pace. Terrakona watched me go, his mismatched eyes bright in the night. When I didn't speak to him, he rested back in a tight coil, but he kept his gaze on me the entire time.

Regal Heights had enough energy to move the ocean, but once we were a few hundred feet from the gates, the thump of the music lessened. It was easier to speak—and think—and that was when Atty turned to me, her fingers laced.

"It's been so long since we could have a private conversation," she said.

"I suppose." I crossed my arms, surprised at how chill the evening could become. With little effort, I kept myself warm. Atty's phoenix magic was passive—she likely wasn't cold. Magics that could create heat were a great boon.

"You said something about your brother?" Atty asked. "His transformation?"

"He and MOS *combine*." I laced my fingers together in demonstration. "Merge. Like Luthair and I used to. I wasn't expecting it. And it happened out of nowhere. MOS reached out a hand and took Ryker straight into her." I shook my head. "I'm sure that sounds... not right... but it's what happened."

Atty held a hand to her mouth. Her long fingers were delicate and smooth—she hadn't been outside much lately.

"Do you think that MOS has a true form?"

Her question got me thinking. "I suspect so."

"And god-creatures?" Atty asked.

I rubbed at the back of my neck. "Uh, *probably*. I mean, I hadn't thought of it." I glanced down at the mark on my chest. "But my mark isn't glowing."

"I've been thinking about documenting all experiences with mystical creatures achieving true form, not just my own." Atty tapped her fingers together. "I mean, there are so many strange creatures in this world. Look at MOS. She's *different*. She's strange. Even her name is strange." Then she smiled at me. "I think... if anyone is going to have a true form god-creature, it'll be you."

I pointed to myself.

She nodded.

Then I laughed. "I don't think so. I mean, Luthair and I were—" I stopped myself cold. I was about to say, *Luthair and I were perfect together.* I hadn't thought about it like that before, and I was surprised by the sudden amount of emotion I felt roiling around in my chest.

I turned away, ice flooding my veins.

"I just doubt it," I lamely finished. "Terrakona is strong, and together, we're powerful, and that's all I've been focusing on. I just need to deal with the Second Ascension. If I can do that without true form, great. If I need true form, then I'll cross that bridge when I get there."

I had made up my mind. Nothing would stop me from ending their whole organization. I'd do whatever it took.

The further we traveled away from the city, the less light we had. The moon and stars offered to be our guide.

But that was when I felt the presence of others. I tensed as we neared an outcropping of rocks that overlooked the canyon. To my surprise, there were two people sitting on the edge.

Zelfree and Calisto.

I had thought they were in the city—in a fortress house, where Zelfree could keep a close eye on Calisto—yet here they were, in the middle of nowhere, at the dead of night. It seemed like an odd choice, but I wasn't about to question Zelfree in front of Atty and Calisto. Instead, I greeted them with a quick nod.

They both sat with their legs dangling into the canyon, the fall to the bottom at least a thousand feet. Certain death, really. Yet neither seemed concerned.

Zelfree jumped to his feet and ran a hand through his hair. His mimic, Traces, purred as she got to her feet and laced herself between his legs. "Oh, look. It's the Warlord and the phoenix arcanist. We were just talking about you."

I met Zelfree's gaze. "You were?"

He huffed and shook his head. "It was in passing." With a hasty gesture of his hand, he motioned to Atty and me. "What're you two discussing?"

"True forms of mystical creatures," Atty replied.

"Of course," Traces sarcastically muttered, rolling her feline eyes. "We're all shocked."

The mention of true forms interested Calisto, though. He hadn't been paying attention to us at all, but then he glanced over his shoulder, his gaze harsh.

"Huh," Zelfree said. He crossed his arms. "Even during the celebration? Atty, what have I told you about the importance of taking a break? You should enjoy life. Adventure. Friends. Food. *Anything*."

"Well, about that." Atty fussed with the blue sleeves of her robes, hesitation in her voice. "I was finding that difficult. And I thought, perhaps, the way to achieve a true form with my phoenix would be through rigorous study. Some legends say that phoenixes are creatures of knowledge."

I could practically hear Zelfree's frustrated thoughts. He clenched his jaw, clearly holding back words.

But Calisto never bothered to limit himself.

"You, lass?" Calisto said as he got to his feet. "A true form phoenix? Never." With a dismissive huff, he slid his hands into the pockets of his trousers.

Atty stood a bit straighter, her nerves melting into irritation. With stiff words, she said, "I didn't come here looking for the advice of a dread pirate."

With a dismissive click of his tongue, Calisto replied, "Then take the advice of someone who *had* a true form eldrin. You're never going to get a true form phoenix through *study*."

Atty gripped her hands together, her knuckles growing white. Then she stepped closer to me and said, "Your eldrin was a man-eater and a monster. Phoenixes are nothing like that." She exhaled as she placed a gentle hand on my shoulder. "And you're a fiend, Calisto. What do you know of other creatures?"

Calisto darkly chuckled, his gaze shifting to the canyon. "I was a mystic seeker for decades, lass. I worked for the best there was. I've seen the true form of dozens of creatures, even a phoenix."

That one statement silenced Atty. Her eyes went wide, and she held her breath.

Zelfree glanced over his shoulder. "You did?"

"That's right," Calisto muttered. "Some lunatic who called himself *Roger the Undying*. His true form phoenix was a sight to see."

"You're a liar," Atty whispered.

Calisto shot her a cold glare. "Trust me—I don't care enough to lie."

"Then... Then what do you have to do?" Atty moved closer to the edge of the canyon, her long hair caught on the breeze. "What was the trick? How did he achieve true form?"

"*I'm a liar*, remember?" Calisto chortled as he shrugged. "What does it matter?"

"If you know, tell her," I growled.

Calisto was silent. At first, I thought he would ignore me, but then he finally exhaled. "Listen, you don't understand what it means to see a mystical creature at its apex. You're soft and blind. The telos of a creature is obvious."

"What does that mean?" Atty asked, her words filled with a mix of hope and confusion.

"It means—phoenixes *rise from the ashes*. They don't *manifest in books*. Rising from the ashes is about rebuilding yourself from nothing." Calisto held up a hand and tightened it into a fist. "It's about being *beaten* but refusing to die. *That's* the telos of a phoenix." He glowered at Atty. "It's a long, rough road of struggle and recovery. You're a prissy little lass. The most you've struggled with is a dull sandwich."

Atty stiffened.

"What did I say?" Zelfree snapped. "Stop antagonizing them. It won't work."

Calisto shook his head. "It's nothing but the truth."

"You don't know that for sure," Atty whispered.

I thought Calisto hadn't heard, but then he replied with a snort and a laugh. No words. No denial, no affirmation. He just didn't care one way or another.

Atty turned to me, her shoulders bunched at the base of her neck. "Volke, I'd like to return to the celebrations."

Her request surprised me, but I wanted to return there as well. "All right."

Then she took my arm and held it close. Her hands trembled again, so I didn't object to her touch. Clearly, she wasn't feeling her usual confident self. Hopefully, she'd feel better alongside the rest of the Frith Guild.

# CHAPTER 43

## A FATHER'S HONOR

Atty and I didn't say a word as we traveled back to the celebrations.

The music had returned in full force by the time we had reached the outer wall. Atty clung to my elbow, and I didn't shoo her away out of politeness, but I figured now was a good time to talk about a different subject.

"So, Evianna and I have been—"

"Do you believe him?" Atty interjected.

I mulled the question over for half a second before replying, "I believe him."

"Even though he's a blackheart?"

"Well, he's... not really the kind of man to lie for the fun of it. And he *does* seem to know a lot about mystical creatures." I had seen his memories. He *had* run with mystic seekers in the past, and mystic seekers were trained in the knowledge of all sorts of creatures. "Also, Theasin wrote a book on mystical creatures, and in it, I remembered him saying that phoenixes required *hope* and *determination* to achieve their true form. Hope and determination are only tested in adversity... Like Calisto said."

"I just don't know what to do with that information." Atty sighed. "Do you?" She stared up at me, her eyes pleading.

"Maybe we should talk about something else. I've been meaning to tell you that—"

"This is important, Volke. Please. Just... I need to find answers. This question has plagued me for so long."

I really didn't know what to say to her. So, in awkward fashion, I said, "Evianna might know what to do. You see, since we've been spending so much time together, *as a couple*, I've come to learn that she's highly educated in all sorts of interesting areas."

That was probably the most bizarre way to convey that information, but I didn't care. At least Atty hadn't interrupted me, and hopefully, this could be resolved once and for all.

"As a couple?" Atty slowly released my elbow. "Oh. I apologize. I should've been more proper." She brushed back her blonde hair, her attention on the ground. "And you're very right. She's highly educated. That's true."

It shocked me that Atty had known nothing about Evianna and me. Atty really had been separating herself from the group so much that even simple information like this came as a surprise.

"You don't have to apologize," I muttered. "I just wanted to let you know. And I do think you should speak to her. And perhaps even Vinder, the minister of Regal Heights. His true form gargoyle is amazing. He might have some advice."

He might also try to throw her into the gorge, but I suspected everything would ultimately be fine.

"And don't worry," I added. "You're one of the most talented arcanists I know. I'm sure you'll figure this all out. Eventually. But I do think Zelfree is right. You should take a break occasionally."

Atty didn't react to my words. She just stared at the ground, not giving me even a nod.

Had she heard me?

I couldn't figure out her expression, but she did seem troubled. Atty had been the one to end things between us—even if she didn't make it clear. She surely couldn't have thought I would wait until she was ready to get back together? Right?

I nervously chuckled and then scooted to the side. "Well, I'm going to go find Evianna now."

That was when Atty broke out of her silent trance. "Wait. Can I come with you?"

"Sure. I'm sure the others will enjoy your company."

"You don't mind? Even though..."

I shook my head. "You're overthinking it. Come with me. No one will be bothered."

Atty replied with a tepid smile and shuffled to my side. As we walked to the bonfire, she said, "You look good with your shirt open, by the way. I'm sure everyone has told you that, but I figured I should voice my approval."

My face heated a bit as we reached the edge of the flames. If I had known this would be so popular with the ladies, I would've done it more often before. Or perhaps they just liked seeing my god-arcanist mark. It was impressive.

The moment Karna spotted me, she smiled with all the fierceness of a shark. Her eyes darted between me and Atty, examining the both of us. Then she leapt up from her seat, grabbed my wrist, and danced closer to the flames, taking me with her.

"*Volkie*, we've been waiting for you."

She sat me down next to Evianna, and for that, I silently thanked her. But then Karna sat on my other side, scooting close. When Atty approached, no one really greeted her. Ryker kept his eyes on the roasting rabbits, and Evianna was focused on me.

"Atty, come try some of the food," I said, drawing her into the moment. "I haven't had any of this, but it looks amazing."

She took a seat close to us, her excitement forced. I wasn't sure what else I could do for her. It surprised me that she had such poor social skills sometimes. Had spending all that time alone stunted her?

I worried.

---

The party lasted until the sun rose.

Which was lunacy.

How did the citizens of Regal Heights have such energy? The music, the dancing, the meat, and the entertainment was nonstop. Even the children stayed up. When I wandered back to my fortress home, I found dozens of people passed out in the alleyways between stone buildings, and even a few curled up on the rabbit fur across the bridges.

What if they rolled off? Was no one concerned?

The guards went around, hitting people with sticks, getting them up on their feet before pushing them toward their homes.

The number of hydras in the city surprised me as well. The giant half-dragons couldn't move well, and some of them acted as if they were drunk. They staggered back and forth, and the many heads argued with themselves.

Raisen stood by the door of my fortress, one of the few hydras that wasn't puking or sleeping in an awkward position. His king head stared at me with focused, gold eyes.

"Warlord," Raisen said, a light hiss in his words. "Did you enjoy the celebrations?"

I nodded. "Where's Hexa? Did she enjoy the party?"

"She hasn't been herself."

Another head chimed in with, "She couldn't celebrate. She was too busy being sad."

A third head said, "Her family comforted her all night."

The king head hissed at the others. Then he turned his

attention to me, glaring. "Warlord, please make sure that we find Vethica. My arcanist feels pathetic and weak for not saving her immediately."

With a sigh, I nodded. I knew how she felt. I had failed to save people in the past, and it hurt, deep in my soul.

"I also need to find Luthair," I muttered.

The eyes on all of Raisen's faces widened. "Ah. Yes. I apologize."

"It's fine. I'm just saying that I have an interest in finding the Second Ascension as well. But I'm not sure what we can do to get this done faster."

"Do you think Vethica is dead?"

I shook my head. "I think the Second Ascension wants *advantages*. They want magical items, mystical creatures, more arcanists... And they want leverage over us. They won't kill Vethica. She's too useful."

I couldn't say the same thing about Luthair. There was a good chance they were just going to kill him and turn him into a trinket or artifact. Or—in the worst-case scenario—he would bond with someone while he was confused.

A true form knightmare could sense lies, though. If any of the Second Ascension tried to trick him, I was certain he would sense it, and then perhaps leave them before anything happened.

But that was me hoping for the best.

I wished he would just come back to us.

"We'll find them," I said, concluding my speech to Raisen. "Don't worry about it."

The six heads of the hydra bowed to me. "Thank you, Warlord." And then Raisen lumbered off, his feet stomping on the stone as he went.

I appreciated that Raisen was looking out for Hexa. After a short moment dwelling on the fact that Hexa's loyalty and gruff kindness were bleeding into Raisen, I went inside and prepared myself for a long and peaceful sleep.

While I slept, I dreamt of true form god-creatures.

This wasn't a dream created by Adelgis's dreamweaving magic—it was just a nonsensical series of images and feelings, woven together like a patchwork blanket.

Terrakona growing larger than the world itself. The fenris wolf shrinking to the size of a snowflake. Evianna bonding with the typhon beast, but her knightmare stayed with her, and became armor for her new giant eldrin.

I woke up at one point in the middle of the day. The pillows covered my entire head, and I flailed my arms, sat up, remembered where I was, and then collapsed back on the mattress. When next I opened my eyes, the sun had already set, and the stars lit up the night sky.

And people were still celebrating.

A low beat of drum music rang out in the gorge beyond my window, my heart beating with the rhythm. The special lights and lanterns were still lit, and colored parchment sailed into the gorge, carried by the wind.

I didn't feel like celebrating a second night in a row.

I woke, bathed, ate some of the food left for me on the silver serving tray near the window, and then dressed. While I had several things to do, my thoughts immediately went to my father. I needed to make magical items, and if everyone else was busy anyway, now was a great time. My father wouldn't be out in the festivities.

Sure enough, when I focused on the tremors of the canyon, the party outside had dulled, but not disappeared, and my father still limped around the study, clearly busy with his work. I hurried to his location, wondering if he had finished with Zelfree's project.

If he had, we could move on to bigger and better things.

The stone fortress was easy to navigate. I made my way down

some stairs, and then a hallway before I reached my father's study. When I placed my hand on the door handle, I thought about the time of day.

It was night.

Had my father been working all day? Had he ever managed to get some rest?

I opened the door and stepped inside, determined to question him. The instant I saw him, however, I knew the answer.

Bags hung under his eyes, and his hair looked greasy from sweat. He limped from one side of the room to the other, grimacing as he went. It took my father a couple of seconds to even realize I had entered the room.

"Ah, I didn't realize I'd have company tonight." Jozé forced a smile. "I thought you'd be celebrating."

I shook my head as I shut the door and wandered inside. The bones of the typhon beast were large, but someone had shattered one of the femurs into splinters. The ivory fragments were piled like wood in the corner of the room, some of them still filled with marrow.

A single fang—like the blade of a scythe—sat near the fireplace.

I admired the bones before stopping near my father's side. "I was hoping to practice my imbuing while everyone else celebrated."

Jozé chuckled. "Oh. I see. You heard I finished my potion and you rushed over here."

"The sinberry potion?"

"That's right."

I crossed my arms and furrowed my brow. "And it works? It'll *permanently* erase someone's memories?"

"I'm fairly certain," Jozé said. But then, with a smile, he added, "It's not like I tested it before I handed it over to Zelfree."

"Well, er, yeah. I'm glad you didn't." I remained tense as I asked, "Do you think... it's a good idea? I mean, what if the Second Ascension gets a hold of this and tries to use it on anyone who opposes them?"

Jozé slowly nodded along with my words. Then he shuffled over to the desk, opened the bottom drawer, and withdrew a glass vial. A black *substance* was inside the vial, thick and opaque. He motioned me over, and once I was by his side, Jozé removed the stopper.

The black contents reeked of death. I gagged and stepped away.

With a sneer, I asked, "Is *that* the potion?"

Jozé laughed. "That's right. Trust me, no one is going to *accidentally* ingest this. It would require an impressive amount of fortitude, and willpower, to gulp this down." Jozé tilted the vial upside down. The liquid was so goopy, it slid out with the speed of tree sap. A small drop hit the desk, almost lumpy, like jam.

"And the disgusting texture," Jozé said, his nose wrinkled. "Trust me when I say, it won't be an effective weapon. I used all the berries Zelfree gave me, and I barely had enough for two potions. Only *two*. The berries were small, and I didn't get much from them."

He shoved the stopper back into the vial and then shoved the sinberry potion into the desk.

"I'm still worried about it," I muttered.

Jozé dwelled on my words before reaching back into the desk and withdrawing the vial a second time. Then he handed it to me. "Take it, boy. Throw it out the window and let the gorge take it. Then you won't have to worry."

I held the palm-sized vial close, my heart beating fast. It was a terrible potion—when would we ever need it again? "Are you sure? I mean, you spent so much time and effort making it. You don't mind if I just throw it away?"

Jozé half-shrugged. "Listen, I made that for Zelfree because he asked. I already gave him one vial of the potion. This is extra. And I don't have any vested interest in what happens to it. I'm not even proud of my work here. I prefer blacksmithing, ya see. Making trinkets and artifacts... *This* is something strange and abstract, and I don't like it."

Since my father didn't care, I walked over to the massive window at the far end of the study and opened it wide. The music from the celebrations, as well as a cold wind, drifted into the room. After a moment of contemplation, I unceremoniously tossed the potion into the canyon.

We didn't need it.

The vial twirled through the air, and then disappeared into the fog. I never heard it hit the bottom, but that was because of the drums and shouting.

Then I shut the window and walked back over to my father. "Well, I was hoping to do some imbuing. Would you mind helping me?"

Jozé nodded once and then motioned to the bone fragments. "I was thinking we could craft some swords, daggers, and shields from these pieces. I'm not entirely familiar with the typhon beast, but Brom and Vinder gave me some insight."

"They did?" I asked, my volume much louder than before.

Did the city founder and minister know things about the typhon beast that I didn't?

Jozé gave me an amused glance. Then he hobbled over, grabbed a bit of bone—something the length of his arm—and brought it over to me. "Apparently, the typhon beast was a creature of consumption. It ate more flesh than any other beast. Its fangs and claws sliced through men and mystical creatures with ease."

"Much like how Retribution cuts through magic?"

Jozé nodded once.

I stared down at the bone, turning it over to look at it from all sides. As I did, Jozé opened a small chest by his desk, and withdrew two star shards. The small crystals were each the size of a finger, but they glittered with an inner power that always impressed me.

"Take these," he said as he handed them over. "I'm curious to see what kind of item we can make with world serpent magic." Then he motioned to the bone. "Don't worry about crafting it into a keen-edged weapon. I'll be able to reshape it afterward. Blue phoenix magic allows me to augment materials —even trinkets and artifacts."

Although I wasn't confident, I placed the star shards on the bone, and then covered them with one hand. When I had done this in the past, I had been grasping around in the dark. I wasn't an expert when it came to this.

Did my imbuing have a creation and destruction path? Probably. But I closed my eyes and pushed that thought out of my head. I would need to focus if I was going to create anything.

"The real trick to imbuing is to be well rested." Jozé sighed. "I'm not setting a good example, unfortunately. But trust me. When you're imbuing, you're pouring your magic into your item. If you're exhausted, you won't be able to control the flow properly, so you need rest first—plenty of food. And a quiet place, if possible."

"Is that why you closed the window?" I asked, keeping my voice low.

"That's right."

"What else should I think about?"

My father patted my shoulder. "Imagine your magic. Evocation is the easiest. You make molten rock, right?"

"From my body, yeah."

Jozé went silent for a few moments, probably mulling it over. Then he said, "That's fine. Imagine the heat, the rock, the earth—imagine it in the bone marrow."

With my eyes firmly shut, I pictured my magic. It was easy. The obsidian spikes, the hard bones, the molten rock—my evocation was deadly, but it also made me stronger than before. A type of offense and defense that most people couldn't handle. How would that mix with the typhon beast?

"Stop," Jozé said. "I can tell you started thinking about something else."

With my eyes still closed, I smirked. "Really? How?"

"You've got an honest face, boy. Wearing your emotions like clothing. And your eyebrows relax whenever you shift focus. I can see it. Don't do that."

Sometimes I hated how much everyone could tell about my mood. In this case, it wasn't that bad. I steadied my thoughts, went back to picturing my evocation, and then pushed my magic outward, straight into the bone fragment.

When I had handled the bones of the apoch dragon, I had felt their power. Touching them had given me the feeling of a slumbering beast briefly awakening. Now, as I imbued these typhon beast bones, I felt it again. As if the bones were reveling in my magic, fighting to live once more. Did pieces of the god-creatures contain parts of their consciousnesses?

No. That was impossible.

Wasn't it?

"You're not focusing again," Jozé said.

I pushed the thought of the typhon beast out of my mind.

As my magic flowed from me, the two star shards melted and sank into the bone, becoming the adhesive that would hold the magic in place. Once they were gone, I couldn't bind any more magic into the item, even though the bones desperately wanted more. I had more magic to give, and I was certain the bones could handle just about any amount of magic, but without more star shards, this was the limit.

Then I opened my eyes and stared down at the bone.

It was ivory bone with veins of red. Those veins pulsed with power, glittering with magic. It was both beautiful and terrifying. They reminded me of veins in a body.

Then again, molten rock was the blood of the world...
Perhaps this was appropriate.

I raised the bone fragment into the air and then swung it around as if it were a real sword. My father stumbled back, hands up in the air.

"Whoa, whoa!" he called out. "Don't get reckless, kid!"

The veins in the bone shard flared bright red as I swung, and a terrible heat exploded from the ivory length, the power so intense that the air seemed to scream, even though I wasn't swinging fast. If not for our magical resistance to heat, both Jozé and I would have been cooked by the sheer power of the trinket.

I slowly lowered the bone shard and gave Jozé a sheepish look.

"Hand it here," he said, motioning with slow movements. "Carefully, please."

I handed the bone fragment over. The glitter of red magic made me smile.

That was when Jozé closed his eyes and held the fragment out in front of him. He had a single star shard, and I wondered if he needed that in order for his augmentation to become permanent. He gritted his teeth, held the bone with both hands, and allowed his magic to work. The bone glowed, as if in the fires of a forge, and became malleable like clay. With expert hands, Jozé molded the bone into a straight and fine edge by pinching the edges with his fingers. The blazing hot sword would've easily burned any other arcanist, but my father was immune to heat.

Once he had finished sharpening the edges, and crafting a tang for a handle, he exhaled and stopped his magic. As the blade cooled, its orange glow faded, letting me get a good look. It was an ivory sword with glittering red veins of power.

A blade from the legendary typhon beast.

Jozé opened his eyes, walked around the desk, rummaged through one of the drawers, and then withdrew a piece of metal.

Steel? I wasn't certain. With more magic, Jozé crafted a handle and affixed it to the edge of the bone blade, finishing the sword in a matter of minutes.

If we had gone to a normal blacksmith, this sword would've taken a few days to craft, no doubt in my mind. And they might not have been able to craft the bone, since it was such an odd material.

Once the steel had cooled a bit, Jozé handed me the blade. "Here. Try it. If the balance is off, let me know."

As I took the blade, Jozé stepped away to give me space. The study was a large room, and it was easy to distance myself from everything around. I swung the sword a few times, pleased with the weight. It was light, but felt sturdy.

The *point of balance* of a sword was the precise location on the blade where its weight was equally distributed to each side. If the point of balance was close to the handle, the wielder wouldn't be able to make quick strikes, but they would be able to make strong swings. If the point of balance was close to the tip, recovering from a strike would take twice as long, as the blade would be a bit unruly.

Which was why most weaponsmiths designed their swords with a point of balance near the center. It helped the wielder make fast, powerful swings, while also recovering quickly to prevent counterattacks.

Retribution was perfectly balanced.

And so was this sword. I swung it with ease, and even slashed through the air without exerting myself. A lightweight blade with a keen edge, and the heat of a volcano. An interesting weapon.

How many of these could we make?

"That's a good weapon," Jozé muttered, scratching at the stubble on his chin. Then he rubbed at his tired eyes. "I'm surprised it went so well so quickly... Your god-arcanist magic is incredible. That sword is just a trinket, but it can express more power than some artifacts."

I nodded along with his words, wondering what effects could be created through different combinations.

Jozé rubbed his forehead, looking slightly dazed. "Working with these god-creature parts is an artificer's dream."

"Can I set this down?" I asked, staring at the red veins.

"On the stone over there. Don't worry—I can craft scabbards that will contain heat."

I set the blade on the floor near the window, on flat, cold stone. Then I walked back over to my father, my thoughts on my artifact sword.

"Have you given thought to how I can improve Retribution with world serpent magic?" I asked.

Jozé nodded once. "It'll require more star shards than you used to craft the weapon. You used ten, didn't you? That's what I remember." He held up a hand, silencing me before I answered. "The more we use, the more magic we can imbue, but only if the base materials can handle it. Since this is the apoch dragon we're talking about, I think it'll work fine, but it's the attunement I'm worried about."

"You've already given this thought?"

"Considerable thought." Jozé waggled a finger as he limped over to the desk. He didn't get anything out of the drawers, he just leaned against the side, his weight obviously too much for his bad leg. He rubbed at his thigh. "I don't want my son defeated on the battlefield because his weapon failed him."

Jozé didn't usually refer to me as *his son*. He did so only occasionally, and every time it happened, my chest tightened. "All right."

"The Autarch has a lot of resources," Jozé whispered, his voice becoming quieter with each word. "He has arcanists, mystical creatures, star shards, gold kirin magic... Even more bones of the apoch dragon. Which means... we must give you the best artifacts we can create."

"I don't think it's necessary."

Jozé gave me a sidelong glance. "I don't want to take any risks. Your friend Adelgis—Theasin's son—gave me an explanation of the Autarch's power base, and I knew once he was finished that you might be in trouble."

"Well, no one has been bonded with their god-creature as long as I have," I stated. "Not even the Autarch. While he might have resources, I think I have a few advantages of my own. You needn't worry so much."

"You tell me that after you've had children of your own."

His statement startled me. I hadn't thought of it like that, but at the same time, I couldn't be coddled. "Have you done this with Ryker?" I asked.

Jozé snorted. Then he opened a drawer and withdrew a sapphire sash. Well, half a sash. It was woven with silver thread, and only partially complete. Blue phoenix feathers were sewn into the beautiful fabric, each shimmering with inner beauty.

"I'm making this for Ryker." Jozé ran his thumb across the bottom of his nose. "I'm not the best at sewing, but I've done my fair share. Once it's complete, I'll use some star shards to create a magical item capable of protecting him from fire."

I crossed my arms, amused by his concern. "Really? I mean, Ryker doesn't fight much. You've seen him."

Jozé shoved the sash back into the desk. "Look, I've seen what his magic can do. The boy will be on the battlefield at some point. Maybe I can't fight with him—and protect him—like a perfect father would, but I want to do *something*, all right, boy?"

I held up a hand. "I wasn't trying to insult you or—"

"When you question whether or not I'd help Ryker, it's like you're calling into question my honor as a father." Jozé forced a quick exhale and then shook his head, his eyelids heavy.

"I didn't mean anything by it, I swear."

He said nothing. The study remained silent as we both dwelled on the conversation. Finally, Jozé said, "I know you didn't mean anything by it." He closed his eyes and then ran a hand down his face, dragging his fingers over his eyes. "Don't bother listening to me. I'm tired. It's late."

I nodded once. "It's fine. I, uh, really appreciate you caring. About me. I thought for a long time that you didn't."

Jozé snapped his gaze up to meet mine. His eyebrows knitted, and I suspected he was about to say something, but I cut him off with, "Ever since I reunited with you, you've been nothing but a concerned father. Thank you for that. Truly." I laughed once. "Sorry for getting you caught up in this battle. And also for getting Devlin's airship blown up. I know that was home for you."

"Don't worry about it, boy," Jozé muttered, his expression softening with a smile. Then he pointed to the blade at my hip. "Let's work on that, shall we?"

I placed my hand on the hilt and nodded.

# CHAPTER 44

## RETRIBUTION, A SWORD WITH NO EQUAL

I drew Retribution and allowed myself to admire the black sword I had created with knightmare magic. In just a moment, the sword Luthair and I had crafted together would be changed forever...

I wanted to commit the way Retribution currently looked to memory.

Then I laid it on the table.

Jozé handed me a pouch containing fifteen star shards, which seemed like a ridiculous amount. I placed the star shards, one after the other, along the length of the blade. Then I rested my fingers on the hilt and closed my eyes.

"Attuning an item to an individual isn't a complicated matter, but it is another step we need to take once you're done," Jozé said.

"All right." I tried to focus on my magic.

"Don't just imagine your evocation this time. Imagine all your magic. Imagine your eldrin."

"Why?"

Jozé walked around to the other side of the desk. I couldn't see him with my eyes closed, but my hearing, and my tremor sense worked just fine.

"You want the power of the apoch dragon bones to be dominant, right? Because the bones absorb and destroy magic? Then you shouldn't focus on any particular aspect of your magic. Give the dragon what it wants. Let it feed on your power in its purest and most complete form. Imagine everything of your eldrin feeding the bones and letting them wake."

"Are the bones... alive?" I asked. "Even when I was making the bone sword, the typhon beast remains felt like they had a personality."

"Mystical creatures are just made of magic, boy. And the magic isn't *dead*. The magic is still there, in the remains, holding a sliver of that creature. That's why they make great trinkets and artifacts."

And why the soul forge could resurrect them.

It made sense now.

They were... magical constructs. The magic that made up their body remained in their body, even after death. But the apoch dragon seemed like the antithesis of that.

It was disconcerting.

"Think about all your magic," Jozé commanded. "Think about it disappearing. Think about it being eaten. If the bones can handle a grand total of twenty-five star shards, you should be able to add your magic to the blade. If the bones can't handle it, then this will fail."

"Will Retribution break?"

Jozé took longer to answer than I liked. "Probably not."

I gritted my teeth, scrunched my eyes tightly closed, and then exhaled. I did as my father wanted. I pictured my magic. Creation, destruction—the choice I had to make. Once I made a decision, one would disappear. Then I thought about my aura, the capstone of my powers. I could eradicate the arcane plague, or change it into something *else*. What if I lost that as well?

It worried me. My salvation or armageddon aura was the key to ending the plague once and for all. I hadn't even started learning it, but I knew I would need to. All the god-arcanists would have to.

Imagining that I would lose it made me uneasy.

And the bones seemed to like that. I had never thought Retribution sinister, but occasionally, I felt the *end of things* deep inside of it. The apoch dragon was death and ruin. Nothing more.

So, instead of running from the feeling of loss and failure, I dwelled on it. That was when I tried to push my magic into the sword, using the star shards as glue. The little crystals melted, spreading across the black blade of my sword. My fears of losing my magic went with them, seeping into the bones that made up the core of Retribution.

Dark, terrible fears.

The knightmare magic inside the blade seemed to flare at the fear I offered. My world serpent magic wasn't replacing my old knightmare magic... Instead, they mixed together, intertwining as they empowered the blade. But the apoch dragon bones wanted *so much* magic.

The fell dragon reminded me of the darkness found between stars—a terrible void that threatened to snuff out all the lights in the night sky. Even now, as the bones absorbed my magic, it was as if it wanted to steal everything I had.

That was probably why I had been able to feel the bones' power when I had been infected with the arcane plague. They were both magics of consumption and death. The pain was excruciating, transcending the physical as it ate at my soul.

My magic was at the very limit of its current capabilities, and the agony had pushed me to the point of collapse. But I managed to hold out until the last star shard melted into the sword.

Then my vision blurred, my strength fading. It felt like my

muscles were burning, as though I had run around Regal Heights for five days straight.

Despite that, I managed to use all fifteen of the star shards. Right at the end, my arms gave out. I grunted as I dropped the sword on the floor. Retribution clattered on the stone, the edges of the blade glowing slightly.

"Are you okay?" Jozé asked.

I shook my head, my arms trembling. "I..."

After two deep breaths, my strength returned in slow amounts. Everything was okay. I just needed rest.

"That was straining," I muttered.

"The powerful artifacts always require a vast amount of concentration and work." Jozé glanced between me and the blade on the floor. "I'm surprised you managed it in the first go. I thought we would have to do this multiple times."

"I just did as you asked. I thought... about losing all my magic."

Jozé knelt and picked up the sword. It took him a bit to stand straight, but he eventually managed it. Then he examined the blade, his scrutinizing gaze landing on the center of the weapon.

"I've never seen this before..."

I stepped close and stared at Retribution. Then I caught my breath.

Where once Retribution's blade had been a shadowy black, now it was the depthless void of space. Thousands of stars marked the center of the blade. It reminded me of the celestial dragon. It was as if someone had torn away a piece of the night sky and fashioned it into a weapon.

On both sides of the blade, where Jozé had carved Retribution's name into the shadow steel, now blazed hundreds of emerald stars. The jade sparks glowed brighter than the other stars, and they rose all the way from the hilt to the tip of the blade. They twisted together in an incredibly ornate design, forming a constellation in the shape of a serpent.

The stars...

Luthair's cape had had stars.

And Terrakona...

It was definitely his image.

"Have *you* ever seen this?" Jozé whispered.

I shook my head. "Never," I said, a little winded from the imbuing.

"The apoch dragon bones could take all that magic... And your world serpent sorcery is powerful. More powerful than I expected. I'm not sure if I should be proud or horrified that you managed this."

I understood what he meant.

Jozé swung the sword once, and dark energy crackled along the edges of the blade, as if the weapon were woken through action. I felt the power of the apoch dragon bones radiating a sense of ravenous hunger and fear.

"Is Retribution okay?" I asked.

Jozé handed the sword to me. When I swung it, the blade felt effortless and light—more so than the bone sword. The point of balance was just as I remembered, and the blade had a sleek but sturdy feel in my hands.

The dark energy crackled again, ready to lash out at whatever the sword touched.

Jozé reached out a hand. I held the sword straight so he could examine it, but to my surprise, he grazed his palm along the edge. The blade cut him with no effort—like Jozé didn't even exist. If I moved the blade too much to one side, it would slice through him in an instant.

Jozé jerked his bleeding hand away, but dark energy swirled around the injury.

Tendrils of that terrifying power leeched into Jozé and tore into his soul, tore at his bond with Tine. The energy stripped magic from him and drew it back into Retribution, leaving only a potent residue tainting his being.

My father sucked in a breath through his teeth, and I quickly sheathed Retribution, hoping it would stop hurting him.

"Father?" I asked, panicked. "Are you okay?"

Jozé held his injured hand close to his chest, forcing himself to breathe. Slowly, but surely, he regained his strength. With a forced smile, he glanced up at me. "Well... that was surprising."

He showed me his palm.

The injury reminded me of the corpses in Thronehold—of the people Theasin had killed by stealing their lifeforces. The area around the cut was blackened, and branching veins of darkness radiated from the wound. They weren't spreading, which eased some of my anxiety.

My father tried to evoke fire. Some white embers sparked from his bloody palm, but not much, like the magic was strangled.

Or dead.

"Are you okay?" I asked as I placed a hand on his shoulder. "Should I... Should I go get someone with healing magic?"

Jozé shook his head and offered a weary smile. "No. No, I'm fine, boy." With a shaky voice, he added, "That sword... It's a blade without equal. I've never seen anything like it."

I swallowed hard as I glanced down at the hilt. The sword had always been deadly, but now it was something more. My father could barely use his magic.

"Can it still be attuned?" I asked.

Jozé stepped close to his desk and leaned against it. "Yes. I'll do that in just a moment. Let me recover a bit. Please."

Guilt flooded me. My father didn't deserve to be injured. I should've been more careful—I should've kept the blade away from him. There were other ways to test it.

"I'll go get Atty," I said. Normally, I would've gotten Zaxis, since he had been the better healer, but that wasn't an option anymore.

"Thank you," he said.

I turned and left the study, both proud of my sword, and worried it might be too much. Then again, everyone was right. The Autarch had more artifacts and weapons than I did. Maybe I would *need* a blade like Retribution to slay the man.

I would eventually find out.

# CHAPTER 45

## TAKING RESPONSIBILITY

After Atty had struggled to heal Jozé, he took Retribution in order to attune it to me. That way, if anyone else tried to wield my blade, they wouldn't be able to. However, since my father was so exhausted, he ended up going to bed just as the sun rose. He would attune my blade later.

While he slept, I decided to imbue more bone fragments. Although imbuing my blade had taken a toll, I had recovered quickly. I decided I could make at least a dozen new weapons before I needed to stop.

Holding the bones was interesting—it made the imbuing process enjoyable. The chaotic magic surging through the fragments of the old typhon beast was so intense, it made my body tingle. It reminded me of the scale I had used to create Forfend, except this power seemed... savage. Brutal.

The typhon beast had been uncontrollable, and I felt it here.

And each bone fragment was more interesting than the last. At first, all the bones I imbued had the red veins across them. But by the fourth one, I started to think of my manipulation. I could manipulate water or terrain, so I decided to think of the ocean and rivers.

The fourth bone shattered in my hands as the star shards melted. It startled me so much, I dropped everything. The bone bits scattered across the stone floor.

When I picked up the fifth bone from the typhon beast, I decided to think of my terrain manipulation. At first, it was going well—my focus was unbroken—but the moment the star shards melted, the bone once again shattered. I didn't understand why, and my father was sleeping, so I didn't have anyone to ask.

Now wasn't the time to expend resources for wild experimentations, so I grabbed two more star shards and imbued them with my evocation, giving them the veins of heat.

**"Warlord, you've been up for some time."**

I grabbed another bone and twirled it around in my hands. "I'll go to sleep soon enough."

**"The sun is straight above us."**

I glanced at the window. He was right. High noon. But I didn't want to stop. If I kept imbuing until sunset, I'd be back on a normal schedule. "I'll be fine."

At first, Terrakona didn't reply. I thought he was satisfied, but then he said, **"The guildmaster of the Frith Guild came to speak with me."**

"Oh?" I grabbed two more star shards and held them tightly in my palms. "Is everything okay?"

**"She suggested we make a pathway to the bottom of the gorge. That way, whoever decides to brave the typhon beast's Trial of Worth will have a way to get there."**

I stopped my work on the bones and thought over the situation. The first typhon beast couldn't escape the gorge and had eventually died. If the second typhon beast walked out of its lair right now, it would be just as trapped as the first.

We *needed* a path for the creature to ascend out of the gorge.

But the gorge was so vast and deep. Creating a path would take weeks—perhaps months—at the minimum. At least, at my current mastery. I wasn't yet proficient enough to open a huge canyon in order to defeat an enemy—which meant I'd have to slowly carve away at the rock, creating a switchback path, or a staircase...

Which gave me an idea.

"Okay," I muttered. "Tomorrow, I'll start on that. It'll give me good practice while we wait for the tracker to figure out where the Second Ascension ran off to."

**"I will help you, Warlord."**

"I'd like that."

Since we had arrived at Regal Heights, Terrakona and I had spent too much time apart. If I was working in the gorge, at least Terrakona would be able to be with me.

Nightfall.

The entire day had been spent exercising my imbuing skills. Overall, I had shattered two bones, and imbued twenty. I left my father's study feeling accomplished. I wished Zaxis had been with me. He needed to practice this, too. Everyone did, really.

I headed for the roof of the fortress. I wanted to stare down into the gorge and get a feeling for the surroundings. Where would I build this new pathway? Did I want it close to Regal Heights? Or farther down Hydra's Gorge? I needed to give the matter serious thought.

When I reached the roof, I took a deep breath of fresh air.

The celebrations had stopped, but the decorations remained. Clearly, everyone was too worn out from the parties to bother removing the wolf lanterns and paper displays.

The wind had scattered some of the parchment, though. Bits of colored wolf decorations were everywhere, even on the roof of my temporary home. I crunched over them as I made my way to the railing. Then I leaned my elbows onto the stone around the edge of the roof, my thoughts distant.

Imbuing all those bones had made me think of the first god-arcanists. The star shards in their time had been corrupted magic. They couldn't make magical items until they had fixed the corruption. And then, sometime afterward, they had been killed by the apoch dragon. They only had a small window of opportunity to imbue anything, and there hadn't been any experts on the matter...

Luvi had left an illusion to instruct me, because he had known there would be more god-arcanists. It occurred to me that I should do the same thing. If I kept a detailed journal about my experiences with my magic, especially item crafting, I could aid the future world serpent arcanist.

Whoever that person would be.

I would've been content to imagine the future until I got tired, but that was when I heard voices drifting up on the wind from the gorge. One of them I recognized immediately. Everett Zelfree. The other... It had to be Calisto, but he whispered most of his words, hiding his tone.

I scooted down the railing, searching for the pair. Now that the partying had come to a stop, it wasn't difficult to sense around, to feel everything that made contact with the ground. To my surprise, Zelfree and Calisto stood on the edge of the gorge, a few inches from the sheer drop off. They were on the outside of the fortress building, on a walkway that led out of the city.

No one else was around.

The distant lantern lights barely provided any illumination. The moon and stars were the greatest source of light.

Zelfree said something, but I couldn't hear the words, just the soft mumble of his voice. I closed my eyes and concentrated, trying to feel the vibrations of his words through his body.

"And then what happened?" Zelfree asked.

His words registered in my mind like I had heard them with my ears. I felt the tiny vibrations caused by his speech and was somehow able to reconstruct them into words, including the tone and inflection, but that was harder. It required all my attention.

"He just kept clinging to me," Calisto replied, too quiet for me to hear with my ears, but the vibrations were clearly there. "I told him to leave me alone. I never wanted him on my ship."

"He probably felt safer with you."

"No one is safe with me."

Their conversation told me that Zelfree hadn't yet given Calisto the sinberry potion. They were too busy discussing the past. I wondered why. Had Zelfree changed his mind about the whole thing?

"Anything else?" Zelfree asked. "That was seriously the last time you felt like you were comfortable with somebody?"

"I'm not like you," Calisto stated as he shifted his weight from one foot to the other. I saw him move, but my magic allowed me to sense it better. "I don't *fit in* anywhere. I had to make my own crew, and do things my own way, before life ever made any sense."

"But you regret most of those decisions?"

At first Calisto didn't answer. Instead of watching them from the railing, I took a seat on the roof, hiding behind the stone bricks. I couldn't see them, and they couldn't see me. But I could still hear and feel them.

It made me feel like Adelgis.

"I regret a lot of things," Calisto replied, his words slow.

"Well, that's why I wanted to bring you out here. I've come up with a solution."

"You're finally going to tell me?"

I closed my eyes, picturing their conversation in my mind's eye. At the same time, I sensed the people inside the fortress. Like my brother and Karna. Their voices were drifting into my perception, and I struggled to keep their words out of my thoughts.

Again, just like Adelgis.

"This here. You should drink this. It smells foul, but I think it's the solution."

A moment later, Calisto snorted. "It smells like a Death Lord's moldy boots."

"It'll make you forget everything. Your time as a dread pirate, your time with Redbeard. Hellion. Markus. Everything. You won't have to keep *suffering through your thoughts*, as you called it."

"For how long?"

"Forever."

The conversation came to a standstill. The two of them didn't say anything, or even move. That was when the voices of everyone else came to me through the vibrations in the stone and metal. Including my brother stammering through a compliment to Karna.

"—w-well, you're beautiful with every hair color." Although I couldn't hear him, Ryker's voice floated into my head. I heard his tone in my imagination.

"You must have a preference," Karna replied, her purr-cadence gravellier when I felt it this way. "Every man has a preference."

"It's your confidence, and, uh, demeanor, that I think is more important than the c-color of your hair. You glow when you're happy. When you're... helping people. Helping me."

I shook my head, dispelling their conversation. Zelfree and Calisto had started talking again, and shifting my focus took a little time.

"Why?" Calisto asked. "*What're you thinking?*"

But now he was speaking loud enough that I could hear him with my ears. Concerned this would turn into a fight, I stood and leaned on the railing again. Zelfree and Calisto were still standing by the edge of the gorge. What if one of them pushed the other?

"I want you to have a chance at a normal life," Zelfree replied. He held the vial in one hand, the black liquid just as thick and disgusting as the potion my father had shown me. "I want you to try."

"No one else wants me to try, Everett."

Zelfree shoved the vial into Calisto's hand. "I don't care what they want. If I have to, I'll leave the Frith Guild and help you find a new life somewhere else."

Calisto ran his free hand through his copper hair, his anger and frustration manifesting as a dark chuckle. "What's wrong with you? The Frith Guild is your life. You've been with them since... since before you were an arcanist."

"I don't care. I'm going to help you this time. No matter what."

Calisto grabbed the collar of Zelfree's shirt, and that was when I thought something might happen. I leapt up onto the railing, prepared to jump down and help Zelfree. It wouldn't be much of a fight—Calisto had no magic—but I wanted to make sure I manipulated the terrain fast enough to stop people from falling.

"The more you do for me, the more pathetic you are," Calisto stated, cold and practically disgusted. "Let me go. You're embarrassing yourself. *Just end this.*"

Zelfree placed a hand on Calisto's wrist. "Lynus, all those years ago... you were right. I took you for granted, and I was so caught up in living an adventure, I failed to realize you needed me."

"That was in the past."

"Just listen. I've made up my mind. I'm going to help you. I don't care if it costs me the Frith Guild or *my dignity*—I'll be there with you."

I glanced around. Where was Traces? But then I found her.

She sat on a boulder nearby, her eyes glowing in the moonlight. The little mimic cat watched the confrontation without blinking.

Calisto released Zelfree's shirt. Then he stepped away, his attention on the vial in his hand. He sighed, one so loud, and tinged with frustration that I thought he was going to go back to yelling. Instead, he just said, "I'm not worth it, Everett."

Apparently, it was Zelfree's turn to yell.

"Curse the abyssal hells, Lynus. *Listen to yourself.* You're talented! You bonded with a manticore, *and you made it true form*. You ran your own ship. You defeated the Dread Pirate Redbeard! You found a world serpent scale, even though the Second Ascension never could. The Autarch saw your talent! That was why he kept you around. That was why he gave you all those assignments and acquiesced to your ridiculous demands."

"I—"

"You're the only one who doesn't see that you've got more to offer the world than death and mayhem!"

The shouting was loud enough that I suspected everyone in Regal Heights was listening to this conversation. Either that, or they were being awoken from their sleep.

I waited, perched on the railing, wondering if anything else would happen. The lull in their conversation made me worry. No one said anything. What were they thinking? I supposed I wasn't completely like Adelgis after all, since I couldn't delve into their minds.

"You can do better than *me*," Calisto said, though I didn't hear it. He spoke so softly.

"That's not how love works."

I almost slipped off the railing. The statement had caught me completely off guard. I flailed and stumbled, and Traces turned her glowing eyes in my direction just as I fell back onto the roof. I hit the stone on my hip, losing a bit of my concentration.

Once I had picked myself back up, I focused my magic a second time. It wasn't appropriate to listen in, but I wanted to know what Calisto would do. I still feared he would throw Zelfree into the gorge for saying such a thing.

"I don't want your damn potion," Calisto said, stiffer and stiller than before. "What an insult that would be to Hellion. And to Markus. To everyone I ever hurt."

"To the people you hurt?"

"They can't escape the pain. Why should I?" Calisto scoffed. Then he unceremoniously tossed the potion off the side of the cliff and straight into the gorge. It fell into the mist, likely shattering near the vial I had thrown. "I've been a coward most of my life, but I'm not so pathetic and craven that I would close my eyes to reality."

"But—" Zelfree began.

"*Listen.* I'm either going to pay for my crimes with my life— a punishment that, for some reason, you can't bring yourself to execute—or I'm going to suffer through all the damn consequences of my actions. *I don't want anything less.* I don't want any more escapes—any more running away. The damn kid called me out and told me how I was trash for letting everyone tear me down, and I'm done with it."

"The... kid?"

"It doesn't matter." Calisto crossed his arms. "Just make up your mind. Push me into the damn gorge or let's get on with this *sad dance of life*. I was never supposed to live this long, but look what you've done."

Zelfree exhaled and stepped close to Calisto. "I can't believe you threw that potion away. It took me a lot of effort to get it."

"Tsk. I can't believe you wanted me to drink it."

"I told you I'd do whatever it took to help. You told me *your thoughts* were driving you insane. How am I supposed to help with that?"

Calisto relaxed— the first time he had done so during the

whole conversation. "I suppose I need to deal with them the old-fashioned way. By sufferin' through them."

When it became apparent that neither of them was going to kill the other, I exhaled and moved away from the railing. At least I had my answer. Zelfree was going to watch Calisto, and hopefully, the former dread pirate would attempt to atone for his crimes for the rest of his life.

And it did seem that Calisto truly did feel remorse. I doubted I would ever set aside my contempt for the man, but I respected his resolve not to take the easy way out. Most men wouldn't have done that...

And since he wasn't an arcanist anymore, he would resume aging as normal, which meant his life would be short. In a few decades, he'd be old and weak, and shortly after, he'd die. I supposed that made Calisto a *lisque*. A companion to an arcanist who wasn't an arcanist—someone who would die much earlier than their partner.

What an odd fate for the man.

There were worse endings. This was probably a kindness the man didn't deserve.

It was more for Zelfree, in reality.

---

When I returned to my room, the door was ajar.

I had been so focused on Zelfree and Calisto's conversation, that I hadn't been paying attention to everyone else in the fortress. When I concentrated, I felt someone on the bed in my room. My throat tightened, and my chest filled with energy ready to burst outward.

Evianna.

Although I was excited that she had come to see me for the night, I didn't want to act *too* excited. I slowly opened the door and stepped inside, surprised to see a single lantern lit and sitting on the nightstand next to the bed. Evianna waited with ten pillows piled around her as she read one of my books on the first god-arcanist.

My thoughts took a poetic turn. Evianna was stunning beyond compare. Karna and Atty were just as beautiful, in their own ways, but their attitudes and mannerisms always felt constructed, like a façade. Evianna was genuine, alight with life and emotion, that enhanced her natural beauty. Her hair and eyes gave her an exotic cast, and the way her skin glowed made her seem more than human.

Something transcendent, unbound by the earth. Magical.

I couldn't quite manage to put it all into words. I rubbed at the back of my neck, worried I might sound too sappy if I tried.

Evianna glanced up as I neared, her cheeks pink and her smile wide. "Volke, there you are. I've been waiting."

"Sorry," I said. Then I hurried over to my side of the mattress and sat on the edge. "Are you going to stay with me tonight?"

Evianna placed a hand on her face and glanced away. "Of course. But you shouldn't say it like that." She waggled a finger. "You should *ask* me to stay. It's, uh, more exciting that way. Women like to be chased."

"Evianna, will you stay the night with me?"

Her face grew red in an instant—which was weird, because she had just told me to do this exact thing. Was she really surprised?

Evianna hid her face in a pillow. Then she carefully lifted her head and smiled. "I'd love to."

She shoved the pillows out of the way, revealing her sleeping wear—a full set of robes. White, silky. Very elegant and classy. She even had a belt. Her outfit made me think I should have been wearing *more* clothing, but that also seemed ridiculous. Instead, I tugged off my shirt, and removed my boots.

Then the shadows flickered, and a chill hung in the corner of the room. Layshl—she was reminding me that she was still here. With a sigh, I hoisted myself on the bed and pulled up the covers.

Evianna quickly cuddled up next to me, her warm breath on my skin a welcome sensation.

I combed her white hair with my hand. She traced my god-arcanist mark with the tips of her delicate fingers.

My heart beat so hard, I doubted either of us would be able to sleep.

"What were you doing before you came to bed?" Evianna asked, obviously trying to distract me.

"Eavesdropping on members of the Frith Guild," I admitted in a sheepish tone.

"Really?" She swirled her fingers on my chest. "Do you do that often?"

"Well, more often than I would like, to be honest."

Evianna stared up at me, her eyes wide with curiosity. "Learn anything interesting?"

I chuckled, and then shrugged. "Well, sure. But, uh, let's keep it between us, shall we?"

———

The next morning came quicker than I had thought it would. I hadn't gotten much sleep, but that was fine. I had spent a long while speaking with Evianna and holding her close. It had felt intimate in a way that nothing before it had.

I left her asleep and headed out toward Hydra's Gorge. The morning was bright and pleasant, and I enjoyed the weather around Regal Heights, even if it was dry and unforgiving in the sun.

I walked all the way out of town to an area of the gorge with a long and wide flatland by the edge. If I rearranged the canyon edge, what kind of consequences would that lead to?

Terrakona made his way around the city, moving around the rocks and boulders with ease, despite his gigantic form. He slithered over to my location, his emerald scales glittering in the daylight. They reminded me more and more of Forfend. How brilliant and thick would they become?

My eldrin stopped near me, his crystal mane practically glowing.

**"Warlord,"** he telepathically said, his voice bright and cheery. **"So you've arrived. This is our first great creation— to rearrange the land and make it our own."**

"I wouldn't have said it like *that*," I muttered. "But we're going to make a path for the typhon beast to walk up. That way, we can get him out of this gorge."

**"The land is ours to control."**

He spoke in such grandiose terms, it sometimes worried me. Was the land really mine? Perhaps it was best I thought that way so I didn't have any mental blocks when it came to my magic. I needed to shape this territory.

"I was thinking we could make a stairway," I said. With a smile, I added, "And I want to shape each of the steps. One by one."

**"Why is that, Warlord?"**

Terrakona tilted his head to the side, asking the question with genuine curiosity.

"There's something on my home island that we call *the Pillar*. Chiseled into each step we have the virtues required to become an arcanist. All one hundred and twelve steps—each one unique."

**"And you wish to make that here?"**

I nodded once.

I knew them all by heart.

The first step? *Integrity. Without it, we cannot have trust.*

The second? *Passion. Without it, we grow complacent.*

The third? *Discipline. Without it, we are not the masters of our own destiny.*

I could go through all of them, anytime, day or night.

"But on my home island, the last couple of steps were ruined." I smiled to myself. "I figured I could make them here... So that this place would have a complete set of stairs."

**"As you wish, Warlord. But it will add time to our construction."**

"I think it's worth it." I motioned to the red, black, and gold stones all around us. "C'mon, Terrakona. We should get to work."

# CHAPTER 46

## CREATING A PATHWAY

Carving out steps in Hydra's Gorge was more difficult than I had thought it would be.

I had to make them large—since I wanted a god-creature to walk up this path—and I didn't want them to take up much space, since I wasn't about to rearrange all of Regal Heights. That meant I had to make them travel down the side of the canyon as one long walkway, parallel with the opposite cliff face.

Not free hanging steps, either. Those would easily break under the weight of a god-creature. I had to carve them into the canyon's side, heading straight down, each step nearly as tall as an adult. Perhaps I would even have to create smaller steps *per* larger step... Which would require a lot of work and effort, but it would all be worth it.

On the Isle of Ruma, the first step of the Pillar, near the ground, was *integrity*, but since I was making this stairway in reverse, I figured I would do it the opposite. The first step at the top was integrity, and I made it twenty people wide—large enough to fit Terrakona easily.

Terrakona snorted and then made the second step, his

magic matching mine perfectly. Afterward, I used my manipulation to carve the virtue about passion deep into the stone.

After a long exhale, I made the third step. Terrakona made the fourth. We chunked away at the side of the gorge, creating smooth surfaces and rounded edges. Since I was trying to be accurate and precise, my full attention was required. With each movement of my hand and body, my magic seeped into the ground and rearranged it as I wanted.

The twenty-third step... *Humor. Without it, we live in a darker world.*

The twenty-fourth step... *Dignity. Without it, we treat ourselves as buffoons.*

The twenty-fifth step... *Tenacity. Without it, we trick ourselves into giving in.*

But that was when I had to stop. Imbuing drained magic directly from an arcanist. The loss of power wasn't permanent, but it took time to recover. I had pushed myself to the absolute limit yesterday... Even an entire night wasn't enough time for me to fully recover.

It was the middle of the day, but I had to rest again.

Terrakona moved up and down the steps, as though testing them out. He slithered effortlessly over each one, his weight held by the structure, the stones smooth enough that they weren't catching on his scales.

But the stairway was barely down the side of the canyon... At this rate, the one hundred and twelve steps wouldn't be enough to reach the bottom. I would have to get creative. Some steps would have to have ramps between them.

This would take longer than I had anticipated.

Whenever the typhon beast awoke, it would have an easy time exiting the gorge. Whenever we were done.

I would've been content to admire my construction for most of the day, but a sudden blast of icy air caught my attention.

Terrakona felt it, too, because he whipped his head to the side and hissed.

A large cluster of ice crystals had formed on the other side of the gorge, right on the edge. The gorge was a mile across, but the fenris wolf and Zaxis were easy to spot. They stood with Illia, Fain, and Adelgis, of all people.

The frozen crystal originated from Zaxis himself. He huffed and grabbed at his chest, frost covering most of his body, including his trousers. He wore no shirt—still—and the rime coated his chest and neck.

"Terrakona," I said. "Can we make a bridge?"

The world serpent flicked out his massive tongue before manipulating the stone. Rocks jutted out of the sides of the canyon and collided in the center, forming an impromptu path. Stone rained down into the mists of the gorge, the crushing impacts echoing up.

Terrakona lowered his head, and I climbed onto his crystal mane, fitting my feet into the latticing. He carried me across the gorge. I remained tense the entire trek, my focus on the vast emptiness beneath us. The stone bridge didn't shake or crumble —we were safe—but part of me couldn't stop thinking about the first typhon beast. It had just *fallen*.

Once we reached the other side, I slid off Terrakona and jogged over to the others. Zaxis and Fain walked around the ice crystals, their attention on the frost and rime. Illia and Adelgis stood off to the side, waiting near Vjorn. The massive fenris wolf watched with his ears erect and his eyes unblinking. He was lying down on a blanket of snow, though, like a pup in a comfortable bed.

"What happened?" I asked as I ran over.

Illia and Adelgis smiled as I approached, both in their usual outfits, even if everyone else was switching to the style of Regal Heights. Illia loved her eyepatch and coat, after all. I rarely saw her without them. And Adelgis definitely preferred the appearance of a scholar—he had been born for the role.

Illia motioned to the ice near the gorge. "Zaxis *accidentally* used too much of his magic."

Nicholin, who sat on her shoulders, shook his little head. "Can you believe this? Look at all that ice he evoked!"

I glanced at the clump of ice near the gorge edge. There was enough to fill a whole single-story house. "I can believe it," I said. "When I first evoked my magma, I practically boiled part of the ocean." And, also, a person. But I wasn't about to mention that last part.

"The *first* time?" Nicholin pretend fainted on Illia's shoulder.

My sister rolled her one eye. "Why couldn't Zaxis do that before?"

"When I evoked my magic, I was under attack." I motioned to the canyon, and then to Regal Heights. "Zaxis has been in a safe area since his bonding. There's less urgency here. We can take our time to learn magics."

"Don't talk to me about *safety*," Zaxis shouted, drawing everyone's attention.

Fain stepped away from the other man, crossing his arms and tucking his frostbitten hands into his armpits. "You need to calm down." Even Fain's voice was elevated, and that almost never happened. His new wizard hat—which he wore with his old sailing outfit—fluttered in the wind but didn't leave his head. "Your magic isn't like it was before, Zaxis. You're going to injure somebody."

The two of them glared at each other for a tense moment. Then Fain turned away and headed for me. He said nothing to Zaxis as he left. Once Fain drew near, he gave Illia an odd glance, and then met my gaze.

In a low voice, he muttered, "Zaxis saw your work on the stairway and decided to *intensify* his training. I've been helping him, but he won't listen to me. Maybe *you'll* get through to him."

Nicholin chimed in with, "It's not you, it's him. Zaxis doesn't listen to anybody. Don't feel bad."

"Thank you for letting me know," I said, ignoring Nicholin. "I'll talk to Zaxis."

Before Fain left, he leaned in closer and said, "Also, he asked me to be one of his knights—to swear myself to him, since my wolf-like eldrin is similar to his. He wasn't thrilled when I said my loyalty was to you, and you alone."

That surprised me. Zaxis wanted *Fain* as a follower? Just because their eldrin were similar?

"Thank you," I said, patting Fain on the shoulder. I wasn't sure what else to say.

Fain nodded, curt and silent. With a smirk, he gave Adelgis an odd look. Then he shrouded himself in invisibility. At first, he walked away, but once he was about thirty feet off, he slowly turned around and snuck back to the group, lingering nearby.

I only knew because of my tremor sense.

Did Fain always do that? Pretend to leave and just hover nearby regardless? It almost made me laugh.

"*He does it most of the time,*" Adelgis telepathically said. "*Fain said he prefers to stay nearby, just in case someone might need his help. His wendigo is close as well.*"

I felt Wraith near the fenris wolf, like a dog sticking close to its pack. But Wraith remained invisible as well, clearly preferring to remain hidden.

Illia watched as Zaxis attempted to create even more ice on top of the amount he had already evoked. She frowned, her lips pursed. Something about this disappointed her, though I didn't know what. Shouldn't she be happy that Zaxis was improving? His magic had clearly grown stronger.

"I'll talk to him," I said as I jogged over.

Illia didn't reply to me. Perhaps she was disappointed as

well? Normally, I could tell with her—we were siblings, after all —but today was different. She seemed reserved and quiet.

Even Nicholin held back his commentary.

As I approached Zaxis, he held up a hand. "Volke, get back. I have this under control."

The ice crystals he had evoked pointed in all directions, like a star cluster sprouting from the ground. The points of the crystals reached up at least ten feet in the air in some directions, a chill mist wafting off the ice. Zaxis stood at the back of the crystal cluster, breathing hard as he tried to evoke something more.

The ice was on the edge of the gorge, half dangling over the cliff.

"Everything okay?" I asked. "It seemed like you and Fain were arguing."

Zaxis snorted. "I said, *I have this under control*."

"What're you doing?"

"Trying to... *create something*." He waved a hand, and another icy spiral lifted out of the cluster, jutting into the sky like a lance erupting from the ground. Then Zaxis exhaled and wheezed, obviously strained by the magic use. "I've got this. Everyone else is... overreacting." He had to keep gulping down air as he spoke.

I glanced around, my eyebrow lifted. "Create what? This... ice?"

"*No*." Zaxis rubbed his red hair with both hands. "I'm trying to figure out my *other* evocation. Vjorn said this was my *destructive* power, but I can't get my creation power to manifest. And now I feel like I'm just creating an *ice wall*. Doesn't that count as creation?"

"Uh, well, I think—"

"And then look at what *you're* doing." Zaxis motioned to the stairway across the gorge. "I need to do something like that. I'm just not strong enough yet. Which is why I need to practice." He flailed his arm to the side, motioning to everyone else with a giant gesture. "But no one wants me to practice too hard because *I'm going to hurt myself* or *I need to rest* or *maybe I'm not emotionally stable.*" He scoffed and huffed and then scoffed again, like he only had those two options to convey his frustrated indignation.

Clearly, he had some issues.

But Zaxis never responded well to me just pointing them out. He hated that.

"What does Vjorn think?" I asked.

Zaxis took a minute to calm himself. He turned to me, almost baffled. "I haven't asked him."

"Terrakona has been helping me since we bonded. If I didn't have him, I wouldn't know what to do with myself."

I was certain that Vjorn would tell Zaxis to relax and take his training at a manageable pace. It wouldn't help us if Zaxis was straining himself just to catch up with me.

Zaxis cracked his knuckles. Then he stared at his eldrin for a long moment before returning his attention to me. In a quiet tone, he said, "Volke... I just..." But Zaxis didn't finish his thought. Something about his expression worried me.

I glanced over my shoulder and met Adelgis's gaze. Since Adelgis had learned to trace god-arcanist magic, he had been able to hear the thoughts of god-arcanists, so surely, he knew what was wrong with Zaxis?

Adelgis shook his head. "*Zaxis doesn't trust his eldrin. He half blames Vjorn for getting Forsythe killed. They don't talk much.*"

Curse the abyssal hells. That was the worst answer I could've heard. No wonder Zaxis was lashing out and not developing his magic. Arcanists and eldrin were fundamentally a team. Zaxis's distrust and resentment could weaken their bond, restricting his power. He probably hated his new evocation—it was *so* different from his old phoenix magic. The complete opposite, in fact.

Maybe that was why Illia was so upset. She already knew Zaxis was having a hard time with everything.

"Uh," I muttered as I glanced at my half-completed walkway. Then I added, "I know you said you wanted to train on your own, but I could use your help."

Zaxis slowly lifted an eyebrow. "*My* help?"

"Yeah. I'm recreating the steps of the Pillar." I motioned to the stairway into the gorge. "And it's really taking a toll. I was probably going to quit for the day. But... I think if you were helping me, perhaps we could do this quicker."

"I don't manipulate stone." Zaxis huffed again. "I don't even know what I manipulate. How am I supposed to help anyone?"

"Well, you can *try* to manipulate something. And your ice can break away some of the stones of the gorge, which would help me alter the terrain faster. And if you did all that, you'd be improving your own magic at the same time."

Zaxis stared at the steps, his brow furrowed. For a long moment, I thought he would reject my offer, but then he half-smiled. "I can't believe you love that Pillar so much. Those words basically run in your blood."

"Yeah." I chuckled and glanced down at my boots. "I think my favorite step is eleven."

"Conviction?" Zaxis mulled it over. "Without it, virtues are just words."

It sometimes surprised me that Zaxis knew the Pillar just as well as I did.

"My favorite is twenty-eight," he said.

I balked immediately. "*Frugality?* Seriously? *That's* your favorite?" I couldn't believe it. Who picked *frugality*?

Zaxis laughed as he punched my shoulder. "You're gullible sometimes. Illia says you'll believe anything if it's said seriously enough."

I half laughed in response. "I don't think that's true..."

"And yeah, I'll help you make a second set of steps. As long as you promise me that you're not going to leave Evianna to elope with your *precious stairway*."

Already, I could tell Zaxis was feeling better. Was it because I had asked him to help me? I didn't know, but I preferred this side of him. It was always easy going when he was in a good mood.

"What's your favorite step for real?" I asked.

Zaxis shrugged with one shoulder. "I don't sit around daydreaming about it like you do, but... I'd say twenty-two."

"Fortitude," I muttered. "Without it, we allow pain to dictate our lives."

His choice felt symbolic to me. Perhaps Zaxis knew it, too. He just seemed so much better after the conversation. I was glad I had come over to see him.

# CHAPTER 47

## THE THIRTY-EIGHTH STRATAGEM

At some point, I asked to borrow Illia's Occult Compass —it could locate nearby mystical creatures so long as we had a part of one. We had the scales and venom of king basilisks, so I thought we might be able to track down Akiva, since he was nearby. Unfortunately, the compass only pointed back to Thronehold.

I supposed that made sense. Akiva wasn't traveling with his gigantic eldrin, Nyre. We would've found their location long ago, even if they were using trinket illusions. He was likely traveling with Orwyn by himself.

Which was good for us. The farther an arcanist was from their eldrin, the weaker their magic became. Akiva wouldn't be as deadly.

I had hoped we could use the compass to find Luthair, but I was quickly reminded it would always just point to Layshl. Frustrated, I pushed the thought out of my mind. If only we had part of the sky titan...

Instead, I focused my energy on things I *could* do.

Unfortunately, I had a million tasks to accomplish, and not

enough time to get them done. And in some instances, I couldn't complete them, because an obstacle was in my path.

I wanted to see Luthair. More than anything. In order to distract myself, I committed all my attention to everything else I *could* do while I waited for information.

Like mastering my magic.

And helping Evianna with her knightmare training.

Zaxis allowed me to teach him a few things, which was also nice. He needed it, and he probably needed more of a distraction than I did. Zaxis's thoughts ran away with him at times.

I also had to make artifacts and trinkets with my father. The more of my magic could be made permanent, the better off we'd be.

And I wanted to have a plan for the typhon beast and its lair. The last few times, we had just rushed in the moment we had found the place. I knew why—with the world serpent, we had been trying to beat the Second Ascension, and with the fenris wolf, we had wanted to see if the pure magic of the lair would cure the plague. In both instances, the bonding had been haphazard. What could I do to make it less so this third time?

Lastly, I had to make a plan for the sky titan arcanist and her cronies. I wanted to be prepared—I wanted to be a tactician, like Luvi. His epic battles were a thing beyond legend, and he claimed to have never been defeated.

Until the apoch dragon.

I wanted to surpass him. I wanted to reach the greatest heights of all time, and put a rest to the plague, and the blackhearts who followed the Autarch, once and for all.

It was just as Devlin had said. *Life is like a boat filling with water, and each day the bucket gets a little smaller*. Thankfully, I had the others to help me. Illia, Adelgis, Fain, Zelfree, Eventide, Ryker, Karna, Terrakona—I had so many people at my side that each day flew by faster than the last.

After a week of working, I had made several dozen magical

items with my father. After a second week, Zaxis and I had created half the steps of the new Pillar. After three weeks, Zaxis had ventured into the hydra caves a second time and defeated two more plague-ridden hydras with the help of Vjorn.

And after four weeks, the tracker extraordinaire, Vika, returned from her long hunt.

The instant she entered Regal Heights, everyone in the city buzzed with excitement. They all knew, apparently, that she was the one in charge of tracking down the Second Ascension's nearby location. I assumed it was because of Hexa. The citizens of Regal Heights were close-knit and talkative. A terrible combination if we wanted to keep a secret.

Vika, her dog eldrin, and Hexa arrived at my fortress home, and I summoned Eventide to join us. Together, we sat down at a long table in the dining hall, and Vika immediately unrolled a leather map and spread it out before us.

The map detailed Hydra's Gorge, Regal Heights, the outskirts of the Rocky Wastes, and a few nearby rivers and lakes. Vika slid her finger over the etchings in the leather, guiding our gaze from the city, all the way into the Rocky Wastes, and then to a river. She only stopped once we reached one of the lakes.

"Do you see this?" Vika asked. She was so tall that she managed to stare down at all of us, including me. "This is Copeland River, which connects to Garnet Lake. There's a series of waterfalls right where they meet. From what I found, the arcanists of the Second Ascension were gathering materials from the caves behind the waterfall."

"What's in the caves?" I asked.

Vika shook her head. "Nothing anymore. But there were several wisps and gloom shrooms. The Second Ascension now has them all."

"But do they have *Vethica*?" Hexa slammed her hand on the map. "Everything else comes second!"

Archnie, the laelaps eldrin, hid behind Vika, his tail tucked between his legs. It made me sad to see a beautiful golden dog so frightened, but Hexa was a competent hydra arcanist. Most people would be afraid when she was angry.

Eventide gently placed a hand on Hexa's shoulder. Without words, they met each other's eyes. Once Hexa had straightened her stance and relaxed, Eventide said, "We'll locate her."

Hexa nodded once. Then she rubbed at the arcanist mark on her forehead. "We've waited too long. Maybe something has happened to her. Or maybe... Or maybe she thinks we don't care about her."

I had all the same thoughts, only about Luthair instead.

"Our primary concern is the sky titan arcanist," Eventide said. "Do you have any idea if she was near these waterfall caves?"

Vika rubbed at her eyebrows. "I know you say she's a god-arcanist, but I haven't heard any word of that. No one in the area —not the other trackers or mystic seekers—have seen even a single footprint of a giant creature near here. Except, of course, your wolf and snake."

"That makes sense," I muttered. "The sky titan doesn't have a body. And it's invisible."

"It doesn't have a *body*?" Vika repeated, her words thick with skepticism.

"It's a beast made completely of wind. If the sky titan arcanist wanted to keep it hidden, she could. Even from trackers. There's no scent to trace, no footprints to uncover." I held up a finger. "The real question is... have you found more signs of the undead?"

Vika slowly nodded. "Ghouls. Plenty of ghouls in the area, even though they haven't been in this area before."

Which meant the Keeper of Corpses was likely nearby. The ghouls answered to him, after all. And the sky titan arcanist. These waterfalls had to be their base of operations. They were close. I could feel it.

"You said there were people near this river and lake?" I asked.

Vika pointed to a small spot on the map marked with a square. "This here is a small fishin' town. They have a trading outpost and a couple hundred people. Why?"

"I wanted them to come to me, but just knowing I'm here doesn't seem to be doing the trick," I said.

Eventide crossed her arms. "When they had Theasin, I'm sure they were a lot more confident. He had bonded before you, and he was the one planning most of their operations. Now that he's gone, they've been less aggressive. I'm sure they're biding their time, waiting for the Autarch to master his magic so he can lead a strike against you."

I smirked as I said, "I agree. But I think they also want to get their hands on more god-creatures."

"What're you sayin'?" Hexa demanded, her eyes narrowed.

"I think we should go to this fishing village and tell the people that we're trying to find the next typhon beast arcanist—that we need unbonded people to head to Regal Heights. We'll tell them we know the location of its lair, and that we have tests to determine their worthiness. I'm sure the sky titan arcanist will hear of it, and that's when she'll come to us."

Eventide mulled over the comments. "That's a risk."

"We have the runestone, don't we? The Second Ascension can't enter unless they take it. Which is why I know they'll come for us."

"They can't afford to lose another god-arcanist. I don't think they'll be flippant with an attack."

I had given this a lot of thought. I knew the patterns of our enemies.

"The Second Ascension always has an escape plan," I said. "Rhys, the weird arcanist who follows the Autarch like a stray mutt, has been there every time they've attacked, even when they assassinated the queen in Thronehold. *But they couldn't attack when the nullstone aura was active over the castle.*"

The others listened to my reasoning, even Vika, who hadn't

been there. Her dog eldrin poked his nose up to the side of the table, sniffing as he, too, listened intently.

"Which means Rhys's magic won't work on nullstone, or the aura it creates when we have enough of it." I pointed to Regal Heights. "If we tell people we know the location of the typhon beast lair and that we have the runestone to open it, I think the sky titan arcanist, Orwyn, will call for help from Rhys. I think she'll come here, hoping to kill me—or at the very least, steal the runestone and go to the lair herself."

Hexa leaned heavily on the table, her eyes wide as she slowly nodded along with my words.

"I think we should gather some nullstone and have it nearby. I think... I can manipulate the terrain to trap Rhys. The nullstone won't work on Orwyn, so we'll actually have to fight her, but if we create a pit with the nullstone, and cover the top, I can open the ground enough to have the other arcanists fall into it. And once there, they won't be able to escape."

Similar to how Luvi had defeated the typhon beast.

"A pit trap?" Vika asked with a partial laugh. "Are you serious? I think people will notice if they're standing on one."

"It'll be giant," I said, circling my finger over a portion of the map. "So large that it'll practically be a field, and then most people wouldn't notice the difference. I think I can do it. I've been practicing. We just need the nullstone."

"Those quarries are deep in the Argo Empire, near Thronehold," Eventide stated.

I sighed and nodded once. "I know. That's the only problem with this plan. I don't know if we can get the nullstone in time."

Eventide grabbed her braid and wrapped the gray hairs around one finger while she stared at the map. With a distant gaze, she seemed to contemplate the situation, her lips thin as she clenched her jaw. Her glowing arcanist mark reminded me that this probably wasn't her first time dealing with overwhelming enemies.

"Brom and Vinder are old friends of mine," Eventide murmured, obviously thinking aloud. "I could speak with them about airships in the nearby area. They were once popular, but most went to distant lands. If we can hire one—maybe even pay them with star shards or god-arcanist imbued trinkets—perhaps we could fly in some materials."

"Nullstone won't travel on an airship," Vika stated. "Not much, anyway. If you gather too much, it'll create its anti-magic aura."

"Sovereign dragon arcanists can attune the stone," Eventide countered, her gaze still distant. "That's how they control the nullstone in the castle—which allows them to suppress it. Perhaps Queen Ladislava will help us, if we ask nicely enough."

"Well, other arcanists can attune it as well—at twice the cost of star shards." My father had taught me that long ago. "But the amount of nullstone I want... we would exhaust all our resources. It probably isn't worth it just to transport some rocks."

Which meant we *should* speak to a dragon arcanist.

I loathed the idea of getting Ladislava involved in this fight, but I thought it just might work. What if we *did* get enough nullstone here to trap some of the Second Ascension? It would be a crushing blow. We would be *one step closer* to ridding the world of their presence.

The thought sent electricity through my veins.

"We should try," I said. "Even if I have to ask the queen nicely."

"She's gonna have you on your knees," Hexa practically spat. With a frown, she added, "I'm sure we could do this without her. I thought *any* dragon could attune the nullstone? Why not get a competent dragon arcanist from some other place?"

"I do know a few who seem to like me," I said, turning to Eventide. "And they swore to help against the Second Ascension, should I call upon them."

But even this was a risk. The other dragon arcanists lived farther away than Ladislava, most on distant islands. She was probably our only hope if we wanted to act quickly.

"I'll ask Brom and Vinder," Eventide finally stated. "If they know of an airship, then we'll move to the next step. Understood?"

We all nodded—even Vika and her dog eldrin.

I turned to her and offered a slight bow. "Thank you so much for your aid."

Both her eyebrows lifted. "Oh, no, thank *you*, Warlord. It's been an honor to work with one of the Frith Guild."

I just hoped everything Vika had brought us was accurate. If it was, perhaps we could ensnare the Second Ascension and bring down another one of their god-arcanists.

## CHAPTER 48

## LUTHAIR'S RETURN

When I returned to the fortress this time, my father's blue phoenix was waiting for me. Tine glittered in the light, more lustrous than any precious gem. Her heron head and long beak were beautiful, and I instinctually leaned down to stroke her sapphire feathers as soon as I drew near.

She fluffed herself under my touch. Soot fell to the ground, her warm body heating further as I ran the tips of my fingers down the length of her back.

"Is everything okay, Tine?" I asked.

"Your father has finished attuning Retribution," she said matter-of-factly. "I came to get you, since my arcanist struggles with the stairs at times."

"Oh, thank you. I'm glad he finished—because I think we might have to deal with the Second Ascension sooner rather than later."

Tine nodded. With a majestic swish and turn, where her peacock tail fluttered outward, she led me into the fortress building. Against the bright red of the bricks, Tine stood out even more. I loved the hue of her blue feathers, and the bright white fire that made up her inner body.

We climbed the stone steps to my father's study. Although I had lived here for longer than a month, the time had flown by so quickly that I had barely registered my surroundings. Now that I was feeling confident, I glanced at the walls, admiring the paintings. They weren't landscapes or portraits—they were paintings of raw metals, jewelry, and breathtaking caves alight with glowing mushrooms and crystals.

I didn't know where the imagery had come from, but I loved it. How had I lived here for over a month and not noticed?

When we reached my father's study, I walked in with a smile.

Jozé stood by his desk. My sword was on the surface, black and speckled with emerald stars that created the serpent constellation in the center. He grazed his fingers along the edge and then glanced at me with an exhausted smile.

"This took longer than I thought it would, boy," he said with a weak chuckle.

I jogged over, excited to see the finished product. The sword didn't look much different from the last time I had seen it, but as I drew close, I sensed the ravenous power deep within the blade. The sword still thirsted for magic.

Tine ran into the study, her wings half opened as she rushed to the desk. Then she rubbed her head along Jozé's leg, similar to a cat greeting its owner. Jozé reached down and scratched at the side of her head.

Then Jozé stood straight, picked up the sword, and handed it over to me. I took it, tested the balance one more time, and then sheathed it, the dark energy crackling with the movement. I felt better knowing I had the sword at my side.

"The blade will burn anyone who touches it," Jozé stated. "I managed to use some of my blue phoenix magic. I think the blade will now burn *anyone*, including those normally immune to flame."

"How did *you* pick it up?" I asked, honestly curious.

Jozé smirked. "Well, I attuned it to your *bloodline*. For multiple reasons. Firstly, so I could still handle the sword, in case we need to do something with it in the future. Secondly, I thought, maybe, you might want to pass the blade down to your own son or daughter."

My chest tightened at the thought. Would I give my blade to someone? I could see myself handing it to a child of mine, when the day came. Hopefully, before I faced the apoch dragon itself.

"Thank you," I said, touched by the gesture. I found myself at a loss for words. Jozé didn't have to go through so much trouble, but he always did.

He waved away my words. "You've grown into an impressive man. You've done me proud."

The quiet that settled between us was a comfortable one. The items we had created over the last few weeks were all around us, evidence of our time together. It almost made me wish Ryker were here.

Or my mother.

But I hadn't given much thought to it until just now. I was finally in a place where I could put that old wound to rest.

Jozé rubbed his brow and then pressed his fingers against his eyelids, struggling to keep sleep at bay. "Well, boy, I think I need to rest. You look after the sword—I hope it serves you well."

"We'll need it soon," I muttered.

"Why's that?"

"The Second Ascension will probably be attacking Regal Heights."

Jozé didn't react to the news. Either he had known it already, or he had suspected. With a sigh, he headed for the door, walking at a slow pace. His blue phoenix stayed by his side as he went. "Be careful, boy. I like this place. I'd hate to see it turn out like Thronehold."

With my sword at my side, I headed to Hydra's Gorge.

Terrakona was there, and so were Zaxis, Vjorn, Illia, and Nicholin. When I approached, Zaxis motioned to the massive canyon. "We only have a few more steps." Then he smirked. "I think we can finish today."

"Good," I said. "Because after that, we need to talk about protecting Regal Heights and also preparing for a war."

The others exchanged quick glances. Then Zaxis crossed his arms. "So, that tracker lady found the Second Ascension, huh?"

"That's right. And we're going to lure them here. But I don't want anyone from the city getting hurt. Which means—"

**"We must be hunters,"** Vjorn said, his voice a low growl. **"We will make this area our stalking grounds. Shaping it for our purposes. Luring our prey into the traps of our devising. Giving them a false sense of security, only to rip it away, along with their lives."**

Sometimes I forgot how grandiose Vjorn could speak. His lust for combat and death wasn't anything like Forsythe's gentle but determined attitude.

"Well, I hadn't thought of it in those terms," I admitted. "But that's close to what I want. We need to outsmart our enemies. We're no longer going to be surprised by *their* tactics. We're going to shock them with a few of our own."

Nicholin clapped his front paws together. "Yes! *Yes.* I like this. We should be the ones *they're* afraid of. They should know that you can't mess with good, hardworking people and get away with it!"

Illia half-smiled. Then she turned to me. "He's still upset his favorite bakery in Throxehold was ruined."

"W-Well, and the peace was disrupted!" Nicholin rubbed at his face. "I was also upset about that."

I didn't care what the reason was. I agreed with Nicholin. We were going to turn this whole war around. But first, we would complete this second Pillar, right here in Regal Heights.

Zaxis hopped down the first step. Each one was large enough that it required a considerable amount of effort for a normal person to jump up one or down to another, and we still had to add ramps and smaller stairways. It wasn't the best-looking staircase ever constructed, but it was massive. The letters carved into each step were the size of my head.

"The last few steps are waiting for us," Zaxis called up, his voice echoing as it went. "Let's go!"

His giant wolf lumbered after him. Terrakona and I went shortly afterward. Illia and Nicholin waited at the top until we were halfway down. Then she concentrated, exhaled, and teleported.

To my surprise, she appeared next to us at the halfway point, her glitter of teleportation wafting around her when she appeared. With a laugh and a wide smile, she turned to us. "Did you see that?" she asked. "I've gotten better."

Zaxis leapt down one more step and then scooped her up into his arms. "I told you! You're getting better at that every day."

She wrapped her arms around his neck. "I've just never made it that far before in one leap. How far do you think that was?"

Nicholin, still on her shoulders, squeaked a bit. "It was *forever* away from the top of the canyon. We did it! And it definitely was a *we* effort, because my awesomeness rubs off on whoever I touch."

I felt awkward watching their celebration. They were so happy and obviously elated to be in each other's arms. I turned my attention to the opposite side of the gorge, muttering things like *congrats* just in case Illia was waiting for my praise.

That was when I noticed an odd feeling.

Something was walking along the bottom of the gorge, between the ghostwood. I had never sensed anyone down there before. With ice in my veins, I stepped off the edge of the steps and used my stone manipulation to create a platform to lower me toward the individual.

Hadn't Brom and Vinder spoken of someone sneaking around Hydra's Gorge? Perhaps this was the villain who was plaguing the hydras. If it was, I'd have to test out the increased effectiveness of Retribution.

"Where are you going, Volke?" Illia called down.

"I'm going to check something," I called back. "I'll meet you at the bottom of the steps."

They didn't question me further.

With my heart beating hard against my ribs, I went straight to the bottom of the gorge and then stepped off my temporary platform. The mist of the ghostwood swirled all around me, limiting my vision. Fortunately, I felt every hesitant step made by the intruder. For some reason, the person walked a few steps and then *disappeared* from my tremor sense before reappearing a few feet off in another direction.

It reminded me of something...

The movement of a knightmare.

Whenever a knightmare stepped through the darkness, they were basically invisible to me. The stealthy movement didn't create any vibrations.

My heart nearly stopped when I realized a *knightmare* was here in the ghostwoods of Hydra's Gorge. Was it Luthair? Had he escaped the Second Ascension and now was just wandering lost in the canyon?

It had to be.

I ran forward, unable to stop smiling. My heart beat hard with each step that brought me closer to the mysterious footfalls. I wove between trees, unbothered by the twisted faces in the bark, and leapt over the roots growing overtop the rocks.

"*Luthair*!" I shouted, my voice carrying far, repeating over and over. "Luthair, is that you?"

Even though the mystical creatures in Thronehold had lost their memories, they still remembered their names. And they still remembered they had bonded with someone. Luthair would still know his name—but would he recognize me? I hoped so. With all my heart.

I literally couldn't run fast enough.

The knightmare stopped moving, but it wasn't far off. It had to have heard me.

I dashed through the last of the ghostwoods and then came to an abrupt stop the moment I reached its last known location. I wildly glanced around, irritated by the cold fog for the first time since seeing Hydra's Gorge.

"Luthair?" I asked.

He had to be hiding in the shadows, where I couldn't sense him.

"Come out," I demanded. "I won't hurt you. I know you don't remember much, but I know you! Please, Luthair. You know I'm not lying—you can sense it! Please, come out and talk to me!"

The gray leaves of the trees rustled in the mist, creating a haunting melody that lingered in the gorge. I kept glancing around, frantic to catch sight of any movement. It was too dark and foggy to see much, however. With my hands clenched into fists, I finally stood still.

"Luthair?" I whispered.

Then it happened.

The darkness around the roots of the trees stirred. They coalesced together in front of me, forming into a suit of armor.

I leapt forward, my heart in my throat, my eyes stinging with tears I tried to hold back, but then I stopped a foot in front of the shadowy creature.

It wasn't Luthair.

My heart sank into my gut, filling my thoughts with anger, even though that was irrational. Why should I be mad because there was a *different* knightmare nearby? I just... I had wanted it to be Luthair so badly.

This knightmare resembled Luthair, but it wasn't the same. It was black plate armor, with raven feathers lining the collar of its cape and hanging from the belt around its waist.

The armor wasn't complete, which meant this knightmare was still young. Small sections of its legs and arms were missing. It was like an invisible person only wearing half a suit of armor made of inky void. The pieces floated around—even the helmet —without anything inside.

"Who are you?" I asked. A second later, I realized it must've sounded rude. "Forgive me. I, uh, thought you were going to be someone else. My name is Volke Savan."

"You may call me Thurin," the knightmare said, his voice masculine and rusty, as though he hadn't spoken in some time. He also had raven feathers emerging from his helmet, creating a crest. "Please, forgive *me*. It has been centuries since last I spoke with anyone."

"Centuries?" I balked. "Why?"

Thurin lifted a gauntleted hand and pointed to the far end of the canyon. "My death... No, the king's murder... It happened over there. He was pushed into the canyon and died when he hit the bottom. It was... his wife. She had grown tired of him."

I crossed my arms and thought back to my time at the bottom of the gorge. I had seen dragon bones down here in an odd pile. I had thought they had all fallen, but now I knew the truth. The king and his eldrin must've been pushed. Had his wife been a powerful arcanist with wind abilities? She had knocked so many down here.

"And you came to life from the dead king's shadow?" I asked.

"That's right. King Nurith. His death was painless and quick, but my hate still burns for those who did him wrong."

Arcanists lived a long time. Perhaps Nurith's wife still lived.

"Why have you stayed in the gorge?" I asked. "You can travel in the shadows. You could've escaped at any time."

"It wasn't until you arrived that I thought I might have a chance. The corruption in the caves deterred me at first. And I cannot move through the shadows very far. My magic is weak— I've never bonded with anyone. I'm young."

I motioned to the area of the gorge with the new stairway. "You can get up there. And perhaps you can join the Frith Guild and find someone to bond with."

"I seek vengeance. A guild will not suit my purposes."

"Oh. Right."

My heart had already fallen into my feet, and hearing that this new knightmare, Thurin, would *also* leave, was somehow another blow to my morale. What if every knightmare I knew eventually left? Even Evianna and her eldrin...

"Volke Savan?" the knightmare asked. "You've grown melancholy."

I ran a hand down my face and forced half a smile. "I'm fine. Forgive me. You just remind me of someone."

"Luthair?"

I quickly lifted my gaze to meet his empty helmet. "You know of him?"

"No. You were yelling his name as you ran through the canyon. It wasn't difficult to piece together this mystery."

His comment made me honestly chuckle. I rubbed at the back of my neck. "Sorry. Yes. I thought you were Luthair. He was a knightmare I knew."

"And you've lost him."

"You could say that. But I'll find him. I swear it."

I spoke the last part like it was a threat, but I hadn't meant to come across so aggressive. It had just slipped out. I hadn't discussed Luthair's death and resurrection with many people— and how his disappearance ate at me—especially not at length. It hurt too much. But in my heart, I knew I would find him. I wouldn't rest until it happened.

Thurin lifted his black cape. The inside lining was a deep red —just like Luthair's had been before he had achieved true form. The raven feathers on his collar shifted with the winds in the gorge. Then Thurin swept the cape in front of him and offered a bow.

"Forgive me again, Volke Savan. I've been away from civilization far too long." He straightened his armor body and dropped the edge of his cape. "I would like to see your guild. There are many questions I have about this world."

"Why didn't you approach me when I first came down here? Or when I excavated all those bones? I was down here for a long time."

Thurin shook his helmet. "I have traveled up and down the gorge for some time, looking for a path that had no corruption. Sometimes I was resting, dwelling on my thoughts. Years pass when there's nothing to do at the bottom of the gorge. I've learned to do nothing for long periods of time."

"I see." Again, I pointed to the staircase. "Then please, come this way. I'm sure Guildmaster Eventide will make sure you're safe and comfortable."

## CHAPTER 49

# PREPARING FOR CONFRONTATION

I took Thurin up the new Pillar steps. Zaxis and Illia regarded him with wide eyes and silent stares. When I passed Vjorn at the top of the steps, the gigantic wolf snorted once and then glanced away, unconcerned. Without much discussion, I brought the new knightmare all the way into Regal Heights. The citizens of the cliffside city only knew of knightmares because of Evianna, so when I brought a new one through town, they pointed and whispered.

I understood the awe they felt. The first time Luthair had emerged from the Endless Mire, I had been in awe. I had also been dying, but that wasn't the point.

Thurin didn't speak much, even as I dropped him off at my fortress home. It was probably for the best. I didn't feel like talking. What was I going to say? Telling stories about Luthair would just dull my enthusiasm. I had to remain positive.

When I returned to Hydra's Gorge, Zaxis had already used his ice to blast away some of the rock. His frost crystals cracked the side of the gorge, sometimes even causing damage to the steps I had already created—which was why they had taken so long to construct.

I didn't mind. He was practicing his magic, and so was I.

The fog at the bottom of the gorge made things a little difficult. Not only was it colder, and darker, but when I tried to create the words on the last two steps, I had to get within inches of the rock to see what I was doing.

The one hundred and eleventh step... *Mercy. Without it, we cannot help others find redemption.*

The one hundred and twelfth step... *Justice. Without it, we cannot differentiate from revenge.*

They had been destroyed on the Isle of Ruma, but now they would be here, forever. Afterward, as I examined my work, I smiled to myself. The two steps reminded me of Calisto.

Once finished, I stepped away and brushed the dirt from my trousers and open shirt.

Illia and Zaxis got close to the steps as well, reading the words and then chortling to themselves. They had never loved the Pillar as much as I did, and I figured they were about to mock me.

"I love it," Nicholin eventually commented from atop Illia's shoulder. "It's exactly what this gross gorge needed."

"Gross?" I asked.

"Yeah. Look at all this fog! And some of these caves stink..."

"That's because of the gas," I said. "It's not safe. You shouldn't be in it for long. Especially the caves, where it's the deadliest. I thought I warned everyone of that?"

Nicholin nodded. "You did. I still wanted to see for myself. Gross."

I had long gone nose-blind to the horrendous smell of the canyon, both the gas and the waste splattered along the stones. Perhaps if other people used the stairs with any regularity, they would clean up this area so that it didn't stink of waste.

Warning signs would have to be made around the deadly caves as well.

"Illia," Zaxis said as he ran a hand through his fiery hair.

Sweat made the locks cling to his face and ears. "What is your favorite step of the Pillar? If you have one, that is."

"Step fifty." Then she faced me with a grin, obviously waiting for me to fill in the rest.

"Honesty," I said. "Without it, we cannot learn the truth about ourselves."

She tapped the side of her head with a finger. "You can always recite those without a second thought."

Zaxis folded his arms over his chest. "Yeah, it's impressive. You always know. At first, I thought it was a little weird, but... You really took every word on that Pillar to heart."

"Wasn't that the point?" I asked with a chuckle.

"Still." Zaxis smiled. "I'm trying to pay you a compliment. Just take it, okay? Let's move on."

His anger over the last few weeks had waned. Zaxis must have felt it, too. He gave me an easy smile and stood closer to me and Illia.

Part of me enjoyed the fact that I had recreated the Pillar with him. It felt like we had done something great, when we had come from a place so tiny. The Isle of Ruma was a backwater location barely anyone had heard of, but here we were, doing amazing things together.

"You have that look in your eyes," Illia said, smirking. "What're you thinking about?"

"Have you ever wondered what people would write about you long after you're gone?" I clasped Illia and Zaxis's shoulders, keeping them close. "It's moments like this, I wonder what they'll say about us."

Zaxis rotated his shoulder. "Okay, this has gone too far. You're not allowed to read any of those *legends of old* stories anymore. They're going to your head."

"Yeah, Zaxis is right, don't talk about our eventual *deaths*," Nicholin chimed in.

Illia chuckled into her hand. Once Zaxis and Nicholin were

done scoffing and booing, she placed her hand on my shoulder. "I enjoyed the sentiment. I hope people write about me as the *untamable beauty who was the true mind behind the god-arcanists.*"

The comment had us laughing again. I enjoyed the camaraderie and how easy it was to speak with both Illia and Zaxis. Sometimes we had disagreements, but in that moment, I felt like there was nothing that could ever really come between us.

It was a rare feeling, one I hadn't really had before.

But we had to get back to business. There were forces in this world that wanted to tear us apart, and I couldn't let that happen.

Determined to make the most of our time before we attracted the Second Ascension, I motioned to the steps. "We should head back into town and start outfitting people."

"For a fight?" Nicholin asked, his voice quiet.

I nodded once. "I think we should pass out trinkets, including some weapons, and then head out to announce that we've found the typhon beast's lair."

The statements settled onto the group like a wet blanket. It was a serious matter, one that we couldn't take lightly. Confrontation was upon us.

"All right," Illia eventually said. "Let's go."

Zaxis cracked his knuckles. "Yeah. I've been thinking this over since I found the plague-ridden hydra. I'm going to make a pistol artifact. Jozé suggested it to me. He said he's made several before."

I nodded—I had used a magical pistol before, but it had been shattered by decay dust. If Zaxis made one that was powered by his god-arcanist magic—and didn't require ammunition other than his evocation—it would be a powerful tool.

"Why a pistol?" Illia asked. "That's the exact opposite of your fighting style."

"My *previous* fighting style." Zaxis glared at his hands. "I want to use my ice more like Vjorn did in his lair. Everything was frozen. It was so cold, the air was almost solid. We were struggling long before we got to him..."

"You can make things *that* cold?"

Zaxis scoffed and then smirked. "I can make *anything* cold. That's the power of the fenris wolf. Haven't you heard the speeches?"

Nicholin straightened himself, ruffled the fur on his body until he looked scraggly, and then said, "Hur, hur, I am winter, *which means I am death itself.*" He spoke in a comically gravelly voice, trying to mimic the ominous tone of the god-creatures. "My frost will kill everything, even happiness and jokes!"

"That's not funny," Zaxis growled.

"Oh, it's pretty funny. Unless the cold has already killed your sense of humor."

Illia hid a chuckle with the back of her hand. I suppressed a smile, not wanting to escalate Zaxis's anger.

"Let's go," Zaxis commanded as he dragged himself up the massive steps. "We have important things to do, and none of you are taking this seriously enough."

I knew he was just angry—because no one was taking this as seriously as I was.

---

The travel to distant towns didn't take long with Terrakona—just an hour at a leisurely pace. His giant size, and ability to rearrange the terrain as he moved, made it an easy trek.

I stood in his mane, my eyes half closed as I enjoyed the breeze and sun. Evianna stood next to me, her white hair fluttering with all the softness of a cloud. When she caught me staring, she smiled.

The short journey allowed me to relax. I was coming to enjoy any chance to visit distant locations and new people. Everything was so beautiful and strange. I was an islander at heart, but my wanderlust could never be sated.

The small town that Vika had spoken about was, in fact, located near a river and a lake. To my surprise, both water sources seemed small and shallow. Well, at least compared to the many lakes and rivers I had seen throughout my life. Perhaps they were just average for this region—it was drier here than most places.

The town by the lake wasn't an impressive one. It was so small, it made the Isle of Ruma look humongous. A collection of houses surrounded three buildings. And that was it. They were made of stone at the base, and wood up top. Some of them were two stories, but I feared for their integrity. If I shook the ground around here, they would surely topple over.

When I stepped off Terrakona, a handful of people came rushing out of the town.

They all knelt as they got close, dropping to one knee and touching their hearts. Several offered greetings, but only one person stood and walked over.

It was a young woman with long chestnut brown hair. She wore a long dress, but I didn't pay much attention to it. I was more intrigued by the mark on her forehead. It was a seven-pointed star with a will-o-wisp wrapped around it.

But I didn't see the wisp anywhere.

"O-Oh, hello, Warlord," the woman said, her hands clenched together in front of her as she approached. With an awkward smile, and a furrowed brow, she continued, "We're so pleased you're here. Forgive everyone. We didn't know that you'd be visiting our tiny village."

"Don't worry about it." I glanced around, wondering if any

other arcanists would approach. "I came here to make an announcement."

The woman's tanned skin paled enough that she almost went white. "Oh, my. W-What kind of announcement?"

"The Frith Guild has located the typhon beast's lair, and we have the runestone needed to open it. Another god-arcanist will soon emerge into this world, but we don't know who." I turned my attention to the frightened villagers who were either hovering around the shabby buildings or kneeling right in front of me. "It could be someone from… whatever the name of this place is."

Terrakona snorted. **"Very diplomatic, Warlord."**

I ignored him.

The woman let out a long sigh. "Oh. Well, that's *good* news. Forgive me. I thought you were going to conquer our village. We call it *East Valley*, not that that's important, of course." She placed a hand over her heart and genuinely smiled this time. "You want to find someone worthy of a god-creature? The mythical typhon beast—a hydra with no equal?"

"You know of the typhon beast?" I asked, honestly surprised.

"Oh, uh, not really. Just that it's the king of hydras. Or so my mother said. I hope I haven't offended you."

I shook my head, disheartened. "No, it's fine. But if you know of anyone who wants to bond with a god-creature, please send them to Regal Heights, all right? And spread the news." I motioned to the surrounding territory. "If you know of any other places with people who want to become a god-arcanist. *West Valley*, perhaps? If such a place exists."

The woman held her hands even tighter together. "Oh, yes. I will. Thank you. Such an honor to have a god-arcanist himself deliver the message."

"I just want to make sure everyone knows it's legitimate," I said.

"Smart. Very smart."

I didn't know if she honestly believed what she was saying, or if she was just saying it to appease me. Either way, as long as the news spread, I was certain the Second Ascension would eventually hear.

I offered the woman a bow, and then turned back for Terrakona.

"W-Wait," she said, stepping closer.

I glanced over my shoulder. "Yes?"

"Can arcanists try? For the g-god-creature, I mean. Is that possible?"

The question didn't sit right with me. All I could think about was Luthair and Forsythe. Eldrin and arcanists were partners, and an arcanist willing to sacrifice their eldrin for a chance at greater power didn't deserve the title. But I shook the thoughts from my head. "Arcanists can offer themselves for judgment in front of the god-creature. So please make sure to tell everyone."

"I will." The woman moved away from me and nervously waved. "Thank you so much for visiting. You can, uh, stay the night, if you wish. We have a single room in the bar we use for any guests."

Terrakona lowered his head and I climbed onto his mane. The smell of dirt and fish reminded me of home, but I didn't want to risk an assassination attempt by the Second Ascension. "No, thank you. I'll be returning to Regal Heights. Thank you for the offer, though."

"Of course." She waved harder as Terrakona lifted his head. "And thank you for not destroying our village! That's very appreciated!"

I chuckled, one eyebrow raised. I wanted to ask, *why would I bother destroying your village?* But that sounded condescending —like the village was so pathetic, it wasn't even worth wrecking.

"Don't mention it," I called out as Terrakona turned to leave.

**"It wouldn't be difficult to destroy them,"** my eldrin said. **"The Children of Balastar are everywhere, it seems. Weak and spread out. Ants without a hill or queen."**

Evianna held on to my arm as we traveled away from East Valley. She couldn't hear Terrakona's telepathic voice—as Terrakona could choose who he spoke to at any given moment —but Evianna could obviously tell I was speaking with him. She said nothing as we traveled, holding me close, waiting for the conversation to end.

"I thought the villagers were pleasant," I said under my breath. "Destroying them never even crossed my mind. Well, except for when the woman suggested it." I should've asked for her name.

**"Sometimes animals cull the weak to strengthen the herd."**

"Good thing we're not animals."

Terrakona snorted, disagreeing at a certain level. He was— obviously—a giant serpent, but he knew what I meant. Our sensibilities were beyond animals. I wouldn't kill people just because they were *weak*. That seemed... like the first step to insanity.

The sun headed down as we made it back to Regal Heights. It still seemed odd how much people feared me upon first meeting, but I was getting over it. I would just have to show them that I was here to be a leader, not a tyrant. And I enjoyed the challenge.

## CHAPTER 50

## ORWYN'S PARLEY

For the next few days, I stayed in Regal Heights, vigilant and tense.

The red jasper runestone—the one for the typhon beast—was on me at all times. Eventide thought it best I kept it close, especially since I had improved my sword. My first thought had been to hide it, but Eventide reminded me that magics could be used to detect its location, even if under a hundred tons of rock.

If we had enough nullstone, perhaps we could hide it from magic, but a tracker, like Vika, could probably still sniff out the runestone. Which was why I had to keep it close.

Whenever I pulled the runestone out to look at it, I admired the etching of the typhon beast itself. The multi-headed beast was fearsome, each head glaring and showing its fangs. Who would bond with it? The thought kept me up at night.

I stayed around my fortress home, especially with my father.

We had crafted several swords, which we handed out to people of the Frith Guild—well, to the people who could wield them. Since the blades were so dangerous, and filled with heat, only individuals who felt confident using them were allowed to take one.

The sovereign dragon scales were used in a suit of black and red armor. I helped by imbuing it with magic, making it heat resistant and tougher than most steel.

Zaxis actually came in and spoke with my father about imbuing items, and he managed to imbue the manticore claws with frigid ice. The knuckle-like weapons reminded me of him, but he didn't take them for himself. Instead, he insisted that Jozé help him with his pistol.

"Pistols use combustion," my father said. "Heat on gunpowder—it explodes to propel the bullet. You want to make an *ice* version? You know that makes no sense, right, boy?"

Zaxis paced around the study, waving his hand at all the items on the bookshelves. "Are you telling me it can't be done? Even after all the amazing trinkets you've created?"

"I'm saying it's not a good concept. What else does fenris wolf magic do?"

Zaxis stopped mid-pace, his shoulders tense. He didn't look at my father. He just stared at the stone floor. "Well, I haven't developed much of anything else."

"No manipulation?"

Zaxis didn't answer.

With a frown, Jozé turned to me, obviously hoping for me to give him an answer. I just shrugged. Zaxis had been learning to evoke frost *well*. He was already creating gigantic structures of ice—practically glaciers—but he had done little else. No illusions. Nothing.

Jozé waved both his hands. "Okay, wait. I think I have an idea. What if *Volke* imbued a pistol, and you imbue the bullets? We can have a gun capable of firing without much gunpowder, and bullets that will transfer a burst of your icy evocation."

For a long moment, Zaxis didn't acknowledge the suggestion. I thought he was going to dismiss it—just because he had been so ornery lately—but he actually nodded. "That's a good idea," he muttered.

"Yeah?" I asked. "Because I think it's a great idea, too."

Zaxis smirked. "Let's do it, then. I want a pistol to rival your sword."

I placed my hand on the hilt of Retribution. "Well, let's not get too hasty..."

The three of us laughed at the comment, and I thought the rest of the day would be spent coming up with plans to make an epic artifact, but that was when the door opened. Eventide stepped inside, her normal exuberance hidden under a serious expression.

She turned to me, her eyes narrowed. "Warlord—we have a problem."

Zaxis and Jozé both turned to face me. I held my breath as I walked over to Eventide, uncertain what she wanted. Once I was close, I asked, "What is it?"

She handed me a letter. The seal on the outside had already been broken, so I couldn't see the design made in wax. I wasn't sure who it had come from.

As soon as I opened it, I recognized the handwriting. The elegant loop of the letters and the precise way everything was written... It was Orwyn. The handwriting matched her letter to the Autarch.

It read:

*To Warlord Volke Savan, the World Serpent Arcanist,*

*My name is Falcon Orwyn Tellia, the Sky Titan Arcanist. Although we serve different organizations and pursue conflicting goals, I humbly request that we meet as equals to parley. As god-*

*arcanists, we stand in a league of our own, and we should be able to come to an agreement that requires no bloodshed.*

*Please meet me in two days' time, at the edge of the Rocky Wastes, where the red sands meet the shrub forest. You may bring Hunter Zaxis Ren, the Fenris Wolf Arcanist, but there is no need to involve anyone else. If you arrive with others, then I will assume you want conflict, and I won't reveal myself. But if you want peace, I will be there, with only my eldrin as companions.*

*I look forward to seeing you and your world serpent.*

*Orwyn Tellia*

I read the letter several times. She wanted to parley? What was there to discuss?

Then again, I *did* want to avoid bloodshed. And what if I could rescue Vethica and Luthair? Nothing would make me happier.

But I didn't trust the Second Ascension. They were cravens, blackhearts, and the scum of the world. They had spread a plague across the land just to further their own sinister goals. They resurrected dead creatures to force them to bond to weak individuals. They had killed the last queen of the Argo Empire and started a civil war.

None of this inspired confidence. A meeting with Orwyn was likely a trap or a scheme. That was the only explanation.

But I was the stronger god-arcanist.

She had a kirin—which would empower her god-arcanist magic—but I had been bonded longer, and now I had

Retribution. If I killed her in a one-on-one fight, perhaps that would be for the best, too. No one in Regal Heights, or the Frith Guild, would be put into harm's way.

"When did this arrive?" I whispered.

Eventide frowned. "This came a few minutes ago from a messenger who was told to give it to the leader of the Frith Guild. That was why I opened it—I thought it was meant for me. Apparently, Orwyn knows the truth of the matter."

I turned the parchment over in my hands, hoping to find more words. Nothing. It was just the note to meet at the edge of the Rocky Wastes.

"Well?" Zaxis demanded. "Is everything okay?"

I folded the letter up and tucked it into the pocket of my trousers. "Yes. But... I'm going to need a favor from you."

Zaxis lifted an eyebrow.

"I need you to come with me to the Rocky Wastes in order to speak with the sky titan arcanist. She's asked for a parley, and I want to see what she says." I walked over to him and then met his gaze. With a serious stare, I added, "A parley is a serious matter of honor—no one is to attack each other. Do you think you can handle that?"

Zaxis hardened his gaze. "I know what a parley is. I can handle it."

"Promise me that you won't attack her. We'll listen to what she has to say and try to come to a peaceful solution."

"I promise," he stated, curt.

With a nod, I turned back to Eventide. "Do you... think you can take the red jasper runestone back? Maybe you, Brom, and Vinder can keep it safe in city hall until I return."

She half-smiled and held out her hand. "Oh, I'm sure those two will love that. They've been a little grumpy about being left out of all the action."

I withdrew the runestone from my belt pouch and placed it in the palm of her hand. "Thank you."

"When will you return?"

"A week at the latest."

The news got everyone silent. While my father seemed relieved, Zaxis didn't seem thrilled. He pursed his lips and glared. His hate for the Second Ascension was unrivaled. I suspected he wanted to fight no matter what.

I turned on my heel and headed for the door.

What would I speak with Orwyn about?

I was honestly curious.

---

The long trek to the Rocky Wastes twisted my insides.

A war raged in my thoughts. A parley was an honorable meeting of two sides—a peaceful moment for two sides to discuss a truce or armistice. Attacking each other during a parley was considered the height of dishonor.

But it would solve so many problems.

We wouldn't even need to bring nullstone to Regal Heights if I killed Orwyn. And with another god-arcanist dead, the Second Ascension would be greatly weakened. We could hunt down the Autarch and end this war once and for all.

But...

Orwyn had said she wanted peace.

Maybe she meant it.

So I had to do my best to win her confidence and convince her that the goals of the Second Ascension were heinous. Maybe she would join me and the Frith Guild. That would be the *best* outcome—it was just the most unlikely.

Zaxis and Vjorn ran alongside me and Terrakona. They never glanced over or ever spoke to us. Even when we stopped to stretch or eat, Zaxis and his wolf were deadly quiet. I knew he was thinking about killing Orwyn as well, but I suspected it wouldn't be as easy as he imagined. I didn't know what the sky titan arcanist was capable of.

It took us a day and half to reach the Rocky Wastes and find where "the red sands met the shrub forest." It was an odd location where the plants grew to the very edge of the bizarre desert. Once we arrived, I slid off Terrakona and stood in the sands, away from any cover or place where an assassin could hide.

Zaxis stayed atop Vjorn, holding on to the chains around his eldrin. He glared at our surroundings, like any rock at any moment could transform into the enemy. The man never relaxed.

We waited for several hours. The sun began to set, and I thought Orwyn might never show herself.

But then a blast of wind rushed over the desert, disturbing the sand to the point I had to cover my eyes. Terrakona roared and Vjorn growled, their aggression so loud, it stung my ears. But then they stopped.

The wind died. The sand rested back on the ground.

When I opened my eyes, there was Orwyn, standing only twenty feet from us, her kirin by her side.

The kirin was a beautiful creature. It had the shape of a horse, but tiny scales covered its body instead of hair. The beast shimmered and moved with the fluidity of a fish, elegant in all regards. Its cloven hooves were similar to a deer's, and its tail reminded me of a lion's. The beast had a horn, like a unicorn in the middle of its forehead, but unlike the unicorn, the horn was twisted into the shape of an antler.

This kirin's horn was made of semi-transparent crystal and glittered with inner power.

Its eyes... reminded me of a starry night.

Mystical. Awe-inspiring.

Orwyn paled in comparison to her elegant eldrin. She was beautiful, for a short and thin woman, but nothing that I cared to admire. Her short strawberry blonde hair fluttered in the gentle breeze. Her locks barely reached the bottom of her chin. And her emerald eyes were clear and a lighter color than Zaxis's green, but they were somewhat vacant, like she was always staring at something right behind me, rather than my face.

Terrakona had said she was a Child of Luvi, and someone worthy of bonding to... But I still didn't care for her. A gut reaction of mine.

Orwyn wore long robes of white and silver, with the front open to expose some of her skin. She also wore a band of cloth over her chest, likely to keep decent, but it didn't completely hide the mark that originated over her heart and continued out to her shoulder, ribs, and arm.

The mark was a twelve-pointed star with a four-winged, two-headed bird wrapped around the points. Well, maybe it was a bird. It was difficult to tell. The creature was abstract. Its extremities half-floating away from its body, like a toy with its limbs held to the torso with string.

I didn't see the sky titan anywhere.

It was invisible, but the mark on Orwyn's chest made me wish I could see it with my own eyes.

Zaxis slid off Vjorn's back and then jogged to my side.

Terrakona and the fenris wolf waited behind us. Together, Zaxis and I walked over to Orwyn, neither of us saying a word. The sunset reflected my mood. The longer I stared at the sky titan arcanist, the darker my thoughts grew.

I tried to keep from spiraling out of control—I needed to remain positive.

But it was difficult.

Once we were within five feet, Zaxis and I came to a halt.

Orwyn glanced between us, her vacant expression reminding me of Adelgis. She was... odd. It was the only word I could use to describe her.

"You came," Orwyn whispered.

"You called for us, didn't you?" Zaxis snapped.

I placed a hand on his shoulder and squeezed. We had to remain diplomatic. We *had* to.

"You wanted to speak with us?" I asked. "You said you thought there was a chance we could avoid bloodshed?"

Orwyn hummed something to herself. Then she laced her fingers together in front of her. The mark on her forehead was a standard arcanist mark—a seven-pointed star with a kirin woven throughout it.

"May I ask you a question first?" Orwyn stared at me with all the charisma of a dead man. Her lack of expression made it difficult to guess at her feelings.

"Sure," I said, my hand on the hilt of Retribution.

"I heard some of the king basilisks came back to life in Thronehold. Is that correct?" She spoke her words slowly and quietly.

"They did."

"And then what happened to them? Were they slain?"

This was a bizarre topic. I had never expected Orwyn to bring this up. To be polite, I responded, "They were confused and lost, and we saved them. Most were taken from the city, but one of them bonded with the guildmaster of the Lamplighters Guild."

"Did you meet a king basilisk named Kezrik?"

The questions grew stranger and more specific—which worried me. Still, I decided to humor her. "Yes. Kezrik was the one who bonded."

Orwyn smiled, which surprised me. She brushed back some of her reddish-blonde hair, her fingers thin and delicate. "Oh, thank the good stars. Akiva has been so worried."

"Akiva *the assassin*?" Zaxis asked, practically scoffing each word. "What does he care?"

"Kezrik was once bonded with one of Akiva's kin, you see. Akiva worried Kezrik would die a second time." Orwyn placed her hands in the middle of her chest, still smiling. "I can't wait to tell him the good news. Akiva will be so happy."

Zaxis and I exchanged a quick, baffled glance. It seemed odd that Orwyn's first priority would be to find out about the king basilisks. Did Akiva mean that much to her? She *had* mentioned him in her letter to the Autarch.

"Was that why you brought us here?" I asked.

Orwyn's smile faded as she lowered her hands. Her kirin shifted on its cloven feet so that it stood closer to her. She stroked its long face.

"I brought you here because I wanted to speak," she said, no emotion in her words. "I believe you two are making a terrible mistake."

I tensed. "What mistake?"

"Not serving the Autarch."

Zaxis couldn't stop himself from laughing. It was cruel and cold, but he laughed for a solid ten seconds. Then he shot her a glare and shook his head. "We could say the same damn thing about *you*. The Autarch is a lunatic."

"Cane Helvetti is a great man. He—"

"Wait," Zaxis interjected. "His name is *Cane Helvetti?*" He snorted another laugh. "No wonder that chump calls himself *the Autarch*. With a name like that, I'd want to hide it, too."

Orwyn frowned slightly, but anger obviously didn't come easily to her. She waited until Zaxis was done with his huffing before she continued with, "Helvetti was chosen by the gold kirin. That means he's destined for greatness. He is the rightful ruler."

"Screw that logic," Zaxis practically shouted. "I'm bonded with a *black wolf*, therefore *I'm* destined to *whoop his ass.*"

I grabbed his shoulder and shoved him back. With a glare, we exchanged tense looks. I wanted him to relax—perhaps Orwyn could give us some insight into what was going on.

Once Zaxis had calmed down, I turned back to Orwyn.

"Sorry about that. Please enlighten us. Why is Helvetti so special? *Besides* the fact that he's bonded with a gold kirin."

The sun finally set, shrouding us in darkness. Orwyn scooted closer—much to my surprise—like she couldn't see us fully. With her hands held in front of her, she replied, "I don't think you understand. Helvetti had a perfect plan to seed the world with endless magic. You see, he explained it all before he began."

"I can't wait to hear it," I said, my voice terse.

"He said that the god-creatures were destined to bond with people who had kirin eldrin." Orwyn touched her kirin with the tips of her delicate fingers. "It makes sense. That way, the arcanist doesn't have to lose their eldrin during the bonding. Did either of you two have kirin?"

Zaxis gritted his teeth. "You know we don't."

"I know." She frowned slightly. "You sullied his hard work with your blundering. The kirin of my village bond only with people meant for leadership. Since you don't have one..."

"Theasin didn't have one," I stated.

"The god-creature was his reward for saving the kirin village. He deserved it."

"Well, we've never seen your village. Besides, I heard several kirin were stolen and sold away by pirates and plague-ridden navy men. Maybe two of those was meant for us, and it's *you* who's sullying everything by fighting against us."

I didn't know if any of that was true... I just hated her logic. And I was right—maybe there was a kirin out there who wanted to bond with Zaxis or me. We would never know. We had never had an opportunity to meet one before Orwyn's.

"The natural order is for kirin arcanists to bond with god-creatures, and since the Autarch can bond with multiple creatures, he should be the one to lead us." Orwyn tilted her head to the side, her eyebrows slowly knitting together. "And with his magic... The Autarch planned to slay the apoch dragon.

That way, the god-creatures could forever seed the world with magic, making it a brighter and better world."

"What're you even talking about?" Zaxis snapped. "Seeding what? With what? Who cares? That doesn't give you the right to spread around a literal *plague*."

"The natural order of things is for sickness to cull the—"

"I'm gonna *natural order your face with my fist* if you don't—"

Again, I grabbed Zaxis's shoulder and jerked him close to me. "Stop." I squeezed my fingers into his flesh. "Calm down. Just let her finish."

He glared at me, ice practically coating some of his bare skin along his chest. Was he *that* upset? I needed him to control himself. It was important.

Zaxis inhaled, relaxed a bit, then returned his attention to Orwyn. He didn't say anything, he just glowered at her. That was probably the best I could hope from him.

"Helvetti was a great healer," Orwyn said. "An apothecary of some renown. He knows what's needed for the world to heal. He says that magic will correct all sicknesses and strife. And that once the god-arcanists work together to cure the plague, we will create something new and grand, like when trinkets and artifacts were first created more than a millennium ago."

Even if all that were true, I still didn't think the death and destruction was worth it.

"If you help Helvetti, we could achieve this easily." Orwyn patted her kirin again, stroking the scales along its back. "My kirin thinks you should both join us." She spoke in a whisper now—I didn't know why. "Lith is talented at finding people with great promise. Lith thinks we shouldn't fight."

"I don't want to fight," I said, my voice calm, even if I hated everything she had said. "But Helvetti's plan is disgusting, and I won't support it. If he continues, I'll have to kill him."

Orwyn stared at me with emerald eyes. She said nothing.

"And if you help him," I continued, "I'll kill you, too."

"Your confidence is misplaced." She held her kirin close.

"I suppose we'll find out."

Orwyn sighed into the scales of her mystical horse. "Akiva told me that you wouldn't listen."

"Akiva is a tool," Zaxis spat.

I shot him a glare. He huffed and crossed his arms, returning to silence.

"Well, now that I've listened to your proposal, why don't you listen to mine?" I asked.

Orwyn kept her attention on her kirin, never replying.

"Join *us*. We'll put an end to the plague, and we'll deal with the apoch dragon when it arrives. Together. There's no need for any more violence. We don't need to force rulers to capitulate to our demands, or wreck cities in order to get the resources we want—we can build a greater world the old-fashioned way."

"And if I say *no*?" Orwyn asked.

"We go back to killing each other, obviously," Zaxis added, calmer than before, but still menacing.

"Akiva said you'd try to kill me here."

I motioned to the desert. "You're free to go at any time. But if I see you again, you won't have my honor to protect you. We'll have to fight. And then we'll see who's stronger."

Orwyn glanced at the Rocky Wastes, her gaze still vacant. Then she pulled herself up onto her kirin. Her strawberry blonde hair swirled into her eyes for a moment, and she brushed it all back.

"Thank you for taking the time to speak with me." She forced a small smile. "Warlord, Hunter—you surprised me. I thought you'd be... more like Theasin. And Helvetti. But you two are so different."

"You can still change your mind," I said.

Orwyn shook her head. "All I know... is my village. And Helvetti. I don't want to question my beliefs now. Not after everything I've done. What kind of god-arcanist would I be then?"

"It's never too late."

"Helvetti says he needs the typhon beast on his side in order to defeat all other god-arcanists..."

The wind picked up worse than before. Sand blasted into the sky, stinging my eyes in an instant. I covered my face and kept my eyes scrunched. The brief sandstorm lasted a full minute before it finally calmed. That was when I opened my eyes again, only to find Orwyn had disappeared.

"Terrakona," I called out. "Did you see where she went?"

**"Yes, Warlord."**

"Where?"

**"She flew off, untethered by gravity. Such is the magic of the sky titan—and why the previous one was called *the Falcon*. I'm afraid we won't be able to follow her in the dark when we have no way to track a tiny bird."**

"How do you know that was why she has the title of Falcon?"

Terrakona growled a bit. **"I'm... not sure, Warlord. The memories are whispered to me, from a time long gone."**

"Memories from the first world serpent?"

**"I believe so."**

This hadn't been the first time Terrakona had been confused about his memories. I wondered why, but I didn't have many theories.

I cursed under my breath and then glanced back in the direction of Regal Heights.

Orwyn and I both had a deep-seated conviction, but mine had been born of experience. I had seen the evils of the world and was determined to right them. Moments of reflection, and even moments of despair, had strengthened my resolve.

But Orwyn...

Her conviction stemmed from a lifetime of platitudes and

speeches. I suspected she hadn't reflected on them, and instead followed her path with blind devotion, hoping whoever led her knew what they were doing. She hadn't thought through the implications or what it might mean for people she had never met. Never reflected or questioned.

The perfect follower.

No wonder the Autarch liked her.

"Let's head out," I said. "I want to get home as soon as possible so we can report this to the others."

**"As you wish,"** Terrakona said as he lowered his head.

Everyone had to know that Orwyn, and her assassin friend, were likely to attack any day now. Although I realized afterward, I hadn't asked about the whereabouts of Vethica, or even if Orwyn knew of Luthair. It frustrated me, but I already knew the answer. She wasn't going to help us.

So I'd have to make sure I followed through on my plans.

One way or another, we'd discover the whereabouts of the Second Ascension.

# CHAPTER 51

## A PHOENIX PISTOL

The moment I returned to Regal Heights, I went straight for Brom and Vinder.

I wanted to take the red jasper runestone and hide it, but another piece of me feared that the Second Ascension would force their way into the typhon beast's lair somehow, like they had with Terrakona's tree lair.

And Akiva was immune to poison gases. He could easily venture into the caves and find the door to the typhon beast's lair, no doubt in my mind. What if he managed to get inside? What if *he* became the typhon beast arcanist? I wouldn't put it past him to murder his own king basilisk just to do it.

I slammed through the doors of city hall and hurried up the stone steps to the main sitting room. I already knew Brom, Vinder, and Eventide were inside, because I felt the footfalls of three people and a gargoyle.

Without thinking, I burst into the room. I should've knocked or announced myself. Vinder jumped from his chair and drew his sword—one of the typhon beast blades I had constructed—heating the room a few degrees with his weapon. Brom withdrew a pistol from the holster on his belt.

Eventide, however, didn't flinch. She seemed to have realized my sudden arrival was not a sign or attack, but just me getting carried away.

"I spoke with the sky titan arcanist," I said, curt. "She's going to attack us to get the runestone. Orwyn made it clear the Second Ascension won't allow us to gain another god-arcanist."

Vinder sheathed his blade and frowned. "We know that, lad. Everyone knows that."

I clenched my jaw as I strode forward. Then I slammed my hand on the stone table in the middle of the room. "We shouldn't wait to have someone bond with it. That was a mistake. We should send people in now, while we build the pit trap for my plan."

"Right now?" Eventide asked as she stood from the red-stone chair. "I think we need more time. William can be brought to the lair, but he's the only one we have who is unbonded. If the typhon beast doesn't bond with him, then—"

"Okay, we can wait for a little while, but it has to be soon. Please." I tried to impart the urgency in my voice, but I knew it came off as demanding. I exhaled, calmed myself, and finished, "I don't want them to get their hands on the beast. According to legend, the Monster was devastating, and I think we need it on our side."

Eventide nodded along with my words. "Some people have arrived in Regal Heights, all hoping to bond with the god-creature. Perhaps we can set up a few small tests to see if they're worthy of the runestone. If yes, we'll escort them into the lair and see if the beast bonds."

"But the poison gas. We need—"

Brom stepped forward, the scar on his face a little distracting. "Don't worry about none of that. I'm a grandmaster hydra arcanist. We're immune to poison gases, and I can make trinkets that grant immunity as well."

"That's right," Vinder stated. "And I can be there to help

people with the awkwardness of the gorge. I'll rearrange the stones in the caves—we can have as many people as we want to try to bond with the creature."

"As long as they're not with the Second Ascension," I said. "Maybe have Adelgis speak with each of the people hoping to bond."

"Of course. Of course."

Although this wasn't what I had imagined for the typhon beast, it was better than nothing. We *couldn't* allow it to bond with anyone in the Second Ascension. In my heart, I knew. We had to protect it at all costs.

---

My anxiety about the bonding felt like a poison slowly sinking into every inch of my body. I needed a distraction, so I headed to my father's study. While I had rushed over to city hall, Zaxis had said he would bring materials to my father. I didn't know what materials, but I would still need to imbue them into whatever kind of gun my father constructed if it was going to become a potent artifact.

With my thoughts focused, I made my way through town, and then to my temporary home. The citizens of Regal Heights waved as I passed. I returned the gesture whenever I noticed them, enjoying the overall friendliness.

When I reached my father's study, I carefully stepped inside and smiled.

Zaxis and my father were standing next to the large desk, their attention on all the creature parts spread out before them. Neither of them glanced up when I entered, but they both mumbled a greeting.

Then my father motioned to a small pile of stone-like scales. "These are from a pyroclastic dragon. *They are basically fire incarnate.* We should make the pistol out of these, and maybe some salamander bits..."

"No," Zaxis growled. "I don't care if the dragon is more magical... I want to use these feathers."

"But phoenixes aren't as specialized. Consider blue phoenix feathers, at least? She specializes in heat. Tine will be happy to provide a few. She'll—"

"*These are from Forsythe,*" Zaxis snapped, cutting him off. He gripped the edge of the desk. "They're the only mystical creature I want."

I walked over to the desk, my attention immediately falling to the scarlet feathers in the middle of all the other mystical creature parts. They shimmered with heat and power— phoenixes were strong. Just below dragons in terms of raw power. Forsythe's feather would make a fine artifact.

But I understood why my father scoffed and pushed away from the desk.

Red phoenixes weren't *the best* option for a pistol. They would work, but if Zaxis wanted *the best,* he should choose the most powerful type of creature he could get his hands on.

If he used the typhon beast's bones to make his pistol...

But I shook the thought away the instant Zaxis scooped up the feathers. He held them with care and concern, as if worried he would ruin them if he was too rough. It reminded me of how I had treated Luthair's cape. I hadn't wanted anything to happen to it.

"I'll imbue the pistol," I said, breaking the silence between them.

Jozé pointed to a nearby bookshelf. "There, boy. I have the frame of a pistol. We just need to combine the parts and imbue it all."

I followed his gesture, grabbed the metal frame of a pistol from the middle shelf, and then brought it over to the desk. Zaxis handed over the three feathers. One had a dot at the end, resembling that of a peacock marking. I took the feathers—which were still warm—and held them close to the frame of the gun.

"How do we combine these?" I asked.

Jozé held out a hand. "Give them here. I can do it. My blue phoenix magic allows me to augment materials, remember?" Once I handed them over, Jozé shot Zaxis a hard look. "Are you *sure* you want to use these feathers? We have better options."

"This is what I want," Zaxis stated. He crossed his arms over his bare chest. "Forsythe gave me the feathers so I could trade them at a market... but I couldn't part with them. Now I don't ever want them out of my sight. If they're part of my pistol, that will be easy."

I appreciated Zaxis's dedication to his previous eldrin. It reminded me of Luthair.

After a short sigh, my father scooped up two star shards from the desk and then held the three feathers and pistol frame close. Then he closed his eyes.

The metal of the frame heated, glowing a bright orange and white. The shine of the superheated metal was almost too bright to look at directly. Then my father heated the feathers, and it was like staring into the sun. The feathers burst into white flames, retaining their shape but somehow burning brighter than I had seen any phoenix burn before.

Jozé wrapped the feathers around the pistol, his skilled fingers tucking them into the metal framework. He wove them around the handle, and then the barrel, and even through the trigger... It took him some effort, and he went to work at a slow and controlled pace. If he dropped the weapon, it would land on stone, so I wasn't worried about anything catching fire.

It took my father several minutes to lace the feathers in place. They were so hot, it was likely they were welded to the metal itself, becoming a single object. When Jozé was finally done, he exhaled slowly and allowed the heat to dissipate.

The resulting pistol looked as if it had been forged out of crimson metal.

The phoenix feathers had been fused into the gun frame. Flourishes of feather ruffles marked the edges of the metal, giving it a wing-like aesthetic.

"The star shards are holding the feathers in place," my father said, a bit breathless. "Volke, you can now imbue the weapon. Please, imagine your molten rock when you do so. We want the pistol to fire without the need for an external heat source."

I took the weapon from him. The pistol likely would've burned a normal person, but it didn't affect me. Then Jozé handed me eleven star shards. I took the tiny crystals and placed them along the barrel of the gun.

After spending so many weeks crafting trinkets, I no longer felt uneasy about imbuing. I closed my eyes, just like before, and cleared my thoughts of all other things. I pictured my magma oozing from the creases in my palm. The destruction... the life blood of the world...

In my heart, I knew I would pick destruction for my evocation.

And creation for my manipulation.

Moving the land and controlling its life blood, were my preferred method of handling problems. Although I liked the idea of controlling the ocean waves, I knew I would have to travel across the land more than the water. And I wanted to build things. Like the staircase down into the Pillar.

"Focus," Jozé chided. "You're not thinking about molten rock."

"R-Right," I sheepishly said. "Sorry."

"Don't mess up my pistol," Zaxis growled. "Forsythe's feathers are in there."

He was right. I didn't want to mess this up.

After a short exhale, I dwelled solely on my molten rock and how the heat had once boiled part of the ocean. My evocation was beyond powerful, and once this weapon had been imbued, it would be beyond powerful as well.

My magic slowly drained from me, like a cup of water being poured into the desert. But unlike with the apoch dragon bones, I could tell the feathers had a limit. The phoenix parts couldn't contain all my power. If I forced too much into them, they would break.

Fortunately, I managed to use all eleven star shards before I reached the feather's breaking point. I smiled as I opened my eyes, proud of myself for getting used to the sensation of imbuing.

The pistol...

The metal frame pulsed like a heartbeat, occasionally crackling with red energy. It now had a smooth, almost organic appearance, as if the pieces had fused wholly into a single object. And the wings designs created by the feathers... they had merged into the image of a majestic phoenix sweeping along the weapon's length.

Was that from the phoenix magic? Since they also had healing magic? Or was it because I had thought of the magma as lifeblood? Either way, the pulse of magic was mystical and beautiful at the same time. Each flare of power brought with it a shimmer of crimson.

Zaxis held out his hand, his eyes wide. I handed him the weapon. He carefully brought it closer to his eyes so he could examine it. "This is amazing."

"You still need to imbue your bullets," Jozé stated. "But I believe this weapon will fire any projectiles with great force—maybe too much force. God-arcanist magic can be a bit unpredictable."

"I like being unpredictable," Zaxis said with a smirk.

"At some point, I'm going to need to attune the pistol to you. I don't know if I'll be able to change it after that... So make sure you're happy with it before we move to that step."

Fatigue gripped me. While I had become better at imbuing trinkets and artifacts, the process still exhausted me. The room spun as I staggered over to the wall and braced myself against it.

"I think I need to sleep for a bit," I said.

Jozé nodded once. "Get some good rest. We'll need you later for some more artificing."

## CHAPTER 52

## SEEDING THE WORLD WITH MAGIC

Over the next week, Eventide, Brom, and Vinder managed to find a small airship that belonged to a traveling merchant. The merchant—a pegasus arcanist—agreed to move nullstone in exchange for some star shards. It would still take time, but it was a start.

I set to work altering a field near Hydra's Gorge. A field just outside the city, on the north edge, the parts closest to the Copeland River and Garnet Lake.

I couldn't take too long manipulating the terrain. The longer I worked, the more likely it was that someone would see what I was doing and deduce the purpose. So, in a single evening, under the cover of darkness, I made a large hole and then covered it with a thin layer of stone, dirt, and grass.

Anyone walking over the hole—which was a few hundred feet wide—wouldn't know the difference. Well, unless they could feel things through tremors. My magic allowed me to detect the hole under the field, but my feet couldn't tell the difference whenever I walked across it.

As the sun began to rise, blanketing the world in calming blues and oranges, I walked back to Regal Heights. Terrakona was just outside the city, beyond the wall, and near the shrubs. He was manipulating the terrain, altering the surrounding area to bring trees together in a small cluster.

When I approached, he stopped his work and turned his massive serpentine head to face me. The morning light glittered through his crystal mane. The core of each crystal was black—much like a knightmare—and I smiled when the dark glimmer caught my eye.

"What're you doing?" I asked.

Terrakona moved his gargantuan body to the side, allowing me a better view of the trees he had collected. They had been pushed together in a haphazard manner, like a child smooshing clumps of wet sand into a pile and calling them a castle.

The roots were poking out of the ground, a couple trees were leaning heavily to one side, and some of the trunks looked to have splintered during the moving process.

**"I'm making a grove, Warlord,"** Terrakona telepathically replied. **"I just need a few more trees."**

Leaves were scattered across the ground from all the force required to move the oak trees. I glanced around, trying to spot something nearby. A couple of trees were in the distance, on the other side of Hydra's Gorge.

"Why are you building a grove?" I asked as I stared at the far-off plants. "This seems like a lot of effort... We aren't staying here forever."

**"True. But they are."**

Terrakona motioned his head at the ground. I walked closer to the crooked trees and stared. To my surprise, four dryads emerged from the ground, each one struggling to burst out of the tightly packed soil. Their waxy green skin and vine hair were all similar, but their eyes set them apart.

Foil had pink flower eyes. Another one had blue flowers for eyes. Another had yellow. And the last had white. They were all disturbingly similar—small, humanoid children with vegetation for bodies.

"*Four*?" I balked. "I thought... But... The last I heard... You had only found two! That was it. Why are there four here, Terrakona?"

The dryads flinched at the sound of my half-yelling. They promptly buried themselves in the dirt again, hiding away from sight. Then they went inactive, like seeds in the ground. That was why I hadn't sensed them with my magic—they weren't making any vibrations. They weren't moving at all.

**"I keep finding them,"** Terrakona said as he lowered his snout to be closer to the ground. He sniffed at the area they had disappeared. **"They have no family or tribe. I wanted to create them a home. A place they could belong."**

The thought gave me hope, but at the same time, I was still baffled as to why they were here. *Four* dryads? In the middle of nowhere? Just appearing around Terrakona? What was going on?

For a brief moment, I thought about running to one of the mystic seekers, but then I realized something. Orwyn had spoken about the god-creatures *seeding the world with magic.* She had said the Autarch wanted the god-arcanists to live so we could add more magic to the world.

Was Terrakona's vast depth of power somehow spilling out of him? Were the dryads being created through fable means? *Progeny* creatures needed parents to breed, but creatures who were born through a *fable* just needed certain conditions to be met, and then they would spawn into the world as infants. Knightmares were born when rulers were murdered... But dryads? Could a fable condition be that the world serpent was alive? Or maybe these were special dryads?

Terrakona manipulated the ground, moving the trees so that they weren't tilted. He went to great lengths to make sure they were neatly positioned in a tight circle. The roots still jutted out of the ground, but he was beginning to get everything in order.

"We should, uh, find people to bond with them," I said. "There are people coming from all over to bond with the typhon beast. Perhaps some of them will be content with dryads."

**"Yes, Warlord. A fantastic idea."**

I made a mental note to tell that to Eventide. She could lead people to this grove so that they could speak with the baby dryads.

I placed a hand on one of Terrakona's emerald scales. "Thank you for watching over them."

**"There is no need for thanks. I merely thought—what would the Warlord do if he found so many lost dryads?"** Terrakona glanced back at me, his serpentine eyes locking with mine. **"We are guardians, aren't we? Leaders. And leaders protect their flock."**

I half smiled as the four dryads slowly poked their heads above the surface. Their hands had claws of bark, and when they blinked, the flowers shifted their petals.

Did all dryads look like this? These ones seemed... different...

"I'm going to rest," I said. "I hope your little dryads enjoy their new home."

**"I do, too, Warlord."**

---

When I slept, I had dreams of magic.

And the Autarch.

For some reason, we were speaking in the middle of a forest, somehow in the same grove that Terrakona had created. I couldn't make out the Autarch's exact words, but we were having a conversation about the necessity of magic.

He made a convincing argument. We needed magic to make the world a greater place—a world safer for all.

Then he said something about culling the weak and making room for the strong. I told him I didn't want that, but then he reminded me that Terrakona wanted something similar, and so did Vjorn. No matter what I said, the Autarch wouldn't listen.

Then the forest was on fire, and up from the flames arose a dragon...

I didn't get a good look at it, other than to remark that it had claws the size of ships, and it swiped its massive hand across the forest, decimating everything it touched. Nothing was left afterward—just rot, ashes, and a field of bones.

When I finally woke, my chest was tight with anxiety. I scrambled to sit up, lost in a mountain of pillows. After a long sigh, I rubbed at my eyes and reminded myself it was all just a terrible dream. The Autarch, and the apoch dragon, were forces of destruction. And it felt like they both disguised their mayhem under the façade of *good* and *necessary*.

I didn't like it.

But I refused to dwell on it for long. Instead, I got up, got dressed, and headed out to complete some of the many tasks I still had remaining to do.

———

At night, when I was done with my training and helping Zaxis, I headed back to my bedroom. Evianna joined me as I walked up the stone steps of the fortress. She told me about the darkness around the canyon, and how some of the shadows were darker than she had ever seen.

"And when I'm in those shadows, my magic is more powerful," she said. "It's like in the caves—where there's no light. Isn't that amazing?"

I forced a smile and nodded. There weren't many steps up to the front door of the fortress, but it felt longer whenever my thoughts dwelled on Luthair. "I do remember that being the case when I was a knightmare arcanist. You should always try to fight in the shadows whenever possible."

"I do." Evianna held on to my arm. "I just have to find places where I can lure villains. I think that's my best plan of action."

I opened the door to the fortress, and we stepped inside. To my surprise, Hexa was waiting there, flanked by two men who had enough muscles for five people. It was the first thing I noticed—their buff physiques were enough to intimidate most. I just wondered how they had gotten to be so *big*. They were almost as wide as they were tall, with solid muscle as dense as rocks.

And they wore the revealing clothing common in Regal Heights. Which just highlighted their considerable bulk and numerous scars. How did they even get into their clothes? The fabric strained over their chests and biceps. It was an honest mystery.

And their curly hair, even *more* sandy brown and cinnamon than Hexa's, had been cut so short, they were almost bald.

"Hexa?" I asked, confused.

The three of them were just standing in the entrance hall, dead in the middle, like they had been waiting for me. Was this... some sort of ambush? Obviously, Hexa wasn't going to hurt me, but I couldn't help but think their motive was sinister.

Hexa stepped forward. She wore hydra-scale armor that hugged her body. She was muscular, too, but not like the men. The purplish scales were layered over each other in a fashionable way, and she kept one of my bone swords in a sheath on her hip.

"Volke," she said. Hexa motioned to the two men on either side of her. "These are my cousins. They're twins. This is Todd d'Tenni, and this is Marx d'Tenni. They've been waiting to meet you."

I hadn't realized until that moment, but both of them were hydra arcanists. Their foreheads were marked with the arcanist star—the etching in their skin prominent. They had been bonded for a long time, then.

And the scars on their arms, chests, and legs reminded me of tiger stripes. A hydra's Trial of Worth required some sort of scarring, and everyone in Regal Heights seemed proud to show the marks off. Hexa's cousins had turned the scars into a piece of artwork on their body, like how some people used tattoos to beautify themselves.

Both of them stepped forward and bowed their heads.

"You're smaller in person," Todd said, one eyebrow up. "But you've got cunning eyes."

Hexa smacked his shoulder. "You heard what Vinder said! You don't need physical strength when you have god-arcanist powers. Volke defeated Vinder without much effort!"

"Impressive," Todd said.

Marx stepped forward and bowed even deeper. "Thank you."

"For?" I asked.

That simple question seemed to confuse him. He processed my words as though this were the first time he had held a conversation.

"For..." Marx narrowed his eyes. "Being a kind god-arcanist. Of course."

I slowly nodded. "Oh. Well, don't worry about it."

Hexa shoved her two cousins behind her. Then she turned to me, her cinnamon hair curlier than ever, bouncing with each turn and slight movement she made. "Don't worry about these two. They just act weird whenever they're nervous. They're both *really* impressive."

Nothing I had seen—outside of their physique—convinced me of that, but I was willing to believe Hexa. She knew the locals better than I did. If she thought they were talented, they probably were.

"I know we're going to face the Second Ascension soon,"

Hexa quickly said before I could add anything to the conversation. She stepped close so that there were only a few inches between us. "I want to be on the front lines. And my cousins are gonna back me up."

I lifted both my eyebrows.

Evianna narrowed her eyes, her attention on Hexa's proximity to me. It almost seemed like Evianna wanted to push Hexa away, but Evianna restrained herself. Instead, she just held my arm tighter.

"I figured you'd fight the Second Ascension," I said.

Hexa shook her head. "Yeah, but I want to be one of the *first* to fight them. Marx and Todd have my back. We're going to do the whole d'Tenni family proud. You'll see."

Her two cousins each smacked a fist into the palm of the other hand.

They were... disturbingly similar. Obviously, they were twins, but it was a little more than that.

"Uh, sure," I said. "I'll try to make sure you're in the thick of it."

Hexa smiled.

Then I asked, "Is there a reason why you want to fight so badly? Other than just wanting to destroy the Second Ascension?"

"I just want to make sure that, whenever we find Vethica, I can tell her—with complete honesty—that I did everything I could to make sure she got home safely." Hexa stepped away, much to Evianna's delight. "And I'm going to do just that. My family has done everything they can to help."

"How so?"

Hexa motioned to her armor. And then to her cousins. "They've spared no expense. Everyone is behind me. Nobody messes with a member of the d'Tenni family and gets away with it."

"We were mad that Hexa left for the Frith Guild years ago,"

Todd stated. "But we're over that now. Hexa needs our help. We'll be there for her."

"Yeah," Marx lamely added.

And that was it. No other deep thoughts from the pair of them.

"All right," I muttered. "I'll keep that in mind when the time comes. And understand that it'll be soon."

Hexa's smile grew cold and serious. "Oh, I know. That's why I waited for you. I wanted to make sure I spoke to you before anything happened." She slapped the arms of her cousins. "C'mon! Let's go get some rest, guys."

They laughed and headed for the front door. Both men said a goodbye but ultimately forgot about me the instant one of them brought up getting some drinks on the way home. They seemed good natured—and somewhat like Hexa—but I wondered how competent they were at fighting.

Hopefully, that was the thing they specialized in.

"Regal Heights is... not my favorite place," Evianna said. She leaned her head on my shoulder. "Promise me that we won't live here when we eventually build a home and settle down."

My face heated. We hadn't talked about building houses together yet. It was heartwarming. "Uh, all right. I kind of like it here, but I understand it's not for everyone."

Together, we continued to my room. Hopefully, we could fill our days with talks about where we were going to live once the Second Ascension had been stopped.

———

A week later, a few hundred people had arrived in Regal Heights, all looking to bond with the typhon beast. It wasn't just locals from nearby villages, either. Mystic seekers from around the area had hurried here as quickly as they could, all claiming they deserved the right to prove themselves to the mighty god-creature.

I allowed Eventide and Adelgis to handle the process. They gave the hopefuls tests of courage and wisdom—things to prove the person hoping to bond would do right with his new magic.

To my surprise, most people didn't like the sound of the typhon beast. When Eventide described the legends to the new arrivals, some actually left. The *monster* of legend was too much, apparently. Some even said they didn't want to bond with a creature who had defied the previous Warlord.

Were the old legends really that bad? Everything the typhon beast had done was in the past. It seemed odd to me that anyone would rethink bonding just because the first typhon beast had been a villain.

Sometimes individuals couldn't escape their past, it seemed. Not even god-creatures.

During the sorting process, where Eventide and Adelgis questioned everyone, I sat on the edge of a nearby fortress building, watching from on high. I kept my shirt closed and wore a cap, so that no one would recognize me.

Illia and Nicholin joined me for the "fun."

One by one, individuals approached Eventide as she stood by a fountain near the edge of the gorge. Adelgis sat on the stones around the edge of the fountain, just a few feet behind her, his expression neutral and almost uninterested.

"No need to be worried," Eventide said.

A short woman with black hair and sunkissed skin replied, "Sorry, guildmaster. I've never, uh, done this before."

"I'll let you in on a secret." Eventide leaned in close. "Neither have I." She smiled and leaned away, her easygoing demeanor so infectious, the other woman was smiling. "Let's just stumble through this together, shall we?"

"A-All right."

"Who would you say is the most important person in your life?"

The short woman didn't require much time to answer. "My husband," she said. "I'd do anything for him."

"And if you saw someone stealing bread from a bakery, but you knew the loaves were old and about to be thrown out anyway, would you report it?"

The woman struggled more with that question. She hemmed and hawed and finally said, "If it was going to be thrown out anyway... I wouldn't say anything."

Illia and I sat a good forty feet up, away from the masses, but still within earshot of the conversation. The citizens of Regal Heights watched from all manner of nearby balconies and windows as well.

"Why is she asking about stealing?" Illia asked, her one eye narrowed.

"I don't know," I muttered. "Probably to see how they would answer."

Footsteps on the roof of our building caught my attention. I glanced over my shoulder, only to see nothing. Someone was invisible. I placed a hand on Retribution and waited.

"Fain?" I asked.

"Yes?"

He allowed his invisibility to drop and appeared a few feet from Illia and me. With slow steps, he approached, his hair disheveled and sticky with sweat. The sunshine over the gorge didn't do him any favors. His frostbitten ears and fingers seemed dried out.

"Eventide is asking those questions to see if they answer truthfully," Fain said.

Nicholin ran his paws over his white and silver fur. "Adelgis will tell her if they're lying?"

"That's right."

Illia sighed. Then she touched her eyepatch and just stared at the next hopeful approaching. "I feel like we should first weed out all the inept people."

Fain shifted his weight from one foot to the other. "Well, I think most of them are ept."

"Is *ept* even a word?" Nicholin whispered, his blue eyes shifting from side to side.

"What makes you think they're talented?" Illia asked, ignoring her eldrin's question.

"They're here, aren't they?" Fain motioned to the line of people waiting to speak to Eventide and Adelgis. "They left their friends, family, and home, all to brave the unknown and prove themselves worthy. Even if they're not skilled, they all have ambition greater than the average man."

"They may just be greedy and delusional."

Fain shook his head. "Maybe some of them. But not all. The real cowards join the Second Ascension. These people are here because they want to prove they're something more than ordinary."

Illia didn't reply, but I could tell she was mulling over his words. It pleased me that they were on speaking terms. She hadn't liked him much at first, but eventually, she had warmed up to Fain.

The rest of the time we just sat in silence, watching the people come and go. None of them seemed like someone worthy of the typhon beast, though. It worried me. They replied tepidly, without much confidence. How would they wield the madness of the deadliest hydra if they couldn't navigate a simple conversation?

It genuinely worried me.

I hoped William was enough for the beast. Then I wouldn't have to fret.

Three days later, Eventide and Adelgis said they had found two individuals whom they thought would impress the typhon beast. They informed me that the city ruler and minister would be willing to take those two, along with William, into the lair first thing in the morning. They would escort everyone to the beast and see what the god-creature thought.

I felt a little hesitant. First off, part of the Trial of Worth was supposed to involve locating the runestone, but we had already done that. Apparently, venturing into the lair with knights was common, even in the old tales, but Brom and Vinder weren't the knights of these individuals, not even William.

I shook the thoughts from my head. We didn't have time to quibble about the properness of the trial. I just hoped the typhon beast wouldn't be offended.

Fortunately, the nullstone arrived as well, attuned so it wouldn't destroy the airship.

I had sent a note with the airship captain—one addressed to Queen Ladislava. I had requested she alter the nullstone for us. We provided the star shards, of course. I was pleased she had decided to cooperate. It was a simple request, after all. There was no need to argue.

Maybe Ladislava had finally realized that.

Everything was in place for us to execute our plans. At dawn, Eventide and the city rulers would approach the typhon beast, and tonight, I would have my trap completed.

There wasn't as much nullstone as I had wanted, but it was enough to fill the pit I had created. I took the rocks, stored them near my fortress home, and waited until the sun went down before moving them. When I was certain no one was watching, I spilled the giant blue and black rocks into the pit.

The suffocating effects of the rocks still bothered me, but they couldn't shut down my magic. I spread them out and then covered the pit again with a thin layer of rock, dirt, and grass, making sure that the field looked decent.

The smell of fresh soil reminded me of the graveyard on the Isle of Ruma. I had forgotten how much I enjoyed the scent. If only I could smell the salt of the ocean... Then it would have been perfect.

I spent all night working on my trap, Terrakona by my side. After some long hours, I was finally satisfied.

"How does it look?" I asked as I motioned to the field.

In all honesty, it looked as good as Terrakona's grove. The grass was in weird lumps, and hills of dirt were scattered around because I couldn't smooth them all without disturbing the trap underneath. If there hadn't been a pit, I could have made the field pristine.

But it would pass for a tilled meadow.

**"I love it,"** Terrakona said, enthusiasm in his telepathic voice. **"We should create more things together."**

I smiled. "Yeah. I'd like that."

When the sun came up, I cursed at myself for not being in the city. I wanted to see William off. But then I caught sight of a horse in the distance, and my thoughts faded.

The animal galloped toward Regal Heights, its rushed movements kicking up dust. The rider urged his mount faster and faster, never slowing.

No one ran that fast to deliver good news.

I closed my eyes and sensed our surroundings. The movement of people in Regal Heights. The breaths of comfortable sleepers. The footfalls of Vjorn, the giant wolf. The guards on their patrol.

And then the rider dismounted near the wall.

His speech...

"Someone tell the Frith Guild," the rider said, the vibrations of his words traveling to me, even if my ears heard nothing. "Our village is being slaughtered! East Valley needs help! I barely got away with my life!"

My heart briefly stopped. The information rocked me, and I

lost concentration. My eyes snapped open as I quickly tried to process the information. Then I motioned for Terrakona to come close.

"They're attacking," I said, my attention on the horizon.

The first sliver of the sun was shining over the distant mountains. Did the Second Ascension know our plan to enter the typhon beast's lair? Was that why they were attacking now? Or had it been a coincidence?

I suspected this was intentional, and it worried me.

**"What's happening, Warlord?"**

"They're killing people. I don't know why." When Terrakona lowered his head, I stepped onto his crystal mane, my hands unsteady. "We have to go."

**"Rushing to meet them wasn't our plan."**

Curse the abyssal hells.

I understood now. The Second Ascension was trying to control the battle by forcing me to leave the city. That had to be it. They were killing people just outside of Regal Heights, hoping I'd rush to their defense.

And I would have to. I couldn't sit by and let people get slaughtered. Fortunately, Zaxis was also a god-arcanist, albeit a new one. He could defend Regal Heights while I dealt with the blackhearts. But first, I had to come up with a plan and get everyone into place.

# CHAPTER 53

## DASTARDLY TACTICS

Terrakona and I stormed over to the walls of Regal Heights. Then Terrakona roared, waking the whole city with a call to war. Vjorn leapt onto the roof of one of the fortified fortresses. He threw his head back and howled, his answer to Terrakona's war cry. The haunting howl was as icy as the god-creature's magic, and I could feel the power and bloodlust behind it.

The citizens of Regal Heights weren't the type to hide, apparently. The few I saw armed themselves with weapons and strapped on lightweight leather armor. It seemed that everyone would fight, if it came down to it, even the older citizens. I swear the elderly in this city thought it was shameful to let the younger generations handle anything. A few old men barked about *how they still had it*, despite their shaky hands and hunched backs.

Seeing the citizens rallying so calmly for war, I felt a little more confident about leaving Regal Heights to deal with the problem at the nearby villages. With my sword, my shield—and the pendant Eventide had crafted for me—I knew I could handle any problem waiting for me.

I briefly considered wearing armor, but I ultimately decided against it.

My evocation had become so powerful that only magic items could hope to withstand it. The Second Ascension would surely bring decay dust and apoch dragon weapons, meaning any magic armor would be worse than useless.

"*Volke?*" Adelgis telepathically asked me.

"Tell Zaxis, Hexa, Evianna, and Fain to stand guard near the city gates." I gritted my teeth and added, "And please let Eventide know what's happening. I know she's in the typhon beast's lair, but still. She needs to know."

"*Of course. What about the others?*"

"Illia and Zelfree should both teleport to me," I said. "Then we'll head for the village."

"*It'll be done.*"

"Karna should remain hidden and hopefully surprise anyone who sneaks in. If Ryker can fight, he should join her."

"*Your brother says he's ready to test his might against the enemy.*"

That surprised me, but I wasn't about to question it. If Ryker thought he could handle a battle, I wanted him to try.

Who else was here who would listen to me? Would the hydra arcanists of the gorge welcome the instructions of the world serpent arcanist? I had to try.

"Adelgis—ask some of the hydra arcanists to wait near the staircase into the gorge. The others should wait in the city itself, preparing for a defense if the enemy gets inside. Let them know that teleportation is an option. They need to stay vigilant."

"*And Atty? She has asked to help with the fighting.*"

Atty...

"Have her go to the steps as well," I said. "Just in case."

Adelgis sent me a telepathic sense of confidence. He would relay my instructions. Confident he could handle it, I held on to Terrakona and waited for Illia and Zelfree. Each second that crept by took a toll on my sanity. I wanted to rush straight to the conflict, but I had to calm myself and wait.

The first world serpent arcanist, Luvi, had been a calculating strategist. He wouldn't have fallen for enemy traps.

Illia and Zelfree appeared next to me, pops of air and glitter heralding their arrival. Both of them landed on Terrakona's mane, crowding my eldrin's head. Terrakona was large, but two people was usually the limit for riding on his mane.

"We're here," Illia said between heavy breaths. "Where are we going?"

I pointed to the distant mountains. "East Village."

"Let's go," Zelfree added.

Traces, his mimic, had transformed into a rizzel. She was just as cute as Nicholin—with white fur, silver stripes. And she was just as large as Nicholin as well, weasel-like and all. Her blue eyes twinkled in the morning light.

"Go, go, go," Nicholin squeaked. "We're ready!"

But before we went anywhere, the shadows around Terrakona shifted and fluttered. Evianna stepped out of the darkness, already merged with her knightmare. She wore the dark shadow-scale armor like a true knight, her confidence radiating through. With careful and controlled movements, Evianna dove into the darkness and then shadow-stepped to the back of my eldrin.

"You're not going without me, Volke Savan," she said in her merged double-voice. "Layshl and I are going to fight by your side no matter what."

We didn't have time to argue the point, but I knew Evianna was a very competent fighter. Perhaps we would need her strength. I nodded once in acknowledgement of her presence.

Terrakona's scales flared as he lunged forward. The ground rearranged itself as he charged forward, heading straight for East Valley. When we had traveled there at a leisurely pace, it had taken an hour, but it would be less than half that time with Terrakona so enraged.

Illia and Zelfree stood close to me, each gripping the crystal lattice of Terrakona's mane like their life depended on it. Nicholin and Traces stayed on their arcanists' shoulders, their heads poked up like meerkats.

Evianna used the shadows to steady herself on Terrakona's back. She had long since become accustomed to his serpentine movements, and she had no trouble keeping her balance. Her knightmare's cowl stayed over her white hair, hiding it from view.

"What's the plan?" Illia asked. "Why me and Zelfree?"

"When we reach the village, I was hoping you could save any citizens who might still be alive," I said, though I knew it was unlikely we would find survivors. "After that, if you could try to capture members of the Second Ascension—I need to question them."

Zelfree nodded once. "All right."

I glanced over my shoulder. "Did you hear that, Evianna? I think your shadow abilities might help with this, too."

She stared up at me. "I understand. We'll save the people first and then attack."

"Right."

"Do you know what we'll find there?" Illia asked.

I shook my head. "I suspect we'll find the sky titan arcanist and her lackeys. The Keeper of Corpses, Akiva, maybe some newer arcanists and plague-ridden monsters."

My words were terse and serious, and Illia listened with an intent expression. This would be dangerous, and I feared for her, Evianna's, and Zelfree's safety, but part of me was also excited.

I couldn't wait to rid the world of more plague-ridden lunatics. And if I managed to fell major members of the Second Ascension, nothing would be better. Especially if they were just slaughtering people to gain my attention. What a cowardly and dastardly tactic.

Beyond reprehensible.

Thankfully, the trek was swift and without issue. I spotted East Valley within fifteen minutes and steeled my heart to the reality of combat. Flames licked the sky—the tiny houses and public buildings were all ablaze. Smoke rose in pillars toward the sun, the dark clouds marring the otherwise beautiful surroundings.

Terrakona went straight to the edge of the town and roared again, announcing his presence to everyone in the area.

Illia teleported away, popping out of existence and heading for the buildings that were still intact. Zelfree grabbed my arm and teleported me to the ground. Then he and Traces disappeared in a flash of glitter, no doubt rushing off to help Illia with my assignment.

Evianna shifted through the darkness, went straight to my side, and then kissed me on the cheek. Her knightmare armor was cold, but her warm breath on my face was a reassurance. We could do this.

"Stay safe," she said. Her merged voice made me smile as it reminded me of Luthair. "I'll be back."

Evianna dove into the shadows and shot off after Zelfree.

Bodies littered the roads of the village. I couldn't stare long, as each one hurt my heart. Women, children... How could anyone do this without feeling the pain and suffering of lost life?

Before I ran into the village, I took a few moments to sense my surroundings. What I felt shocked me. There were multiple people here—and large beasts—but they were in the buildings, hiding among the flames, but I had expected that. And the shouts for help, the cries of innocents... I had expected that, too.

What surprised me was the argument I sensed from the other side of the village. Two individuals were yelling, their voices shrill and grating, enough that the vibrations of their words were clear amidst the mayhem.

"What have you done?" someone shouted.

I couldn't hear them, but their words were distinct thanks to my tremor sense. However, I couldn't identify them.

"Everything is in order," a second person answered, also yelling. "The Warlord is here! Now face him, empowered by the death."

"Did Orwyn order this? I agreed to serve *her*, not *you*."

"You will serve no one if you don't slay the world serpent arcanist."

"The people here... You've made a tactical error!"

"Culling the weak to fuel our strength. Their blood is a chum that attracts the Warlord, and it's a fuel that empowers our allies. We need it."

I had heard enough. Whoever had killed these people—just to get my attention—would pay with their lives. They would pay for their wanton destruction.

I opened my eyes and clenched my hands into fists. Then I waved my hand and manipulated the ground, knocking over two nearby houses. They were on fire, but the monsters within told me they were just hiding places for villains. Sure enough, the roof collapsed on top of giant salamanders, their red-hot scales glowing bright. They screeched and exhaled flames into the sky, but the ground under their feet gave out, and they struggled to move.

**"Warlord?"**

"Don't worry about me," I said. "Rid the village of these blackhearts. Kill all the plague-ridden creatures."

**"As you command."**

Terrakona lunged forward and bit down on one. Normally, salamanders were too hot for creatures to touch, but my eldrin was immune to such paltry heat. Terrakona's fangs sank into the creature, and his venom killed the monster instantly. The arcanist, half-buried in rubble, hadn't even had time to react.

I smashed another house with a mere flick of my wrist, collapsing the building onto a plague-ridden griffin and its arcanist. The griffin burst out, laughing. It was a twisted beast—it had six legs, two of which were eagle legs with feathers and talons. The extra legs came out near the wings, however, in odd directions not useful for walking. The beast's lion head was larger than normal, bloated with excess blood, like its very face would pop if struck too hard.

When the griffin rushed for me, I evoked magma from the palm of my hand. I threw it at the creature, and the glob of white-hot molten rock striking its chest and burning into the monster. Regardless of the grievous injury, it continued its charge, giggling the entire way, as though its death were the funniest joke of all.

With its four claws, it leapt at me.

I withdrew Retribution, and in one clean slice, separated the beast's head from its body. The crackle of powerful energy electrified the air. The griffin still slammed into me, the claws weakly scraping across my body and tearing my shirt. I shoved the dead body away, coated in tainted blood but unconcerned.

But a small part of me worried for both Illia and Zelfree.

I couldn't focus on it, though. The faster I dealt with the enemy, the less likely any harm would come to my allies.

A pop of air drew my attention to the center of the village. I thought it would be Illia or Zelfree, but it wasn't. Instead, a weaselly man with long robes and a frail body stood near a building on fire. Ten kitchens' worth of grease coated his shoulder-length hair. His sunken eyes were so beady, they were almost disappearing into his cheeks.

The arcanist mark on his forehead... It was a rizzel. But the star looked odd. Crooked. Twisted. I was too far away to see for sure, but something was off.

I recognized the man. Rhys. The righthand man of the Autarch.

And everything about Rhys, since the first time I had seen him in Thronehold, had always been off.

He was the man I wanted to trap. He was the one who always managed to get some of the Second Ascension out of harm's way. He had even taken the corpse of the soul forge before we could get it for our own purposes.

Rhys had to go.

"False Warlord," Rhys called out, his voice as grimy as his appearance. "You're early. But it matters not. You've ruined the Autarch's plan—*a plan that took decades to craft*. You will be wiped from our new pantheon."

I stepped forward, well aware that Terrakona was close.

**"Shall I kill him?"** Terrakona asked telepathically.

"Continue killing the other arcanists," I whispered. "I'll handle this."

**"As you wish, Warlord. But once I'm done, I'll be by your side."**

Terrakona smashed another building, killing yet another mystical creature with his deadly fangs. What surprised me was the lack of reaction from Rhys. The twisted man just smiled, as though everything here was exactly what he wanted.

"You don't frighten me," I replied, just loud enough for him to hear.

"Common last words muttered by arrogant fools." Rhys motioned to our surroundings. "Welcome to your grave."

When I took another step, my heart beat fast, but not in a normal pattern. The irregular thumping in my chest was concerning, because it meant only one thing.

Akiva the King Basilisk Arcanist... He had created a magical aura. The *Requiem Aura* was unique to king basilisk arcanists. While their aura was active, nearby deaths improved the physical prowess of the arcanist. They ran faster, were stronger, and had unbelievable amounts of endurance.

I had seen Akiva use it to kill the Grandmaster Inquisitor in Thronehold. Akiva had been too fast, and too strong, for the ancient arcanist to handle.

And now I stood in a field of death. Bodies littered the streets, and Terrakona continued to create more corpses as Rhys and I spoke.

The more death nearby, the stronger Akiva became...

Which was why they had killed so many people. Not only to draw me here, but to empower Akiva. But he was so far away from his eldrin. Would he have the strength to face me? I supposed we would find out. A one-on-one fight with a king basilisk arcanist would be a good test of my new might.

But then a blast of wind kicked up embers and spread the smoke. I half-covered my eyes, never taking my attention off Rhys. Had Orwyn finally arrived to help with this showdown?

I caught my breath when I glanced up.

It wasn't Orwyn.

It was a twilight dragon. The mighty Hasdrubal, King Odion's faithful eldrin. The beast landed on a ramshackle building, the roof sagging under his weight. Odion rode atop his dragon's back, his white armor and sword beautiful.

Unfortunately, I couldn't say the same thing about his plague-ridden eldrin.

# Chapter 54

# Showdown In East Valley

Poor Hasdrubal.

Twilight dragons were majestic creatures of both light and darkness. In the daytime, their scales were white. At night, their scales shifted color, becoming as black as the sky.

As a plague-ridden monster, the creature's scales were confused. The majority of the dragon's scales were white, but some had shifted back to black, like a reverse-colored night sky, where the stars were black and the void between them was whiter than ivory.

Twilight dragons also had two heads. According to myth, the heads represented the sun and moon. Apparently, there was some truth in that because the plague-ridden monster had "horns" jutting from his two heads that reminded me of those celestial bodies.

One head had a horn protruding from its chin, and another on its forehead, both curved, like a crescent. It was as if someone had slammed a deformed moon through the beast's skull.

The second head had horns bursting out from all points. One horn jutted out of the eye of the creature, half-blinding it.

The horns were pointed and straight, like a sunburst had exploded deep within the creature's brain.

Hasdrubal's wings molted feathers at a shocking rate, each one laced with blood. With shambling movements, the twilight dragon slid off the rickety building and slammed to the ground.

"Here we are," one head said, laughing.

"Let's see... *how you suffer*," the other head hissed.

Odion slid off the back of his eldrin. "Ever since I met you, Warlord, my life has been a living nightmare. You are a force from the abyssal hells—the Second Ascension is correct. You never should've had this power."

Both the heads of the twilight dragon roared, and Terrakona replied in kind.

But Hasdrubal's roar had clearly been a signal.

Before either Terrakona or I could react, two of the burning buildings exploded outward. Pyroclastic dragons—their bodies warped and twisted by the arcane plague. Each was little more than a draconic skeleton carved out of basalt. Magma poured from their chests as if it were blood from a beating heart. One had second set of arms. The other had tusks like a boar, its eyes weeping molten rock like fiery tears.

They hadn't moved or even breathed, which was how I had missed them.

They had just been lying in wait, ready for the signal so they, too, could attack.

Every remaining Second Ascension member in the village emerged from their hiding places and charged. Not at me—they charged at Terrakona. They were arcanists, some with salamanders and pyroclastic dragons, things immune to flame, or twisted griffins, beasts who could fly.

"Terrakona!" I shouted.

**"These fiends are rushing toward their deaths."**

"I'll help. Let's group up and—"

**"You told me to handle the other arcanists in the village—and that's what I intend to do."**

I gritted my teeth, worried for Terrakona, but he rushed forward before I could say anything else. With all the might of a god-creature, the world serpent clashed with the dragons. Then he whipped his tail around to catch the salamanders, slamming three of them into the ground.

I couldn't keep watching him. I had my own battle to fight.

My heart continued to beat at an irregular pace, which meant Akiva's aura was still in effect. He was nearby, strengthening himself, and I had a plague-ridden twilight dragon to contend with.

Rhys held out a hand. "*Do it*. Just as we discussed."

The twilight dragon evoked an orb of darkness, his corrupted magic laced with malice. It enveloped all of East Valley in an inky void that my eyes couldn't pierce. If I had been thinking, I would've asked Evianna to help me with a bit of knightmare augmentation—I could've seen in the darkness, then —but since she hadn't, I was blind.

But not without sight.

I closed my eyes and hefted my shield, Forfend, onto my left arm. With Retribution in my other hand, I was ready for the fight.

They had planned this. They wanted to trap me and Terrakona. They had killed the villagers to get me away from Regal Heights, and now they were going to ambush me with multiple powerful arcanists, one of whom was using the deaths of the villagers to fuel his magic to new heights.

But I felt the rumble of the dragon's steps, Odion's quick footfalls as he ran toward me, and the soft steps of Akiva as he snuck up from behind.

Although they thought me blind, nothing could be further from the truth.

Akiva attacked first. He lunged at me, faster than any normal man. I pivoted on my heel to face him, raising my shield as I unleashed a wave of magma. Akiva's knife struck the surface of Forfend with enough force that he hurt my shoulder. I stumbled back a few feet.

I couldn't see him, but I knew it was him.

I knew.

And Forfend was damaged afterward—scratched across the surface—so the knife had to have been made of apoch dragon bones.

Then Akiva struck again. I managed to block, but again, my shoulder was bruised from the effort. King basilisk venom appeared out of thin air and flew toward me. Obviously, Akiva's invisibility didn't extend to things that lifted his person.

Again, I managed to block with my shield, but I wasn't as worried. Terrakona had been able to live through king basilisk venom, so there was a possibility I was immune as well—though testing it hadn't been in on my priority list.

But Akiva had only thrown the venom as a feint. He shot right, and then aimed for my sword. I thought he would cut me, but instead, he tried to rip Retribution from my hand.

Akiva grabbed the hilt and handle.

That was when Akiva yelled and leapt away, his charred flesh a distinct smell that mixed with the ashes of the village.

I couldn't enjoy my tiny victory for very long. Hasdrubal stormed toward me, his two heads weeping blood from his bizarre horns. I manipulated the ground, trapping the dragon's feet in place. But then the beast dove into the darkness, just like Evianna—the whole dragon! Right into the shadows. Hasdrubal was larger than an elephant, but he still melted into the void and then stepped out of the darkness right next to me.

With Retribution in hand, I slashed at his moon-head. I caught the beast and removed the lower part of his jaw in one quick and effortless strike.

With a shrill laugh, Hasdrubal whipped the head away from

me. But the sunburst-head dove in and bit my shoulder. His fangs sank deep, piercing part of my body, but not my bones. *It burned*.

But it had been a terrible mistake on his part.

I placed my palm on the dragon's face and evoked molten rock. The heat melted through Hasdrubal's scales and bones, right into the flesh. The melting flesh smelled like cooked meat.

When the monster reared his second head back, I jumped for his body, hoping to kill him in one blow with my sword. But my shoulder hurt, and I hesitated for a moment while I pushed through the pain.

That allowed Odion to emerge from the shadows right next to me. He manipulated the darkness and created black knives that shot up from the ground—a reverse rain where the blades went straight to the sky at a deadly speed. They cut into my chest, arms, and legs—slicing through my skin and muscle. Each one stung more than the last, but my adrenaline made the pain seem momentary, even if I was bleeding more with each new cut.

I evoked more magma and threw it around, creating pools of molten rock. I wanted to keep Odion from reaching me. That was when the obsidian sprouted from my elbows, knuckles, and shoulder. Whenever I evoked too much, it was as if my whole body underwent a transformation. My bones were coated in basalt, and obsidian stones rose from my skin like spines.

I grew my own armor.

But the shadow knives continued to shoot up from the ground. They couldn't harm the obsidian or basalt, but they stung my skin, and a few got close to my eyes.

Bleeding out was a real problem. I couldn't allow it to happen.

I activated the pendant Eventide had given me. It was an atlas turtle pendant made with true form atlas turtle magic—a barrier sprang to life around me. It blocked the darkness, stopping the knives.

Once the darkness had stopped its assault, I ended the protection of the pendant. Finally able to concentrate, I lunged toward Hasdrubal. My sword crackled with power as I drove it forward. I stabbed Hasdrubal in the chest with all my might. Retribution slid into the dragon's body as though it weren't even there.

The plague-ridden monster laughed as the orb of darkness disappeared.

The flames of the burning city came back into my view. Smoke wafted all around us, but I didn't need to breathe. I didn't inhale the clouds of ash and debris.

With a quick glance, I checked on Terrakona. His hardened scales defended him well against the half dozen mystical creatures. He was so large that his enemies were slowly dying to his attacks. Terrakona was winning.

I returned my attention to my own fight.

Hasdrubal hadn't yet died. The beast tried to evoke light, but I dragged my blade out the side of the monster's chest, slicing up the body, cutting through ribs, his heart, and even his shoulder. Blood gushed onto the ruined road as the dragon collapsed to the side.

My sword... it hungered for the magic.

It wanted it all. I had the urge to continue stabbing the beast, even though he was already dying.

"*Hasdrubal!*"

Odion dove at me and swung his sword. I stepped back, dodging the blow, but my tremor sense told me that Akiva was getting closer. The assassin snuck up behind me, and to my horror, I still couldn't see him with my eyes. He was invisible. Was it a trinket? Or an artifact? King basilisks didn't normally have the magic to hide themselves like that.

"You're a blight," Odion said through clenched teeth, tears streaming down his face. "A curse upon the land."

He sounded touched in the head, no doubt from the plague.

But now that his eldrin was dying, Odion *might* be able to be saved.

When he swung his sword, I slashed with Retribution and cut his blade clean in half.

But that cost me.

Akiva attacked in just that moment. He didn't try to take Retribution—not after what had happened last time. Instead, he stabbed me in the back with a stiletto, the thin dagger sinking deep into the soft parts of my back.

I clenched my jaw and grunted, the agony a sharp spike that shot through my spine. Even with my obsidian and basalt, it wasn't enough to defend me from the little knife.

Akiva pulled it out and stabbed again—so fast, I couldn't dodge.

And then Odion attacked me from the front.

Well, he tried.

The darkness sprang to life all around us. Tendrils of shadows lashed out and grabbed Odion's limbs. He was dragged away from the battlefield, flailing and thrashing the entire time.

"No!" he screamed. "*No*! Hasdrubal! That dastard deserves to die for what he's done!"

Evianna stood twenty feet away, her hand up, her knightmare's cape fluttering in the ember-filled wind. She had been the one to drag Odion away, chaining him with the very shadows he had once commanded.

Akiva leapt around me, faster and faster, his requiem aura still causing my heart to beat bizarrely. Hasdrubal's death gave Akiva more power, and he stabbed with his stiletto again, catching me right in the side.

He was too fast for me to keep up. And although I could sense his movement with my magic, I still couldn't see him.

What if I died the same way the Grandmaster Inquisitor had?

*No*! I refused!

I evoked magma—but way more than I thought. It poured not just from my palm, but from every pore in my body, gushing outward in an eruption of power that superheated the air around me. The lava splashed across the ground, creating heatwaves and burning through the cobblestone of the roads and melting the debris of buildings.

Akiva had to back away. He leapt, jumped to the side, and tried to rush at me from behind, all within a second or two. But I had thoroughly surrounded myself with my magma. Which meant he would have to leap over it to get to me—and he couldn't alter his trajectory much once he was in the air.

I swung Retribution, trying to time my attack just right.

The edge of my blade caught Akiva as he flew toward me. I sliced his arm and ribs, almost taking off his limb. He shouted as he half-collided into me. His dagger caught part of my neck—the man had been going for a killing blow.

But the knife just cut through part of my skin.

Akiva's invisibility vanished.

He stumbled, almost fell into the magma, and instead leapt over it just in time to hit the road. His concentration was shattered. His requiem aura faded.

My heartbeat went back to normal.

Akiva took in ragged breaths as he tried to stand.

The wound across his ribs...

Akiva wore armor made of gray king basilisk scales. It was normally fitted close to his body, but the entire side of it was ruined. His skin appeared sickly and rotted, and Akiva's hands shook as he tried to touch the injury. Dark energy crackled off my blade and flared to life around Akiva's body.

I stepped forward, thinking I would kill the man, but my legs almost gave out under me.

That was when I glanced down. I hadn't realized how cut up I was...

I had lost so much blood. Injuries covered my whole body,

and it took me a bit to understand. It was as if I had been chewed up and spit out. The entire fight had lasted but mere minutes, but the intensity—and our sheer determination to kill each other—had made it a brutal fight.

Akiva forced himself to his feet, trembling the entire time. His fingers grazed his injury, and he stared at it with an emotionless expression, despite his dire state.

The man was tall and impressive—even on the brink of death, the man seemed to push forward, fueled by some sort of desire I didn't understand. If his king basilisk had been here, he would've been frightening, but even then, I refused to lose to the likes of him.

My glowing pools of molten rock lit up the whole area.

Hasdrubal lay half melted in one, his dragon scales glittering under the flights of embers.

I tightened my grip on my sword and stumbled forward.

**"Warlord!"**

Rhys teleported next to Akiva. Then he held up a hand and evoked white flames straight at me.

Terrakona, having killed the many creatures out for his life, slammed his tail between me and Rhys. His scales blocked the white fire, negating the attack, much like my shield would have. Just as Terrakona went to flick his tail, Rhys teleported himself, and Akiva, away.

This was what I had been afraid of. I ground my teeth, hating the fact that he had managed to get away. Somehow, I would have to lure him toward my trap. But how? I had to get him!

Terrakona slithered his body over the lava, coiling around me like a protective mother. His rune-covered tongue flicked out of his mouth, close to my body.

**"Your injuries... You must rest."**

"We have to return to Regal Heights." I glanced up at him, the heat of the battle leaving my body. I felt the injuries more than ever. "But first, snuff out the flames around the village. Make sure all survivors are okay."

**"Are you certain?"**

"Are all the plague-ridden arcanists dead?" I asked.

**"I crushed every single one and burned those who weren't immune. Their ashes won't spread the plague any longer."**

"Thank you." I rubbed at my forehead, my vision blurring a bit. "Quickly. The fires. I want to make it back to the city as soon as possible."

With a snort—which blew all over me—Terrakona uncoiled himself and went for the fires in the village. His magic was strong, and I knew he could clear East Valley quickly.

Evianna emerged from the darkness, rising out of the void like only a knightmare could. She stepped close to my side and offered her shoulder. I held on to her, but I offered a smile. "I can heal quickly," I muttered.

"I know," Evianna and Layshl replied in their merged voice. "But I'm here for you. Rely on me when you need to."

My thoughts immediately went to Odion. The King of Javin was on his back, in the middle of the ruined road, shadows tethering him in place. He thrashed and fought, struggling against his restraints, his eyes on the smoke-filled sky. He practically foamed at the mouth as he strained himself with each half-kick of his legs.

Odion's plague-ridden dragon was no more, but I suspected the madness had taken him.

I didn't know what to do with him.

Leave him here?

I forced myself to concentrate. With a wave of my hand, I trapped him in the ground, having rock form over his legs and arms. He wouldn't be able to move until I returned.

"You're a monster!" Odion yelled, his voice mixing with the roar of flames all around us. "You ruin everything! *Everything*!"

Two pops of teleportation—and little clouds of glitter—and Zelfree and Illia were also by my side. They stepped close, both of them staring at me with furrowed brows.

"Are you okay?" Illia asked.

I nodded once. "I'll be fine. I just need time to heal."

"We found a few survivors. They're okay. Safe. Away from the fighting."

"Good."

Zelfree withdrew a handkerchief from his coat and pressed it against the injury on my neck. "*Think*, lad. You can't just let your healing sustain you. Some injuries are worse than others. Hold this close."

I placed my hand on the handkerchief, stemming the blood flow. "Thank you."

"Don't thank me. Just do better in the future. You're the Warlord, remember? Don't go visiting the abyssal hells before it's time to conquer the place."

I smiled at the comment. Zelfree always had a way of motivating me to do better. Even now, when he was technically the weaker arcanist.

Like a true mentor.

"Once Terrakona is done, we need to hurry back to Regal Heights," I said. "I haven't seen Orwyn. I'm afraid... I'm afraid she took the Keeper of Corpses and went into the city."

The news caused everyone to grow quiet.

The moment Terrakona finished with his work, he rushed back to my side. Then we left the village and went straight for Regal Heights.

I just hoped we wouldn't be too late.

## CHAPTER 55

# FIGHTING THE SKY TITAN
# ARCANIST

In my mind, I hadn't been injured when I finally faced off against Orwyn. When I had played the fight out in my head, I had won easily and without struggle because I had prepared myself for weeks ahead of time.

But this was different. Terrakona and I had been pulled away from the city—a plot created by our enemies. The Second Ascension had tried to use Akiva and Odion to kill me, but they hadn't been prepared for my powerful magic and improved artifact.

Unfortunately, now they knew. And I suspected Rhys had gone straight to Orwyn to report what he had seen. If they attacked now, they would do so in a careful manner.

As we approached the city, I spotted Zaxis and his fenris wolf first. The dark fur of the massive wolf fluttered with the breeze, but as I drew closer, the winds picked up. I shielded my eyes as I reached the walls of Regal Heights. The citizens had barricaded themselves inside their fortress homes, and I suspected no amount of gale force winds would disturb them.

Zaxis ran to me. Terrakona lowered his head so we could speak.

"Is everything okay?" Zaxis asked. He gave me the once-over and tensed. "What happened? Are you injured? Should I get Atty?"

Zelfree held up a hand. Now that we were closer to the city, his mimic transformed. Traces melted out of her white and silver fur and then grew brilliant red feathers, shifting forms as easily as a person changed clothes. Her wings were elegant, her beak and talons were metallic, and her eyes golden.

Zelfree's arcanist mark shifted with the change. Now his seven-pointed star was laced with a bird instead of the ferret-like rizzel.

Then Zelfree placed a hand on my shoulder and healed me of my minor injuries.

It wasn't entirely needed. I had already healed most of it, but I still appreciated the gesture. My bloodstained clothes probably made me look worse than I was.

The winds...

A howl whipped through Hydra's Gorge. It felt like a storm brewing out at sea. We weren't anywhere near the ocean, though. It had to be the power of the sky titan, but I had no idea where it was originating from.

"*Volke,*" Adelgis said, his telepathic voice panicked. "*We have several problems.*"

"What is it?" I asked.

"*Eventide says the typhon beast isn't... it isn't well.*"

"What do you mean?"

"*It's upset. Enraged. Eventide and the others made it through the lair, but the typhon beast is speaking in madness. He's not plague-ridden, that's impossible. He's just... He isn't cooperating. He won't bond with anyone.*"

I didn't know what to do about that. The typhon beast from legend had been rather destructive and insane. Was the monster *inherently* evil? Could nothing be done to fix it?

"*And Rhys is nearby. He's teleported several arcanists to the far edge of the city. Orwyn and her sky titan are near your trap—I suspect they know you were working on something there, and they think you're hiding something important, rather than creating a trap. This will work out for you, but you must hurry."*

That... wasn't what I had been expecting. They thought I was hiding something? I had been creating their prison. Amusing they would jump to terrible conclusions. But it meant I had to get to them before they discovered my ruse.

"Tell everyone in town to be prepared for a surprise attack," I said.

"*I have.*"

"Thank you, Adelgis."

"Adelgis?" Evianna asked. She glanced up at me from the back of Terrakona. "Has he given you news?"

I motioned to the distant field I had created. The nullstone trap was perfect. If Rhys was there, perhaps there was still a chance we could catch the man.

"The sky titan arcanist," I muttered. "She's there. *Let's go.*"

Illia, Zelfree, and Evianna stayed on Terrakona to travel with me, while Zaxis and his fenris wolf ran alongside me, no doubt prepared for a real battle. Zaxis even withdrew his pistol from a holster on his belt. The red-metal gun gleamed with inner power, much like my sword.

I hoped everyone still wore the rings I had given them—the knight trinkets with my symbol etched into the side. It allowed faster healing and some protections.

I didn't want to lose anyone else.

The field was a massive square of land over a pit of nullstone. It was hundreds of feet on each side, and while I could tell it was odd when looking at it from up high, I suspected most individuals walking on land couldn't discern too much of a difference from the surrounding landscape.

It didn't matter anymore, though.

I spotted Orwyn in the middle of the field. She was with her kirin, her short hair and robes fluttering about with the strong winds. There was someone else with her as well. A young man.

And a pile of bodies.

That was no doubt the Keeper of Corpses and his arcanist.

When Terrakona rushed over, the winds suddenly died down. Completely. There wasn't a breeze at all as we entered the makeshift field and approached the sky titan arcanist.

There was nothing around us. No trees. No rocks. No rivers.

Just an open field.

A false meadow.

The perfect battlefield.

Vjorn kept pace with Terrakona as we slowed and then eventually stopped fifty feet from Orwyn and her kirin.

Her majestic dragon horse glittered in the morning light. With a snort and whinny, it nuzzled its snout against Orwyn's cheek. She patted her creature and whispered something to it before turning her vacant expression toward me.

The young man behind her was sickly. He had a shriveled leg he tried to hide with long trousers, but it wasn't enough. His shrunken chest gave him a bit of a hunchback, and his face seemed out of alignment.

The star on his forehead...

Ryker's was the only other mark I had ever seen that had nine points. The Mother of Shapeshifters was a child of gods, which meant the Keeper of Corpses was likely one as well.

The piles of black and rotted bodies were likely the creature. They were just lying around, like garbage, sitting at the feet of the twisted man and his shriveled leg.

"Warlord," Orwyn called out. "Please. Give me the red jasper runestone... and leave this place. We can avoid bloodshed."

Terrakona lowered his head. I leapt off his mane and hit the ground, confident in my capabilities. I might have just been in a fight, but a second wind filled my veins with icy hate. I was ready.

"*Avoid bloodshed*?" I repeated. "Are you insane? I saw what you did in East Valley. Those corpses are on your hands."

Orwyn stopped stroking her scaled horse. She stared at me with emerald eyes, her brow furrowed. "Rhys was in charge of drawing you away. He claimed he could slay you without my involvement. I didn't know he would be killing people to lure you out of the city."

"What did you think he was going to do?" I asked, my voice terse, my anger barely restrained.

"I wrote you a letter, and you came. I thought... Rhys might do the same. You're quite trusting."

The young man with the short leg huffed. "I tried to tell Rhys that was insanity, but he insisted."

Orwyn frowned. "You didn't tell him to stop, Ezril?"

"I did. But he said we were *culling the weak*. Disgusting."

Ezril was the Keeper of Corpses arcanist.

With a glare, Zaxis pointed at him. "You're standing in a pile of bodies, *fool*. Don't tell me you find Rhys's tactics disgusting."

Ezril smirked, his misshapen face twisting a bit. Then he waved his hands at his body, stopping to show off his odd leg and small chest. "Trust me. I'm not a fan of anyone claiming to *cull the weak*. Do you know who everyone thinks should go first in that situation? The sick kids. *Like me*. So, *no*. I'm not a fan of Rhys's tactics."

Orwyn shook her head, her frown deepening.

"And my corpses are from a time long gone," Ezril continued. "Ancient warriors who will kill you all if you think to fight me and the sky titan arcanist."

"If you truly disagree with Rhys, we don't have to fight," I said.

Orwyn motioned to the canyon. "Give us the red jasper runestone, and we'll leave. But I can't go without it."

Zaxis leapt off his god-creature and hit the ground right next to me. Then he brushed himself off, clearly accustomed to wearing no shirt at this point. He motioned to the arcanist mark on his chest. "You're not just going to fight one god-arcanist. You've made an enemy of two today. Surrender. *Or else.*"

Part of me wanted to wait. Rhys wasn't here.

Then again... He always appeared whenever someone in the Second Ascension was in trouble. He would show up if Orwyn needed help. Which meant we needed to go through with this fight. We needed to beat her.

Zelfree, Illia, and Evianna also dismounted my eldrin. They stood around our god-creatures, waiting for the order to attack.

I still hadn't seen the sky titan. The lack of wind bothered me, but what was I supposed to do? If it wasn't going to show itself, we were going to have to force the issue.

I pulled Retribution from its sheath and put Forfend back on my arm.

"You heard the Hunter," I said.

Zaxis half turned to me with a smile.

"Surrender," I continued. "Or else."

Orwyn placed a delicate hand on her cheek. With a slight frown, she turned her attention to the ground. "I'm so sorry. I'll try to make this as painless as possible."

She waved a hand, and I thought she was going to evoke something. I tensed, raised my shield, and readied myself to counter. Instead, she just kept her hand out in the air, her fingers spread apart.

"*Sytheria*s, *the sky titan*—end this. Please."

And then... it was as if someone had taken away the volume of the world.

The rush of the wind, the shouts of panicked people, the breaths of my team—all was devoured by absolute quiet. I had never realized how much I *could* hear, how much sound I unconsciously ignored, until it had been stolen.

All I heard now was a ringing in my ears and the thunder of

blood roaring through my head. We were trapped in a void of silence.

And that wasn't all. I couldn't breathe. Anytime I tried to intake air, my breath stopped, as though controlled so *completely*, that it wouldn't answer the summons of my lungs. But... I forced myself to remain calm. I didn't need air. I didn't actually need to breathe. It was my passive world serpent ability. Terrakona had once likened me to a rock, and the material of the world didn't need to breathe to survive.

So neither did I.

But when I glanced around, I knew that wasn't true for everyone else.

They pointed and waved their hands, trying to get my attention. Each one was trying to indicate that they couldn't speak or take in breath. Evianna touched her neck, Illia mouthed the problem to me.

Even Zaxis pointed, his jaw clenched.

The rings I had given them all glowed with faint light. The rings might let them last a little longer, even without breath, but I wasn't certain.

Then Zaxis lifted his pistol and tried to fire. But... the fire snuffed immediately, strangled out by the air. Not even the fire could breathe, and without that, the flames of the phoenix magic—enhanced by my god-arcanist magic—couldn't function.

The sky titan had total and utter control of the wind and air all around us.

And I had no idea where it was. I glanced around, looking toward the sky, but I saw nothing. Just the clear blue weather around Regal Heights. This was the nightmare I had feared— what was the sky titan's weakness?

But did that mean that the sky titan was going to kill the Keeper of Corpses and its arcanist as well?

I glanced over at the misshapen man.

The corpses around his feet rose up and formed the shape of a four-legged monster. The bodies of dozens of men wrapped together, the bones linking to form the body and spine. Rib cages of warriors made up the monster's chest, and bits of flesh strung it all together.

But then, just like with MOS, the corpse-beast merged with Ezril. Unlike Ryker, Ezril's merge was over almost before I realized it had happened. They merged nearly as fast as Luthair and I had been able to.

The corpses wrapped around Ezril, encasing him in rot and undead body parts. The bones laced together and formed a golem of meat, rotted muscle, and white bone. Ezril had been five and a half feet before—but now he was eleven feet of undead power.

His "skull" was made up of three corpses, their arms and legs put together in such a way as to create "eyes" and a makeshift mouth. The tongue was just arms held together with sinew.

Perhaps the sky titan could select who was affected by this suffocation, but I doubted it. More likely, the Keeper of Corpses and his arcanist didn't need air, a trait common among undead.

Orwyn must have planned this entire strategy out beforehand. She had brought only one ally with her—someone who didn't need to breathe.

Did she know *I* didn't need to breathe?

Probably not.

Which meant I had an advantage she hadn't accounted for.

I just had to take advantage of it.

# CHAPTER 56

## THE TYPHON BEAST

It had been less than six seconds since Orwyn had started the fight, and we were already on the back foot. We had to recover the momentum and fast.

We were on a time limit.

Zaxis didn't need any instruction. He couldn't breathe, but he wasn't going to let that stop him.

With an amazing amount of energy for someone who couldn't take in breath, Zaxis leapt forward and blasted out an epic amount of ice. Frost crystals lanced up from the ground, forming a long line of ice. It went straight for Orwyn, but she jumped into the sky.

She created a tornado of wind around her. The gust took her —and her kirin—straight up, allowing her to avoid the blast of ice. She "rode" her kirin like it was a pegasus without wings.

Undeterred, Zaxis blasted more ice at the Keeper of Corpses. The crystals raced along the ground and slammed into the corpse-golem. The eleven-foot-tall beast stumbled and then clawed at the frost. It held him in place.

Vjorn lunged forward to help his arcanist, but that was when the wind around him picked up to hurricane levels. Vjorn was thrown backward, despite his massive size. When he slammed to the ground, frost and ice chilled the earth around him.

Twisters of wind formed around us, threatening to pull everyone in and hold them there. Even I lost a bit of footing before I manipulated the ground to grab my feet and anchor me in place.

Terrakona rushed toward the twisters. When he collided with the winds, his adamant scales shattered the magic of the tornados, ending them all at once. But then more whirlwinds appeared, all at the edge of the battlefield, then moving toward us. Terrakona whirled, shifting his strategy to defense. With incredible dexterity, Terrakona contorted and wove his body across the battlefield, using his tail and head to intercept the whirlwinds.

The sky titan was near, I just couldn't see it. That monster's primary goal in this fight was clearly to deal with the giant eldrin on the battlefield, all while slowly suffocating everyone else.

When Vjorn got back to his feet, his frost coated the surrounding area, making the winds fly slower. But still—he was on the defensive as well.

Ignoring the chaos around me, I advanced, holding Retribution and evoking magma in my free hand. I worried the strange suffocation effect would suppress my magic as well. It had snuffed out Zaxis's pistol—could it end my magma? But my molten rock oozed from my palms, dripping to the fake field at my feet. The heat was there—but the flames were snuffed out a second after they sprouted across the grass.

But that meant my molten rock wasn't affected by the air-control.

I could still use this.

Unfortunately, when both Zelfree and Illia tried their evocation, it stuttered out. Phoenix fire was *normal* flame, and the rizzel's white flame was also a type of fire. The sky titan's magic altered the air so that their magic ended seconds after they tried to use it.

Evianna, on the other hand, suffered no such restriction. She evoked terrors. She dove into the darkness, emerged near the Keeper of Corpses, and unleashed literal nightmares all around them. The flesh-golem stumbled, grabbing at its massive head.

I ran to join her. Retribution's hunger was a roar echoing in my mind. The shade of the long dead apoch dragon thirsted for magic, and that terrible energy crackled up and down the blade, yearning to feast.

Lunging forward, I slashed at one of the undead-golem's legs. I removed the leg in a single strike. The corpse bits rearranged themselves—faster than I had expected—helping the golem to maintain balance as it stumbled forward.

Zaxis evoked more ice, and finally, the creature slipped and crashed to the ground. I couldn't hear the impact—something about the air prevented all that.

Ice crystals slammed into the monster's head, freezing everything in place.

Then the corpses rearranged themselves. Several arms reached out of the body and clawed at the ice, freeing a large portion of the creature so it could stand.

Then the Keeper of Corpses evoked rot. Deadly, black vapors poured from the undead creature, spreading out all around him.

The grass died. Parts of my skin flaked off, and my eyes burned. I leapt away from the monster, and so did everyone else. The rot spread onto my body, like a horrendous rash that was changing my skin color.

From the sky, Orwyn waved her hand. Then her kirin's twisted horn lit up with power—clearly giving Orwyn more strength.

A blast of pure wind shot toward us. It struck Zelfree, the wind so forceful, it "cut" into his chest, creating a large wound. Zelfree staggered backward. He healed himself with his phoenix magic and my knight trinket ring, but Orwyn did it again, cutting him open with pure wind.

Zelfree tried to run off and heal, but there was nowhere to hide. Vjorn and Terrakona were fighting all around us, slamming into the whirlwinds, while Orwyn watched everything from the sky, circling at a leisurely speed. We had no rocks or trees for cover, and even if we had, the Keeper of Corpses was rotting everything away with his deadly evocation.

Orwyn shot wind at Zelfree, cutting him over and over, but he didn't have the means to attack back.

Traces couldn't fly.

The wind worked against her, never allowing her wings to work properly. She flapped her phoenix wings, half taking off and then tumbling to the ground. The fire at the center of her body flickered out. Her soot stopped.

Transforming would cost her strength and breath—something she didn't have. And Zelfree's options were limited. Traces couldn't mimic the god-creatures, so all that was left was Evianna's young knightmare or Illia's limited rizzel.

And then Traces collapsed. Once she did, she transformed back into a mimic—becoming a small feline with gray fur.

That was when Zelfree lost his healing. He hit the ground on his knees, unable to stop the assault. Although I couldn't say anything, Terrakona knew what to do. He rushed over and guarded both Traces and Zelfree, protecting them from Orwyn's blasts.

Her magic did nothing to Terrakona.

But Terrakona couldn't seem to reach her, either. When he evoked vegetation, two trees appeared on his back. Vines lashed out, trying to grab her, but Orwyn was nimble.

She was *the Falcon*. She dodged each attempt and just flew higher, far out of our range.

Illia attempted to manipulate gravity—she lifted herself off the ground, slowly but surely. But that was when the winds took her. She flew across the battlefield and slammed into the ground. With gritted teeth, she jumped up and teleported back to my side, but it was obvious the suffocation was getting to her. Without Illia's evocation or manipulation, Orwyn had the advantage.

And I was certain Illia wouldn't risk teleporting. It would only take a few seconds of falling before she hit the ground—teleporting into the sky wasn't an option.

I ran forward once the rot had dissipated and cut off another leg from the Keeper of Corpses. That maniac barely noticed. He just rearranged his body and reattached the leg—the corpses stitching themselves together—or he simply created another. He was an undead amalgamation that seemed designed to just keep us busy until we ran out of breath.

I tried to use my magma evocation on him, but blasts of wind knocked aside all those attacks and kept the worst of my heat away from Ezril.

Whenever the Keeper of Corpses evoked rot, I had to jump away and allow my skin to heal before I got in close again.

I could open the ground and trap him with my nullstone, but... Would it work on him? And even if it did, I wouldn't catch Rhys, then.

Evianna struggled to fight. The rot harmed Layshl, and Evianna shook from so long without breathing. I motioned her away, telling her to abandon the fight, and instead of arguing with me, she dove into the darkness and left.

Thank the good stars.

Nicholin held up his paws and tried to reverse the gravity—perhaps to pull Orwyn down—but she was too far away, and his manipulation was too weak. His little arms shook, and he couldn't yank her from her kirin perch.

And Illia was the next to collapse.

Both she and Nicholin had been holding their breath, but they were at their limit. They looked like they were about to teleport away—to save themselves—but they just couldn't muster the strength. They both hit the ground, Illia's face purple and her knight trinket ring slowly dimming as the last of its power faded.

If Zaxis could have yelled, he would have. Instead, his shout just left him more breathless than before. He silently roared and then evoked a blizzard's worth of ice. It reminded me of my time in the ocean, when I had evoked so much molten rock, I had caused the water to boil.

This was just in reverse.

Ice coated the ground. Crystals jutted into the sky. Snowflakes came into existence around us, spreading out, lowering the temperature. Even the light seemed to dim. The cold became so much, I had to evoke my magma just to keep warm.

And then it got colder.

And colder.

The Keeper of Corpses struggled to move. The bodies that made up its monster form were becoming frozen solid. With each step, it moved slower.

Then it was done. It became frozen to the ground, unable to move.

Orwyn attempted to blast wind at Zaxis.

But Vjorn leapt in the way, taking the strike. When Orwyn evoked more wind, Vjorn protected his arcanist, shielding Zaxis no matter what and adding his own power to the winter storm Zaxis was summoning.

That was when I saw it.

The sky titan.

Through the blizzard, through the cold, there was an outline of something in the sky right above us. It was a four-winged creature the size of an inn, in the slight shape of a bird. And it was freezing over.

My eyes widened as I realized something crucial. The sky titan couldn't be harmed by physical means—*but the sheer cold of the winter winds was freezing it, making it solid*. And the body of the beast was literally appearing before our eyes. Zaxis's magic was so cold, the sky titan couldn't handle it.

Although I couldn't speak to Zaxis, I motioned to our surroundings. Then I pointed at the outline of the sky titan— how the frost was covering the beast and giving it form. Zaxis's eyes widened.

He knew.

I knew.

We had a plan.

Zaxis evoked more and more ice. He was getting so good at it, that my entire false field was covered in snow and crystals. We stood in a frozen landscape, the dead of winter. The fenris wolf was right—it was a killer. Snow piled into hills, and a flurry of snowflakes fell to the ground, smothering the grass.

Terrakona wrapped up both Zelfree and Illia and their eldrin and then rushed to get them away from everything. I didn't know how much territory Orwyn's air-manipulation covered, but I suspected it wasn't too far. Terrakona could save them.

I hoped.

The more ice was evoked, the more frozen the sky titan became. That was when I manipulated the stone—careful not to break my trap—and lifted myself into the air with a pillar of rock. I went so fast, and so sudden, Orwyn and her god-creature didn't have enough time to process the change.

I evoked molten rock from every crease in my body, creating an eruption of heat that splattered across the frozen sky titan.

And in that moment, something happened. I felt it deep within as my magic fundamentally shifted. I grazed something perfect as my evocation's power, so long divided, became whole. I felt the power of my vegetation evocation crisping and burning, being devoured by the destructive magic. At the same time, the lost magic had become fuel to make my destruction burn brighter.

My creation evocation was lost forever, but the power of my destructive evocation now seemed endless.

My blazing molten rock melted straight through the sky titan.

The impossible cold had been enough to make the god-creature just barely tangible. And now my evocation split the newly corporeal bird apart, searing through its four-winged body. Magma ate away at its form, melting into the creature and becoming part of the vortex that made up its body.

My magma hovered in the air because the beast was invisible, but I watched the lava eat away at the titan's insides.

I tumbled back to the ground, falling like a rock. I hit the ground with the force to break bones, but I felt nothing. No breaks, no snaps. I leapt to my feet and whirled around.

Zaxis's face had become just as purple as Illia's.

He couldn't go much longer.

But he had given me his all.

When we met each other's gazes, Zaxis gave me a thumbs up... and then also collapsed. Vjorn fell to the ground next to his arcanist, unwilling to leave.

The sky titan tried to fly off, but both the magma and the frigid cold had mixed together to create a hurricane effect. The "air" inside the creature's body had become a storm.

While the beast struggled to control itself, I lifted up another rock pillar and leapt at it.

I swung Retribution, cutting into the sky titan with my black blade. The magic-eating properties of my weapon drained the massive, invisible god-creature. I felt the magic siphon away from the sky titan, quickly and violently.

Then Orwyn slammed me with wind. I hit the ground, parts of my skin sliced open from the air strike. But my bones weren't broken. Instead of obsidian and basalt... my body felt like metal. Like steel made into something living. An increased effect of the destructive magma.

The sky titan hit the ground with the force of a hurricane.

Then the air returned to normal. I took in a deep breath. And my hearing returned at the same time.

Orwyn fell from the sky. She gasped as she plummeted, but otherwise made no sound. She hit my makeshift field, along with her kirin... The multiple cracks of bone sent a shiver down my spine. No one should fall from that height. If she was still alive, it would be a miracle.

Then again, god-arcanists had improved healing. Perhaps she was broken now, but in a few hours, when her bones mended, she would be fine.

Why had she fallen? Had she lost her concentration after seeing her eldrin wounded? That was my only explanation. Or... perhaps I had killed the sky titan. Either way... she wasn't about to do anything anytime soon.

I ran over to Zaxis first, just to make sure he was okay. He was on the ground, his mouth hanging open, his color slowly returning. When I shook him, his eyes fluttered open, but he was obviously confused.

"Did you get her?" he asked between deep gulps of breath.

I smirked. "Yup. We did it. The fight is over."

"*Teamwork*," Zaxis wheezed. Then he gave me another thumbs up from the ground.

I patted his shoulder, making sure he was okay and in one piece. That was when Zaxis slowly withdrew his pistol from the holster on his belt and fired it—from the hip—into the wall of my pit trap.

The resulting *bang* and echo were the only sound for a few miles.

"What was that?" I asked.

"Heh." Zaxis closed his eyes as he smirked. "At least... I got to fire it once. That's all I wanted."

I chuckled and shook my head. Zaxis was too much sometimes. He was too exhausted to even stand, but he still wanted to shoot his damn pistol.

The Keeper of Corpses lay frozen on the ground, a mountain of rotted bodies. It would take a while for him to thaw, most likely.

That was when I heard a pop of air and tensed. Without even glancing around, I immediately stood. I held Retribution close as I caught sight of Rhys and Akiva. They had teleported to the field, no doubt to take Orwyn to safety.

Rhys seemed healthy—uninjured. But Akiva wasn't as lucky. The sword wound I had given him was still there. The side of his ribs looked as though they had become infected, his skin black and green around the injury. Akiva took ragged breaths, sweat dappling his skin.

And Orwyn's sky titan...

I couldn't see it anymore, but I felt its air body around us. The creature was basically incorporeal, which meant we could be inside it without really noticing. And it was around us—we were all walking inside its torso, basically.

Rhys and Akiva were close to Orwyn. Too close. If I didn't act now, I might lose them. I held up a hand and manipulated the field. I shattered the thin layer of rock that kept us above the nullstone.

Everything broke apart, like a dramatic earthquake. The stone splintered and crumbled, causing me, Vjorn, Zaxis, Rhys, Akiva, the Keeper of Corpses, Orwyn, her kirin, and the body of the sky titan to fall into the pit.

It was a short fall—thankfully. Just fifteen feet. It still hurt my legs, especially my knees. I collapsed on the bluish-black nullstones, hating their anti-magic effect. But it didn't shut down my magic, which was all I cared about.

Zaxis hit the nullstone face-first, which hadn't been intentional. His nose exploded with blood, and then he rolled to his side, groaning. Vjorn hit next to him, but he managed to just slump into a comfortable position.

I didn't see what had happened to the others. My attention went immediately to Rhys. He stumbled around, trying to get to his feet, his greasy hair flung over his face, as if it were a dirty mop wig.

It was only then that I glanced over to Orwyn.

She was slowly getting to her feet! How? I had seen her fall! She had hit the ground so hard. But there she was, slowly getting up, along with her kirin. The brilliant dragon horse whinnied and cried as it helped her.

Did the kirin... Did it strengthen the healing effect of the god-creatures? Was that how Orwyn was healing so quickly?

Panic overtook me. If Orwyn used her abilities to fly Rhys out of this pit, I would lose him *again*. I couldn't have that. I had to stop her—right here, right now.

I evoked my magma, but where once I had to create small globs to throw, now it emerged like a stream or a splatter—a spray of molten rock that flew a great distance, deadly and burning.

My aim was perfect. It would have struck her head and ended this, but I hadn't expected Akiva to leap in the way of my attack.

Despite the injury to his ribs from our previous fight, and the fact that he had just fallen into this pit trap, Akiva had forced himself to his feet and leapt in the way in the molten rock, taking the hit on his arm, upper leg, and part of his side. He blocked any of the evocation from reaching Orwyn.

Then he cried out, collapsing to the ground, his body shaking.

Orwyn's emerald eyes went wide. She couldn't stop looking at him, her hands trembling. Her expression haunted me. I had never seen her emote so much. Her horror seemed genuine and thorough—and before I could evoke more magma, she waved her hands, and wind erupted throughout the nullstone pit.

Just like I had feared, she flew out of the pit, taking people with her.

To my surprise—she only took the Keeper of Corpses, Akiva, and her kirin. They shot out of the pit and flew off into the sky. But not Rhys. She had left him... like she just didn't care.

Rhys stumbled into a sitting position. He stared at the sky, clearly in disbelief.

"Come back here," Rhys shrieked. "*You can't leave me here! The Autarch will hear of this! How dare you!*" But then he ran out of breath. He gasped and took in ragged breaths. "The Autarch... The Autarch won't stand for this!"

Currently, he wasn't worth my time. I had other priorities.

"Terrakona?" I called out, wanting to see my eldrin. "Terrakona?"

But he didn't answer. My heart beat harder against my ribs as I manipulated the rocks and created a small staircase out of the pit. Then I lifted Zaxis and Vjorn out of the trap. I set them on the outside, walked up the stairs, and took a deep breath.

Once on the edge of the pit, I removed the stairs, preventing Rhys from escaping.

As I exited the nullstone pit, Adelgis's telepathy reached me.

"*Volke, please come quick.*"

"What's wrong?" I asked.

"*It's the typhon beast. It... it stormed out of its lair. The gigantic hydra walked up the stairs you created and it's heading into the city. Terrakona is on his way, but I don't know who else can handle this. Please—the beast is out of control and rampaging.*"

I whipped my attention over to Regal Heights. The city sat across the gorge, off in the distance. Sure enough, a massive creature was heading toward the fancy side, smashing rocks as it charged forward.

A hundred-headed monster.

The typhon beast.

# CHAPTER 57

## THE TYPHON BEAST ARCANIST

T stared at the typhon beast in the distance, wondering how fast I could get to Regal Heights without Terrakona. My eldrin had taken Zelfree and Illia away during the fighting. He probably still had them—he was almost to the gates.

That was when Evianna lifted out of the shadows. She still wore her knightmare, merged together, which meant they lived and died as a single being. When Evianna turned to me, she held out her hand.

"Let's go together," Evianna and Layshl said in their merged voice. "We need to stop that monster."

I took her hand. "Thank you."

Evianna pulled me into her arms. She held me close, resting her cheek on my chest, only for a moment. Then we dove into the darkness together, the cold comfort of the shadows a welcome reprieve. We traveled for some distance—a couple hundred feet—before Evianna had to emerge again. I was impressed. She had really improved the distance she could shadow-step.

Then we dove again. And again. Like a whale traveling across the ocean, emerging above the waves for breath.

When we finally reached the gates of the city, we met up with Terrakona. He glared out across the gorge, watching the typhon beast approach the first of the houses.

**"Warlord,"** Terrakona said telepathically. **"The typhon beast is unstable. Shall we destroy it?"**

"No," I immediately replied.

**"But it has come to kill. Can't you smell its hunger? Its hate?"**

"I need to speak with it first."

I pushed my way through the gate guards and then past the citizens of Regal Heights. Hundreds of people were outside their homes with bags over their shoulders and small crates in their arms. They were prepared to abandon the city only if the typhon beast actually made it over to where they were.

I ran down the long road built next to the edge of the gorge and then across one of the metal bridges. Evianna stayed with me, effortlessly keeping pace. I didn't want to travel through the darkness because I wanted to keep my eyes on the city itself.

That was when the typhon beast reached a distant building. The massive creature crashed into the stone, shattering a wall of the fortress. The rocks clattered down the edge of the gorge, their thunderous destruction loud enough for everyone to hear.

When I drew close, I finally got a good look at the typhon beast.

The god-creature was definitely the monster of legend. It had one hundred heads, but ninety-nine of them were small and snake-like, similar to the heads of a medusa's hair. They were a mane of snakes around a singular dragon head. The necks of the creature—even the dragon head—were considerable. It was a ball of writhing flesh. The snakes wrapped around each other, some reaching out and snapping at nearby objects.

When birds shot into the air, trying to flee, the snake heads independently struck out and gobbled a few dozen down.

The typhon beast had runes glowing on the foreheads of the

ninety-nine snake heads. They flicked and sparked with magic, each one different. The snakes chittered and spoke at maddening rates, so quick and whispered, I couldn't distinguish between them.

The typhon beast's scales were dark green and black, and it walked on six impressive legs, like the king basilisks. The beast's tail was longer than the rest of the body and ended in spines, each point deadly sharp.

The fenris wolf wasn't as large as Terrakona, but the typhon beast... It was damn near as large, just *muscled and wide* instead of *long*. The beast lumbered with significant weight behind it, crushing small stones under its feet.

The typhon beast screamed. First the main head, then the many snake heads. It was a song of suffering. Then the monster smashed a second fortress building, its front claws ripping at the bricks and tossing them to the side.

That was when Hexa and her family—along with their hydras— rushed up the road. They beat me to the scene, but that was fine. As long as someone slowed the typhon beast and stopped it from harming Regal Heights.

Hexa swung one of the bone swords. Heat and flames scorched the air. The typhon beast screamed and snapped its many heads at her. She fought three heads while two snake heads bit at her arms and legs.

Raisen lunged forward and crunched a typhon beast head, but then he was swarmed by the mane of snakes. They bit him repeatedly. Thankfully, he was immune to venom. Unfortunately, he wasn't immune to bleeding out. After a dozen bites, blood poured from him at a fearsome rate.

Hexa's cousins dove into the fray. They also swung the swords I had crafted. When they connected, they lopped off a snake head without much problem. But then the snake heads grew back in a matter of seconds—bursting out of the old flesh and knitting bone and muscle.

The fighting was so fierce that the typhon beast stopped its assault on the buildings. It swiped its tail, knocked two of the hydras away—one almost tumbled into the gorge—and then snapped at Hexa. The beast wasn't disturbed by the fight. It barely seemed to notice that its heads were being cut.

Hexa evoked deadly gas.

That also didn't work.

The typhon beast breathed it in without fear. The gas never slowed it, not even for a moment.

As I dashed up a stone stairway, getting closer to the conflict, the ninety-nine snake heads starting chittering. They snapped their fangs in time with each other, louder and louder, their frantic mutterings disturbing.

The chittering pierced my ears and went straight to my thoughts. My vision blurred, and halfway up a flight of stone steps, I lost my balance and collapsed. Evianna grabbed me and helped me to my feet. She wobbled a bit as well, but less than I did, and I suspected it was because her knightmare was merged with her, giving her strength.

We were close to the beast and the hydras. Just a few more steps, and I might be able to speak with it.

Hexa and her cousins managed to back the monster away from the ruined building, but then the beast slammed itself forward, landing on the hydras and their arcanists, half-crushing them. Then it thrashed with its claws, raking the hydras and their arcanists, shredding flesh from their bodies.

And then I was finally close enough! I reached out to manipulate the stone. I created sand under the back legs of the beast, and when it sank down, I trapped it in rock. Hexa managed to free herself. She slashed with her sword, cutting through half the beast's leg, freeing her cousins in the process.

Their hydras scrambled away, each one heavy and large. They didn't move quickly, but it was fast enough to avoid the grasping claws of the enraged typhon beast.

Then the stones around the gorge started to rearrange themselves.

It wasn't my doing...

Brom, Vinder, and Eventide rushed up behind the beast, obviously having sprinted from the stairway into the gorge. They were panting and taking in deep breaths. Impressive for two men, and one woman, with such old appearances.

That was when the typhon beast screamed again.

Fire erupted out of each of its mouths, a river of flame flooding a portion of Regal Heights. The heat didn't bother me, but Evianna had to dive into the shadows to avoid the fiery torrent.

My clothes mostly burned, but then I hefted my shield. Forfend absorbed the magic of the fire and stored it deep within.

Once the typhon beast stopped breathing fire, I ran up to the roof of my fortress home. It brought me closer to eye height with the creature's main head.

I rushed over to the railing.

"Wait!" I shouted. "Stop! Mighty typhon beast—we're not your enemy!"

My yelling caught everyone's attention. Brom and Vinder stood in a defensive position around Eventide. Even Evianna remained quiet and behind me, obviously waiting to see what would happen.

The typhon beast...

Its eyes were reptilian—something I had come to admire— but its pupils were angry slits. Its dragon head snarled, and the chittering of the many snakes lessened.

**"Here you are, Warlord,"** the typhon beast stated, its dragon head speaking with a dark and low voice. **"Face me. You will die this day."**

My whole body tensed, my heart fluttering with panic. I didn't want to kill this god-creature. Why did we have to fight?

"But why?" was all I could ask.

**"Look at what you've done!"** the beast yelled.

I glanced around, honestly confused. Everyone in the gorge town was just as baffled as I was. Why was the typhon beast here? Why had it left its lair without an arcanist?

After a shake of my head, I said, "I don't understand. What's wrong? I want to help you."

**"Help me? *Help me*?"** The typhon beast swished its head from side to side. **"No. You threw me into that pit. My *blood* stains the rocks of this canyon."** It motioned to the red rocks in the gorge. **"Look! Look at my suffering. You hated me. You tried to kill me. I am... I am... a monster."**

The last part was laced with confusion, like even the typhon beast didn't know what it was talking about. Then the beast breathed flame once again, washing my fortress residence with fire so hot, I thought its might melt the windows. Again, it didn't bother me, but instead of defending, I just stood there.

My shirt turned to ash, and my trousers were mostly charred... I knew now why Zaxis had insisted on crafting fireproof armor.

"Stop!" I called out. "I didn't try to kill you!"

**"Liar! Liar! I remember... It... It's all I could think about!"**

All it could think about?

But then it struck me. Sometimes, both Vjorn and Terrakona had memories that seemed to belong to the first god-creatures. Terrakona remembered things that only the first world serpent knew. He said they were like memories drifting to him from an ancient time.

But...

The first typhon beast had been stuck in a canyon for years. *Years*. So, if *this* typhon beast had any memories from the first beast, they were probably all terrible and filled with suffering.

**"You tried to kill me,"** the beast said. **"You tried to kill me!"**

"That wasn't me!" I shouted back. "My name is Volke Savan! I'm not Luvi. Please, listen. You're just confused!"

**"You..."**

The ninety-nine snake heads hissed and screeched, and then they all started speaking at once. Some of them whispered, some of them shouted. They all tried to voice an opinion, and it was enough to give me a headache.

"I'm the *second* world serpent arcanist," I called up to the beast. "Please, calm down. Tell me your name."

Everyone in Regal Heights watched the exchange with bated breath. The crowds barely moved. Even the children watched in awe as I tried to calm the massive monster.

The typhon beast hissed, but the noise faded away. Then it snorted. **"I am the second typhon beast. My name... My name is Xor. You are... a Child of Balastar. Not a Child of Luvi."** Xor's main head seemed to grasp what was happening. **"Not Luvi..."**

This god-creature was tortured. He couldn't seem to think straight, but he seemed to be pulling out of it.

How terrible a life Xor must have had. All his old memories were painful and sad—and probably filled with loneliness. Everyone had hated the first typhon beast. Xor carried that with him? He hated me because of it?

"Everything will be okay," I said, holding my hands up. "Please. Listen. You're just bothered by your memories. They're not even really yours. They're memories from the first typhon beast."

**"Memories..."**

"Yes. Please believe me. I want to help."

**"The memories..."** Xor closed his dragon eyes. The snakes did the same. For a short second, I thought the creature might try to sleep. Then Xor opened his eyes. **"Yes. You are correct, Child of Balastar. These memories haunt me. They're not mine. They just linger... like ghosts. Whispering."**

I smiled.

This was working! I was getting through to him!

"We'll find you an arcanist," I said. "You just need to relax."

But that seemed to agitate the beast again.

His snakes hissed, and his dragon head flashed its deadly fangs. **"No. My arcanist lives! I feel his presence. *The Monster*. I must find him!"**

What? This creature clearly wasn't bonded with anyone. He looked like a baby, even if he was gigantic. His young dragon face and the small snakes of his mane, all told me that this wasn't a mature typhon beast.

"W-Wait! The Monster is dead! Just like Luvi. He's not—"

The typhon beast yanked his back feet out of the stone holding him. He stomped around, cracking the roads and shaking my fortress home. He was so strong—and sturdy—that I feared he might cause an earthquake.

Windows cracked and exploded on both sides of the gorge.

Xor roared, his frustration apparent.

I was about to pull out my blade and fight the beast in order to calm him, but that was when he suddenly went quiet. All his heads stopped talking. The typhon beast held his breath, his many eyes drifting down to the road.

I glanced over the railing, wondering what had caught Xor's attention.

Calisto.

The man had leapt out of a broken window, no doubt about to escape. But now he just stood on the road, thirty feet from the beast. With wide eyes, Calisto stared at the monstrous god-creature. The typhon beast met his gaze, still not speaking or making any noise.

Then Xor hissed. **"There you are. The Monster."**

Calisto tensed, and I felt his heart racing through the many vibrations in the ground. Everyone waited, stunned, watching with rapt attention.

**"Haunted by dark thoughts... Haunted by terrible memories... You are my arcanist."** Xor stomped forward until there was barely any distance between them.

Haunted by dark thoughts?

The typhon beast reached out with a clawed hand. Calisto turned, as if he would run, but the monster grabbed him and lifted him from the road. Calisto struggled, but Xor didn't care.

**"Tormented by the past,"** the typhon beast said with a dark murmur. **"Just like me. Your soul is what I want. I've... I've come here to find you, as the oldest source of light as my witness."**

I caught my breath.

*Calisto?* The typhon beast arcanist? That couldn't be possible.

"*Let me go,*" Calisto growled.

Xor held him closer, practically crushing the man in his clawed grip. **"You want redemption? I must... make up for my past... for the terrible memories. You must help me. Only you understand. Child of... Child of..."**

It seemed as though the beast was still confused. He was struggling to maintain his coherent speech.

## CHAPTER 58

### A DESPERATE PLEA

No one said anything.

Not Eventide, not Brom or Vinder... The citizens of Regal Heights watched from a safe distance, some on balconies, some on the opposite edge of the gorge. No one had seen anything quite like this—not even me.

Every other god-creature had waited until someone came into its lair to bond. But the typhon beast had been so tormented, and so disturbed, that he had rushed out of his lair and gone straight to the person he wanted to bond with.

Was Xor in that much pain? Did he think bonding would relieve some of that?

**"With the oldest source of light as our witness, I intend to intertwine our destinies."**

The world shuddered with magic as Xor offered to bond.

This couldn't be happening. This had been one of my greatest fears from the moment I had learned god-creatures had come into the world—that someone like *Calisto* would somehow manage to bond with one.

But...

Nothing happened.

There was no flash of light, no black sky.

Calisto closed his eyes... denying the bond. If he didn't accept, nothing would come of this. The god-creatures couldn't force themselves on anyone. No matter how much Xor wanted Calisto as an arcanist, it had to be mutual.

The typhon beast roared, and another shudder of powerful magic rocked the nearby area. Would Calisto reject the creature again? After everything we had discussed?

*"Just do it,"* I yelled, both furious that this would happen, and even more furious that Calisto would try to refuse. "If you're not going to die, you might as well live for something! *Help us!"*

Calisto snapped his eyes open.

Then...

A wave of magic blasted throughout the gorge. Rocks tumbled into the canyon, the mist cleared for a moment, and the air howled in all directions. I closed my eyes and held on to the railing of the building.

The sun disappeared, transforming the blue sky into a dark one.

No matter how many times I saw this, it never became mundane. Somehow, the epic nature of the god-creatures affected the very world itself. They spawned magical creatures— like Terrakona's dryads—stole the sun and had control over the elements. No wonder the Autarch had done everything he could to bring them back.

A pillar of red light shot into the air. The beam of illumination brightened the area, blanketing us in crimson.

But a few seconds later, the light vanished. The sun melted back into the sky, dispelling the darkness.

Xor set Calisto back on the ground. The dread pirate stumbled and then pulled on the robe-like clothes of Regal Heights. He easily moved them off his chest, exposing his new god-arcanist mark—a twelve-pointed star spiraling outward, over his ribs, arm, and shoulder. The typhon beast was laced throughout the mark, all one hundred heads.

**"A lifetime I have waited,"** Xor said with a roar. **"Soon, I will have my redemption. Soon, I will erase these haunting memories! We will change the world until it sees!"**

Unlike Vjorn and Terrakona, who had been obsessed with leadership and greater things, Xor seemed more focused on himself. He didn't speak in grandiose terms, just about his own personal state of life. Was that intentional? Or was it because the first typhon beast arcanist had been such a lunatic?

I didn't know.

And now that the beast had bonded, Vinder immediately started using his true form gargoyle magic to fix the shattered buildings. The stones rearranged themselves, fixing into place to undo all of the beast's destruction.

And while I could've helped, exhaustion stole all my willpower. I rubbed at my forehead, taking in slow breaths.

**"Warlord... We have another god-arcanist on our side."**

I smiled to myself. "That's right."

**"The Second Ascension will grow desperate."**

The Second Ascension... I had left Rhys in the pit. I would have to collect him and bring him back to city hall in Regal Heights. The man had a thousand questions to answer. Whether he wanted to or not.

---

With my remaining strength, I went back to my pit trap, encased Rhys in nullstone, and then dragged him back to Regal Heights. He would be subdued, and then Eventide and Adelgis would handle his interrogation.

As much as I would've appreciated torturing him for information, that wasn't necessary. Adelgis would discover all his secrets.

While I traveled to the city, the man shrieked and flailed, his threats always involving the Autarch himself.

*The Autarch would make us suffer for this.*

*The Autarch would kill us for this.*

*The Autarch would explode the city, slay our favorite pets, and light all our left shoes on fire.*

It was tiring—and also predictable. After the tenth hypothetical scenario where the Autarch would punish us for whatever we had done, I started to ignore it all. By the time I brought Rhys to the city, he was hoarse from yelling and barely able to move.

Eventide, Brom, and Vinder took him, and I left everything in their hands.

But then I went back to get Odion, and that drained me more than Rhys. The King of Javin wasn't himself. He barely moved, he barely spoke... and when I locked him away, his gaze was clouded with lunacy.

I tried not to think about it.

Then I went to my home, climbed the stairs to my bedroom, and threw myself on the bed. I didn't even bother with new clothes. I smeared blood, dirt, and ash all over the sheets as I curled up and immediately went to sleep.

I had no dreams. My rest happened in an instant.

One moment, I closed my eyes. A minute later, I opened them, and the sun had already gone down.

I had slept for over eleven hours. All in one sitting. And I still felt tired. With a hard swallow—my mouth dry—I rolled to my side and closed my eyes again.

Another two hours, and I woke again.

The moon shone through my cracked windows. Hydra's Gorge was just as beautiful as I had remembered. I sat up, ready to deal with any situation, my energy recovered.

After a long stretch, with which I groaned and held my arms to the air, I finally got to my feet. The fights replayed in my mind as I gathered new clothes. With Retribution and Forfend on my person, I dwelled on Akiva and Odion... Orwyn and the Keeper of Corpses...

My only regret was that Orwyn had gotten away. I wanted to get her and all her followers. The Autarch didn't deserve to have another god-arcanist on his side. He deserved nothing, and I was determined to stop him no matter what.

**"You frequently dwell,"** Terrakona telepathically said.

With a new button-up shirt, black trousers, and a belt for Retribution, I smoothed my clothing. "Do you know what I'm thinking?"

**"I feel parts of your passion and emotions. You regret. I sense it."**

"I wanted to get the sky titan and remove it from play. Orwyn's powers are too dangerous. What if she turns that on a city, like Theasin did with his? I don't want to even think about it."

**"Hm."**

Ready to face the world, I headed for the door. As I placed my hand on the cold metal handle, Adelgis's voice also rang in my mind.

*"Volke... You should come to the city gates."*

"Why?" I asked aloud.

*"Orwyn is heading our way. She's not shielding her thoughts from me anymore. She wants to speak with you."*

Invigorated, I threw open the door and rushed into the hall. I flew down the stairs, two at a time, and then hit the ground and ran out to the road. Instead of taking the normal walkways, I leapt off the edge of the gorge and manipulated the rocks to jut out of the cliff face. They caught me before I fell too far, and I used the stone to create a quick bridge.

I dashed across, stepped onto the road again, and headed for the main gate.

The night sky was clear and perfect, the stars glittering as though to lead the way. They felt stronger, somehow. More vibrant. The presence of the stars gave me more energy than ever before.

When I reached the gates, I slowed my run and came to a stop.

"She's coming?" I asked through strained breaths.

*"She's almost here. I've also asked Atty to meet you there."*

"What? Why? I can—"

But before I voiced any more of my concerns, the winds picked up. I withdrew Retribution and hung Forfend on my arm. Terrakona was curled around his makeshift grove, not too far away. He held up his head, his crystal mane shimmering in the moonlight.

A gust of wind washed over me as Orwyn descended from the sky. She rode on the back of her kirin, but she wasn't holding it. Instead, she had her arms wrapped around the sickly body of Akiva.

When they landed, dust kicked up all around us.

The gate guards pointed and gasped, but I motioned them to stand back.

Orwyn dismounted from her dragon-horse. She struggled to hold Akiva, and he half-slumped to the ground, his eyes barely open.

His ribs were still marked with Retribution's magic-eating damage. And his arm, leg, and gut were burnt to the point of revulsion. His flesh reminded me of raw sausage. He had taken that injury to save Orwyn... but he obviously couldn't handle it.

Orwyn fidgeted with the sleeves of her robes. Then she fussed with Akiva's armor. He collapsed to the ground, unable to stand.

"What're you doing?" he growled, his voice rough.

Orwyn ignored him. She turned to me, her eyes wide and glazed with tears. "Warlord..." She stepped closer, her hands up.

I hefted my weapon. I didn't know where her sky titan was,

but I suspected it was close, ready to suffocate the citizens of Regal Heights.

Orwyn flinched away from me, her stare half vacant, but also laced with worry. "He's dying," she whispered. "I didn't know who else to turn to..."

"*Don't*," Akiva hissed from the dirt. He held an arm over his ruined body, unable to speak further.

With my sword at the ready, I slowly lifted an eyebrow. "You came here because he's injured?"

Our recent battles had probably cost the Second Ascension all the assets they had in the region. Orwyn would have to fly hundreds of miles to find someplace guaranteed to have a healer. Akiva didn't have that much time. She really had no choice but to come to me.

"He won't last much longer. Please, Warlord. I... I don't want to watch him die. Help me."

"You tried to kill us. Akiva got damn close. What makes you think I would help him?"

"I..."

A harsh chill swept over the area. I glanced over my shoulder to find Vjorn standing at the gates, his massive wolf form intimidating in the dead of night. His eyes glowed like the moon, his ears erect.

Zaxis leapt off his back and landed on the ground with confidence. When he strode forward, he glanced between Orwyn and me. Then he offered me a smirk and came to a stop standing near me.

"Do you need help?" he asked. "We can defeat her sky titan a second time."

Orwyn motioned to Akiva's limp and dying body. "We won't have time for fighting. *Please*. Akiva won't last much longer."

Zaxis stared at Akiva's crumpled body and then frowned. "He's dying?"

"Yes."

He scoffed. "Good."

The reply struck at Orwyn's composure. Her lips trembled, and her hands shook. She hurried to Akiva's side and held his arm. Her delicate fingers gently grazed the side of his face. She whispered comforting words.

I slowly lowered my blade. After a sigh, I said, "Our phoenix arcanist is on her way."

Orwyn snapped her emerald eyes up at me, meeting my gaze. She didn't say anything. She just stared in disbelief.

The chill of the fenris wolf, mixed with the normal cold of the night, made for a frigid atmosphere. I heated myself with my empowered evocation, defeating the chill temperature in an instant.

Before Atty reached us, Hexa came running to the gate. She pushed her way past the gate guards and then ran to my side. With her teeth gritted, she pointed at Orwyn. "Adelgis was right! There she is!" Hexa smacked my shoulder. "We have to get her. We—"

I held her arm.

Hexa stopped talking, her brow furrowed.

"It's okay," I said. "Calm down. We're going to help her."

"*What*?" Hexa balked.

Zaxis narrowed his eyes, his facial expression saying the same damn thing. When I shot him a sideways glance, he huffed and crossed his arms.

"Yeah," he said, loudly. "We're going to help Orwyn. Whatever Volke says."

Whenever Zaxis wasn't fighting against me, we always did a great job of supporting each other. It was so unfortunate that Zaxis considered everything a competition.

"Why?" Hexa asked.

"Because she's going to tell us where the Second Ascension is hiding Vethica." I turned back to face Orwyn. She kept her slender fingers on Akiva's arm. "That's the price for our healing. You have to help us find our missing comrades."

I thought she would protest, but Orwyn just nodded her head. "I accept. Please, just help him. I'll tell you everything you want to know."

Akiva growled something, but he clearly didn't have the strength, or state of mind, to make it coherent. Orwyn tightened her grip on him. "Don't you remember how you felt when you lost your family? I don't want to feel that way."

Akiva closed his eyes, his face wan and dappled in sweat. The tension in his muscles faded, and it seemed to me as though he had accepted his fate. Either *we* would heal him, or he would die. There were no other options.

"*Where's Vethica?*" Hexa demanded, clearly unmoved by Orwyn's distress. "She's a khepera arcanist! The Second Ascension took her."

"She's north, near Deadman's Bluff. There's a castle town there, with an underground dungeon. The Autarch uses it to store people and things they dig up from the oceans."

Deadman's Bluff?

That was a cursed location according to the sailors who came through the Isle of Ruma. A bluff was a type of rounded cliff that hung over the ocean. Deadman's Bluff had gotten its name from the many pirates who had been hanged at the gallows at the edge of the cliff overlooking the waves.

Hexa turned to me, her smile so bright, it practically lit up the night. She slapped her hands together and then said, "We did it! We have our location. We have to go!"

I slowly nodded.

Deadman's Bluff was farther north than Thronehold. Which meant we had gone the wrong direction to find Vethica. But I didn't say that—I just forced myself to return Hexa's smile. With Terrakona and Vjorn, we could make the trek easily.

"I told you we'd find her," I said.

Hexa hopped once and then went hurrying back into Regal Heights. Then she shouted, "I'm going to wake everyone! We'll leave within the hour!"

We didn't even have a discussion about it. Then again, I didn't blame her. If Luthair were nearby, I would've done the same thing.

Which reminded me...

"Orwyn," I asked. "Before the phoenix arcanist arrives... Please tell me. Have you seen a true form knightmare? He was resurrected during the attack on Thronehold. I've been looking for him."

Orwyn glanced over, silent tears streaming down her cheeks. She rubbed them away as she said, "You mean your first eldrin, Luthair? Oh, yes, Warlord. I saw him. Just like the khepera arcanist, he was taken to Deadman's Bluff so that he could meet the Autarch."

My gut twisted, and I lost the ability to breathe.

After a harsh swallow, during which I cleared the wooly feeling from my mouth, I asked, "You're sure?"

"I'm very certain, Warlord. He's probably still there. Even as we speak."

I turned on my heel, my heart starting up again at a fierce rate. We had to leave Regal Heights—perhaps faster than within the hour.

Luthair was waiting for me.

# THANK YOU SO MUCH FOR READING!

**Please consider leaving a review**—any and all feedback is much appreciated!

**The final act of Volke's story... And showdown with the legendary apoch dragon.**

**To find out more about Shami Stovall and the Frith Chronicles, take a look at her website:**

https://sastovallauthor.com/newsletter/

**To help Shami Stovall (and see advanced chapters ahead of time) take a look at her Patreon:**
https://www.patreon.com/shamistovall

**Want more arcanist novels? Good news! Academy Arcanist, the spin-off series, will be releasing soon! Join a whole new cast of arcanists on a fun adventure (set in the future of the Frith Chronicles).**

**See you at Astra Academy!**

# About the Author

Shami Stovall is a multi-award-winning author of fantasy and science fiction, with several best-selling novels under her belt. Before that, she taught history and criminal law at the college level, and loved every second. When she's not reading fascinating articles and books about ancient China or the Byzantine Empire, Stovall can be found playing way too many video games, especially RPGs and tactics simulators.

If you want to contact her, you can do so at the following locations:

**Website:** https://sastovallauthor.com
**Email:** s.adelle.s@gmail.com

CPSIA information can be obtained
at www.ICGtesting.com
Printed in the USA
BVHW042206251122
652843BV00005B/175